WHEN HE'S TORN

The Olympus Pride Series, Book 5

SUZANNE WRIGHT

The characters and events portrayed in this book are fictitious. Any similarity to real persons, living or dead, is coincidental and not intended by the author.

Cover design: J Wright

ISBN: 9798386188085

Imprint: Independently Published

For Sally
*(Hi Sal! *huge wave*)*

CHAPTER ONE

"You need to get rid of them."

Pausing with her spoon hovering above her cake, Bailey frowned at the brunette sitting opposite her. "What? Why?"

"They're freaking out the rest of the pride."

"How? It's not like they're bothering anybody."

Havana shot her an impatient look. "Absolutely *anyone* would be bothered that snakes are nesting in their building."

"They're not nesting … as such," fudged Bailey, holding her paper bowl closer to her chest. "They just want some company, so they come sleep at my apartment now and then." She paused as a gaggle of squealing kids ran by, dragging party streamers through the air. "Is that so terrible?"

"Yes," Havana insisted, plucking a spring roll from the paper plate on the table in front of her. "Because they go slithering through air vents and pay visits to the other residents."

"They're just being neighborly."

"*Bailey*."

Right then, the DJ on the stage spoke into the mic, and the song changed into something even more upbeat. Whistles of approval went up, and then more asses left seats as the number of dancers increased.

Pride events were often held here at the Tavern, their pride-owned local hangout. This evening, they were celebrating the sixtieth birthday of one of their submissives, Clarence. He seemed to be having an absolute blast—if he wasn't dancing to the blaring music, he was singing on the karaoke. The songs were mostly hits from the 70s and 80s.

Slicing her plastic spoon into her cake, Bailey scooped up a chunk and shoveled it into her mouth. The tastes of frosting, jam, cream, and moist sponge burst on her tongue. Chewing, she glanced around to see that most of the partygoers who were not on the dancefloor had congregated into small groups that either sat at tables, stood around talking, or even played pool. Most of the kids had fled to the arcade area, but some were dashing around the place like their asses were on fire.

Bailey's inner serpent wasn't keen on all the noise. But though the venue was super loud, it was loud in a happy way. There was lots of laughter and singing and light-hearted chatter.

As always, the omegas had gone *all* out when it came to the decorations. Birthday banners were pinned above the bar and stage. String lights and lanterns hung on the brick walls, skirting the sports paraphernalia and widescreen TVs. A white and blue balloon arch was positioned near the buffet table. More white and blue balloons were tied to pretty weights and set on tables, along with confetti and LED candles.

One of the burgundy-cushioned booths was all but overflowing with various sized gifts covered in glossy wrapping paper. There was also a stack of envelopes and several gift bags.

"I'm serious, Bailey." Havana bit into her spring roll. "I need you to get on top of the situation."

"I can't help it that full-blooded snakes are drawn to me. They're drawn to *all* snake shifters."

"I know that. But I also know that they'll heed your mamba if she puts on a dominance display to scare them off. Have her get rid of them."

"She doesn't want to. They're her friends."

Havana fired an incredulous look Bailey's way. "Her friends?"

"And they haven't bitten anyone." At least not yet.

"But they might, mightn't they?"

Probably. "Of course not."

Havana snorted, flicking her maple-brown hair over her shoulder. "Well, forgive me if I'm not confident of that. No, don't argue, they need to go."

"I can't believe you want to isolate my snake from others." Bailey sank her plastic spoon into her slice of cake extra hard. "Don't you care that she gets lonely?"

Havana crossed her almond-shaped bluish-gray eyes and then bit into her spring roll again. "She does *not* get lonely. She prefers her own company. The only reason she likes being around others is that she finds humor in stirring the pot. As do you."

So true.

"Your mamba urged them to take a hike last time. What's the difference?"

"You were my roommate back then, and my snake is protective of you." The devil shifter was not only Bailey's Alpha female but her honorary sister. "I live alone now."

"If you discount the numerous snakes nesting in your apartment, yes, you do."

"I told you, they're not nesting." Per se.

Havana gave an impatient shake of the head. "Just get rid of them."

"Fine. But my mamba is *not* happy about this." Bailey scooped up more cake with her spoon and then shoved it into her mouth. "And I'm honestly pretty surprised that the pride went whining to you about it. The majority of them are pallas cats. Those things fear nothing."

'Undauntable' was one of many descriptors that could be given to pallas cat shifters. They were as brash and bad-tempered as they were disturbingly vicious. The latter particularly applied to their inner animals.

The small, adorable fluffballs were pound for pound one of the strongest of the shifter breeds. More, they were so downright batshit they would attack with a feral, unchecked, demonic fury even if their enemies were stronger, bigger, and outnumbered them. Pallas cats either didn't or couldn't muster any fucks to give, which she could respect.

"First of all, you have to stop referring to them as things," said Havana. "Second of all, they're not afraid of the snakes. They simply don't want said snakes making a home for themselves in their building. Which is reasonable. Not that I'd expect you to understand that, since you and 'reasonable' are pretty much strangers. So you'll have to take my word for it."

"But—"

"No, stop being difficult."

"I can't. Your frustration warms the coldest parts of my soul."

Havana reached over and flicked her on the forehead.

"Ow. That hurt, you know." Her hands occupied, Bailey couldn't rub at the smarting spot, so she just spooned the last of her cake and wolfed it down.

"Good. It was supposed to."

Aspen materialized and retook her seat beside Havana, her usual smile absent. "I could throttle her."

Feeling her brow crease, Bailey put her empty bowl on the table. "Who? Why? What?"

Aspen held up her cell phone. "I just spoke to Corbin," she said, referring to a male grizzly shifter who was both their boss and their savior. "He's been trying to call you. Where's your cell?"

"In a bag of rice on my kitchen counter," replied Bailey.

"You dropped it in water *again*?"

"Only the mop bucket. I didn't drop it in the toilet this time. Why was Corbin trying to call me?"

Aspen rested her phone on the table. "Apparently, Ginny is insisting to all and sundry at the rec center that *you're* responsible for the recent attack on Jackson."

Bailey almost chuckled in sheer surprise. "Me? Is she kidding?"

"Nope. She's convinced of it. She claims it's another of your attempts to punish him for cheating on you with her."

Bailey snorted, and her mamba flicked her gaze skyward. "That happened *yonks* ago. Hey, I'd have no problem nonetheless kicking his ass. I'd also enjoy it." Her ex would deserve it for sure. "But I wouldn't blindside him. I'd make sure he saw me coming. And I definitely wouldn't leave him for dead in an alley. I don't kill those who wrong me. It's more entertaining to break their mind."

"Yeah, for you. But not everyone operates that way."

"They should. They'd enjoy life so much more."

Havana cut in, "No one at the center will heed Ginny. They know that jumping someone from behind isn't your style, Bailey." Pausing, she batted salt off the golden-brown skin of her arm. "Plus, considering you were at a mating ceremony the evening he was attacked, you have plenty of alibis."

"I'm not worried that the members of the center will believe her. But I don't like that she's trying to stir up drama there." Owned and managed by Corbin, the rec center gave loners a place where they could relax, make friends, and be safe.

Bailey and her girls had once been loners in need of somewhere to go as children. Corbin had been the one to take them in. They'd worked at the center for years. And they hadn't retired even after they joined the Olympus Pride when Havana mated its Alpha male, Tate.

"According to Corbin," Aspen began, absently skimming her fingers through the dark, sleek, choppy layers of her long, angled bob, "Jackson is saying that he thinks it was a random attack. He's probably right. Sad as it is, it isn't uncommon for loners to be targeted by packs or prides or whatever."

Bailey gave a slow nod. Having no protection, loners were easy prey. She herself had been "preyed on" from time to time over the years. It had never ended well for those who'd thought to come at her.

Havana chomped down the last of her food. "I doubt Ginny's as angry about the attack as she claims to be." She focused her gaze on Bailey. "I think she's just throwing accusations your way to get back at you for tormenting her all these months."

"Probably," said Bailey. "She was seething when all I did was laugh at her for starting the petition to have me fired from the center. Though why she thought I'd be upset, I don't know."

"Most people would be," said Havana. "But since it's well-known that you feed off the frustration of others and find their subsequent reactions amusing, yeah, I have no idea why she expected you to be upset."

People could be so weird.

Aspen went to speak, but then a waitress appeared at their table with a black, garbage bag.

"Any trash?" asked Therese, her powder-blue eyes bright and clear.

Bailey handed over her spoon and empty bowl. "I like the nose piercing. It suits you."

Tentatively touching the rhinestone ring, the slim blonde flashed her a smile. "Thank you. I'm still not used to it yet, but I love it already. My cat thinks it looks stupid, though."

Havana laughed. "No offense, but pallas cats are disapproving creatures in general, so I wouldn't worry about it."

Loosely stroking a fist down her golden-blonde ponytail, Therese gave a sheepish smile. "Disapproving indeed. Mine is always grumpy anyway—it comes with being latent," she said with acceptance, not resentment, though it couldn't be easy to resign yourself to being unable to release your inner animal. She quickly bagged every bit of trash on the table. "You girls need anything else?"

"I'm good," replied Bailey. Both Havana and Aspen echoed her sentiment.

"All right, just holler if you change your mind." Therese turned to leave, almost bumping into two other females who'd appeared at the table. "Sorry, my bad."

"No problem," said Blair, their Beta female.

Similarly, Livy—who was the birthday boy's mate—assured her, "It's fine." She stepped aside to allow the waitress to pass and then turned to face Bailey and her girls. "Hello, ladies," she greeted, a bowl in hand. "Thank you so much for coming. My Clarence really appreciates it."

Havana waved off her thanks. "Of course we came. It's his birthday. And you made chocolate fudge cake. We were never going to miss that."

Visibly pleased by the compliment, Livy patted the back of her dark, asymmetrical bob before cutting her blue gaze to Bailey. "Well, don't you look pretty tonight."

"And every other night," said Bailey. "You and I have that in common."

Livy chuckled. "I like this one, Havana." She set a bowl of pecan pie in front of Bailey. "Here. I know it's your favorite, so I saved you a slice. Enjoy." With that, she left.

Her mouth curved, Blair stared after the woman as she took the chair beside Bailey. "She's so sweet."

"I know," said Aspen. "I want her to adopt me."

Bailey peered into the bowl, her nose wrinkling. "She's always feeding me."

Blair's brow furrowed. "Feeding you?"

"Yes. She comes to my apartment with homemade casseroles and stuff, saying she had them *lying around*. Sometimes, she just stops by to 'chat.' Like we're old friends. And she'll always bring a cupcake or something." Bailey rubbed at her neck. "It feels weird."

Aspen snorted. "Of course someone being nice to you feels weird. You're not used to it. People are usually threatening to end your existence."

"I like it better that way." Bailey swiped the bowl from the table and lifted the plastic fork. "Things get boring otherwise."

Blair gave her a playful nudge. "If Livy was unmated, I'd say you were being courted. Hmm, maybe she's got her eye on you for one of her sons."

Bailey froze, her fork wedged in her pie. "What?" Her snake also stiffened, equally wary.

"She did the same thing years ago with Colby, who's now happily mated to Livy's eldest son, Matthew," explained Blair, her green eyes twinkling. "Livy knew he had a huge thing for Colby, so she gently pushed them together. I remember watching it all go down, wishing *my* mother could be so supportive of my choice of mate."

The nineteen-year-old bush dog shifter might not have mated their Beta male, Luke, until recently, but they'd been part of each other's lives since they met when Blair was twelve. "Maybe Livy has you in mind for Deke," Blair added.

Bailey blessed her face for not flushing. Just the mention of the male enforcer made her belly do a dumb little flutter. And that was some bullshit right there. Never before in her life had a guy made her stomach do *anything.*

It was annoying, but unfortunately not enough to dim his appeal for her. There was a reason that Bailey called him Eye Candy, and it wasn't merely to poke at him. Truly, Deke Hammond was a treat for the eyes.

Big and broad and inked, he was packed with muscle. He had the eyes of a predator—focused, intense, and filled with an animal cunning that spoke to her snake. Those same eyes were a vivid caramel-brown that looked a lustrous gold in some lighting.

The angles of his ruggedly masculine face were hard and sharp. His short hair was dark as molasses, much like the light layer of scruff that darkened his strong jaw. His bottom lip was slightly fuller than his top one, and she wanted to lick both. Maybe even nibble on them a little.

She'd never admit it aloud, but Bailey loved his voice. It was rough and scratchy; all thorns and barbs. It could make any girl's skin break out in a shiver.

Unlike most, he wasn't one little bit unnerved by her inner snake. But then, Deke never seemed rattled by anything. The tough bastard was so damn steady and sure of himself.

For Bailey, there was something unbelievably enticing about his air of cool stoicism, even with its underlying sense of danger. Or maybe *because* of that danger. But no one else needed to know that, including her friends.

Bailey chomped down some pie. "It's not that."

"It could be," argued Blair. "It would make sense."

"How? Livy knows perfectly well that he promised himself to Therese's bestie. Dayna Something-Or-Other." And if Bailey's stomach cramped each time she thought of it, well, it just meant she had gas.

"Not quite. He's not in a long-distance relationship with Dayna. He simply agreed to wait for her to come home rather than move on while she was gone—it was to see if they had the potential to build something real. But according to Colby, Livy is of the opinion that he needs to untangle himself from Dayna."

"Why?"

"She feels that Dayna doesn't deserve her boy, considering she's been content to stay away for so long. Maybe Livy also thinks that you'll fit him better." Blair sighed. "I kind of feel bad for him right now. Touch-hunger can't be any fun."

Bailey had personally never experienced it, but she'd heard it was hell. Touch was a need for shifters. Highly tactile, they didn't function well without both social and sexual contact. And if they were deprived of either, they'd be hit by touch-hunger at some point. They'd then have to deal with irritating stuff like hot flushes, night sweats, and their libido sporadically kicking into overdrive.

There were some exceptions where a lack of sexual touch was concerned, such as when a shifter was provided with enough social touch by their true mate—something that would be very potent for them—to compensate for it. Which was why Blair and Luke had been spared it during the years they were unmated.

From what Bailey had learned, Deke and this Dayna person had agreed to only sleep with others when touch-hunger came calling. Apparently, he usually did exactly that. This time, though, he appeared to be fighting it.

"I don't know why he won't just go work it off in some female's bed. He's been like this for *weeks*. It's not as if he's short of offers." Bailey stomach twisted again. More gas.

Havana looked at her. "The only outlet he's currently getting for all the tension is from his verbal spars with you, which is why I didn't tell you to dial it down and give him a break. He needs whatever release valve he can get."

Blair fiddled with the end of her pale-blonde braid. "I personally think Bailey should just go fuck his brains out and be done with it."

Bailey almost dropped her fork. "What?"

Aspen barked a laugh. "I happen to agree. No, don't say you don't like him *that way*, Bailey. We know you too well."

Which was terribly unfortunate at times. "I like his butt, that's all." It was spectacular. "And I still say he's not worthy of it."

"You can't *possibly* hold it against him that he asks you to reflect on your behavior," said Aspen.

"Yeah? Watch me." Bailey shoved more pie into her mouth.

The bearcat sighed and shook her head.

"You can hold a grudge and *still* help him work off the touch-hunger, Bailey," said Blair. "He'd bone you no problem."

"Are you kidding? The dude is *no* fan of mine. He wouldn't even fuck me if the survival of his species depended on it." Bailey dug her fork into her pie again. "Besides, I'm not interested in sleeping with someone who spends most of his time glaring at me in disapproval. It hurts."

Aspen cast her an exasperated look. "You love that you irritate him. You purposely set out to do it."

True. "I do that to everyone," Bailey reminded her.

"Yeah, but you put in a little extra effort when it comes to him," said Aspen.

Hmm, maybe. In her defense, her mamba always egged her on. Peer pressure was no easy thing to fight for Bailey, she was very sensitive to such … Damn, she couldn't even finish the thought without inwardly laughing it was so ridiculous. The truth was that she only responded to pressure if she *wanted* to.

"I don't know why you're so sure he's not into you, Bailey," said Blair. "I've seen the way he looks at you."

Bailey flicked up a brow. "Like he wants to squeeze my throat until I stop breathing?"

"The *other* way he looks at you. Like he wants to get all up in your business. And now that you're no longer dating Shay …" Blair shrugged.

The mention of Shay made Bailey's lips thin. Hey, he was a decent guy. And not boring, which she liked. But he'd regularly made a point of talking about Deke, always watching her carefully while a knowing smirk played around the edges of his mouth.

"Believe what you want," began Bailey, waving her fork dismissively, "but I'm telling you, Deke loathes me. He thinks I'm evil."

"No, he doesn't," Havana assured her.

Bailey snorted. "He splashed me with holy water to, and I quote, 'see what happened.' He claimed to be disappointed when I didn't burst into flames."

Aspen's mouth curved. "I swear, he can be almost as bad as you sometimes." She paused. "If you were to ease your foot off the taunting-him-pedal, he'd probably be a lot nicer. Maybe give him a reprieve."

"I wouldn't give him the steam off my shit. Besides, Deke doesn't do 'nice.'"

He was a *good* guy, but nothing close to pleasant. Gruff and unpolished, he had zero time for subtlety. In fact, he was as aloof and superior as any feline. Not to mention rude and finicky. And he could ignore you like only a cat could. But people tended to find his rough exterior endearing.

"Well, whatever the case," began Havana, "I'm thinking Blair's right that Livy's chosen Bailey for Deke."

Blair nodded, her eyes dancing. "Be warned, Bailey—Livy might be a submissive shifter, but she's no pushover. That woman is as persistent as a damn wolverine, and she loves her children *fiercely*. If she has truly decided that you're what Deke needs, she'll stop at nothing to make sure he has you."

"I'm kind of excited to see how this all plays out," said Aspen, smiling and rubbing her hands together.

"It's going to be fun," Havana asserted, her mouth hitched up.

"Excuse me," Bailey cut in, "but nothing is going to 'play out.' Even if you're right that Livy's up to something, it still won't amount to anything. I'll just tell her to back off, and she will."

Giving Bailey a pitying look, Blair gently patted her on the head. "You're so pretty."

"Don't make me burp in your face." Catching movement from her peripheral vision, Bailey looked to see a tall, stocky figure stride into the bar. She tensed. She knew that walk. Knew that nape tattoo. Knew that scraggly haircut.

Bailey hissed right along with her inner serpent, who recognized him just the same. "That motherfucker."

Havana stiffened. "Who?"

"Remember my cousin who died shortly before we joined the pride?"

The devil nodded. "Yeah."

"Well, he ain't dead." Bailey lurched to her feet. "He's also standing *right there*."

Setting three shot glasses down on the bar, the bartender sighed at Deke. "Whiskey is not going to help with your little problem."

Deke wouldn't consider touch-hunger "little," but whatever. "I wouldn't have thought that you cared." He and Gerard didn't exactly see eye to eye.

"I don't." The bartender gave a superior sniff. "I'm just stating what should be obvious."

Well, of course Deke didn't need telling that alcohol wouldn't solve his issue. Only one thing would, and Gerard was the last person Deke would have expected to recommend it. "You're actually urging me to sleep with a woman who isn't Dayna?"

The other male usually gave him judgmental, disapproving looks—offended on her behalf, despite that she and Deke had an "understanding" where touch-hunger was concerned.

Gerard parted his lips to speak again. His words didn't come out. His gaze slid to something behind Deke, and he then snapped his mouth shut.

Glancing over his shoulder, Deke almost groaned. Both his Alpha and Beta male were approaching, looks of resolve etched into their faces. And he knew they would once more pester him to "open up." More, he knew his time for putting them off was over. He could see that in the hard sets of their jaw.

The bartender melted away as the two males closed in on Deke.

One hand splayed on the bar, Deke lifted a shot glass and then flicked his Alpha a brief look. "This isn't the time or the place to have the conversation you want to have." He knocked back his whiskey, relishing the burn as it slid down his throat.

Luke snorted, propping his hip against the bar. "At no point has *any* time or place suited you when we've questioned you in the past."

Fair point.

"We're not going to let you blow us off, so don't bother trying," stated Tate. "I warned you that we'd only give you so much time to get your mental shit together."

Inwardly cursing, Deke placed his glass on the bar.

"You haven't been yourself lately. *Then* you got hit by touch-hunger. But instead of addressing it, you seem intent on ignoring it. Which makes no sense." Tate folded his arms, his gaze steely. "Tell us what's going on."

Deke looked from one Devereaux male to the other. The brothers were very similar in appearance. Tall, dark, broad, and blue-eyed. Tate carried a little more muscle than his younger brother, but both were well-built. "You're really gonna push me to talk about this here and now, at my dad's birthday party?"

"Yes," replied Tate. "Because it means you can't leave and avoid our questions this time."

Fuck, Deke should have anticipated that they'd corner him now. They were sneaky that way. He grabbed a waiting shot of whiskey from the bar and tossed it back.

Luke sighed. "No amount of alcohol is going to make the touch-hunger go away."

"Helps take the edge off, though." Cricking his neck, he set down his empty glass beside the other. Usually, he wasn't much of a drinker. He'd knock back some beers while shooting the shit with his pride mates now and then, but that was pretty much it. Until recently. He'd take whatever relief from the touch-hunger he could get.

Generally, Deke could go seven months without sexual touch before it became an issue. Whenever touch-hunger had struck in the past, he'd instantly worked it off—sometimes it had taken days, sometimes it had taken weeks. But this time, he was having … difficulties alleviating it. As such, since it hit him a few weeks ago, his body had been in a constant edgy state.

He always felt jittery and antsy. Like he'd overloaded on caffeine and energy drinks. He sometimes woke in the night, sweating but without a fever.

Worse, the touch-hunger would randomly flare up, assailing him with relentless sensations … just as it had mere minutes ago. His skin was now hot and prickly. His head pounded and felt tight with pressure. Little itches kept racing over his flesh.

More, such raw need coursed through him that his dick was painfully hard. He knew from experience that no amount of attention from his hand would ease it. Because it was *his* hand, not that of another.

Being around so many unmated females didn't help—it often caused the touch-hunger to flare up. As if his body sensed that a solution to its issue was close by; as if it was trying to drive him to reach for that solution.

Deke rubbed at his forehead. He wanted to go home. Be alone. Get away from the noise and activity. He felt so overstimulated that his nerve endings were raw and his senses felt sharper.

"We're not doing this to be nosy," said Luke. "We're concerned. We want to help."

Deke considered blowing the brothers off. Again. But it would be a fruitless endeavor—he saw that clearly.

It also seemed like a shitty thing to do when over and over they'd respected his wish to be left alone. That couldn't have been easy for them—particularly since they were both born-alphas and, as such, authoritarianism was written into their damn DNA.

Even now, they weren't calling rank and imperiously demanding answers. They were merely pushing for Deke to confide in them so that he wouldn't have to deal with his issue alone. In that sense, they were only doing what he'd do if the situation were reversed. Pride looked after pride.

"Seriously, why won't you ease the touch-hunger?" Tate pushed.

Deke reluctantly replied through gritted teeth, "Because I can't. My cat won't have any of it."

Tate's lips parted. "What?"

"He's constantly in a fucking snit," Deke explained. "Doesn't want anyone near him—male or female. He's always on edge; always either pacing up and down or stiffly crouched in a corner. Honestly, you'd think he was trapped. That's how he acts. Like a caged wild animal."

Luke stared at him, clearly at a loss. "What sparked this?"

Deke shrugged. "I have no idea. Seriously. It wasn't so bad at first. He was just tetchier than usual. But it got worse as time went on, until he was wound so tight he kept starting fights with other cats for the release. Then he pulled inward, wanting nothing to do with anyone. But I didn't think he'd still act so withdrawn when touch-hunger became a problem—I thought he'd want it to be dealt with."

Tate edged closer, his arms slipping to his sides. "Is it because of Dayna? Does he miss her or something?"

Deke slid Gerard a quick look, ensuring he was out of hearing range, since the bartender was a close friend of Dayna's and would report back anything he heard. "No." Deke paused as a scuttling sensation raced up his arm. He ground his teeth against the itch. "He didn't even fight me when I made the official decision to pull out of the vow I made to her." A decision he hadn't yet shared with her, but he would.

Tate's brows flew up. "You've pulled out?"

Deke blinked. "You sound pleased."

Tate's compact shoulders lifted and fell in an easy, fluid movement. "You're a man of your word, Deke—you don't like to break it; I respect that. But I don't think it's fair that you're expected to stick to it in this situation. I mean, she wasn't supposed to stay away for so long. Don't get me wrong, I'm not criticizing her for being hesitant to leave Australia—she's taking care of her family. But she told you she'd be gone a year at most."

Not told. *Sworn.* And yet, over two and a half years later, she still hadn't returned.

Intent on finding his true mate, he'd always made a point of keeping his relationships short and shallow. But he'd unexpectedly grown close to Dayna. Maybe because they'd been friends for years prior to them sharing a bed.

When her pregnant sister unexpectedly lost her mate, Dayna had chosen to temporarily move to Australia to be at her sibling's side. But she hadn't wanted her and Deke to throw away what they'd been building, so she'd asked him to wait for her. He'd agreed, and they'd made a promise to only sleep with others when touch-hunger came calling.

"At this point," Tate went on, "I'm not even sure she intends to return."

Deke slugged back his last shot. "I believe she wants to. But I also think that she's finding it hard to drum up the will to leave, and I get it. Evan might be her nephew, but she's co-parented him since he was born. Really, she's been more of a mom to him than her sister has." He set his glass back on the bar.

Luke tilted his head. "How did she handle you pulling out of the vow?"

"She doesn't know it's my intention yet. I video-called her a few days ago to tell her, but it turns out that her great-uncle just died, and so his mate—unable and uninterested in fighting the breaking of the mating bond—is now dying. What kind of a dick would I be if I broke it to her now that I was done waiting for her to come home?" Deke plucked at his tee. Like his skin, it felt too tight; felt confining. "I should have done it months ago, really."

"You should have done it a year and a half ago, when she failed to come home like she'd said she would," maintained Luke.

"If I'd known she'd stay in Australia this long, I wouldn't have made her any promises." He would have thought it pointless for them both. "Countless times I considered bowing out. But then I'd feel like a piece of shit for not supporting her at a time when she's so busy supporting others. And I worried it would make Dayna feel pressured to return before she's ready."

"I get it, Deke. But it isn't fair to you that you've had to put your life on pause. It's not for you to be her rock." Luke pushed away from the bar, straightening. "Unless you think she's your true mate?"

Deke scratched at his cheek. "I once thought she might be. She's the only woman I've ever really clicked with. But she's been gone a while, and I haven't struggled to deal with it. Neither has my cat."

Puffing out a breath, Tate rocked forward slightly on the balls of his feet. "And here I thought you were just struggling with your attraction to Bailey."

Deke's head flinched back slightly. "Bailey?"

"You want her," said Tate. "That much is obvious."

Deke felt his mouth firm. Yeah, it was obvious. It was also a goddamn mystery.

Not that she wasn't attractive. Bailey was a pretty thing. Not classically beautiful, but striking. Arresting. And far too fucking tempting.

Her dark deep-set eyes were set into an oval face that boasted high cheekbones, elegantly arched brows, and a full, upturned mouth. Her obsidian hair seamlessly blended into a striking silver and tumbled down her back, sleek and ruler-straight. The warm tones of her smooth, flawless skin hinted at her Japanese ancestry.

Average height, she was also slender and supple. Her breasts were high and delightfully perky. And fuck, she had a great ass—tight and round.

Despite being a dominant female shifter, she didn't give off a predatory vibe. She had "innocence" written all over her. Looked as sweet as she did helpless. There would be no way to guess that the female was a ferocious, cunning, bloodthirsty creature who picked fights simply for something to do.

Provocation was not required with Bailey—even with no motive, she had zero problem drawing first blood. Or tossing out logic. Or dicking with people. Or waving her crazy flag high in the air.

Yeah, there was nothing innocent about Bailey Bryant.

But his cock gave not one fuck about that. Nor did it give a single shit that she set his damn teeth on edge—always pushing his buttons and not taking him or his authority seriously. The woman didn't really take *anything* seriously, from what he could tell.

She was like no one he'd ever met. There was no real way to handle her. Deke could be sure of it, because he'd tried. No avenue he'd used had been effective. Not glaring, not ignoring her, not blowing her off, not riling her, not calling her on her crap, *nothing*.

In sum, attempting to handle Bailey was much like trying to dish out orders to a full-blooded cat. They'd just twitch the tip of their tail and walk away—having better shit to do than deal with you.

It made no logical sense to him that, despite it all, he found it impossible to dislike her. Or that she was such a temptation to him he actually worried that, should he be caught in a moment of weakness, he might make a move on her regardless of the vow he'd made to Dayna.

Deke *never* broke his word. Ever. But Bailey had made him consider it more than once, and so he couldn't help feeling a little resentful toward her.

Tate tipped his head to the side. "Would your cat be down with you spending a night in her bed?"

Deke shook his head. "He often wants to bite her—and not in a good way. In any case, it doesn't matter, because she wouldn't be down with it either. The woman doesn't like me."

She didn't even refer to him by his own damn name. She addressed him with dismissive terms such as Boy Toy and Eye Candy. She might as well say, Oh Depthless One. "Plus, there's Shay to consider. She only recently stopped dating him."

Tate's brow inched up. "Do you realize that you barely got out the latter two words without grinding your teeth?"

Yeah, well, Deke didn't like thinking of her with others. It wasn't that he felt possessive of her. But the thought of other males touching her made his hackles rise—it was difficult to explain.

"Your mom likes her," Tate casually threw in.

Deke exhaled heavily. "I know." She often raved about the mamba. Well, Bailey possessed a lot of the traits that pallas cats found admirable—namely viciousness, ferocity, and fierceness.

Luke rubbed at his chin, his eyes dancing. "Livy also keeps taking food to her apartment."

Deke almost rocked back on his heels. "What?"

"Oh, yeah," said Luke, nodding. "Your mom frequently knocks on her door. Colby mentioned it."

"Jesus," Deke muttered, thrusting a hand through his hair. Why his mother thought that the mamba would make a good match for him, he had no clue. They were far from compatible. Complete opposites, really.

Bailey was more likely to shoot him in the face than let him touch her, and he couldn't envision himself spending any real length of time around her without putting duct tape over her mouth. They had only two things in common: They possessed an ill temper, and they were seriously unforgiving.

His cat often snarled at her, irritated by how she dismissed and poked at Deke. And considering her snake had launched herself at Deke with lethal intent on numerous occasions, he felt he could safely conclude that the mamba would have no more interest in him than Bailey would. So. Yeah. His mother was aiming her arrow at the wrong female.

"Back to the subject of Dayna," began Tate, "do you think she'll take your decision well?"

Deke pursed his lips. "I would have said yes, considering it'll mean she won't feel torn between me and Evan any longer. But I've offered to free her from her promise numerous times in the past, making it clear that there'd be no anger on my part. She always turned down my offer, swearing she'll be home 'soon' and asking me to wait."

At this point, Deke didn't understand why. They didn't video-call as often as they used to. In fact, weeks at a time could go by before he heard from or contacted her. So he obviously wasn't on her mind, just as she wasn't on his.

Luke set his hands on his hips. "Did your cat's weird behavior begin after you officially decided to break away from her?"

"No." Deke ground his teeth as an itch built on his nape. "It was happening before then. It didn't coincide with anything else that was going on at the time. I don't know why he's acting this way, but nothing helps."

"So you don't think he'd calm down if Dayna came home?" asked Luke.

"No. He's not upset with her. He's not *anything* with her." It wasn't until the skin of his nape began to sting that Deke realized he was scratching it hard. He lowered his arms to his sides. "Don't get me wrong, he respects and likes Dayna. But he doesn't pine for her. The thought of scrapping the agreement doesn't bother him one way or the other."

Tate leaned his side against the bar and braced his arm on it. "There's no one he calms down around?"

"No," replied Deke. "And he goes nuts whenever I even think of bedding a female. Like he doesn't want the intimacy. Not even to alleviate the touch-hunger."

Tate twisted his mouth. "Maybe he's acting this way because he's tired of waiting for his true mate to come along. It might be that he's withdrawn from everyone because the only touch he wants is that of his mate."

Deke frowned, considering that. "It's possible."

"I'd ask why you didn't tell us about all this sooner, but I can understand why you kept quiet." Tate paused. "There was a point where my own cat had similar issues, though not to this severity. Confessing weakness to other predators isn't something we do. I protected my cat just the same as you're protecting …" He trailed off, his brows snapping together. He whirled on the spot and began scanning their surroundings. "My mate is pissed about something; I can feel it through our bond."

Deke swept his gaze around the Tavern, searching, searching—*there.* He frowned as he took in the scene. Blair stood off to the side, her eyes wide in what appeared to be bafflement as both Havana and Aspen stood at Bailey's back. The latter two females seemed to be silently raging as the black mamba shifter argued with an unfamiliar male.

A male who was *too far up* in her personal space for Deke's liking.

Before he knew it, he was on the move.

CHAPTER TWO

Should he mind his own business and return to the bar? Probably. Bailey would have said so. She'd repeatedly told him to not stick his nose where it didn't belong.

But no way was he going to hang back while another male was so aggressively invading her personal space. So Deke kept striding over there, his back teeth locked. All the while, his cat moodily prowled beneath his skin as he snarled at the spectacle up ahead of them.

Deke could only assume that Camden had felt his mate's anger, because the tiger shifter appeared at Aspen's side just as Deke approached the group with the Devereaux brothers close behind. The noise level in the Tavern was so loud that it wasn't until he neared them that Deke could hear any of what was being said.

"You didn't go to my funeral," the stranger complained, leaning toward Bailey. "Or the one before that."

"I went to your first funeral," Bailey told him. "Though that was because I thought there was a ninety percent chance you were actually dead."

"You didn't even cry," griped the male.

Her face scrunched up. "What was there to cry about?"

Reaching them, Deke slid a hand between their bodies to plant a hand on the guy's chest. "Move back."

Dark eyes so very like Bailey's slammed on Deke. "What?"

"I don't like how close you are to her. Move. Back." Deke lowered his hand when the male did just that. "Now maybe you can tell me who the hell you are."

"Name's Roman," he replied, glancing around and taking in the number of people crowding him—a number that increased by two when Tate's guards, Isaiah and Farrell, joined them. "I'm her cousin, so you can relax—I ain't gonna hurt her."

Deke blinked. Cousin? His cat faltered, just as surprised. Loners generally had no contact with family members, and Bailey had been a loner for most of her life. Or so Deke had assumed—he wasn't entirely sure.

Bailey didn't volunteer much personal information about herself. And he'd made a point of not digging for any, not wanting to feed his curiosity about her.

Deke was just about to ask if Roman was a lone shifter when Havana took an aggressive step forward, sidling up to Bailey protectively.

"You have some balls coming here," the Alpha female all but growled, glaring at Roman. "Big, giant, hairy ones. Because I *know* I told you to stay away from Bailey."

It wasn't surprising that Roman tensed—devil shifters were renowned for having explosive tempers. "I got a situation," he defended.

Aspen huffed, her face dark with anger. "You always do. If it isn't cash you want, it's a place to lie low or a bullshit alibi."

He pointed at Bailey. "And she turns me away every time." It was a genuine whine.

"Yet, you keep coming back," Camden bit out. "Explain."

Blair lifted a hand. "I'm sorry to cut in, but I have to know why someone would have one funeral, let alone multiple, when they're not actually dead."

Deke had been asking himself that very same question.

Havana cast her a humorless smile. "Well, Roman here has a habit of pissing off the wrong humans. So he fakes his death, waits for the heat to cool, and then crawls back out of his hidey hole."

What a goddamn tool.

"What is it you want?" Bailey asked her cousin, setting her hands on her slim hips. "Just spit it out so I can say no and you can leave."

Roman gave her a pleading look. "Bay, I need your help. These people … they don't show mercy."

Her eyes narrowed. "What people?"

Shifting nervously, Roman rubbed at the side of his neck. "Ugh … the Westwood Pack. I kind of owe their Alpha money."

Bailey felt her lips part in complete shock. "You dumb motherfucker."

A lover of casinos, Roman wasn't a stranger to borrowing massive amounts of money. Generally, he lost as many bets as he won. And since he quickly squandered his winnings on more bets, he often found himself in debt to the wrong humans. But he generally didn't borrow cash from shifters. And borrowing money from the Westwood Pack? Epic mistake.

Deke frowned at him. "Jackals? You screwed over jackals? Seriously?"

She understood his disbelief. Most breeds of shifter tended to steer clear of jackals—their kind had a tendency toward cruelty and maliciousness. They would stab you in the back without hesitation, even if you were one of their own.

Roman ignored Deke, focused on Bailey. "I need somewhere to stay. Somewhere they won't come looking for me."

"They'll question every living relative you have, me included," she pointed out, her voice icily calm. "You know that." Hence why her snake was furious—he'd effectively brought danger to her doorstep, and he clearly didn't care. "You came to me because you think they won't tangle with a pallas cat pride." *Asshole.*

Roman lifted his shoulders. "Well, they won't."

"Wrong," Deke stated. "They'll do whatever they have to do to get back what they're owed."

Her thoughts exactly. Jackals did *not* let such things go.

"You have a nest," Camden said to Roman, a bite to his voice—the tiger wasn't a fan of her family, much like most people. "Why not ask them for help?"

"I did," Roman replied. "They told me I was on my own with this."

Not a shocker. The Umber Nest were tight. But they wouldn't back you if you bit off more than the nest as a whole could chew. They'd leave you to clean up your own mess and accept the consequences. In some situations, they'd even wash their hands of not only you but your children if necessary. Much as they'd done to Bailey after her parents—

She slammed a door on that mental path.

"Come on, Bay, you know what it's like to be alone," he wheedled.

Havana hissed. "Don't you *dare* try playing that card. You being told by your Alpha to deal with your own shit is nothing remotely close to the life of a lone shifter."

Roman spluttered. "I never meant that—"

"I'm going to save Bailey the trouble of dealing with you," Tate interjected. "We're not going to welcome you into our pride. We're not going to grant you protection from the Westwood Pack. We're not going to give you a place to hide. We're not going to help you in any way, shape, or form."

Just as Roman had never helped Bailey over the years. None of the nest had. It wasn't as if they hadn't known where she was. They'd been the ones to deliver her to Corbin.

Roman swallowed. "They'll kill me, Bay."

"Only if they find you." Bailey paused. "So make sure they don't find you." Considering he was a master at hiding, she was relatively confident that the jackals wouldn't.

Tate gestured at the exit. "Go. And stay gone."

Roman waited a long moment, as if sure Bailey would speak up for him. She didn't. She merely stared at him. Spitting out a curse, the male angrily stalked out of the Tavern.

Maybe some would have felt guilty for turning him away. Bailey didn't. Nor did she see why she should feel bad. After all, no one from the Umber Nest had been there for her when she'd needed them—on the contrary, they'd freaking abandoned her. And by hypocritically asking her to have his back, Roman clearly didn't give a single, miniscule shit that it would mean *she'd* be in danger as well. Her welfare meant zilch to him.

Feeling the weight of someone's gaze, she looked to see that Deke was staring at her—and not in a flattering way. It was one of his piercing stares. As if he was trying to see through her and didn't particularly like that he wanted to.

Her snake pinned her own unblinking gaze right on this cat who both annoyed and intrigued her in equal measures.

"I didn't know you had contact with any of your relatives," he said.

She blinked. "Why would you?"

He let out a grunt. "Do you see or hear from any of them often?"

"Depends on your personal definition of 'often,' I guess."

Deke watched as Bailey took a deliberate step away from him—a common thing of late. Likely aware that him being in close proximity to unmated females aggravated the touch-hunger, she purposely avoided coming too close to him. He appreciated it.

Yet he didn't.

Because the physical distance somehow irritated him. But right now, as touch-hunger rode him *hard* and his cock began to ache like a mother, he was grateful for it.

Deke was about to call her on her evasive answer, but then Blair moved to her side and asked, "Do you think the jackals will really come here to speak with you?"

"Yes," Bailey simply replied.

Havana gave her a pointed look. "If they show when you're on your lonesome, *text me*. Don't try to deal with them alone."

"Sure thing." Bailey sighed. "Anyone need a drink? Because I need a drink." With that, she walked off.

Havana, Aspen, and Blair were quick to follow her to the bar, clearly concerned. Deke joined Camden, Tate, and Luke in trailing behind them.

Watching as the mamba knocked back shot after shot, Deke could easily sense that—despite how she casually talked and laughed—she was *pissed*. Her girls didn't speak of Roman or the jackals; they tried distracting her with other matters, and their mates took their lead.

Deke, too, kept his questions to himself. So many danced around his head …

Why hadn't her cousin's nest taken her in when she'd become a lone shifter? Or had she always been a loner? Had the nest in fact offered her a place in it but she'd refused? Why wasn't she willingly in contact with her relatives?

See, this was why he rarely asked her or others about her. It only made him want to know more. She was a puzzle. One he'd strived to understand but couldn't.

He half-expected her to get blitzed, but she didn't. She switched to water at one point, clearly intent on being vigilant. She took her role as Havana's bodyguard seriously.

When Tate had first made Bailey an enforcer, Deke hadn't really expected the Alpha to give her any responsibilities beyond being a guard for Havana. He also hadn't expected her to last long in the position—she seemed to get bored fast. But Tate had called on her several times, utilizing the many skills that Deke would never have guessed she possessed. And if she was bored by the job, she hadn't let it become a factor.

Deke had quickly learned that Bailey might be a handful, but she never let down either Havana or Aspen. If they needed something, she was on it. Say what you want about the mamba, but she had a steadfast loyalty to those she loved.

As the hours went on, she loosened up, her temper cooling. He'd noticed that hers tended to run quick and hot. She wasn't one to stew for long.

By the time the party died down, she was back to her old self, though a little quieter than usual. Introspective, maybe. She was probably plotting something.

After wishing his father a happy birthday once again, Deke, along with Bailey, Aspen, Camden, and the Alphas, piled out of the Tavern with Isaiah and Farrell taking up the rear. As the cool evening breeze stroked over Deke's heated skin, he tipped his face up to enjoy more of it, uncaring that it carried the scents of fuel and car exhaust.

As a group, they all stalked along the sidewalk. It was late, so the bus stop was empty, the cart vendors were gone, and the store security shutters were down. A few pedestrians roamed the sidewalks, and two hung near the stoplights. Other than that, the street was empty.

Light spilled out of the windows of the apartments above the stores, casting shadows on the sidewalk. Each of the premises were owned by the pride. There were many, including a coffeehouse, a bakery, a bookstore, and an antique shop. Most of the employees were pride members. Others were lone shifters or even humans.

Of a daytime, the street was often hectic. The stores received a lot of custom—not only from the pride, but from outsiders. So cars would be parked in every space, and the bus stop was often crowded.

In front of him, Bailey shuddered. "Damn, it's chilly tonight."

"It's not that bad," said Camden beside her. "As soon as fall hits, you're always shivering."

Bailey rubbed at her upper arms. "I'm a snake shifter. I don't like to be cold."

"Then it would have made sense for you to bring a jacket," Deke chipped in.

Without altering her pace, Bailey glanced at him over her shoulder. "You butt into my conversations a lot. What do you get out of it?"

"Your annoyance," he said.

"Gotcha." She faced forward.

Deke ground his teeth. She said it with complete understanding. Like they were on the same wavelength when they absolutely were not. He didn't get off on riling people unless they were Bailey—she was the single exception.

As they reached the corner of the street, the Alphas and guards headed to the nearby cul-de-sac where they lived. Deke and the others crossed to one of the two pride-owned apartment buildings. He'd been on high alert for any signs of Roman, but the walk was uneventful.

Inside the complex, the four of them trickled into the elevator. Deke and Camden pressed the buttons for their respective floors.

Deke stood apart from the others to avoid any incidental touches. It wasn't enough to stop the touch-hunger from flaring up, though. Because the scents of the other three shifters bounced around the confined space, and one of those shifters was an unmated female.

His arousal ramped up. His nerve-endings sang. His flesh turned fever-hot. The skin around his rock-hard cock suddenly felt too tight.

Silently cursing to himself, he focused on the changing numbers on the digital screen. The elevator smoothed to a stop on Aspen and Camden's floor. The couple said their goodnights and exited the elevator.

Then he and Bailey were alone.

She hummed low as the elevator once more began to ascend, adjusting the straps of her dress and bra. She began studying her reflection in the mirrored wall, baring her teeth to rub at one of them.

He felt a muscle in his cheek twitch. She often did stuff like that when no one else was around but them. Hummed or muttered to herself or demonstrated other types of behavior that people generally did when alone—dismissing his presence so easily.

He wasn't going to react. He wasn't going to say a word. Not even now, while touch-hunger clawed at him so hard that agitation was a drumbeat in his blood.

Finally, the elevator halted again. She strode out first, still humming. He followed, wondering why the universe had thought it would be amusing to stick them on the same floor.

As she was approaching her apartment, her neighbor's door swung open. An elderly woman dressed in a long robe stepped out, her gray hair in rollers, and pinned an angry gaze on Bailey. "There you are. There was another damn snake in my apartment earlier. I opened the lid of my toilet and got the surprise of my life."

"It just wanted to say hi, Vera," Bailey told her, pulling her keys out of her purse.

"Say hi? It hissed at me."

"No one likes being looked at when they're using the toilet, jeez."

Halting near his front door, Deke sighed. *Unreal.*

"You need to chase these things out of the building," snapped Vera. "If you don't, I'll make sure *you're* the one who's thrown out."

A creepy smile slowly crept onto Bailey's face. Like *seriously* creepy. One that was freakishly wide but didn't reach her eyes. No, her eyes looked dead.

Not good. He'd seen the mamba bite people in the past while wearing that very expression.

He began heading toward them just as Vera's scowl faltered at the sight of Bailey's smile. She tightened the belt of her robe and took a nervous step back.

She *should* be nervous. No shifter took kindly to someone threatening to chase them out of their territory—whether it be an apartment, a stretch of land, or a cardboard box. But one who'd once been a loner like Bailey would be even more territorial, because they'd spent years moving from home to home, never quite settling ... until now. They would not let *anyone* take their personal slice of territory from them.

Reaching the mamba, Deke began shepherding her toward her apartment even as he said, "Vera, go inside." He swiped the keys from Bailey's hand. She didn't react. Didn't even look at him. Her gaze was fixed on her neighbor.

"Try to have me evicted if you'd like," said Bailey, her voice dangerously calm, her words coming out slow and flat.

Having unlocked her front door, he tried urging her inside, but her attention was still fixed on Vera.

"It would be a mistake, of course," Bailey told her. "Because it's not the *full*-blooded snakes you need to worry about. They're not the only ones who can travel through the vents."

Vera swallowed hard and retreated into her home.

Deke ushered Bailey into her own apartment, kicking her door shut behind him. "You were thinking of biting her, weren't you?"

"It crossed my mind. She would have deserved it." Bailey tossed her purse on an amethyst-colored armchair that matched the camel-back sofa. "No one gets to take my home from me."

"You can relax. She won't really try to have you evicted. She probably just thought that the threat would light a fire under your ass." He placed her set of keys on the black glass coffee table. "The fact is, you *do* need to get the full-blooded snakes out of the building. They can't nest in your apartment."

"I don't have any here."

"There's one right over there on top of the bookcase."

She flapped a hand. "That's just Clive. He comes and goes every now and then. That's not nesting. Hey, do me a solid and take your mom's dish with you when you go." She pointed toward the kitchen area. "It's on the countertop. I don't know why she keeps bringing me food, but it's weirding me out." She rolled her shoulders. "Make it stop."

Deke stared at her for a moment. He hadn't thought there was anything that could truly ruffle Bailey. Oh, she often freaked whenever Blair dislocated her joints, but Bailey was also morbidly fascinated by it. The displays of kindness from his mother, however? Yeah, they actually made her uncomfortable.

Amused, he said, "Now that's just ungrateful. She's doing a very nice thing."

"Exactly. It's weird."

He felt his mouth curve. "So there is something that gets to you. Nice gestures."

Her lips flattened. "You need to stop smiling like that."

"Like what?"

"All smug and superior." Bailey didn't care that he apparently felt he was oh-so-much better than her. But her serpent? That was a whole other matter. "It makes my snake want to eat your head."

"Why just my head?"

"I don't know. That's her business."

"Her business?"

Bailey shrugged. "I don't question her motivations or interfere with her choices." Her mamba granted her that same courtesy. They had each other's back, no matter what.

"Maybe you *should* interfere."

"I don't see why." Her snake always had shit covered.

"Maybe because she lunges at people and tries to bite them," he sniped.

Ooh, she did like it when he got all snarky. She knew his surliness partly came from the touch-hunger—it was clear to sense that it had a firm grip on him. His cheeks were flushed, his pupils were dilated, his muscles were bunched, and he was exuding a restless energy.

"Like me, for instance," he added. "She's come at me more than once."

"Well, maybe if you didn't call her Hissy Elliot—"

"It's just a pet name."

"—she'd leave you alone. I say 'maybe.' Probably not, though. She doesn't like you being near me."

He frowned. "Why?"

"She's protective of me. You hate me. Ergo …"

His frown deepened. "I don't hate you. There are times I want to shake you so bad it actually takes my breath away. But I don't hate you. Actually, it's the other way around. *You* loathe *me*."

"No, I don't. I wouldn't waste that kind of emotional energy on you."

"Waste? Oh, well, that's very—" Pain smacked into Deke's head like a thunderclap, making his vision go gray around the edges. *Fuck, fuck, fuck.* His cat lurched up to shoulder some of the pain, moodily baring his teeth at Bailey, blaming her. Unfair, yeah, but the feline didn't care.

Her eyes narrowed. "You're in some serious pain."

In more ways than one, now that his level of arousal was reaching new limits. It didn't help that she smelled like a fucking dream. *Mandarin and orange blossoms.* He should leave. Being here, being around *her*, only made things worse.

At the same time, though, her company gave him a sort of … mental release. He could spar with her. Argue with her. Rile her up. Not have to worry about adopting the social niceties that others obsessed over—Bailey didn't give a rat's furry ass how rude he was.

"Why won't you just go fuck the touch-hunger out of your system?" she asked, clearly baffled. "This is seriously not the time to take a vow of celibacy. It'll just keep getting worse."

"Thanks for letting me know," he deadpanned.

Ignoring that, she went on, "I don't get it. You're a dick, but you're not stupid."

"A dick?"

"Why make this harder for yourself?" She dropped her gaze to his crotch. "Like *literally* harder. You a masochist? Is that it? I never considered that before. Probably should have. Makes sense. You into kinky stuff, too? I had a friend who liked to wear cock cages. He also liked being choked during sex, according to his ex. Not to the point where he passed out or anything, though he apparently did once almost—"

"Stop talking about sex," he gritted out, because his cock hurt so much at this point that it would hurt to walk.

"If even hearing someone talk about it is making things worse, you need to address the matter fast."

He felt his nostrils flare. "I don't remember asking for your advice."

"That's because you didn't."

"Then why give it?"

"I'm a giving person."

"You give people problems and headaches—that's about it."

She smiled. "It takes the kind of skill you'll never master."

He clenched his jaw. "I really want to shake you right now." Really, really hard.

"Then my work here is done." She wiggled her fingers. "See you around, Eye Candy. Don't forget the dish."

It was amazing how much one measly little form of address could piss him off so tremendously. And her tone … God, that fucking tone that disdained him so effortlessly. Like he was some pretty boy with no depth of character or purpose in life.

It made him want to grab her by the throat. And then maybe squeeze just a little. Or kiss her. Or both. "My name is Deke."

She sniffed. "So?"

This was seriously the wrong time for her to taunt him. His level of tolerance was at an all-time low. So much pent-up irritation was coiled in his stomach, pushing for a release. He crossed to her. "So use it."

"Why?"

He dipped his head. "You don't want to keep goading me, Bailey," he warned. "You wouldn't like what happened if you pushed me too far."

Her eyes lit up with interest. "Ooh, what would happen?" She clasped her hands in front of her. "Would there be bloodshed?"

"Depends."

"On what, Boy Toy?"

He inched a little closer. "On whether you're much of a scratcher when you come."

She did a slow blink, clearly taken aback. But then she snorted. "Like you'd ever put any part of yourself near my lady bits. Like I'd even *let* you or—*what the hell*?"

Deke really hadn't meant to cup her pussy. It had happened before he could stop it. And now, as the heat of her warmed his palm even through her underwear and dress, he didn't want to let go. "Looks like you were wrong on both counts."

Her eyes went wide, and she smiled. "You're being brilliantly bold. I'm quite proud of you right now. Didn't think you had it in you. Go you!"

He stared at her, momentarily lost for words. "You're not normal."

Her smile ramped up. "I know. I kind of thought we'd already established that. Now, are you going to make me come, or are you just all talk?" It wasn't a question. No, she was quite sure he'd back off.

His cat peeled back his upper lip, urging Deke to teach her a lesson. The animal wanted to show her that he and Deke weren't so weak-willed. Wanted her to realize that she was wrong to dismiss them. Wanted her to actually *see* them rather than look *through* them.

Deke stared deep into her eyes. "You don't know me as well as you think you do."

She gave him a sympathetic smile. "Too proud to back down, huh? Okay, I'll take pity on you and—"

He ground the heel of his palm against her clit.

She double-blinked, a light gasp escaping her. "Well, now. You're just full of surprises tonight."

Agreed. He was surprising even himself.

"But let's face it, you don't want this to go any further, so I think you should—"

He rubbed at her clit again, eliciting another soft gasp from her. "You have no fucking clue what I want."

His cat growled, butting him, urging him to teach her that he wasn't to be underestimated … which was right when the spicy scent of feminine arousal rose up to greet him. And something in Deke quite simply snapped.

Bailey froze as—with a snarl that fairly rang with power and dominance—Deke locked his mouth with hers. But her stillness lasted only seconds. Because then the sexually charged tension between them exploded, and all her thoughts scattered.

It wasn't a kiss. It was a hot, heavy, collision of tongues, lips, and teeth. They savagely ate at each other's mouths, inhibited.

She gripped his upper arms, grinding against the big, warm hand roughly gliding over her clit. Each grind shot to her hardening nipples and made her core pang in need. She couldn't quite believe this was happening, but she wasn't about to stop it.

His free hand tangled in her hair and sharply angled her head, allowing him to thrust his tongue deeper. He feasted on her with so much intensity and desperation, like she was the first woman he'd seen in decades. Her scalp stung from his harsh hold, but she liked the burn. Liked the blatant boldness—one that both surprised and impressed her snake—with which he took Bailey over.

The hand cupping her pussy disappeared.

What the …?

In one swift move, he shoved that same hand up her dress and thrust it into her panties. Firmly palming her pussy, he spread his fingers, parting her folds, exposing the supersensitive nerves between them to the cool air … and then jammed a finger inside her.

Bailey jolted with a gasp that he swallowed, his pupils *blown*. Her muscles rippled around the invading digit as it began to fuck in and out of her. His gaze locked on her own, he kept his mouth pressed to hers as he pumped.

Moaning, she arched into every thrust, digging her nails into his arms. Every drive of his finger hit just the right spot, pushing her closer and closer to coming.

She wanted to pull his cock out of his jeans. Wanted to feel him in her hand. Wanted to jerk him off and give him the relief he'd—for some mysterious reason—been depriving himself of.

But considering he was knee-deep in touch-hunger, he'd come pretty quickly, and she didn't trust the mean bastard not to walk out as soon as he'd had an orgasm. As such, she'd wait until she'd had her own. It really wouldn't be long …

Fingers slipped out of her hair and trailed down her face. His mouth followed, giving her suckling little kisses. He moved as if to coast his lips down her neck. She hissed, not trusting him enough to let his teeth near her throat.

He snapped his hand around her neck. "Behave." He shoved a second finger into her pussy.

Three thrusts later, she imploded with a choked cry as pure pleasure flooded her. Even as her inner muscles spasmed like crazy, she tore open his fly and then fisted his cock as it sprang out. The guttural sound that sawed out of his throat was a growl, a groan, and a *demand* all wrapped into one. Her snake liked it.

Bailey tightened her grip and pumped. Fast. Knowing he needed 'rough' to get off while in this state.

He fucked her fist, grunting into her mouth. And then he was coming with a snarl. Ropes of warm come splashed onto her fingers and dress.

As every bit of tension seemed to leach from his body, he dropped his forehead to her temple and panted out long, heavy breaths. Not quite in control of her own breathing, she released his cock and wiped her hand on her dress.

Moments later, as his fingers slipped out of her, Bailey blew out a breath. "Well, that was weird."

His head reared back, and he frowned at her in affront. "Weird?"

"It's not every day a girl gets sent to O-town by a dude who has more than once threatened to choke her."

Backing up, he shook his head and tucked away his cock. He looked as if he might lick his fingers clean, but then he wiped them on his jeans instead.

She studied him carefully as he refastened his fly, noting that the almost manic energy he'd carried earlier was now absent. The touch-hunger had subsided, then. For now, at least. There, she'd done her good deed for the decade.

She noted something else as well. "You're dying to hightail it out of here." It was written all over his face. No surprise there, though. If it hadn't been for the touch-hunger, he likely wouldn't have touched her at all. "Having regrets, huh?"

"No. I've wanted to get my hands and mouth on you since the first day we met."

She blinked at the unashamed, matter-of-fact statement.

"But my cat …"

She nodded as realization hit her. "Oh, he doesn't like me." Her snake flicked out her tongue, all "*well, fuck him*."

Deke sighed, looking tired. "Right now, he doesn't like anyone."

Her instincts stirred. Something was going on with his cat. Something that was making the feline want zero physical contact. "That's why you haven't worked off the touch-hunger."

A muscle in his cheek ticked.

She wasn't surprised that he didn't confirm it. He would never trust her with his animal's secrets. To be fair, that went both ways.

"I've got to go." He flexed the hand that had moments ago sent her soaring. "Get rid of the snakes."

"At the moment, the only ones here are Clive and that monster in your jeans."

A breath whistled out from between his gritted teeth. "Jesus. Right, I'm leaving." He stalked to the door and pulled it open. Half-turning, he met her gaze, his own still a little blissed out from his orgasm. He parted his lips as if to speak, but then he sighed instead.

She smiled at the impatient sound. "Nighty, night."

He grunted. "Whatever." He left, pulling the door closed behind him.

She couldn't help but chuckle at the rude bastard. A bastard who'd given her a very delightful orgasm and hungrily ate at her mouth like he'd never tasted anything better. How sad that it wouldn't happen again.

CHAPTER THREE

Hearing footfalls head his way the next afternoon, Deke turned away from the coffeehouse's front window mere moments before the waitress placed a mug of black coffee on his table.

Cassandra gave him a bright smile. "Here."

Looking up at his pride mate, Deke tipped his chin at her in thanks.

Resting a hand on the back of the chair across from him, she tilted her head to study him carefully, making her high pink ponytail hang to the side. "How are you doing?"

"Fine." He flexed his fingers, restlessness still living and breathing in his system. But the arousal had subsided, and he no longer felt so uncomfortable in his own skin that he was tempted to claw it off. Which, of course, was courtesy of last night's orgasm. Something he'd told himself he wouldn't think about, because that only led to his cock stirring, and he'd had enough of walking around with a constant hard-on.

"You don't look fine. You look tense as a bow."

Well, if memories of last night would stop crawling to the forefront of his mind, he'd be a lot more relaxed. Jesus, he hadn't come that hard in … he couldn't even remember. Maybe never.

What else could he have expected, though? He'd practically been dancing on the edge of an orgasm for weeks. He'd been wound so tight it almost hurt. *Coming* had almost hurt it was that intense. He'd felt wrung dry afterward.

But he'd be lying if he said that his release would have been so violent and mind-numbing at the touch of just *any* woman. That it had been Bailey's hand wrapped around his dick, Bailey's pussy rippling around his fingers, Bailey's taste on his tongue had magnified the moment.

He could still vividly remember the feel of her hot inner walls clenching his fingers so tight he was surprised they hadn't gone numb. He'd wanted to feel those same muscles clamped around his cock, but it hadn't been possible.

The only reason his cat had allowed Deke to touch her in the first place was that he'd been determined to make his point. Once the moment was over, he'd hissed at Bailey and whipped his tail aggressively … leaving Deke no choice but to back off and take it no further.

Now his cat was back to being averse at even the *thought* of another person's touch. Which was a real fucking problem, because the touch-hunger would flare up again at some point. And likely without warning. That was usually how it went—there was no build-up; it struck out of nowhere, and it struck hard.

Deke inwardly sighed. He had no idea what to do about his cat. No clue if there was anything that could help.

Cassandra slipped onto the chair opposite him. "Why are you doing this to yourself?" she asked, her pale-green eyes soft with concern. "You know you could come to me to work off the touch-hunger, right? There'd be no strings, just like last time."

Deke's cat hissed, unsheathing the tips of his claws. But even if the feline hadn't been so against it, even if Deke had thought it fair to sleep with one woman when his mind was on another, he would have turned down Cassandra's offer. He made a point of not working off touch-hunger with the same female twice. It seemed disrespectful.

"It's bad enough that I'd be sleeping with someone purely to get rid of the touch-hunger—I'm using them, plain and simple," he said. "I'm not going to use the same person repeatedly like it's all they're good for."

"I wouldn't see it that way. And don't forget, I'd be using you too," she added, smiling. "The difference is that I don't have touch-hunger. I just want emotionless sex."

"You wound me."

She snorted. "Doubtful."

He lifted his mug and took a sip of his coffee. "It wouldn't be good to put yourself on my mother's radar all over again." Back then, Livy had done her best to coax him and Cassandra to turn their arrangement into something more—it had driven them both nuts.

"I guess," uttered Cassandra.

"I'm pretty sure that Sam wouldn't like it if I took you up on your offer anyway." Deke slid the healer a brief look. The trim Asian male was leaning against the counter, his dark eyes on Cassandra … and not looking too pleased about her sitting with Deke.

Her lips hiked up. "He's hot, no doubt about it. And a total sweetheart. But he's not dominant enough for my cat's liking. She's frustratingly picky that way, as you know."

The bell above the door chimed.

Looking behind her, Deke saw Shay breeze inside. The very sight of the newcomer made Deke's cat narrow his eyes and let out a rumbly growl of agitation. This had been a "thing" for months now, and Deke was damn tired of it.

Shay had been a good friend of his for years. His cat had never had a problem with the other male … until Shay first began sleeping with Bailey. Even now, despite that the pair were no longer sharing a bed, the feline bristled just *looking* at him.

Really, Deke's cat could be weird where Bailey was concerned. Before becoming strangely averse to sexual intimacy, the feline had been intrigued by and attracted to her, even though she made him crazy. Though he hadn't pushed Deke to pursue her, he also had never liked when she was with other men; never liked that she evidently saw a value in them that she didn't seem to see in Deke or his cat. This hadn't changed.

Shay's gaze swept the space, pausing when it landed on Deke. His eyes widened slightly in what seemed like pleasant surprise. He began heading Deke's way, which only made his inner cat growl again. Louder.

Cassandra stood, giving Deke a too-quick smile. "You know where to find me if you change your mind," she quietly said.

He gave her a subtle nod, though he wouldn't accept her offer at a later date.

Reaching them, Shay beamed. "Hey, D. Cassandra, you look gorgeous as usual."

"Always the charmer," she said with a playful huff.

"Any chance of a pumpkin spiced latte?" Shay asked her, skimming his fingers through his tousled brown hair as he took the seat she'd vacated.

"Give me five minutes and I'll bring it right to you." She then strode off.

Turning to Deke, Shay snorted at whatever he saw on his face. "Don't look *too* pleased to see me," he said, his voice dry.

Deke grunted. "I'm not in the best mood."

"When are you ever?" Shay teased.

"Also, you're annoying."

The other male grinned. "God, you're a rude bastard. Good thing I'm used to it."

"Does that mean you're not going to go away?"

"Yup. You're a big boy, you can handle a little company and conversation. I can't remember the last time we shot the shit. It was before I started dating Bailey."

Deke felt his back teeth lock, and his cat bared a fang.

A smile pulled at Shay's mouth. "I heard something went down between her and some dude at your dad's party. No one seems to know exactly what got said or who he is. Care to share?"

"No." Unlike many of his pride, Deke wasn't one to gossip.

Shay snickered. "Fine. I'm more intrigued about something else I heard anyway. See, apparently, your body language was all kinds of protective. You didn't seem to like seeing another dude so close to her."

"Of course I didn't like it. He was practically in her face."

"Hmm. I think it was more than that, though. It might not be obvious to those who don't know you," he went on, lowering his voice, "but you have a little thing for the mamba. No, don't deny it—we both know you'd be lying."

Biting back a growl, Deke calmly took a sip of his drink.

"I have to ask …" Shay leaned forward. "Why aren't you exploiting this opportunity you have to go after what you want without breaking your vow to Dayna?"

Deke felt his nostrils flare slightly. "Leave it, Shay."

"But I don't get it. It makes no sense to me—if for no other reason than it's only logical to get *something* good out of being struck by touch-hunger." Shay paused as Cassandra materialized with his drink. He cast her a grateful smile and waited for her to walk away before then refocusing on Deke. "Seriously, why not just do it?"

"This isn't your business."

"Since when would I let something like that bother me?"

Deke rolled his eyes.

Shay leaned away, his face scrunching up. "You're not holding back from Bailey because you mistakenly think I'll otherwise be hurt, are you? I like her, but I was no more serious about her than she was about me. Which made it easy to back off when I realized you had a thing for her." Humor glimmered in his eyes. "I don't think I've ever seen you jealous before."

Deke frowned. "I wasn't jealous."

"Oh, how you lie."

Okay. Fine. He'd been jealous. So what?

"You hid it well at first. If I'd sensed it sooner, I'd have broken it off with her quicker." Shay sobered. "You know that, right? You know I wouldn't date someone you were interested in?"

"I'm not interested in anything but changing this subject."

"Tell me you know I wouldn't have touched her if I'd seen you were so into her," Shay persisted.

"Okay, three things. One, I'm not as into her as I think you believe." Deke sounded convincing even to his own ears. "Two, even if I was, I'd have been in no position to expect you to stay away from her, given I made a promise to Dayna. Three, yes, I *do* know you'd have kept your distance from a woman if you thought I had more interest in her than you did. Now, if it's all the same to you, I'd prefer to talk about something else. How's your mom? I heard she had a fall."

Shay stared at him, his lips pursed. Finally, he sat back with a resigned sigh. "Fine, we'll change the subject."

Between sips of their drinks, they talked of general things. Shay occasionally tried circling back to the topic of Bailey, but Deke was having none of it, so the other male eventually relented. Once their mugs were empty, they exited the coffeehouse and then said their goodbyes.

Deke had taken two steps toward his apartment building when he heard someone call his name. Half-turning, he found a petite brunette speed-walking in his direction, a huge-ass smile of excitement on her face.

She stopped in front of him. *Human*, his nose told him. "I came to surprise you. I was going to head to your building, but then I saw you from across the street and, gah, this is nuts!" She slapped her hands on her reddening cheeks. "I can't believe you're *right there*." She moved as if to hug him.

"I know you?" he asked, almost taking a step back.

She blinked, her body tensing, her smile faltering. "I … What?"

"Do I know you?" He didn't believe so. He was good with faces, but nothing about hers tickled his memory. He didn't recognize her scent either, and neither did his cat. Yet, she was looking at him as if they were well-acquainted.

She cleared her throat. "Deke, it's me."

"And who is me?"

A frown slipped over her face. "Are … are you trying to be funny?"

"No."

"I know my hairstyle is different—I went to the salon yesterday—but you can't *not* recognize me."

"From where?"

Her mouth flattened. "My pictures, obviously."

Okay, now he was beyond confused. He turned to fully face her. "What pictures?"

Her hands fisted at her sides. "This isn't funny, Deke."

"No, it ain't," he agreed.

"What game are you playing?"

"Woman, no joke, I don't know you. I have no clue how you could know me."

Her nostrils flared. "It's Maisy."

"I don't know any Maisy."

Red flags of anger stained her cheeks. "There's no way to *not* know someone you've been in a relationship with for the past three months."

He felt his head jerk. "What the fuck?"

The anger began to melt from her expression as a glint of confused panic entered her eyes. "You're Deke. Deke Hammond. Right?"

"Right."

"You're thirty-five. You like hiking. Hate bad food service. You have two brothers—one older, one younger. Right?"

His nape prickled. "How do you know all that?"

"Because you told me. It was you. It *has* to have been you." With an unsteady hand, she yanked her phone out of her purse, tapped on the screen a few times, and then held it up. "Look. That's you."

Recognizing the social media profile on the screen, he went to confirm it, but then something caught his eye. His brows snapped together as a shocked anger flamed to life in his belly. "The fuck?"

"What? What is it?"

"That isn't me. Same name, same pictures, same general info. But it's not my profile." The posts weren't his. *Someone* was clearly posing as him online. "Son of a bitch," he breathed.

She stared at him, horror making her jaw drop. "Oh, God. Your … your voice sounds different, but I didn't think anything of it. Most voices sound different over the phone."

Sensing she was going to bolt out of mortification, he said, "Let me get this straight. You're in an online relationship with this person here?"

She shoved a hand into her hair. "You—they—contacted me through this profile. We connected. We grew close … Why would someone do this?"

"I don't know." But he'd goddamn find out. "Let's go somewhere and talk. I've got questions I'm gonna need to ask you."

"Come on, Bailey, really?"

Pausing scribbling on the sheet of paper tacked to the office corkboard, Bailey looked at the grizzly shifter who was stalking into the room. "What?"

Corbin gave her an incredulous look. "You're actually signing the petition to have you fired?"

"I'm feeling left out."

Shaking his head, he took a seat behind his desk.

"Why haven't you taken the petition down?" Havana asked him from the chair directly opposite him.

Corbin cast a quick glance at Bailey. "She asked me not to."

Well, of course she had. "It's wise to know who your enemies are."

Havana inclined her head, allowing that.

"I thought you three would have left by now—your shift is over." Corbin rested his clasped hands on the surface of the table, his gaze cautious as it settled on Bailey. "I'm guessing you want to talk about Ginny's recent allegation. You should be aware that she's made several calls to the staff here—me included—swearing you're responsible for the attack on Jackson."

"Unbelievable," muttered Aspen, stood beside Havana's chair. "Do any of the staff believe that Ginny's right?"

He snorted. "No. They know full well that Bailey isn't a person who'll hide her crimes. As one of the staff said … '*Bailey won't stab a person—metaphorical or otherwise—in the back; she'll aim right for their fucking eye.*'"

Smiling, Bailey put a hand to her chest. "Aw, that's sweet. Also accurate." She'd actually gone for someone's eye a time or two. There was nothing quite like feeling an eyeball *pop*. "That's not why I'm here, though."

Corbin's brow inched up. "Oh?"

She crossed to his desk and set down the pen she'd used to doodle her name on the petition. "My cousin made a reappearance. The one who keeps dying."

The grizzly's mouth tightened. "What did the little bastard want this time?"

"Protection," replied Bailey, moving to stand near Havana. "He owes the Westwood jackals a shit ton of cash."

Corbin's brows flew together. "Jackals? You shitting me?"

"Nu-uh."

The grizzly shook his head again, grim. "I should be surprised, but he isn't the brightest bulb. What's truly surprising is that he's lived this long."

"I had the same thought," muttered Aspen.

"I'm guessing you all sent Roman on his way," he hedged.

"Good guess," said Bailey. "The jackals will probably want to talk to me at some point—they'll hardly overlook his debt; they'll try to hunt him down. Much as it pisses me off, it's possible that they'll come looking for me here, so I wanted to give you a heads-up. Actually, there's a chance Roman might show here too. It would be wiser for him to go to ground, but he could think he can convince me to change my mind."

"If that little shit stain comes here, he'll wish he hadn't." Corbin cricked his neck. "That nest of his is a joke."

Totally. Even *thinking* of the Umber Nest made her snake want to bite someone. Anyone would do, really.

The way Bailey saw it, she'd been better off with Corbin than growing up with that bunch of selfish assholes. That didn't make her anger at the choices they'd made years ago any less potent, though. Nor did it make much of a difference to her mamba.

Havana twisted her mouth. "I don't think we'll have to worry that the jackals will do anything stupid. They're not going to struggle to believe she turned Roman away, because when they look into his relatives and learn of her existence, they'll also learn that the Umber Nest fucked her over. The jackals will see that she has no motivation to help anyone from the nest."

Aspen nodded. "And even if they aren't willing to dismiss that she's aiding Roman, I don't see them attacking her or anything. Their pack might be tough, but Roman was right about one thing—they won't want trouble with a pride mostly made up of pallas cats."

"Still," began Corbin, "be ready for trouble all the same. The Westwood Pack have a bad reputation, and jackals don't always do what you'd expect."

"Yeah, that species can be pretty unpredictable." Bailey grinned, adding,

"Like me."

"Should you really be so proud of that?" Corbin questioned. "I'm thinking no."

"I'm thinking yes."

He playfully scoffed. "Of course you are." He straightened in his seat. "Hopefully, the entire situation blows over very soon. Be sure to keep me updated."

Bailey saluted him. "Will do, Paddington."

He shot her a look of mock annoyance. "Paddington Bear is not a grizzly."

"So?"

"So there's no sense in—You know what, forget it. I've come to accept that the concept of logic will always escape you."

Bailey grinned again. "Took your sweet time."

Snorting, Havana stood. "Come on, let's go."

Outside, Bailey and her girls headed straight for the car she'd been assigned by the pride. Like all the other pride-owned vehicles, it boasted bulletproof windows.

As they decided to drop by the pride's bakery, she didn't drive Havana straight home as she usually did. Instead, Bailey parked her car in the lot outside her apartment building and then walked with Aspen and Havana to the bakery.

As they entered, the scents of coffee, yeasty dough, spices, and fresh bread washed over Bailey. She inhaled it all, loving it. Her snake wasn't as equal a fan, finding no such things appetizing.

The place was at its busiest around noon, but though it was after six in the evening, there were still plenty of patrons sitting around or standing in the line at the counter. The sounds of dishware clattering, background music, and the tumbling of a dough mixer filled the space.

After Bailey and her girls bought both a drink and one of the baked treats from behind the glass counter, they claimed a table.

Peeling the crackly wax paper from her lemon muffin, Bailey hummed in delight. "So, we still on for movie night tomorrow?"

"Absolutely," said Havana, lifting her éclair from her plate. "We'll have it at my place."

"Good. I like your TV best."

"I don't know why. It's no different than your own."

"Some things cannot be explained, they just *are*."

Havana sighed, flapping her free hand. "Whatever."

"Goddamn shitbag," Aspen muttered under her breath, her upper lip peeling back in disgust.

Bailey frowned. "What? Who?"

Tearing open a sugar packet a little too hard, the bearcat tipped her chin toward a member of the line. "Check out his neck tattoo."

Catching sight of what was basically the no-smoking sign only it featured a wolf's head rather than a cigarette, Bailey had to bite back a growl. Her snake flicked out her tongue, feeling nothing but pure scorn. The sigil was commonly worn by anti-shifter extremists.

The hateful, fanatic humans were very much in favor of culling the shifter population—particularly by attacking them, bombing their territories, and insisting that mated couples be restricted to having only one child.

More, the extremists appealed for shifters to be electronically chipped, unallowed to leave their territory, prohibited from mating with humans, and placed on a register like sex offenders.

Grave mistake.

Because shifters were predators. They didn't run or hide or play nice. They fought violence with violence. So they'd formed the Movement, a group which had no issue eliminating entire factions of extremists and assassinating those in power.

Preferring to keep the identities of their members private, the Movement often recruited unmated lone shifters since they were able to more easily fly under the radar. The group had recruited Bailey, Havana, Aspen, and Camden many years ago. While the four had appeared to live simple lives to the outside world, they'd actually done plenty of Movement-work in the background.

Members weren't considered disposable soldiers. The group was a family who looked out for each other. They also didn't allow members to perform more than eight years of service, wanting shifters to go find their mates rather than dedicate their lives to dealing with asshole-extremists.

Not many people outside the group knew that Bailey, her girls, and Camden were once part of it. Only Corbin, Tate, and Luke. As such, most had no idea that the four ex-members were trained in all kinds of shit that came in real handy at times.

"They all need shooting," declared Havana before taking a hard bite of her éclair.

"If the dude knew he was currently surrounded by shifters, he wouldn't be so at ease," Aspen asserted, pouring sugar into her cup of coffee.

"I hope someone spits all over his order." Havana licked at the small blob of crème that got stuck to the corner of her mouth. "A little rat poison wouldn't hurt either."

"My thoughts exactly." Aspen tipped some milk into her drink and then stirred it with a teaspoon. "Going by the look on Jessie's face, she's considering it."

"I wouldn't be surprised if she did." The female was as fierce as her mate, Farrell, who was also the pride's head enforcer. Bailey took a bite of her muffin, almost moaning in delight as the warm, lemony filling hit her tongue.

"On another note … I got finger-fucked by Deke last night."

Havana's éclair slipped out of her hands. "*What?*"

"And I jacked him off," Bailey added.

"*What?*" demanded Aspen.

"It was totally unexpected, I—"

Aspen slammed up a hand. "Wait, slow down, are you serious right now?"

"Deadly." Bailey had done her upmost best to put the encounter out of her mind but, yeah, she'd failed. Especially that damn kiss—it kept replaying in her mind.

No one had ever kissed her like that. As if every ounce of their focus had been on tasting and exploring and feasting on her mouth, like nothing had ever been more important. A girl could easily get addicted to something like that.

Havana did a slow blink. "Oh my God, you're not kidding."

Her eyes glinting with avid interest, Aspen leaned forward. "How did all that come about?"

Bailey took another bite out of her muffin. "He followed me into my apartment to make sure I didn't bite Vera—it was a close call. She threatened to have me evicted. Can you believe that?" Her snake was still stewing over that.

Havana clicked her fingers. "Focus, Bailey. We're talking about Deke."

Setting down her muffin, Bailey rolled her eyes. "We talked. Well, bickered. I called him Eye Candy. He got all frowny. Then he warned me not to keep pushing him or I'd regret it."

"So you kept pushing him," guessed Aspen, breaking off a small piece of her white-chocolate-chip cookie.

"Of course." Bailey lifted her bottle of water and unscrewed the cap. "I asked if there'd be bloodshed. He said it depended on whether I was a scratcher when I came. I snorted and told him there was no way he'd touch me like that. Next thing I knew, his hand was down south. He didn't do anything at first, just kept his hand there."

Pausing, Bailey sipped her water while her friends gawked at her. "I have to say, I was very impressed that he went that far. I didn't think he'd dare. I have to salute the guy for being so ballsy."

Havana waved that away. "Salute him later. I want to hear what happened next."

"Nosy heifer," teased Bailey, setting down her bottle. "I guess his pride got in the way, because he wouldn't back down. It probably didn't help that he was dealing with touch-hunger. He kissed the breath from my damn lungs, and then somehow his fingers ended up inside me. After I came, I jerked him off." She shrugged.

"Genuinely?" asked Havana, leaning forward in her seat. "This really happened?"

Bailey dipped her chin. "It really happened."

The devil eyed her carefully. "You're not lying?"

"Why would I lie?"

"Because you sometimes make stuff up when you're bored."

"I don't like having nothing to do," Bailey defended.

"Woman, be real, did you and Deke honestly give each other hand jobs last night?"

"We honestly did."

Her lips parting, Havana sat back in her chair. "Well, hell and damn."

"Yes indeed." Aspen tossed a broken-off piece of cookie into her mouth. "I don't know what to say except 'wow.'"

Frowning, Bailey bit into her muffin again. "Then why didn't you just say 'wow' and nothing else?"

Aspen pulled a face. "Do you have to be annoying all the time?"

"It brings me joy," said Bailey. "Don't you want me to be happy?"

"No, not really."

Havana cut in, "We're wandering off the subject; I'm not ready for that yet." She shot Bailey a glare. "I can't believe you're only telling us *now* that you and Deke got your hands a *good* kind of dirty last night."

Bailey frowned. "Why?"

"Besties don't wait to share intriguing stuff with each other." The devil lifted what was left of her éclair. "Why did you both stop at foreplay?"

"He didn't want it to go any further." Bailey told herself that it didn't bother her, but though she was a tip-top liar, she wasn't very good at bullshitting herself.

Havana's eyes narrowed. "Did you say something to piss him off?"

"No." Bailey chucked what was left of her muffin into her mouth. "He just isn't interested."

"I highly doubt that. Like, I couldn't doubt it more."

"Same here," said Aspen before taking a sip of her coffee. "Maybe he wants to clear things with Shay first; make sure the guy won't be upset by it."

Havana pointed at the bearcat. "Hmm, yes, it could be that. Deke's loyal to his friends. Whatever the case, it's obvious now that he does want to be up in her business."

Bailey snickered. "Uh, wrong. I'm not saying he isn't attracted to me." She knew he was, since he'd made it clear last night that he'd wanted her from day one. She wouldn't have thought it would matter much to her snake either way, but the mamba liked that a whole lot. "I just don't think he's happy about it. Probably because he doesn't like me as a person."

Her nose wrinkling, Aspen sipped her drink again. "I don't think he dislikes you, but I do think it's possible that he begrudges being attracted to you. And I think that's because he's all tangled up in a promise he made to another woman."

"But while dealing with touch-hunger, he can act on what he wants," Havana added.

"He didn't, though, did he? He kept his distance from me all these weeks," Bailey pointed out. "He had no intention of coming to me at any point. He never meant for last night to happen. And, hello, has it not occurred to you that maybe I don't want to be used as a mere sexual plaything while someone gets rid of their touch-hunger?"

Aspen let out a low snort. "No. You like being a plaything. And you've helped guys through touch-hunger before. You enjoyed it."

Yeah, she did. "They fuck like savages. It's ace." She liked her sex rough and raw, and she made no apologies for it. She didn't see why anyone should have to.

"So then I'm not seeing why you'd have a problem giving Deke a helping hand." Aspen set down her mug, flicking up a brow. "Unless you're worried you'll get attached?"

Bailey felt her brow crease. "To what?"

"To him," replied Aspen, enunciating each word like Bailey was slow on the uptake. "Emotionally."

Bailey started to laugh. "Get the fuck out of here."

Aspen's eyes widened. "Hey, it's possible."

"Yeah, nah."

"You bonded with us," said Aspen, gesturing from herself to Havana.

"That was an accident."

"Well, maybe you'll accidentally bond with Deke just the same." Impatience rippled across the bearcat's face. "Why are you still laughing? It could happen."

Not likely. Her snake couldn't believe the woman was even suggesting it. "How could I actually bond with someone who I once begged the universe to make fall face-first into a steaming pile of horse shit?"

Aspen looked at Havana. "That sounds like love to me."

"Agreed." The devil ate the last of her pastry. "The bond is already forming."

Bailey crossed her eyes. "God, you're such dorks."

Havana used a napkin to wipe her fingers. "I'm thinking I should invite Deke round for movie night."

Bailey tensed, pausing in reaching for her water bottle. "What?"

Aspen enthusiastically nodded at Havana. "He can hang with Tate and Camden on the deck."

"That's what I'm thinking," said the Alpha female.

"But why invite him?" asked Bailey.

Havana smiled. "I want to watch you two together."

"Like, in bed?"

"What? No, you freak." Havana tossed the napkin at her. "I want to see how your interactions go now that you've touched each other's no-no places."

Bailey did a slow blink and then shrugged. "Well, whatever works for ya." Hearing her cell ping, she fished it out of her purse to find that she had a text from Tate. She read it quickly and then said, "Huh."

"What?" asked Havana.

Bailey lifted her head and met the devil's gaze. "I've been summoned by your mate. He wants me to head to your place right now. Am I in trouble?"

"Is there a reason that you should be?"

Probably. "Not that I know of."

"Then maybe he just wants your help with something." Havana stood. "Let's go find out."

CHAPTER FOUR

Letting out a little shudder as a cool breeze whispered over her, Bailey stuffed her hands in her jacket pockets as she walked into the cute cul-de-sac where the Alphas lived. Every house was owned by the pride and inhabited by one or more of the members. They also currently boasted fall decorations.

Artificial autumn wreaths hung on doors. Pumpkins and colorful planters lined porches. Leaf garlands formed arches around doorways.

Only 6:30pm, it wasn't dark yet. Still, due to the time of year, dusk was already beginning to fall. As such, the lampposts were lit, casting light over the sidewalk—making the wet ground look sleek and shimmery. The rain had stopped, and Bailey hoped it didn't start up again. She wasn't a fan of being caught in it.

Reaching the Alpha pair's house, Bailey followed Havana up the creaky porch steps. The devil shifter had pulled out her own fall decorations. Lanterns sat either side of the pumpkin towers that flanked the front door. Baskets of harvest foliage rested on the porch near the two chairs that Havana had covered with orange and red tartan blankets.

Guarding the house, Farrell currently sat on one of the aforementioned chairs, idly rocking forwards and backwards. Also guarding the house, Isaiah watched from a chair on his own porch.

Most single shifters chose to live in one of the apartment buildings, but Isaiah had recently moved next-door. *How* he was single, Bailey did not know. The dude was hotter than hot, and he had the whole bad-boy thing going on.

Both males tipped their chin in greeting. The girls returned their hellos while Havana unlocked the front door, her hand gently steadying the swaying wreath.

Bailey followed her Alpha female into the house, conscious of Aspen closing the door behind them. Only two people were in the living room—Tate and Deke. Both stood near the fireplace wearing severe expressions.

Bailey's pulse did an irritating little skip at the sight of Deke. She ignored it, of course.

His eyes latched on hers, dark and brooding and far too piercing. She ignored that, too.

But there was no way to ignore her body's reaction to the intense eye-contact. A rush of sexual awareness pulsed through her system. Because now she knew how hot and demanding his mouth could be, how talented his hands were, how long and thick the dick in his pants happened to be. And she was far too eager for a repeat—something she'd likely never get, if only because his cat wouldn't allow her close again.

That his feline had such an issue with Bailey galled her inner mamba. Offended on Bailey's behalf, the snake wanted to whip his furry head with her tail.

Though Deke appeared pissed about something, he didn't seem to be as tightly wound today in a physical sense, so the orgasm that Bailey had given him was apparently still helping with the touch-hunger to some extent.

"What's going on?" asked Havana, looking from one male to the other.

"We need Bailey's hacking skills." Tate slid his gaze to Bailey and then gestured at the laptop on the coffee table.

She perched herself on the sofa and then set the laptop on her lap. A tap of the space bar took the computer off its standby mode, and the blank screen was then quickly replaced by a very familiar NetherVille profile. She quickly scanned it and then looked up at Deke, who was still staring at her. "This isn't you."

His brow pinched. "How do you know?"

"You don't have *that* many friends."

Tate barked a shocked laugh that cracked his serious expression.

Deke shot him the world's worst glower.

"And there's no way you'd post inspirational memes," Bailey went on. The cranky cat rolled his eyes at that stuff. "Also, there are no posts on your page that are written by pride members."

Swiping his hand down his face as if to wipe away his amused smile, Tate focused on her. "You're right, it isn't him. We need to know who created this profile, and then we need to deal with them."

Bailey instantly got to work, flicking Deke a brief look as she guessed, "They did more than simply clone your profile, huh?"

He inclined his head, his lips thinning. "Posing as me, they entered into an online relationship with a human female."

Bailey's fingers halted. "Say what?"

"You're not serious," burst out Havana.

A muscle in his cheek ticked. "Couldn't be more serious."

"Fuck me," Aspen breathed. "Did he also tell her you're a pallas cat?"

Deke shook his head. "No. She has no clue that I'm a shifter or part of a pride. Also, he didn't give her my *exact* address—only the location of my apartment building. But he was otherwise pretty detailed in his descriptions of me and my life."

Holy hell, what a freaking doozy. No wonder Deke looked ready to snap someone's neck. She'd totally help him do it.

Havana perched her hands on her hips. "How did you find out?"

"The human tracked me down to 'surprise' me, having no clue that she's been duped for the past three months," he replied. "I took her to the hole-in-the wall café not far from here away from acute shifter hearing to get the full story from her."

"And?" prodded Havana.

Deke rolled his shoulders, wishing he could easily shake off the anger that had settled in his gut. The same emotion kept knifing through his cat, awakening its primal need to hunt. "This person contacted her via NetherVille three months ago. They got talking. Exchanged phone numbers. They text and call each other on a daily basis. Have heart-to-hearts. He even wrote her poetry."

"So he's a regular Romeo," said Aspen.

"She showed me some of the messages he sent her. The guy is smooth. Always compliments and builds her up. Always says the right thing at the right time." *So very unlike me,* thought Deke. He could never be called verbally smooth.

"I take it they never video-called," said Havana.

"No, they did," Deke told her. "But the image of his face was always pixelated, so she never saw him clearly. Fed up of him making excuses as to why he couldn't meet up with her, she decided to come to him. Me."

"That's some wild shit," commented Bailey without looking away from the laptop, her fingers deftly flying over the keys at such an incredible speed that his cat begrudgingly respected it.

Deke had once asked where she'd learned to hack. Her response? Prison.

It was the same answer she gave him whenever he asked where she'd acquired any of the impressive skills he'd come to realize that she possessed. Havana, Aspen, and Camden were equally skilled in various areas, and all were vague about how that came about.

Returning his attention to the subject at hand, Deke continued, "Maisy gave me the number he's been using to call and text her. I had River look it up," he said, referring to a member of their pride who was also part of the human police force. "It's one of those virtual numbers you can get for free online."

"Then there's no way to trace it back to whoever's using it," groused

Bailey.

"River said as much." Deke scraped a hand over his jaw. "I think it's highly possible that I know the person who contacted Maisy. He told her things about me that were more than just basic details. This person could even be part of the pride." The mere idea that Deke made his stomach twist viciously.

Havana let out a harsh curse. "Did you call him?"

"Almost. I held back because I don't want him to know I'm aware of what he's doing." Not yet, anyway. "If I'd called him, he would have deactivated his profile before Bailey had a chance to hack into it."

"Maisy might confront him," Aspen warned. "If she does, he'll cover his tracks."

Deke had already anticipated that, which was why … "I asked her not to. She agreed."

"Where is Maisy now?" asked Havana.

"She left in a hurry after I finished questioning her." She'd dashed out so fast Deke was surprised she hadn't left skid marks on the floor. "She was as humiliated as she was shocked."

Aspen crossed her arms over her chest. "The question on my mind is … *why* would someone do this?"

Tate twisted his mouth. "It's hard to say, isn't it? Identity theft is serious, and this whole thing is messed up for certain. But it could be that our boy didn't deliberately set out to hurt anyone; he just wanted an escape from being himself, or he struggles with women in the real world so tried forming an online relationship using someone else's pictures."

Havana gave a slow nod. "Most people go catfishing for the latter reason. It's usually nothing personal to whoever they're posing as, so it could be that—"

"Okay, here we go," Bailey all but sang. "We've got a name, an email address, a physical address, and a phone number. Quick warning, Hammond: It would seem you were right, you do know them." She twisted the laptop to face him.

Deke ground his teeth as betrayal knifed through his chest. *Son of a bitch.* His cat unsheathed his claws with a furious hiss. Neither the feline nor Deke were anything close to friends with this male, but it was still their pride mate. That clearly meant nothing to this asshole.

Havana frowned. "AJ?" She looked at Deke. "Didn't you once beat him up?"

His fingers contracting like claws, Deke gave a curt nod. "It happened years ago, way before you joined the pride."

"What brought it on?" asked the devil shifter.

"He cheated on my cousin, who was more like a sister to me."

Aspen let out a soft whistle. "So he has a hard-on for you big time, then?"

"Yes. And not only because I worked him over. I forbade him from going near her again, so he blames me for her now being mated to someone else in another pride. He's also convinced that the reason he didn't get an enforcer position is that I requested he be turned down, which isn't true." As Bailey twisted the laptop back to face her, Deke asked her, "How long has this profile been live?"

"Just over three months," replied the mamba, drumming her fingers on the outer side of her thigh—the movements slow, sharp, somehow menacing.

He had the feeling that she was imagining slicing them down AJ's face. Well, Bailey might not be the most ethical creature, but she would never condone betrayal.

"He wasted no time in finding himself an online girlfriend," Aspen mused.

"No, he didn't." Tate licked his front teeth. "We need to have a chat with AJ."

Deke couldn't agree more.

Bailey pointed at the phone number on the screen. "Is this the one he used to contact Maisy?"

Deke dipped his chin.

For a long moment, she merely stared at the laptop. "Huh."

"Huh, what?" Deke pushed.

She scratched her cheek. "It's weird. The profile info, I mean."

Deke felt his brow pinch. "In what way?"

"Well, he used a fake phone number. And the email address features your name, so that's obviously something he created purely for the profile. AJ has clearly taken those measures to protect his true ID just in case the Maisy thing came to light and his account was hacked. Why would he do that … but then include his real name and physical address? Why not type in *your* name and address, or some bullshit details? Why point a finger in his own direction? It makes zero sense to me."

Deke blinked twice, and his cat paused in his pacing.

"You know," began Havana, folding her arms, "it *is* weird. He could have as easily used a fake name. Why didn't he?"

"Maybe he did," said Bailey.

Deke frowned down at her. "What?"

"Maybe this guy here isn't really AJ," Bailey elaborated. "Maybe someone is using him as a scapegoat, counting on you to be so blinded by your dynamic with him that you'll find it simple to believe he's at fault." She shrugged. "It's just something to consider."

Deke had to admit—though he wouldn't aloud—that she made a good point. Why only make a half-assed attempt at hiding your ID?

"We'll get a better idea of what's happening after we speak with AJ," Tate stated. "He's never been a good liar." The Alpha male looked at Bailey. "Whoever this is, I doubt he's virtually wooing other women as well, but I need you to go through his inbox and check his messages to be sure. Also, it would be helpful if you could hack into his email address to check if he's been communicating with women that way."

She gave a lazy salute. "Will do."

"Can you get it done before we're back?" Deke asked her. "He'll deactivate the profile and the email address once he realizes we're onto him."

She waved his concern away. "I'll change the passwords before I skim through the content. That way, AJ can't log into them, so he'll be unable to deactivate them."

Tate gave a satisfied nod and then sliced his gaze back to Deke. "Let's go pay AJ a visit."

The breath gusted out of AJ's lungs as Deke slammed the male against the wall, fisting his tee. His eyes wide with fright, AJ lifted his hands, trying to lean away from Deke even though there was nowhere to go. "What the hell, man?"

A growl sawed at the back of Deke's throat—a sound that came from both him and his cat. "I don't know where you got the idea that you'd get away with what you did, but you were dead wrong."

AJ shrank back, his shoulders rising to his ears. "Get away with what? What are you talking about?"

"The game's up, AJ," said Tate, sidling up to Deke. "We know."

"Know what?" AJ practically whined, a quake in his voice.

"Maisy paid me a visit," Deke told him.

The male's brow furrowed. "Who the hell is Maisy?"

Deke narrowed his eyes. The guy looked genuinely confused. "You don't recognize the name? You should. You've been in an online relationship with her for the past three months."

AJ gaped. "I haven't talked to any women online."

"That's not what the evidence would suggest."

"Evidence?"

"Everything points to *you* setting up the fake profile."

AJ spluttered. "What profile?"

Deke moved his face closer to AJ's, who jerkily flinched. "The one that's almost a direct copy of mine on NetherVille. You pretended to be me. You picked up a human female—"

"Whoa, whoa, that's bullshit, man!" the other male cried, his eyes popping open even wider. "No way would I do that!"

"Bailey hacked into the account. All your details were there."

Blanching, AJ vigorously shook his head. "I swear to Christ, I never set up any social media profiles in anyone's name but mine."

Deke exchanged a look with his Alpha. Unless AJ had developed acting skills all of a sudden, he was speaking the truth.

Tate pinned his gaze on AJ. "What's your email address and phone number?"

Stuttering, the other male rattled both off. Neither matched the email address and phone number that were used when creating the social media profile.

Tate looked at Deke. "I'm going to call the other number. Let's see if someone answers." He punched in the number and then put his cell to his ear. No sounds of a phone ringing came from anywhere in the apartment, though he supposed that the cell could be on silent mode.

Deke squinted at AJ. "If you're telling the truth, it would seem that someone is using you as their scapegoat."

AJ swallowed. "I'm not lying, I *swear*."

Tate sighed when no one answered the phone. He swiped his thumb across the screen and then pocketed it. "For now, we'll say we believe you. But we'll be looking deeper into this. If we find out you lied to us here today, what follows will be a far worse punishment than you can imagine. So if you have anything to confess, now is the time to do it."

"I didn't create the profile," AJ swore, his hands trembling, beads of sweat dotting his forehead.

Deke released the guy's tee and stepped back. "You'd better not be bullshitting us, AJ. I beat your ass once. I'll happily do it again." He and Tate exchanged another look and then left, shutting the door behind them.

Striding down the hallway, Deke rubbed the back of his neck. "I don't think it was him."

"Neither do I," said Tate. "His shock and confusion were real. Hopefully Bailey finds something to help point us in the direction of who did do it."

The two males left the complex and returned to the Alpha pair's house. The moment they entered the living room, Havana looked up from her seat on the sofa and asked, "What did he say?"

"He point-blank denied it," replied Tate. "I don't believe he was lying." He sat beside her and rested his hand on her thigh. "His reactions were genuine."

Deke crossed to Bailey, ignoring how his gut clenched at the sight of her; ignoring how his cat tensed at the close proximity. "Did you find anything?"

"Not really," the mamba replied, her gaze on the laptop screen. "He messaged other women on NetherVille, but the conversations never went past light flirting and they stopped a couple of weeks after he and Maisy got cozy. As for his email account … the personal info used to create it was the same used to create the fake profile. I went through his emails. Nothing there but spam and social media notifications."

"Shit," Deke muttered.

Bailey met his gaze. "The messages he sent to Maisy contained a *lot* of info about you. He talked about your family and your childhood with so much emotion it's honestly like he slipped into your skin. It's no wonder he fooled the human. I'll be genuinely shocked if this isn't a member of the pride, because I don't see how else they can so accurately pose as you."

"The question of *why* he did it remains unanswered," said Aspen, sitting in the armchair with one leg crossed over the other. "It's possible that—as Tate earlier pointed out—it could be someone who simply wanted to pose as another guy to score women online."

"They're no innocent, though," Bailey piped up. "If we're right and AJ's innocent in this, someone set him up to take the fall. That was a step they didn't need to take."

Tate inclined his head. "They could have just made up a name instead." He turned to Deke. "Let's assume for a second that this person did it to strike out at you. Who would do that?"

Deke shrugged. "No clue."

"The profile was created a little over three months ago," Tate went on. "What was going on in your life back then?"

Deke pursed his lips. "Not much."

"You had a ding-dong with Gerard at the Tavern," Bailey recalled.

Havana's gaze sharpened. "Oh yeah. It was about Dayna, right?"

"Pretty much," replied Deke. "He overheard Cassandra offering to help me with the touch-hunger, and he made some crack about how only an asshole would hold Dayna to a promise while he's sleeping with other women. I asked if he cared to repeat himself. But you know Gerard—he tosses out sly remarks and then immediately pulls in on himself and acts as if he said jack."

Tate nodded. "So you let it slide."

"Yeah. But then he accidentally-on-purpose knocked over my bottle of beer as he was placing it on the bar. He stuttered and stammered and apologized, but I wasn't buying his act. I told him I'd rip him a new one if he pulled a stunt like that again, and that was it."

"Am I right in guessing he's got a thing for Dayna?" asked Bailey.

"She was with Gerard before moving onto Deke," Tate told her. "Some think that Gerard never quite got over her, though he swears they're better off as friends." He paused. "Anything else happen back then, Deke?"

Scratching at his suddenly itchy nape, Deke replied, "I briefly argued with Sam, but it was just a misunderstanding. Nothing for him to retaliate over."

"What sort of misunderstanding?" asked Tate.

"You know he has a thing for Cassandra, right? He saw me having lunch with her at the deli one time. He thought it was a date. It wasn't. I'd headed there alone, and she'd joined me when she'd spotted me there. He turned up at my apartment later that day and confronted me, accusing me of leading her on." Sam might be a healer, but he was no softie. Even though he wasn't a dominant shifter, he didn't hold back if he had something to say—especially in the defense of others.

Bailey frowned. "Leading her on? So, what, she'd totally hop on the Deke train if it wasn't for Dayna?"

He stared down at her, feeling his brow crease. "The Deke train?"

"It whistles and chugs and everything," said the mamba.

Tate's mouth quirked. "I wouldn't say Cassandra's into Deke, but she has a soft spot for him. I can see why Sam would have viewed him as a threat." He sliced his gaze to Deke. "Did he warn you away from her?"

"Not in so many words," replied Deke. "He said if I had any decency in me and I respected her at all, I wouldn't play with her feelings. I explained that he'd mistaken what he'd seen. He accused me of lying at first. Hence why it turned into an argument." And why his cat was growling at the memory—the feline never appreciated having his integrity questioned. "But I eventually got through to him, and then he turned all sheepish and apologetic."

Tate's thoughtful hum came out low. "You're right, that's not something he'd retaliate over. There's no need to."

Havana pulled in a long breath. "Well, at least the whole catfish thing is over. The profile is down. The email account is deactivated. Maisy knows the score. We can keep looking into who might have created the profile—"

"But we might never find out," Deke finished. Noticing that Bailey was staring off into space, he poked her shoulder. "Are you even listening?"

She blinked at him. "There's no D in refrigerator. So why the hell is there a D in fridge? It's not like it would otherwise have been pronounced differently, is it?"

He felt his brows snap together. "That's what you're focusing on right now? Silent letters?"

"Well, they're *everywhere*. Castle. Ballet. Climb. Knee. Conscience." Bailey lifted her shoulders. "Why put letters in places they don't need to be?"

Jesus Christ. "Why do you care?" Deke shot back.

She inched up her chin. "I don't see how that's your business."

"Fine," he bit out.

"Fine."

"Fine."

She cast him a superior look. "You already said that."

"Felt like saying it again."

"Uh, okay, parrot."

It took everything Deke had not to grab a fistful of her hair, bend over, and slam his mouth on hers. To give his frustration the outlet he most wanted. To remind her of what had happened last night, because, with the way she was acting, he could honestly believe she'd forgotten.

Really, he should be keeping a physical distance from her. Her scent and proximity were making him feel even antsier than usual. Plus, the tension between them was more sexually charged than ever. All of that would likely trigger the touch-hunger to flare up again.

But it was galling him big time that she behaved as though last night hadn't made an impression on her. No, as if *he* hadn't made an impression. It was pricking at not only *his* pride but that of his cat, driving them both to want to get up in her space and provoke some sort of reaction from her; to get under her skin and push her into losing her infamous temper.

Bailey closed the laptop. "We should probably ask the rest of the pride to check if anyone has cloned their profile as well. It might not be that Deke is the only one."

Havana's brows inched up. "That's true."

"It would be good if there are others," said Bailey.

Deke felt his face scrunch up. "How could it possibly be good?"

"Our boy was careful with your profile; he left no crumbs to lead us to him," she replied. "But he could have made a mistake with others; could have gotten cocky or careless. Then we'd have something on him, and then I could dig out my poleaxe and go stab a fucker."

Deke almost did a double-take. "You have a poleaxe?"

She looked up at him, her brows sliding together. "You don't?"

"Of course not."

"Huh. Well, that's weird."

"*Weird*?"

She tipped her head to the side. "You don't think so?"

"What I think is that you want to drive me batshit."

"Well, it *is* on my list."

Yeah, that had become apparent. "Any particular reason why?"

"Not one that you'd understand."

"In other words, it isn't rational."

Bailey pursed her lips. "Maybe not to you. You like things to make sense."

"People generally do."

"I don't."

"You're a special case."

Hiding a smile—God, he was so fun to mess with—Bailey wrinkled her nose at his prickly tone. "You don't mean that in a good way, do you?"

"No," he curtly replied.

Bailey only let out a snort of amusement. His level of surliness never failed to tickle her. "Are you trying to hurt my feelings?"

"I gave up on that a long time ago. You're impervious to insults." He looked at Tate. "I'm heading home. Later."

The Alpha male pushed out of his seat and walked him to the door.

Seeing that both Havana and Aspen were staring at her, Bailey frowned. "What?"

"There's still some mighty tension between you and Deke," said Havana, keeping her voice too low to carry to the guys.

Aspen nodded, rising from her seat to move closer. "And it's even more electric than before. What are you going to do about it? You could say nothing, but then you'd be lying."

Not much liking the taunting glint in Aspen's eyes, Bailey didn't respond. She merely began examining her nails.

"Don't you have anything to say?" asked Aspen.

"About what?" Bailey asked distractedly.

"You. Deke. The mighty tension."

"Oh." Bailey didn't look up from her nails. "No, nothing."

Setting her hands on her hips, Aspen began tapping her foot. "You're not fooling us. We know you're not as aloof about this as you'd like us to believe."

Bailey flexed her fingers, still eyeing her nails. "Hmm."

"We're not buying it, Bailey."

"'Kay."

Aspen's foot stilled. "I mean it, you ain't fooling us."

"Uh-huh."

"*You're not*," the bearcat ground out.

"Hmm."

Havana sighed and lifted a hand. "Aspen, don't bother."

"But I hate when she's in '*I can't hear you mode*,'" griped the bearcat, sliding her hands down to her sides and balling them up into fists.

"Which is why she does it," said Havana. "Leave her be for now."

"Can I slap her first? Please?"

"No," the Alpha female firmly stated.

Aspen let out a moan of complaint, her shoulders drooping. "But I really want to."

"It's still a no."

The bearcat turned to Bailey. "You won't care if I slap you, will you?"

"Huh," was all Bailey said.

Aspen growled. "*Oh my God, stop being a little bitch*!"

CHAPTER FIVE

Staring down at the screen of his ringing cell a few days later, Deke cursed beneath his breath. *Dayna.*

Not that he didn't like speaking with her; it would just be difficult to act normal when, unbeknownst to her, he'd made the official decision to pull out of their vow. He was good at deception, but he didn't like to mislead people.

His moody cat turned his back on her, uninterested in giving his time or attention to her or anyone else. The feline really needed to get over his shit.

A glass of orange juice in hand, Deke sank onto his gray leather sofa as he accepted the call with a swipe of his thumb.

Usually, Dayna would be wearing a wide smile. This morning, a frown creased her face.

She looked nothing like the black mamba shifter who took up more of his mental space than he'd like. Dayna's wide-set eyes were a startling blue. Faint freckles dusted her narrow, elfin face. Her auburn, corkscrew curls fountained down her back and would bounce with each jerk or tilt of her head.

"God, Deke, I can't believe you didn't tell me," she complained, leaning the phone against something to hold it up.

He blinked. "Well, good morning to you, too."

"I just heard from Therese. She said someone did a fake profile of you and used it to seduce some poor human woman. What the hell?"

Deke grunted, feeling his mouth tighten. "Yeah, the situation is fucked."

"Do you really think it was someone in the pride?"

He'd been asked that question over and over by various members. They didn't want to believe that one of their own would do something so messed up to a fellow pride mate. The code they lived by was to protect, support, and look out for each other. Inter-pride squabbles were one thing. This was something much bigger.

"I do, yes." But as yet, Deke had no way to prove it. There were no instances of other pride members having their profiles cloned, so there was nothing else to hack; no more trails to follow.

"How come you didn't call me and let me know what happened?" The demand was softly spoken, but it was a demand all the same. And it got his back up.

"This isn't some minor thing, Deke."

True, but he hadn't wanted to contact her for the same reason he'd hesitated to answer her call. Besides … "It is compared to what's currently going on in your life—you recently lost your great-uncle. Plus, the profile has been deleted and so the whole thing is over now."

She leaned forward. "Do you have any suspects?"

No, he didn't. But that wasn't something that Deke could or would share with anyone outside the Alphas' immediate circle. They always kept such speculations private, no matter the scenario. It wasn't fair to publicly label someone a suspect unless you had a strong case. It could also be dangerous, since some pride mates would target said suspects even if there was no proof of guilt.

He lifted his glass to his mouth. "You know I can't tell you that." He took a swig of his juice.

"Oh come on, who am I going to tell?"

"Therese, for one. Who'd then tell everyone else." She was one of the pride's most notorious gossips.

"I'll keep it to myself, I promise." Dayna doodled a cross over her heart with her fingertip.

He gave her a pointed look. "This is need-to-know info. You don't need to know," he stated, calm and firm.

She let out a put-out sound. "Well, that's rude. *And* unfair."

He felt his mouth tighten. "What's unfair is that you're asking me to give you information that my Alphas have trusted me to keep private." And he didn't fucking appreciate that she'd expect him to go against his word; that she didn't respect how seriously he took his position.

She sighed, her shoulders drooping, her face falling. "I'm sorry, I'm sorry. I didn't mean to offend you."

"Apology accepted. Now can we talk about something else? We haven't spoken in weeks. How are you?"

Her expression softened. "I'm fine. What about you? Is the touch-hunger any better?"

With the exception of the ever-present restlessness, it hadn't been too bad after what happened between him and Bailey. But it had increasingly worsened as the days went by, and now he was back to being a walking hard-on. "No."

A shifty expression crossed Dayna's face, and the muscles there tightened. "Gerard mentioned that there was a short period where it eased a little. I'm guessing that means you had sex recently," she said, her voice so flat he would have missed the note of jealousy there if he hadn't known her so well.

His cat bristled, feeling she had no right to her possessiveness after being gone for so long. Deke didn't disagree. Especially since she hadn't been celibate herself when in his physical condition.

In the beginning, he'd felt jealous knowing that other men were touching her. But over time, it had bothered him less and less until, now, it didn't affect him at all.

"I'm right, aren't I?" she pushed.

Instead of responding, Deke took another swig of his juice.

Dayna's chin inched up. "Who was she? Someone in the pride?"

He sighed. "Let's not do this, Dayna."

"I'm simply curious."

"You're always 'simply curious.' Then you're always upset if I satisfy that curiosity, and you go weeks without speaking to me. So let's not go into detail."

"I just want to know if she's from the pride."

Tough. Because he didn't want to talk to her about Bailey or what happened between them. He felt … weirdly protective of the memory. Even a little possessive of it. He wanted to keep it all to himself. "What difference does it make?"

"I'd prefer to know *before* I return if one of my pride mates have been …" She trailed off and swallowed hard. "I wouldn't want to be the only person who didn't know."

"I get it." And if he wasn't intending to pull out of the promise he'd made to Dayna, he might have told her. "But I'd rather not get into it."

"So she *is* from the pride."

"Jesus, Dayna, can we talk about something else?"

A pinched look came over her face. "My friends will tell me if you don't."

He only shrugged. Her friends didn't know shit. And he couldn't imagine Bailey sharing it with her or anyone else except for maybe Havana and Aspen.

Dayna gave him a wounded look. "How do you think it makes me feel that I heard about the fake profile from Therese instead of you?"

"How do you think it makes me feel that you have your friends keep tabs on me?" he shot back.

She pressed her lips tightly shut.

"We can either bicker, or we can talk. I'd rather we talked. You haven't even mentioned Evan. He's usually the first topic you hit. How is he?"

Dayna looked as though she might fight the switch in topic, but then she exhaled heavily and replied, "He's fine." Her lips hitched up slightly as she added, "He's loving the ball pit I bought him."

Deke remained silent as she chatted away about the toddler, so much love shining in her eyes. It didn't surprise him that she'd bonded so tightly to the kid. Much like Deke, she didn't let many people get close to her and was reserved with most. But if she considered you one of hers to protect or take care of, she would give as much of herself to you as you needed.

She blew out a breath, making some of her curls flutter. "It's going to hurt to leave him."

Deke lifted his shoulders. "So stay."

She blinked. "What?"

He downed the last of his juice and then set his glass on the chestnut coffee table in front of him. "If it'll hurt you that much to leave, stay with him. You can't tell me you haven't considered it. Anyone in your situation would."

A line dented her brow. "I don't know how I should feel about you encouraging me to stay here. I would have thought you wouldn't want that."

"We were friends before we were anything else, Dayna. I want you to do what's best for you, not for me. I don't think you returning would be best for you. I think you'd just be sad and wish you could go back. Am I wrong?"

Pulling her arms close to her body, she let her head drop forward. "I don't know." The words were soft. Quiet. Pained.

"If the reason you're so conflicted is that you feel you owe it to me to come back, you don't."

After a few moments, she lifted her head and bit down on her lower lip. "Maybe you could come out here."

He held back a sigh. "We've talked about this before."

"You could be an enforcer here once you got settled and won the Alpha's trust."

"It's not just about my position." She knew that already. "I don't want to relocate. I don't want to leave my family any more than you want to leave yours. I've told you this many times."

Her face hardened. "So *I* have to be the one who gives everything up?"

Annoyance flared through him. "You don't have to give up anything. I'm not insisting that you come back. I never did." Not even when he'd wished she would.

The anger drained out of her, and her shoulders slumped. "I know, I know. I don't think I'd have been so patient in your shoes. I'm sorry for snapping at you. I'm upset about other things. My great-uncle's mate slipped away in her sleep yesterday. I knew she would, and we weren't close or anything, but it was still hard."

Not good with stuff like this, Deke could only think to say, "I'm sorry."

"She lived a long, fulfilling life. They both did. That makes it easier." Her head turned to the side as someone spoke in the background, the words muffled. Dayna turned back to him. "I have to go."

Deke gave a slow nod. "Take care."

"You, too." She smiled and then ended the call.

Puffing out a breath, he let his head fall back. He'd been on the verge of telling her to stay with Evan; that there was no point in her coming home if she was only doing so for Deke. But he'd held back the words, not wanting to kick her while she was already down. He'd give it a few weeks, and then he'd tell her.

He didn't believe she'd be devastated by his decision, but it was bound to sting. He hoped she didn't ask him to reconsider, because he couldn't. More, he *shouldn't.* Not when another woman constantly invaded his thoughts.

He hadn't seen Bailey since the day he'd discovered the profile. He'd been invited to a movie night at the Alphas' place that evening, but he'd declined the invitation, needing a little space from the mamba. He'd thought it would help prolong the break he was having from the relentless arousal, but it hadn't. Maybe because his thoughts kept dancing back to that evening he'd blown his load all over her after feeling her come around his fingers.

Cursing his cock for throbbing at the memory, Deke righted his head and stood, determined to put Bailey out of his mind … and utterly clueless as to why such a thing couldn't be simple.

"Bailey, if you're drawing boobs on that board again I *swear* …"

Turning the smoothie menu toward her Alpha female, Bailey said, "I only did a few decorative swirls this time."

"Why bother?" asked Havana.

"Why not bother? They look pretty."

There was a loud *twang* followed by a "Shit, sorry." Seeing that one of the guys working out had lost control of a resistance band and sent it sailing through the air toward another of the rec center's regulars, Bailey winced. "I did that to a guy once."

"You did it on purpose," said Havana, her eyes dancing.

"I was just testing Randy's balance." The band had wacked his head, knocked his equilibrium, and caused him to trip on the treadmill. He'd gone ass over tit. "I wouldn't have if he hadn't upset Aspen." The guy was Camden's ex and had blamed Aspen for the whole "ex" part. Randy no longer came to the center these days, which was awesome.

Bailey returned the menu to its spot beside the tip jar and then placed the chalk beneath the counter. They didn't only sell smoothies; they sold other stuff such as hydration drinks, active wear, energy bars, and even weight-lifting belts.

The center's fitness area was often busy. There was an array of equipment, such as cardio machines, exercise benches, and towers of weights and dumbbells. PTs spotted and fired instructions at clients. Wall-mounted TVs played low near the cardio machines.

A highly intolerant creature, her mamba didn't like working shifts here. The scents of sweat, metal, rubber mats, and antibacterial cleaner overpowered the air. More, it could be seriously noisy. There was constant heavy breathing, grunting, beeping, feet thumping, and metallic clanging.

Havana propped her hip against the side of the counter. "So … have you seen anything of Deke over the past few days?"

Bailey's belly did a ridiculous little flutter. Ugh. She shook her head. "Nope."

"Not at all? You guys live on the same floor."

"I live on the same floor as several people. Days go by when I don't see them either." Truthfully, she'd considered checking on him a time or two. But she'd vetoed the idea, knowing he wouldn't want her company.

"I saw him yesterday. He's not doing so good. The touch-hunger's bad again."

Bailey tensed, and her snake lifted her head in interest.

"I don't understand why he's not doing anything about it." Havana paused. "But I think *you* do."

Bailey forced herself not to tense. "Why?"

"Because you don't seem confused by it anymore." The devil shifter straightened. "Tell me what's wrong so I can help him."

"If he wants to tell you, he will."

"I'm his Alpha female. It's my job to look out for him."

"Then go do it. But don't ask me to betray his confidence—I'm not gonna."

Her lips quirking, Havana gave a slow shake of her head. "And he thinks you have no morals." She exhaled heavily. "Have you had any more visits from Livy?"

Bailey felt her mouth briefly flatten. "She came to see me yesterday. She brought food again."

Havana hummed, clearly amused. "You're being courted by proxy. You realize that, right?"

"But why would she do that?" Bailey raised her shoulders. "It can't have escaped her notice that he likes control, so she has to see that me and him don't suit."

Havana casually braced a hand on her hip. "Deke's a highly dominant male who likes control, yes. But he also not only thrives on being challenged, he needs it—he'll otherwise feel bored and restless. So it stands to reason that he'll need a partner who challenges him or he'll lose interest in them fast. Livy will know that, just as she'll know that you are anything but easy to handle."

"But still, who'd want me as a partner for their son? *I* wouldn't." Not if she wanted her kid to be happy anyway.

"She likes you. Which shows good judgement on her part. You might be a nut, but you're an awesome nut."

Bailey felt her lips curve. "Aw, thanks. You're awesome, too." She held out her arms. "Can we hug?"

Havana's good humor fled in an instant. "No."

Bailey choked back a laugh. Her Alpha was not at all touchy-feely. "But it—"

"No."

Sighing, Bailey dropped her arms. "You're supposed to love me."

"I do love you. I'm just not gonna hug you."

Noticing one of the center's staff members, Jonesy, heading their way, Bailey raised her brow. "Yo, what's up?"

The barely eighteen-year-old jaguar replied, "Corbin wants to speak to you in his office."

Bailey exchanged a look with Havana and then slid her gaze back to Jonesy. "Do you know what it's about?"

"No, but …" He licked his lips. "There are some people in his office with him. Ginny's one of them."

Her mamba's head jerked, and Bailey inwardly groaned. The little witch had probably come here to push Corbin into firing Bailey, since the phone calls had failed to work.

Havana swore. "You can hold the fort here, right, Jonesy?"

He blinked twice. "Uh, yeah, sure."

"Great." She turned to Bailey. "I'm coming with you."

Unbothered either way, Bailey said nothing as she and her Alpha skirted the counter.

As they walked off, Havana looked at her askance. "Are you thinking what I'm thinking?"

"That I should have carved a dick onto Ginny's forehead?"

The devil's brows dipped. "No. I'm thinking there's a good chance that the people with her are Jackson's relatives."

"You think she'd bring them here?"

"If they wanted to question you, this would be the easiest way for them to get to you. I can totally see her pushing them to come at you. In their shoes, if I had someone repeatedly insisting that you're the person who hurt my relative, I'd want to speak to you myself and ask you a few questions."

Actually, Bailey would do the same. No, scrap that. If someone left one of her loved ones for dead, she'd tie any possible suspect to a chair and interrogate their ass until she felt positive they were innocent.

A mere minute later, they arrived at Corbin's office. Havana's quick knock earned them a "Come in." She opened the door, and Bailey followed her inside. Her inner snake coiled her body tight, not liking the scene before them.

Ginny stood off to the side, her eyes hard, her mouth tight, her arms folded. Two males stood in front of Corbin's desk, their posture strong and vigilant.

All heads turned as Bailey and Havana waltzed into the room. Taking in the features of the two strangers, Bailey felt her eyes narrow. Yeah, these were Jackson's relatives all right. The resemblance was plain to see.

Bailey closed the door behind her and pinned her gaze on Corbin. "Jonesy said you wanted to talk to me."

Havana swept her eyes over the others in the room. "What's all this?"

Corbin cleared his throat. "Well—"

"*You're* Bailey?" one of the males cut in, sounding as stunned as he looked. "Bailey Bryant?"

His relative seemed equally dumbfounded. Obviously she wasn't what they'd expected. Well, since Ginny had no doubt painted her as an evil crone, it was no surprise. She'd been told many times that she looked as if butter wouldn't melt in her mouth.

Bailey had used it to her advantage during her years working for the Movement, and it had eventually become instinctive for her to give off a harmless air. Many were fooled by it; didn't see the danger. Which suited her just fine.

"One and the very same," Bailey affirmed. "Is there a problem?"

It was Corbin who spoke, "Ginny brought some people to the center in the hope of finding you." He did *not* look happy about it. "These are Jackson's brothers, Jarrett and Keaton. I intercepted them during their search and then brought them to my office. I *did* think of tossing them all out of the building instead, but I would prefer that they speak with you in an environment such as this rather than them catching you while you're alone."

Appreciating his protectiveness, Bailey gave him a brief nod before turning to the brothers. "My guess is that you're here to ask questions that a certain someone put in your head. Go for it," she invited.

The brothers exchanged a look, seeming taken aback that she hadn't clammed up, gone on the defensive, and sent them away.

Keaton cleared his throat, regarding her with something close to distaste—he tried to hide it, but not hard enough. "We've heard a lot about the … activity that went on between you and Jackson since your fallout."

"I can imagine." Jackson was a total whiner, and Ginny had probably been more than happy to fill in any gaps.

"For the record, he doesn't believe you're the one who jumped him. I trust his judgement. But I'm not entirely convinced, and I'm a man who likes to cover his bases," explained Keaton, all reasonable. But she could tell that he did suspect her.

"And we have to consider that you certainly have a history of targeting him," added Jarrett, his voice clipped—he clearly had no more respect for her than his brother did. "Where were you the evening that Jackson was attacked?"

"At the afterparty of a mating ceremony," replied Bailey.

"Which means she has literally hundreds of alibis," Havana chipped in.

Both Keaton and Jarrett blinked, surprised.

Bailey winged up a brow. "Ginny didn't tell you? Because I know that Corbin made her aware of it."

Jarrett fixed an intent stare on Ginny. "You failed to mention any of that."

With a defensive sniff, Ginny inched up her chin and nervously scraped her fingers through her teal bob. "Assuming it's even true, it doesn't mean she didn't leave the party at some point, does it? She's a snake. They're sneaky. She could have left without anyone noticing."

"But I didn't," said Bailey. "You'd *love* for it to have been me, but I don't think you're really so convinced that it was. I think you're using this as an excuse to dick with me."

"I second that," Havana piped up, glaring at the bitch. "And if you genuinely gave a damn about Jackson, you wouldn't take advantage of his pain this way."

Ginny's face hardened. "Don't twist what's happening here. I'm trying to help his family bring him justice. He could have *died.* And all because she can't handle that he didn't love her as she did him."

Bailey almost took a step back in sheer surprise. "Love?" Her snake would have laughed if she could.

"You wanted to take him as your mate," accused Ginny.

Bailey looked at Havana. "I totally didn't see her pulling something like that out of her butthole."

The Alpha shrugged. "People can surprise you that way."

"If you didn't care for him," Jarrett interjected, a challenging note to his tone, "why did you react so badly to him cheating on you?"

Bailey met his gaze. "I don't tolerate betrayal. He knew that. He took his mental safety into his own hands when he slept with her." He'd basically signed up for some psychological torture.

Havana looked from one brother to the other. "You're wasting your time here. The odds are that Jackson was targeted by a shifter or two who felt like kicking the shit out of him and took it too far."

Ginny's hands fisted at her sides. "The culprit is standing *right there.*" She turned to Keaton and Jarrett. "Don't be fooled by Bailey's exterior. She's the reincarnation of Rasputin." Ginny tore a sheet of paper from the corkboard. "Look, I started this petition to have her fired. See how many signatures are on it."

Jarrett took it from her and scanned it. His eyes flicked up to Bailey. "You signed this yourself. Six times."

Bailey lifted and dropped one shoulder. "I like to be included in things."

"It's true that there are a fair few signatures on there," said Havana. "Ginny and her friends not only scribbled their names on it but a bunch of fake names."

Ginny's mouth fell open. "That's a lie!"

"No, it isn't," snapped Havana before turning back to Keaton and Jarrett. "Like I told you once before, Bailey had nothing to do with Jackson's attack. She was at a pride event all day long. There's an endless amount of witnesses who can confirm that."

"But they're all from your pride. They'd lie for her." Ginny jabbed a finger in Bailey's direction. "You wanted revenge on Jackson, so you went after it just like you always do. You've been punishing him for God knows how long."

"But I never tried to kill him, did I? No, I toyed with him. That's what I do." Bailey had perfected the art of it when young. "I will do a lot of things to get revenge—I'm a black mamba, after all—but what I don't do is cut my enjoyment short by ending my enemy's life. And where's the fun in coming at someone from behind anyway? Makes the whole thing too easy. I like a challenge."

"Ask around the center," Havana invited, again focused on Jackson's brothers. "The people here know Bailey. You won't find anyone who believes that she's responsible for what happened to Jackson. The only person who'll finger her as the culprit is Ginny."

Ginny scowled. "I—"

"Need to shut the fuck up," Havana finished, a growl building in her throat, Alpha vibes spilling from her. "I am just about done listening to you toss unfounded accusations around. It. Ends. Now."

Ginny snapped her mouth shut, finally showing some damn sense. No one wanted to tangle with a devil shifter—particularly not an Alpha.

Corbin pushed out of his chair. "It would be best if you all left," he told Ginny and her companions.

The brothers flicked Bailey one last hard look before stalking out of the office. Ginny trailed behind them, her head held high, avoiding everyone's gaze. She also slammed the door shut on her way out.

Exhaling heavily, Corbin rubbed at his nape. "I'm sorry about that scene, Bailey. I would have thrown them out—"

"It's fine, I get why you didn't," Bailey told him, waving off the unnecessary apology.

"Just so you're aware, I made it clear to Ginny before you entered the office that she's barred from this day forward." Corbin's face tightened. "What she's doing isn't simply a bitchy game, it's dangerous."

Very much so. Shifters craved blood and violence during times of injustice. Yearned for vengeance on a massive scale. That Jackson had almost been killed was enough of an injustice. That his would-be-killer roamed free was yet another. His family would be craving retribution … and Ginny was trying to sic them on Bailey like junkyard dogs.

One corner of Corbin's mouth very briefly hiked up as he regarded Bailey carefully. "I'm proud of you for not leaping at her just now."

Bailey shrugged. "She was braced for that. It's no fun when people are braced for it."

He gave her a flat look. "Ruin my illusions that you're maturing, why don't you."

Snorting, Havana put a hand on Bailey's shoulder. "Come on, let's get back to the smoothie bar. Hopefully Jackson's brothers will leave you alone after this. If they don't, I won't be so nice next time."

Neither would Bailey.

The rest of her shift went without incident. It didn't seem that Keaton and Jarrett hung around to question members of the rec center, but she couldn't say for sure. If they did, no one mentioned it to her.

Later on, after they'd finished their shifts, Aspen and Camden left in their own vehicle while Bailey drove Havana home. Bailey then headed to the nearby parking lot of her apartment building. Having whipped her car into the closest available space, she cut the engine and slid out of the vehicle. She began walking toward her complex … just as two unfamiliar males stepped out from between two cars up ahead.

They turned to fully face her, their gazes hard and inscrutable. Bailey went on high alert, and her snake's head snapped up. Both males looked neat and polished with their slicked-back dark hair, clean shaven face, and tailored suits.

She slowed her pace as she neared them, dragging in a subtle breath through her nose, pulling their scents into her lungs. *Jackals.* Her snake tensed, flicking out her tongue.

The taller of the two males cocked his head as he studied Bailey. "You don't look much like your cousin. The eyes, though … They're the same."

Coming to a stop before the jackals, Bailey asked, "Who might you be?"

The taller dude nodded. "I'm Amiri." He tipped his head toward his pack mate. "This is Lincoln," he added, all forced friendliness. "We're from the Westwood Pack. How's Roman doing?"

She gave a slight, uncaring shrug. "Don't know. Don't care."

Lincoln's eyes narrowed. "You're aware he isn't actually dead, then?"

"I'm aware," she confirmed. "And before you ask, yes, I've seen him recently."

Amiri's gaze sharpened. "When?"

"Last week," she replied. "He came to my pride seeking protection from your pack. Given I have no love for him, I sent him on his way."

Lincoln cast her a doubtful look. "You sent away your own cousin?"

"I feel no loyalty toward anyone in my old nest."

Amiri dug his tongue into the tip of one incisor. "I heard what they did after your parents were killed. Cold to the bone, it was. But Roman was young back then. Not part of the decision to banish you."

"But he turned his back on me like they did, so …" And Bailey wasn't what anyone could call a forgiving person.

"In your position, I would have no time for anyone from that nest," said Lincoln. "But some people will protect family, regardless of past betrayals."

Possibly. "I'm not *some people*."

"So you say," said Lincoln, clearly still dubious.

She sighed at him, annoyed. "Dude, I can't help you. Like I said, I sent him on his way. I'm not going to keep repeating myself. If you struggle to believe me, go ask my Alphas. You know what pride I belong to or you wouldn't have located me here, so you'll know who they are. They were around when Roman showed up. Tate very firmly ordered him to leave and not return."

Amiri hummed. "And you have no idea where your cousin could be?"

She shook her head. "Nope."

"He gave you no hints?" asked Lincoln.

"He wouldn't have trusted me with any." Would she have given away his location? Probably not. But he wouldn't have risked it.

Amiri reached into the inside pocket of his jacket and pulled out a business card. "If he contacts you, I'd appreciate it if you gave us a call."

She took the card. A number was printed on it—nothing more.

Amiri straightened the lapels of his jacket. "Things between you and my pack don't need to be unpleasant. We have no issue with you, providing you don't stand in our way. Believe me when I tell you that Roman would not be worth the consequences."

She narrowed her eyes, and her snake coiled her muscles as if to spring. "And believe me when I tell you that you'd forfeit your life if you came for me."

Amiri's lips quirked. "A mamba through and through."

"Is everything all right here?" a new voice asked as a figure silently approached.

Bailey gave the newcomer a too-quick smile. "Everything's fine, Gerard, thanks."

Despite her assurance, he glared at the jackals. "I think it's best that you left."

"Do you?" asked Lincoln, a smirk playing around the edges of his mouth. "Well, then, lucky for you we're about to leave." He returned his gaze to Bailey. "We'll be in touch, just in case you lose Amiri's number or forget to contact us with something you might learn." With that, the two jackals walked away.

Gerard turned to her. "You sure you're all right?"

"Positive. But thanks for stepping in all the same." Watching the two jackals head to a parked town car, Bailey exhaled heavily. This day really had sucked so far.

CHAPTER SIX

Forking the last piece of his steak, Deke flicked his mother a look. "Will you stop it already?"

Livy blinked, all innocence. "What? A mother can't look at her son?"

She wasn't looking at him; she was *staring* at him. A sure sign that she wanted to get something off her chest. He suspected this was why he'd been invited to join his parents and younger brother for dinner.

Deke inwardly muttered a curse. He was not in the mood for whatever this was. His earlier annoyance at Dayna seemed to have fed his sense of restlessness, and the touch-hunger was now once more raging. More, his cat was crouched within him, tense as a bow, rumbling low growls for seemingly no reason.

Deke had only accepted his parents' invitation because he'd known they'd otherwise turn up at his apartment, determined to check on him due to the touch-hunger issue. Still, he was now wishing he hadn't. He shook his head at his mother, exasperated. "Just say whatever it is you want to say."

"I always intended to," she said a little primly.

At the opposite end of the dining table from her, his father let out a low chuckle. Clarence wasn't wrong when he called Livy a firecracker. She was full of spirit and attitude, but the older male loved that about her.

Twisting in her seat to better face Deke, she leaned toward him slightly, resting her lower arm on the table. "Have you given any thought into what I said last week about Dayna?"

Deke bit back a sigh, and his cat bared a fang at the mention of the other female. In actuality, Livy hadn't "said" anything about Dayna. She'd *yelled* about how Deke needed to "be done with her already." The look his brother,

Cash, shot him suggested he was having that same thought.

Deke had already decided before then that he needed to pull back from Dayna, but he hadn't told his mother that.

He wouldn't tell her now either.

Because she would tell her sister, who'd tell her mate, who'd tell his father, and so on and so on … until eventually it got back to Dayna. She should hear it from Deke first. He already didn't like that he'd spoken of his intentions to Tate and Luke before he had her. It didn't seem right.

Deke dipped his piece of steak in what was left of his pepper sauce. "Trust me to do what's right for me."

Livy's lips thinned, and her hands balled up. "Two and a half years she's stayed away. That's not someone who deserves you."

For God's sake. "Mom," he drawled, a warning note to his voice that told her to let it go.

Livy ignored it, a flush of annoyance staining her cheeks. "She has her reasons for not returning, I know. But she could have let you go at some point. She could have said, 'Look, I can't break away from my family yet, but if you're unattached when I return to the US, I'll come to you.' That would have been the decent thing to do. But she held you to your word instead."

"Mom, seriously, leave it."

"You wouldn't have done that to her. No way. But she's too possessive to let you move on, and this is her way of making sure you don't."

He briefly flicked his gaze to the ceiling. "*Mom.*" Inside him, his cat unsheathed the tips of his claws, *far* from in the mood to deal with any nagging.

"The only time she seemed to show any real intention of coming back was last time you were dealing with touch-hunger." With a little sniff, Livy folded her arms. "If you ask me, she did that for one reason only—to make sure you didn't consider choosing to pursue something with Cassandra."

Deke harbored that same suspicion. Dayna had made a few sarcastic comments back then such as how nice it was that he and Cassandra "got along so well." He hadn't told Dayna who was helping him burn off the touch-hunger. She had discovered it via Therese and Gerard.

"Is that the kind of person who deserves to have you wait for them?" Livy asked, her tone sharp. "Someone who gets your hopes up when she thinks you might otherwise choose another woman?"

Rather than explain that, no, he didn't—hence why he'd first considered pulling out of the vow back then—he shoved his steak into his mouth. "We don't need to have this conversation again."

"We do if you and Dayna are still bound up in a ridiculous promise." Then she went into yet another full-on rant about Dayna.

He met Cash's eyes. The little shit was on the verge of laughing.

Of course, Deke could easily shut this crap down. All he'd need to do would be to let out a few dominant vibes—as a submissive, his mother would falter under the weight of them. But he would never use his dominance against her that way. Not purposely, at least. He'd done it accidentally as a juvenile on a few occasions, and he'd hated himself each time.

Using another way to handle the situation, Deke tossed out, "She wants me to move to Australia."

Livy's back went ramrod straight. "If you say you're going, I will beat you with a pot."

He fought a grin, lowering his cutlery to his now empty plate. "That's not an incentive for me to stay."

"I mean it, Deke," she clipped. "You are not leaving us. Not to be with someone who clearly doesn't love you the way you deserve to be loved."

"I heard Australia's a beautiful place."

"And if you loved her, you'd find it unbearable to be away from her, but you're managing it well enough—that's telling."

"Australia's looking more beautiful by the second."

Clarence chuckled into his glass.

Livy shot her mate a hard look. "This isn't funny."

Struggling to wipe his amusement from his expression, Clarence set down his drink. "Let's just do as our boy asked and trust him to do what's right for him."

"No," she snapped.

A knock came at the front door.

"I'll get it." Livy stiffly stood, her gaze hard on Deke once more. "But this conversation is not over."

Watching her all but stomp out of the room, Deke sank back into his chair with a rough sigh. The woman might be submissive, but she mentally backed down for no one. When she got an idea in her head, there was no getting it out. Unfortunately for her, she'd passed her tenacity onto him, so she rarely succeeded in changing his mind on anything.

"You're not really thinking of packing your stuff and jetting off to Australia, are you?" asked Cash.

"Nah," replied Deke. "Just wanted to see her face turn purple."

"Bailey, hi!"

Deke's gut clenched at his mother's booming welcome.

"Hi, Mrs. D," said Bailey, her voice making his cat go completely rigid. "I wanted to bring your plate—"

"It's just wonderful to see you," Livy practically sang. "Come on in."

Bailey cleared her throat. "Well, actually, I was gonna—"

There was the sound of the front door shutting, and then two sets of footfalls.

Deke felt his muscles tighten. He did *not* need to be around Bailey right now. His body was already a hot fucking mess. Her close proximity would only make it worse. And yet, his pulse did a pleased little jump of anticipation.

His mother all but shoved her into the dining room, beaming like a loon. "Look who's here, everyone."

Clarence and Cash called out their hellos, flashing her warm smiles. Deke merely grunted.

Bailey lifted her hand in greeting. "Yo."

Curling her arm around the mamba's shoulders, Livy asked, "Have you eaten yet?"

Bailey nodded. "Yup, I'm good."

"What about dessert?"

"Uh …"

"You'll have some with us," Livy declared, herding her toward the table. "Here, you can sit with Cash."

Deke felt his upper lip try to quiver. He'd expected his mother to direct Bailey to the empty seat beside *him*. Which, yeah, would have annoyed him. But it annoyed him more to see Bailey sitting beside his brother, who instantly gave her his full attention—something Livy obviously hoped would spark some jealousy in Deke. Yeah, he knew what she was doing.

That didn't mean it wasn't working.

In fact, it was working a little too well—a darkly primitive jealousy began to slink through his system, heating his blood and twisting his stomach, as she and Cash nattered away to each other like old friends.

His cat's fur puffed up. The feline might not particularly want her attention, but nor did he want her so focused on another male. And he wasn't pleased that she clearly hadn't learned her lesson that Deke wasn't a person she should dismiss. That was exactly what she was presently doing: Acting as if he wasn't there.

He drew in a calming breath. It was a mistake. Because he got a lungful of her scent, and it made his body tighten. Harden. Burn.

Meanwhile, his mother collected all the plates with a smile, looking rather pleased with herself and shooting Deke the occasional smug smirk. He ignored that, fixing a glare on the main source of his frust—

He bit back a hiss as electrically charged arousal fired through him. He held his body still, subtly breathing through the hot, crackly wave as he waited for it to subside. His skin suddenly felt too tight, as if being stretched from the inside out.

Hearing his cell chime, Deke forced his muscles to unlock as he fished it out of his pocket. It was a message from Tate: *Keep a lookout for jackals. Bailey told Havana that two of the Westwood Pack earlier approached her in the parking lot outside your complex to question her.*

Deke went motionless, anger bubbling in his gut. His cat rose to his feet in a slow, menacing move.

Another message came through: *They didn't threaten or attempt to hurt her, but they made it clear they'd be back.*

Then the assholes didn't have a lick of sense, because if she didn't chase them off herself, the pride would do it for her. *Descriptions?*

Dark hair. Tall. Trim. No facial hair. Black suits.

I'll keep an eye out for them.

Also, remember Ginny from the rec center? The one who wants Bailey fired?

Yes. Deke had spotted the woman a time or two when he'd gone to the rec center to either keep watch over Havana or escort her home. *She slept with the guy Bailey was dating, the one who recently got jumped, right?*

Yeah, her. She blames Bailey for the attack. She turned up at the center today with his two brothers, who seem as suspicious of Bailey as Ginny.

Deke ground his teeth, and his cat spat a hiss. They might not have warm, fuzzy feelings for the mamba, but they didn't like that anyone would think to come at her that way. *I'll keep a lookout for them as well.*

A bowl of warm apple pie was placed in front of him by his still smirking mother.

He returned his cell to his pocket as he eyed Bailey, who was snickering at something Cash said. A simple sight, yet the vision of her so at ease with another male made his jaw clench. She'd never been that way around Deke. And vice versa, really.

Much as he wanted more info on what happened at both the center and the parking lot, he wouldn't ask her about it here. He'd do it when they were away from ears that didn't belong to people who weren't part of the Alphas' inner circle.

A prickly itch scuttled across his chest. Deke rubbed at it, trying not to scratch, and then grabbed his spoon. "Why do you have a rabbit's foot hanging on your necklace?"

Her dark eyes flew to his. "One of the Phoenix wolves told me they give the wearer good luck."

"How? The animal wasn't exactly lucky in life. It died and then had its foot removed."

"For the greater good." Bailey lifted the spoon from her own bowl. "It now provides others with good fortune."

"Again, I'm not seeing how. And please tell me you didn't capture, kill, and butcher that rabbit yourself."

"Okay, I won't tell you."

Chuckling, Livy retook her seat at the table. "You two …" Pausing, she turned to Bailey. "So, what have you been up to today?"

"Just working," Bailey replied, spooning some apple pie.

Livy fussed with the position of her bowl. "How long have you worked at the rec center?"

The mamba shoveled pie into her mouth. "Since I was sixteen."

"You lived with Corbin before that, didn't you?"

"At his house, yeah. It's a sort of foster home for homeless lone shifter children." Bailey scooped up more pie with her spoon. "He's the best."

"Were you always a loner before going to live with him?"

"No, not always." Chewing more of her dessert, Bailey glanced at everyone apart from Deke. "Were you all born and bred into the pride?"

"We were," Clarence confirmed, smiling.

Livy's own mouth curved. "Clarence and I were … what's the term for it? Frenemies. We were frenemies when we were children."

Bailey's brows hiked up. "Really?"

Livy nodded. "Teenage hormones changed that. I told him when we were fourteen that I was going to claim him one day."

"And she did." Clarence closed his mouth around his spoonful of dessert and chewed. "I went along with it."

Livy narrowed her eyes. "You eagerly claimed me right back, you liar."

"Of course I did; I'm not a stupid man."

Deke scoffed down his pie as his parents threw casual questions at Bailey. She answered each without really giving away much. It was impressive. It also made him yet again wonder why she bothered to be evasive.

Perhaps sensing the weight of his attention, she looked his way. He didn't drop his gaze, just kept on staring. She raised a questioning brow. He answered her with a slight shrug of one shoulder.

A slow smile crept on her face. "Every time we do this staring thing, I feel our connection growing."

He glowered. "Don't make me drug your drink with holy water—I'm pretty sure it would kill you."

"Nah, I've built up a tolerance to it. Not that I'm buying you want me dead. You'd miss me if I was gone."

"Like I'd miss a kick to the crotch."

She wagged a finger. "You secretly adore me. Admit it. You've wondered if we're meant to be."

"I've wondered if you're an omen that the Day of Judgement is almost upon us."

"Flatterer."

He let out a short, jagged growl.

Bailey couldn't help but grin. This was going a *long* way to improving her mood. She'd originally intended to not stay, but then she'd spotted Deke at the table, saw his face darken, and chose to instead stick around merely to make him snap. Her snake loved that it was working.

"Have you ever been normal?" he sniped.

She grimaced. "And fall into society's trap? No, thanks."

"Society's trap?"

"Encouraging people to be normal is literally just encouraging them to conform. Blend. Follow. Obey. Be part of the world's flock of sheep. I'd rather be the predator that hangs not far from the flock, does its own thing, and bites any sheep that piss it off." She paused. "Why are you pulling that face?"

He rubbed at his nape. "I find myself agreeing with you. I don't like it."

"It does feel kind of weird," said Bailey with a slight shudder. "Stop it."

Cash snickered, almost spitting out his food.

Deke merely grunted before going back to his pie. So she once more began talking to Cash. The twenty-one year old broke female hearts regularly. If she'd been a few years younger … well, nothing. She wouldn't have been interested, because she'd never get involved with a guy when it was his brother she most wanted, even though said brother had no interest in her.

I've wanted to get my hands and mouth on you since the first day we met.

Okay, so it wasn't that he had zero interest in her. It was simply that he didn't wish to do anything about it—probably because he didn't like being around her. That might have hurt if she wasn't well-accustomed to people not wanting her around. Her parents had introduced her to that concept when she was a kid.

Feeling eyes on her, she turned her head without thinking … and found Deke's gaze locked on her. Again. And not in a good way. Her snake reared up, watching him carefully.

He flicked a look at her loaded spoon. "You don't have to eat it if you don't want it."

Bailey's brow pinched. "Why wouldn't I want it?"

"Because it's been sitting on your spoon for the past ten minutes."

"I'm talking with your brother. It's rude to talk and eat at the same time."

His brows drew together. "Since when do you care what's rude?"

"I didn't say I *care*."

He sighed and looked away.

How fun. "You just want me to hurry and finish so I'll leave," she accused.

Frowning, he met her eyes again. "Makes no difference to me whether you're here or not."

"Yeah, you look fine with it."

A choked laugh crawled up Clarence's throat.

"We need to have you over more often," Cash said to her.

Deke's frown slid to him. "She's too old for you."

Cash's brow furrowed. "Maybe I want a sugar mama. Or sugar *mamba*."

Bailey pointed at him. "Ha. Good one."

Inwardly seething, Deke watched as—between bites of her dessert—Bailey chatted with his parents and Cash, again neatly dodging anything too personal. It seemed an instinctive act on her part.

He didn't get why she made a point of holding so much back. And it was strange to watch her be so mindful of what came out of her mouth. Bailey wasn't exactly a person who generally minded her words.

Was it that she had things she wished to hide? Was it that there were things in her past she found too painful to speak of? And why did he care?

Hot pain lanced through his head, almost making him swear beneath his breath. More, a spurt of arousal pulsed through his blood and went straight to his hard cock. His shaft throbbed, his foreskin uncomfortably tight.

He clenched his teeth as he rode the wave, staying as still as possible to keep anyone from sensing it. Even with his cat coming close to the surface to help him shoulder the discomfort, it wasn't easy to bear it—especially in silence.

Bailey's gaze snapped to him and narrowed. He could see that he wasn't fooling her, but he had no idea how she'd sensed his issue. Nobody else at the table had. He was good at hiding his pain.

Keeping his expression blank, he steadily stared back at her. Anyone else would have averted their gaze—he'd been told many times that he held such intense eye-contact it was a little unnerving. Which wasn't purposeful on his part, he'd apparently done it since he was a toddler. His parents had found it hilarious.

Bailey didn't shift in her seat or look away, though. Her unblinking stare held his just fine. Eventually, she let out a prissy little sniff and turned away, as if bored.

Again with the fucking dismissiveness.

His fingers flexed beneath the table as he imagined wrapping them around her throat and giving it a little squeeze. Or maybe just slamming his mouth on hers and—

His cat bared a fang, rejecting the idea instantly.

Just then, Bailey turned to his mother. "Thanks so much for dessert, Livy. It was awesome." She pushed out of her seat.

Livy frowned. "You're leaving already?"

"Yeah, I gotta get going."

Deke stood as well, ignoring how the abrupt move aggravated the dull ache in his head, grateful his long-sleeved tee hid his erection. "Same." He had some questions he needed to ask her.

His mother smiled, apparently mollified by the idea that he was leaving with Bailey. He gave his head a minute shake.

After goodbyes were exchanged, he and Bailey left his parents' apartment and made a beeline for the elevator. "What exactly happened with the jackals earlier?"

She shot him a sideways glance. "I'm guessing Havana mentioned it to Tate and then he mentioned it to you."

The Alpha male made a point of keeping his enforcers well informed on any issue that might affect the pride, so she shouldn't be surprised.

"What happened?" Deke pushed.

"Not much. They asked where Roman was. I told them I didn't know.

They seemed dubious about it, so I said they should ask my Alphas. Instead, they gave me a card with a number on to call if Roman gets in touch. And they made it clear that they'd be back. Gerard hurried them along, but I think they would have left without trouble anyway."

"Gerard?" he repeated.

"Yes. He appeared shortly after I was given the business card."

"Did all that happen before or after you were questioned by Ginny and your ex's brothers?"

Bailey narrowed her eyes. "Tate told you about that, too, huh."

"He keeps all his enforcers up to speed on anything important."

Reaching the elevator, she pressed the "up" button. "I wouldn't really call anything Ginny does 'important.' And to answer your question, my little meet and greet with the jackals happened after."

The elevator doors had glided open, and they both stepped inside.

"Do you think she truly believes you're Jackson's attacker?" he asked, pressing the button on the panel to take them to their floor.

"Nope, not even a little."

"What about his brothers?"

"It's hard to say," she said as the elevator smoothly began to ascend. "They don't seem to be certain I'm responsible for what happened to Jackson, but I'm not sure they're convinced of my innocence either. I don't think they know what to believe."

Deke went to speak, but then the ache in his head sharpened and began pulsing fast—telling him that his libido would soon lose its shit. He clamped his lips shut to hold back a pained groan. His cat's attempt to help him bear the pain didn't work this time.

Deke silently cursed. He blamed her damn scent. It was as delectable as it was feminine, and he wanted to drown in it. The sooner he got into his apartment and away from the temptation of her, the better.

He blinked hard, forcing himself to concentrate on the subject at hand. "I wouldn't have thought Ginny would be so stupid as to pull a stunt like this. It's not like she isn't aware that you'll make her pay one way or the other, and it's never wise to anger a pallas cat pride."

"True." Bailey paused as the elevator doors opened. "But she's feeling all big and brave because Jackson's brothers are at her back," she went on as they stepped out and began striding down the hallway. "Speaking of brothers … I like yours. Cash, I mean. He's cute."

Deke tensed, and his cat bared his teeth. "Don't even think about it." The words came out on an animalistic growl.

"What?"

"Dicking with me by pretending you're interested in my brother."

"What makes you think it would be a pretense? And what has your cat got against me getting hot and heavy with your brother?"

Stopping outside his apartment, he raised a brow. "Didn't we already establish that it's not wise of you to push me too far?"

Her gaze turned inward, as if she was searching her memories. "Oh, yeah, right, I forgot about that."

Forgot? Yeah, he needed to ring her little neck. Instead, he yanked his keys out of his pocket. "Did you get rid of the snakes?"

Walking on ahead of him, she paused as she glanced over her shoulder. "Well … you took yours with you when you left my place days ago, and Clive—"

"Jesus, forget it."

She snickered.

"You know something? You're a—" He cut off as the ache in his head seemed to *explode*, and then it was thundering through his skull. The pain was so excruciating that it made his vision blur, his knees shake, and his head go hot. Black spots danced in front of his eyes, and he would have swayed if he hadn't planted his feet.

Fuck, fuck, fuck.

"Easy, big guy," said Bailey, practically lunging to his side.

"I'm fine," he gritted out.

"Never said you weren't."

"You can go."

"Thanks so much." Ignoring his death glare, Bailey scooped up the keys he'd dropped, unlocked his door, and then herded him inside … briefly marveling over how it wasn't all that dissimilar to what he'd done for her a few nights ago.

His eyes went cat—the warning to leave the apartment very clear.

She scowled at the animal. "Oh, get over yourself."

A growl rumbled out of Deke that came from his feline.

Even as her snake coiled to strike, Bailey put her hands on her hips. "Why are you being a dick?" she asked the cat. "He's in pain. You're in pain. But you're so busy stewing on your own bullshit that you—"

A warm, strong hand snapped around her throat as a very feline hiss escaped through Deke's teeth, his cat still very much in charge.

Her snake lifted her body, wanting to strike at the animal. "Hiss all you want. But if you hurt me I will *ream* your ass."

Just like that, the hand disappeared from her throat and the cat let out an offended growl … as if affronted that she'd think it would cause her physical pain.

Deke's eyes squeezed tightly closed. When his lids lifted long moments later, his eyes were their normal caramel-brown. He dragged in breath after breath, clearly trying to ride out the pain.

"You need to go, Bailey." His voice was full of smoke and glass shards. "I can't calm him or the touch-hunger down while you're here."

She doubted he'd manage either of those things easily even if she wasn't here. He was in a bad way, and she knew he'd probably be like this for hours upon hours.

Bailey was a bitch. Owned it. Was proud of it. Nurtured it, even. But she wasn't cold-hearted. She didn't want to leave him like this. There was really only one way she could help, though. And as an idea occurred to her, she thought she might just be able to give him that help.

Her self-respect reared up, reminding her that he'd never touch her under other circumstances; he might want her, but he didn't approve of her. That knowledge wasn't exactly uplifting, but neither were her failed attempts to quash her attraction to him. She'd tried so hard. Again and again. But it hadn't worked.

Their little sexual encounter a few days ago had made things worse. For her, kisses had always been a mundane part of the foreplay "dance." They were always the same, no matter her partner.

She'd never fell into a kiss. Never lost herself in one. Never had one that shot her arousal straight into the stratosphere like goddamn sex magic.

With Deke, it was different. There had not been one thing mundane about the kiss. It hadn't felt like a mere means to an end. And it had been *nothing* like any kiss she'd had before.

She often tried telling herself that she was remembering it wrong; that it couldn't have been *that* amazing. Not really. Surely.

But while she was talented at bullshitting others, she'd never been good at lying to herself. And now that she knew how hard he could make her come *just from a hand job,* she couldn't help but wonder how much more intense it would be if they took things up a notch.

It was hard *not* to wonder when she was such a curious creature by nature. Her curiosity often got the better of her. "Not knowing" could drive her nuts, and then things would play on her mind until she found answers.

That's all this is, she decided. *All this would stop if I just satisfied my curiosity.*

The infamous kiss would cease surging to the front of her mind. She would quit wondering just how hot they'd burn the sheets. She would be able to ignore the weird sexual energy that crackled between them—hell, a night with him might even extinguish it.

And it wasn't like she hadn't helped guys work off touch-hunger before. Not that it had been a charitable act on her part—nah, she loved how elemental sex could be when touch-hunger was in play. It wouldn't be a selfless act now either. At the same time, though, she truly did *want* to help him.

Leaving him like this would be hard, because it wasn't just any guy. It was Deke. Even her snake wouldn't feel good about walking away when he was clearly in agony. His own inner animal, however, could be a real problem.

"Why doesn't your cat want anyone getting too close these days?"

"He just doesn't," Deke evaded, backing away while swiping a hand down his face—pain was etched into every line.

Poor bastard. "But he didn't interfere when you and me got handsy at my apartment."

"Only because he was mad at you for dismissing me. He wanted to teach you a lesson."

Ah. She hummed, thoughtful. "I have an idea."

"I'm literally afraid to ask what it is," he said, his voice dry.

"If I made your cat mad again, made him want to repeat that lesson he pushed you to teach me … he might let you fuck me, mightn't he?"

Deke stiffened from head to toe. "What?"

"It wouldn't be a pity fuck. Don't get me wrong, I'm all for helping you. But that's mostly for selfish reasons—guys wound tight with touch-hunger fuck like *masters.*"

His brow creased. "You don't even like me."

"You don't like me. Didn't stop you from giving me an orgasm once before."

The tips of his fingers twitched. "You couldn't make my cat angry enough to be interested in fucking. Nobody could."

That wasn't a no to sex, she noted. "You sure?"

"I'm sure."

Oh, how he underestimated her. "All right, if you say so. Personally, though … I think you're just worried that you're not dominant enough to handle me." She folded her arms and walked further into his apartment. "I guess it's a fair concern. I mean, I'm not convinced you can either."

A growl grated the back of his throat.

She pivoted to face him again. "And I'm not easy to please in bed. A guy has to know what he's doing. It would be fair to say you're out of practice, wouldn't it?"

His eyes turned cat once more, and the animal glared at her.

She arched a brow at the feline. "Still intent on having 'nobody can touch me' tantrums like a little bitch?"

Again, there was a guttural growl.

"You don't expect me to be afraid of an itty, bitty cat, do you? *Come on.*"

A hiss sounded this time.

She looked at her nails. "Well, if you're really not up for getting down and dirty, I guess I could go see Cash. Or maybe even Shay."

He moved fast. *Wicked* fast. Then Deke's body was again all up in her space and his hand was curled tight around her throat, his cat still in charge. And the air instantly turned thick and static—not with a bad tension: with a very sexual tension.

Two blinks later, Deke was staring down at her, his eyes twin pools of heat. "You have no clue what you're doing," he said, his voice like crushed gravel. "No clue how hard and rough I'd use you."

"So show me," she dared.

His grip on her throat flexed, and she thought he'd let her go. Thought he'd step back and urge her to leave.

He didn't.

He cursed, tightened his hold, dragged her closer, and then brought his mouth crashing down on hers.

Oh, Lord above, the kiss went from zero to a hundred in a second flat. And it was just as she remembered—feral, bruising, uninhibited. His free arm became a band around her waist, pinning her against him. She wrapped her own arms around his neck, arching into him, her breath hitching as she brushed against his hard cock.

He kissed her so hard and long her lips throbbed. As if he was determined to imprint his own on them. The whole time, she ground against him, craving the friction, feeling herself become damp.

Her lungs burning for air, she pulled her mouth free ... at which point he jerkily whipped off her tee and began impatiently stalking forward, forcing her to back up. Catching her by her hips, he brought her to a sharp halt, none-too-gently twirled her around, and then bent her over the back of the sofa ... all in the space of what felt like three seconds.

She blinked. *Well.*

A growl vibrating in his throat, he roughly shoved down her leggings and panties. A hand boldly cupped her pussy from behind and swiped a finger between her folds, finding her slick. That same finger plunged inside her, and another abruptly drove deep mere seconds afterwards.

"Fuck them," he rumbled, the words so gruff they were barely comprehensible.

With pleasure. She threw her hips back again and again, taking his fingers as deep as she could; listening as he snapped open the buttons of his fly with his free hand in one swift, almost violent movement.

Something hard and warm then bumped the globe of her ass. His fingers disappeared, quickly replaced by the blunt head of his cock. Oh, now they were getting somewhere.

He gripped her ass tight. "Should have done this years ago." He rammed his hips forward, burying himself balls-deep in a single, forceful thrust.

Bailey jolted with a shuddering breath as she found herself speared by at least nine solid inches of thick, long cock. Damn, he had some girth on him. How awesome.

She didn't like that he was holding himself so still. She could almost *feel* him trying to gather his control so he didn't take her too hard. Neither she nor her snake wanted or required him to be careful. "Remember you said you don't hate me?"

"Yes," he grunted.

"Fuck me like you do."

He snarled deep in his throat. And then he was brutally pounding into her, cramming every wide inch of his shaft inside her again and again. It chafed and strained against her tight, super-sensitized inner walls. She had no complaints, though. Not when he tunneled so deep, his angle *perfect.* She didn't just take it, she reveled in it.

"Never fucked a pussy this tight." Deke groaned as her inner walls rippled around his dick. Too many times he'd wondered—even jerked off thinking about—how it'd feel to be buried so deep inside her. The moment felt almost surreal, because he'd never thought it would really happen. Not when he'd been so sure she despised him with every breath she took.

How this was happening when his cat was having a weird fucking crisis, Deke didn't know. It shouldn't have been possible that she could manage to anger his cat to such an extent that it would fall for her trick—the animal wasn't exactly easy to manipulate.

But she'd kept pushing and pushing, goading and goading, until anger and arousal blended. His cat's protests died as the feline sought an outlet. *This* outlet. And now, everything Deke felt where she was concerned just spilled out of him.

Need.

Frustration.

Desperation.

Possession—a feeling that had solidified in his veins the moment he'd jammed his cock inside her.

Still hammering hard and deep, he smoothed a hand up her sleek back, unsheathed the tips of his claws, and then sliced into her bra. It fell to the floor beneath her in pieces.

She grumbled something about it being her favorite bra—he didn't properly take in the words, his focus ensnared by the score marks he'd accidentally left on her back. They were only thin red lines that would be gone within the hour, but they made his balls tighten and his cock ache.

Spitting out a low curse, he began yanking her back each time he savagely thrust forward. Her now-free pretty breasts bounced with each thrust. If he hadn't needed to be inside her so damn badly, he'd have earlier lavished some serious attention on them before bending her over the sofa. But his control had been wafer-thin—still was. Hell, it would have been so fragile even if he *hadn't* been riddled with touch-hunger, because this was Bailey.

As he caught sight of her slipping a hand beneath her, he gently batted it aside. "No touching your clit."

"What? Why not?"

"You're going to come just from my dick pounding into you, that's why." He clamped his hands around her shoulders and fucked her harder.

She gasped. "Don't be such a bossy shit."

He fisted her hair and snatched back her head. "You knew what you were getting into. No use bitching about it now." He slammed into her faster and faster, ramming deeper and deeper … until her inner muscles trembled as they became hotter and tighter. "Yeah, come."

Her back wrenched, arching like a bow, as she hoarsely cried out. Her pussy squeezed and contracted around him, dragging him with her.

Deke's release thundered through him—strong, violent, blinding. His come erupted out of him in hot bursts, filling her. And when his brain switched back on moments later, he realized that his teeth were buried in the back of her shoulder.

Fuck.

He gently detached his teeth from her flesh. He'd marked her. *Marked* her. It was deep, too. Not so deep as to scar, but it wasn't going to fade anytime soon.

Even as he called himself all kinds of stupid, he couldn't regret it. He liked the look of his brand on her skin. His cat, however, wasn't pleased; wasn't in a mental place where he could lay any kind of claim, big or small, to anyone—he wanted only to be alone.

As his cock softened, Deke pulled out and stepped back, still panting.

Breathing a little raggedly herself, Bailey stood upright and yanked up her underwear and leggings. Turning, she didn't berate him for biting her, as he'd expected. No, she smirked and said, "You seriously underestimated my ability to make your cat crazy. Why is that?"

He narrowed his eyes, tucking his cock back into his jeans. "I wouldn't be too smug about it, if I were you."

"Why not?" she asked, gathering the torn pieces of her bra from the floor.

"Because you're now marked. You know what that means for you? It means you're fucked. My cat isn't going to let anyone else touch you while you're wearing my mark. Neither will I." No shifter would.

She gave him a flat look, clearly unbothered how he felt. "The only way you and your cat can ensure that is if *you* keep me sexually occupied. Your animal wouldn't be down with that."

His cat did in fact bare a fang at the idea, but it was an act of annoyed resignation rather than a protest. "He'll allow it." Begrudgingly.

Her brows arched. "Is that so?"

"Yes, it is." A good thing, since Deke had lost the will and ability to fight his need for her any longer. "So, we understand each other?"

"Understand what?"

"No other male touches you while that mark is there," he stated, adamant. "Only me."

She folded her arms. "Look, I'm fine with us doing the dirty while you work off your touch-hunger—I told you that already. But you've been battling it for weeks, so it will probably take just as long to settle. And I'm not seeing how we can stretch it out for *that* length of time. Because once the bite on my shoulder has faded—which will only take a few days—your cat will be back to 'no one gets close.'"

"So I'll mark you again. And again and again. However many times I need to."

She twisted her mouth. "Something tells me that Dayna wouldn't like that you're branding another female."

Definitely not, but … "She'd like the thought of me in constant pain even less." He considered telling her that Dayna wouldn't be in the picture much longer, but he couldn't yet. Not until Dayna herself was made aware of it.

Bailey stared at him for a long moment. "All right. I take it you want us to keep this to ourselves, since your mom—who's pretty much wooing me on your behalf—would otherwise pounce on the whole thing."

"Yes, she'd read too much into it. Then she'd up the courting ante and drive us both crazy. If you want to tell your girls and feel you can trust them to keep it to themselves, fine."

"They wouldn't say a word."

He snared her gaze with his own as he said, "Be warned: I'm going to fuck you often. Hard. Anyway I can get you. And it won't stop anytime soon—like you pointed out, it could take weeks for the touch-hunger to pass. Once it does, we'll each go our own way."

"Works for me. If we're really going to do this, we need ground rules, though."

He felt his forehead crease. "Ground rules?"

"No permanent marks. No butt stuff. No sleeping in my bed overnight."

In other words, she didn't want to encourage any possessiveness or cross the casual line. "You like boundaries, don't you, Bailey?

"Yup." She arched a *You got a problem with that?* brow.

"Whatever." He ate up the small space between them with one step. "Now, I got no clue why you righted your clothes but take them off. I'm fucking you again before you leave, and I want you to be stark naked when I do."

CHAPTER SEVEN

Sitting in a booth nestled against the window of the pride's diner the following day, Deke took a bite of his burger, relishing the tastes of grilled meat, soft bun, warm cheese, and fried onions. Not much of a cook, he often ate dinner either here or at the steakhouse. He hadn't done it as often since touch-hunger rose up, though—crowded places only made him more antsy, especially if unmated females were around.

But his body felt much more settled after last night. And not merely in a sexual sense. It honestly felt as if he hadn't breathed so easily in weeks.

The diner was always relatively busy in the evenings, so waitresses currently walked back and forth—jotting down orders, pouring coffee, or delivering food and drinks.

Most of the customers were from the pride. Others were human cops and truckers, or shifters from outside the pride. Some people sat at the counter or at tables while others were tucked in booths.

His cat generally liked it here. Liked its atmosphere, its metro décor, and having pride mates close by.

But right then, the feline was in a black mood after spending part of the day dealing with a bunch of the pride's juveniles—two of whom actually aspired to be enforcers—who were constantly fighting amongst themselves over fuck-all. His cat had little tolerance for petty matters, especially these days. Disciplining the juveniles hadn't placated him.

As such, right now, *everything* around the feline annoyed it. The chatter. The laughter. The meat sizzling. The cutlery clinking. The background music. Even the scents of coffee and spices and bacon grease.

But then, his feline was never really happy these days. Maybe if the cat wasn't mysteriously battling intimacy, his mood would have improved after Deke so thoroughly fucked Bailey last night. Bending her over his sofa had only been the beginning. He'd taken her on his bed. Against the hallway wall. On the kitchen counter. He'd also licked her to orgasm during their shower, after which she'd brought him to climax with her clever little hand.

His cock stirred in his jeans at the memories. Fuck, she'd felt good. *Tasted* good.

They might not get along so well in general. But in the bedroom, they were in sync. And the knowledge that he'd soon have her again had simmered in his blood all damn day.

She'd agreed to come to his apartment again tonight. Agreed a little too easily, despite being an awkward minx the majority of the time. He figured it was because she'd rather they didn't have sex in *her* apartment.

The mamba had solid boundaries, it would seem.

It suited his cat—the feline needed his space; likely wouldn't react well to anyone taking up too much of it. At the same time, though, the feline was insulted that she wished to keep him and Deke at a distance.

The cat still wasn't pleased with him for biting her. Deke still couldn't find it in him to regret it. Especially when it now meant he could get rid of the touch-hunger.

He took another bite of his burger and then lowered it to the plain white dish. It surprised Deke that she hadn't railed his ass for marking her. Most females would have. But then, Bailey wasn't like most. The things that generally pissed people off quite often made her laugh.

Deke lifted his glass of soda just as the bell above the door chimed. A figure in a blue waterproof coat strolled inside, traffic sounds following behind him until the door gently swung closed. He lowered his hood with a little shudder and wiped at the droplets of rain on his face. *Sam.*

Calling out brief hellos to pride members, the healer walked further inside. His step faltered as he caught sight of Deke, and his default smile strangely wavered. But Sam quickly bolstered his smile and stopped at Deke's table. "Hey there."

He gave a short nod. "Sam."

The healer glanced at his plate and hummed. "I'm hankering for a cheeseburger myself."

"Solid choice." Deke took a swig of his soda. "It's damn good."

Cocking his head, Sam studied him closely. "You seem better today. Less edgy. My healer-senses aren't going crazy around you."

It didn't take a genius to guess what Sam suspected. "I'm not sleeping with Cassandra," Deke told him.

Sam flashed him a warmer smile, but Deke couldn't say for sure that the healer truly believed him. "I'll let you get back to your meal." He then strode off.

With an inward sigh, Deke took another swig of his drink. The bell above the door dinged again as yet another person swanned inside. Deke tensed, his grip tightening on his glass. *Maisy.*

They'd made no plans to contact each other, so he could only assume that whoever was behind the fake profile had pulled another stunt that she felt the need to share. *Shit.*

She hung her jacket on the rack by the door and then leaned her collapsed umbrella against the wall. Her gaze landed straight on him, and she then crossed to his booth, her steps slow and hesitant. She cleared her throat and then offered him a shaky smile. "Hi."

Before he had a chance to speak, she dropped onto the other side of his booth, making the leather cushion creak slightly. His cat snarled—not only at her close proximity, but at how she'd so boldly joined them uninvited as if it were her right.

She held her purse against her chest. "I, um, I saw you through the window. I … I thought we could talk."

Feeling his brow furrow, Deke set down his glass. "Talk?"

The sound of rubber soles squeaking along the checkered tile floor quickly preceded the appearance of one of the waitresses, Hilda. She gave Maisy a quick onceover, flicked him a curious look, and then smiled at the human. "What can I get you?"

"Uh, just coffee, please."

Hilda lifted a brow at him. "Need anything else, Deke?"

"I'm good," he replied.

The waitress disappeared.

Maisy placed her purse on the seat beside her and then nervously rubbed her thighs. She cast him another trembly smile but didn't speak. Just sat there. As if they did this shit all the time. As if her approaching him in public to chat was the complete norm for them.

Why would she even be in this area? If what she'd told him about herself was true, she lived two hours away.

Hilda reappeared and set both a steaming mug and a small jug of creamer in front of Maisy. "Enjoy." Hilda gave him one last questioning look but then melted away.

Maisy went about prepping her coffee, still not saying a word.

Not impressed that she seemed to be dragging this out—he was trying to eat his dinner, for fuck's sake—he prodded, "You said you wanted to talk. About what?"

Stirring her drink, she replied, "He called me a few days ago. Deke Two, I mean. That's what I started referring to him as in my head."

A civil title. Deke tended to mentally refer to him with curse words.

She lay her spoon down on the table. "I hadn't intended to confront him over the catfishing, I didn't want to give him the satisfaction. I'd blocked his number so he couldn't contact me. But he called from a withheld number and, not realizing it was him, I answered. God, just hearing his voice made me so mad. I *blew up*."

Pausing, she took a sip of her coffee. "He insisted that though he lied about his identity, he hadn't lied when he claimed he loved me. He said that he would never play me that way. As if he hadn't already played me simply by pretending to be somebody else." She shook her head, clearly pained. "I eventually hung up on him. He hasn't texted or called me since, so I'm guessing he accepted that the gig was up."

Hopefully the son of a bitch truly *had* accepted it. Deke had considered deactivating his own profile so that no one could create another replica of it, but he would be damned if he'd allow the fucker to have that level of influence over his actions.

She sipped her coffee again. "So, how is your day going?"

He blinked at the mundane, casually spoken question.

"I, uh, I tried adding you as a friend on NetherVille. Not sure if you noticed."

He hadn't, actually. He didn't use the site much.

She briefly averted her gaze. "I thought maybe it might be nice for us to keep in touch."

"Why?" he asked, though he suspected he knew the answer; suspected it would also explain why she'd come here.

She hesitated. "A person can never have too many friends, right?"

His cat bristled at the soft smile she gave him. It was a smile reserved for people who knew each other well, not for those who were relative strangers.

Deke sat back in his seat. "I'm not him."

Maisy's brow puckered. "What?"

"The guy you were talking to all these months and grew to care about. I'm not him."

"Well, of course you're not." She put down her cup. "I wouldn't be here if you were—he needs to have his head examined."

Unsure if she was being deliberately obtuse, Deke clarified, "What I mean is … the personality you fell for was *his*, not mine. You probably feel like you know me. You don't."

"I *kind* of do."

"You know things about me. That's not the same."

"But he did mimic you."

And so she thought there was a chance that she and Deke would suit each other.

"In a way, I *was* talking to you," she added, a belligerent little lift to her chin.

"No, Maisy, you weren't. The details he gave you about me—they were all surface. His own personality leaked through. I know that for certain, because you showed me many of the messages he sent you. A lot of the things he did and said aren't things I would have."

"Maybe not *totally*, but—"

"I'm not a guy who'd seek out an online relationship. Sending sweet, flowery texts isn't my style either. I wouldn't stay awake until the early hours of the morning talking to someone on the phone. I don't much like talking on the phone *period*."

"What if—"

"His sense of humor is nothing like mine. The advice he gave you on this or that wasn't the kind that I'd have given you. His goals and dreams definitely aren't in line with my own—I'm not looking to get married, go on road trips, climb Mount Everest, or move to Italy one day."

She swallowed hard. "Okay, so I don't really know you," she reluctantly relented, "but would it really be so bad for us to get to know each other?"

He sighed. "Look, I get it. You cared for him. A lot. And all the emotion you invested in him is tied up in my pictures." It had to be easy for her to feel comfortable with Deke; to imagine them together because she'd been doing it for so long. "But it wouldn't be healthy for you to have any contact with me when you're trying to heal from what he did."

With a frustrated groan, Maisy dipped her head and buried her face in her hands.

The bell chimed again as the door once more swung open. Traffic noise swept in, overridden by a female laugh. A laugh he knew well. So he wasn't the least bit surprised to see Bailey file into the diner with Havana and Aspen.

His gut clenched at the sight of the mamba. Her gaze did a predatory scan of the large space. Her gaze halted on him and then narrowed as it took in Maisy. Bailey sniffed … and went right back to scanning the diner in an act of pure dismissal.

Predictably, his cat bared his teeth. Deke really was going to throttle her later. Or maybe just fuck her until she couldn't take it anymore.

Her mouth curved, and he tracked her gaze to see that Blair and Elle were waving from their table in the far corner. Bailey and her girls began making their way to said table. Havana and Aspen noticed him, and both sent a pretty smile his way. Bailey pointedly ignored him once more.

Yeah, he was going to pound into her until she could no longer take it.

Maisy lifted her head and dropped her hands. "I get what you're saying, Deke. I do. But I can't see it being a big deal for us to strike up a friendship."

Jesus Christ.

Bailey didn't care that Deke was having dinner with another female. Nope. Not in the slightest. It mattered not one iota to her.

Me thinks I doth protest too much.

What-the-fuck-ever.

Taking a mental dump over the questions that tried flowing to the forefront of her mind—who was the bitch? Why was he meeting her? Was it Dayna? Did the asshole have another female lined up to help him with the touch-hunger—Bailey continued heading toward Blair and Elle. The latter female was the sister of Tate, Luke, and the youngest of the Devereaux brothers, Damian.

She hadn't told her girls what went down last night, or about the agreement that she and Deke had made. Mostly because it would annoy them to find out days later. But also because part of her suspected that, in the light of day, he'd change his mind. She'd find out soon enough. For now, she'd ignore him.

Reaching Blair and Elle's table, she smiled. Both women were slouched back in their seats, a hand on their stomach, empty plates in front of them.

"Hey, it's great to see you guys," said Elle. "You should sit with us."

Shedding her jacket, Havana frowned. "You're not done eating?"

"Not yet." Blair slurped some milkshake through a straw. "We're just giving ourselves a break before we order dessert."

"I highly recommend the chili," Elle told them. "Bailey, before you settle, maybe you can go rescue Deke."

Pausing in hooking her damp coat over the back of a chair, Bailey tilted her head. "Huh?"

Elle leaned forward. "I think the brunette with him is Maisy."

Aspen's brows shot up as she plopped her butt on a chair. "Really?"

Bailey took a long look at the other female. "Yep, that's her, all right. I saw her NetherVille profile photo." She hadn't recognized the human on first entering the diner—she'd only had a view of her back.

"Thought so," said Elle. "I'm not good enough at lip reading to know what they're talking about, but I was pretty sure he said 'Maisy' at one point."

"I wonder why they're meeting up," said Havana, shuffling forward in her seat slightly.

"I don't think it was arranged," Blair claimed. "He was sitting alone, and she just turned up. He looked surprised. Then awkward. Now he's looking impatient and annoyed. I think she's coming onto him."

Bailey was thinking the same thing. There was pure longing in the human's eyes—eyes that were regarding him with more familiarity than a stranger should.

"Go save him, Bailey," Elle urged. "Just walk over there and act as if you're his girlfriend. It'll make her back off. I'd do it myself, but you're on your feet, so …"

Every female at the table looked at Bailey, expectant. Aspen was all-out smirking, clearly thinking that Bailey would refuse. *Pfft.* Like she'd pass on an opportunity to dick with him. This could be fun.

"I'll be back in a sec." Humming to herself, she headed to his table. Both he and Maisy looked up. The human's eyes widened in surprise. Deke's narrowed in what appeared to be suspicion. Ha. She did love that he was so wary of her motives at all times.

Bailey sidled up to his chair and bent down just enough to press a kiss to his cheek. "Sorry I'm late. Who's your friend?"

Deke curled an arm around her waist and gripped her opposite hip, clearly deciding to play along. "Bailey, Maisy. Maisy, Bailey."

Ignoring that even through her clothes his grip was like a red-hot brand that she'd swear she could feel *beneath* her skin, she smiled at the human. "Yo."

Maisy's brow creased as she turned to him. "Your online profile says you're single."

"Oh, I'm sorry, are you a prospective play partner?" Bailey asked her. "Deke, you should have told me you were interviewing one today." She frowned down at him. "Did you forget or something?"

He watched Bailey for a long moment. "Yes," he finally said, his voice hesitant.

Bailey turned back to Maisy. "Just to be clear, we're not officially in a relationship. I'm just one of their current toys. Deke and Isaiah have … specifications for whatever partner they'll eventually commit to."

Maisy frowned. "Isaiah?"

Bailey lifted a hand. "Don't get me wrong, I'd have no problem being part of a triad. But I don't meet their *other* specifications."

"Specifications?" the human echoed.

"I'm no virgin, for one. I don't get off on pain, for another. Swinging ain't really my jam either. And I'm not good at puppy play—I kept laughing instead of barking, and I got stage fright every time I was supposed to pee on the newspaper." She chuckled to herself and then looked down at Deke. "Remember that?"

He stared up at her, his eyes narrowing even further. "I remember."

"Your punishment was a little harsh." Bailey gave him a playful look of admonishment and then turned back to Maisy. "Outdoor kennels are *seriously* cold. Especially when you're naked. Then again, it was better than when he poured candle wax on my nipples. I got him back for that, though. Poured it on his balls. But he likes pain, so it worked out well for all, I guess." She cocked her head. "What kind of kinks are you into?"

Maisy opened and closed her mouth a few times. "Uh …" She glanced around, as if hoping someone would save her from the conversation. Abruptly, she stood. "I have to run."

Bailey frowned. "So soon?"

"Yes." Forcing a smile, Maisy quickly edged out of the booth, hooking the strap of her purse over her shoulder. "It was nice to meet you, Bailey. Deke, it was good to see you, I hope you enjoy what's left of your dinner. You both take care now." She rushed to the doorway, grabbed her jacket and umbrella, and then scampered out of the diner.

Releasing her hip with a sigh, Deke fired a glare at Bailey. "You enjoyed that, didn't you?"

She smiled, shrugging. "A girl has to get her kicks where she can."

"Does she really, though?"

"Yes." Bailey glanced at the door. "Am I right in guessing she was looking to start something with you?"

He exhaled heavily. "You are. I think it's safe to say that you officially changed her mind."

"Then my work here is done. Peace out."

He fisted the bottom of her tee before she could walk away. "Don't forget about tonight," he said, lowering his voice, his eyes heating.

Huh. It turned out that Bailey hadn't needed to worry that he would change his mind. Well, how about that. "I won't. Ten pm at your place, right?"

His jaw tightened. "I said eight pm. As you well know."

"I'm pretty sure you said ten."

"No, you're not. You're just trying to irritate me. And don't think you won't pay for it later." The sexual implication there made her blood sing.

"I feel I should tell you that punishments don't really work on me. They just encourage me to be more difficult."

His lips flattened. "So, basically, you're just testing in every way a person could be testing?"

"That's pretty much how it goes, yes." She nudged his upper arm with her elbow, giving him a taunting smile. "But you want to fuck me anyway."

"I *will* fuck you anyway. Again."

"Then I'll see you at ten."

His eyelid twitched. "*Eight*."

"Dude, are you sure you didn't say ten?"

He growled. "Do you want me to throw something at you?"

"Not particularly."

"Then don't push me."

"Fine. Whatever. See you at nine."

"Bailey, I *swear* ..."

She only laughed and walked away.

CHAPTER EIGHT

Staring up at Deke's ceiling four evenings later, Bailey struggled to catch her breath as she recovered from a monumental orgasm. It had torn through her body and sucked every bit of strength from it. She had all but melted into the mattress, and Deke had slumped over her like a dead weight.

Well, damnedy damn.

"The paint on your ceiling is chipped," she rasped.

"Thanks for letting me know," he slurred, his breath fanning her throat. "I'll get right on it."

She let out a soft, weak snort.

After several nights of being railed by his cock repeatedly, she ached in places she didn't know possible. But she wasn't so sore that she needed a break. At least not at the moment.

His touch-hunger hadn't yet receded, but his general restlessness wasn't quite as acute. Also, he was having less flare-ups, and they seemed to pass quicker. All good news for him. Not so much for her libido.

Considering they'd rutted like animals in practically every position possible, it could definitely be said that her sexual curiosity had been well and truly satisfied where he was concerned. The problem? Her curiosity was the only thing that had been permanently satiated. Her body continued to burn for the broody son of a bitch.

The weird energy between them hadn't disappeared. But it had changed. Lost its rough edge. Perhaps because it was no longer colored by carnal needs going unanswered.

Havana would probably be able to better explain it, but Bailey hadn't told her girls about her little arrangement with Deke. They'd only make a big deal out of it, and it would be more amusing to let them learn of it later on anyway—they'd get all het up about her keeping it from them. She did love it when people got het up about stuff.

Above her, Deke lifted his head. Eyes all warm and slumberous caught hers. The feverish glitter that had been present in those eyes when she'd first walked into the apartment earlier was gone, telling her that his touch-hunger had eased for now.

"My cervix is concerned that your cock wants to hammer a hole into it," she said, her voice lazy.

One corner of his mouth pulled up. "Then maybe stop asking me to fuck you harder and deeper."

"It just slips out."

Shaking his head, he withdrew his softening dick and then fell to his back on the mattress beside her. A breath rattled out of his lungs. "I came so hard my damn gums are tingling."

Letting her eyes fall shut, she said, "Tingling is always good."

He let out a sort of gruff hum. "You've got a lot of stamina. I wasn't sure you'd be able to keep up."

"Ye have so little faith in me."

"I know."

She barked a laugh at the unrepentant admission. She wasn't sure what it said about her that his rudeness tickled her so much. It had stopped bothering her snake. The serpent didn't see him as a threat to Bailey anymore, feeling confident he didn't actually hate her.

"But the main reason I figured you'd struggle to keep up is that people dealing with touch-hunger can go all night."

"They can indeed."

He went still. "You helped someone through touch-hunger before?" he asked, his voice dropping an octave.

"Uh-huh."

"How many?" The question was *all* demand.

Opening her eyes, she turned her head to look at him. Still flat on his back, he had his gaze locked on her. His expression was closed over, but his jaw was tight.

"I already told you I'd helped others." Well, she'd insinuated it. "I made the comment that guys with touch-hunger fucked like masters."

"How many?" he repeated.

"Why?" she asked.

"Because I want to know."

"Why?"

"Because I'm interested."

"Why?"

Exasperation flickered across his face. "Will you just answer the question?"

She huffed. "Three."

His back teeth locked, and his eyelids drooped slightly. "Did any of them mark you?"

"Why?"

"*Bailey.*"

"No, jeez." As of tonight, *he'd* bitten her twice. The back of her shoulder still smarted from where he'd renewed his bite. Other than that, he hadn't marked her again.

She was covered in fingerprint bruises, though. Which was really only to be expected, given how wild things got between them. There was plenty of grabbing and hauling and squeezing.

He rolled onto his side to face her. "Why aren't you pissed that I marked you?"

She frowned. "We already established that you'd have to do it again once it faded or your cat would become a problem, remember?"

"I mean the first time I bit you. You weren't angry. Why not?"

"You didn't do it on purpose. You lost control." She felt her mouth curve. "How can I not find that amusing, considering you're all about control?" In her opinion, it was good for the uptight ass to lose it occasionally.

He studied her intently. "I'm not the only one here who likes having control over themselves at all times, though, am I? You never fully let go. No matter how much you're trembling and moaning, no matter how desperate you are to come, no matter how long I've kept you on the edge of an orgasm, you cling to whatever thread of control you have left."

"*You* hold back, too. Why wouldn't we? This thing we have isn't serious. And you're planning to mate another female." *Skank*, she thought, her stomach cramping. Gas again.

His brows flew together. "Mate?"

"Why else would you wait so long for her?" The promise he'd made to Dayna—in Bailey's view, at least—was kind of extreme.

"It was never about mating. It was about not giving up on what we had merely because she'd need to be gone a year."

Bailey's brow wrinkled. "But it's well-known in the pride that you're set on finding your true mate, so you surely wouldn't have made Dayna such a promise unless she meant enough to you that you'd put it aside. Or is it that you think *she's* your predestined mate?"

"At one point, I did think it was possible. That was mostly why I agreed to wait rather than move on. It didn't seem that big of a deal to wait anyway, since I wouldn't have jumped straight into another female's bed anyway—I would have held off a few months, maybe longer. In the grand scheme of things, what were an extra several months on top of that?"

Well, when he put it like that, it really didn't seem extreme that he'd agreed to wait for Dayna. Bailey wasn't sure she would have in his shoes.

"But when it didn't prove difficult for me or my cat to be so far apart from her, I figured it was highly unlikely that she's my mate. Still, I wasn't certain. There seemed no harm in nonetheless waiting for her to come back." He paused. "I didn't think she'd stay away so long. But one year became two, and then two and a half."

"And yet, you're still committed to the promise you made to her." Bailey returned her gaze to the ceiling. "Noble. Sort of."

"What do you mean, *sort of*?"

"Well, there's nobly sticking to a vow because it means something to you. And there's sticking to a vow purely to *be* noble. What's the point if the vow itself isn't as important as it once was?"

"You don't think I've kept my word for the right reason?"

Bailey rolled to face him, snaring his gaze. "If Dayna mattered so much to you, if some part of you thought she could be your mate, you wouldn't be lying here with me. You'd be wherever she is."

Damn if Deke could deny that. He couldn't deny any of what Bailey said. The mamba was bang on the mark.

Though Dayna sometimes suggested he join her in Australia, she hadn't asked him to go with her when she'd first left. She'd claimed there'd be no point in him going, because she'd be focused on her sister. But if she had requested that he accompany her, he wouldn't have left his life behind to be at her side.

By the same token, she wouldn't have stayed if he'd asked it of her. They simply hadn't been each other's priority. But they'd both thought that might change if they gave it a chance, so that was what they'd chosen to do.

And he hadn't wanted to risk that he'd otherwise be obliviously letting his true mate walk away from him. People didn't always recognize them straight away—they could even be in contact with them for years before becoming aware of it.

However, there had come a point where he'd stopped keeping his promise for the right reason. It hadn't been about wanting to further explore what they'd started anymore, or about him having suspicions that she could be his predestined mate—those suspicions had died. It had been about his sense of honor, and how he hadn't wanted to effectively abandon her when she needed someone to be there for her.

"How come you don't just fly out to see each other whenever touch-hunger strikes?"

He sighed. "I thought about it the first time. But I knew she'd bug me to stay in Australia with her. I wouldn't have, so we'd have argued. Just like we often argue when she suggests I move there via video-calls. There seemed nothing positive in going to see her."

"She never offered to come here for a quick visit?"

"No. She probably worried that I'd ask her to stay, and she wasn't ready to leave her nephew for good."

"Is she gonna be ready anytime soon?"

He had no clue, but it didn't really matter anymore. Not when he'd made the official decision to not spend more of his time waiting for Dayna to return. But he wasn't willing to share with Bailey what he hadn't yet shared with Dayna. As such, Deke didn't answer her question. Instead, he noted, "You don't usually ask me personal questions."

She shrugged one shoulder. "I'm bored."

He felt his eyes almost bug out of his head. Inside him, his cat did a double-take. "*Bored?*" In his bed and bored?

"Well, your cock isn't in me anymore, so …"

He did a slow blink. "The only thing about me that you find entertaining is my cock?"

"Why do you say that like it's a bad thing?"

A low growl pouring out of him, Deke pushed her onto her back and covered her body with his once more. Settling his hips between her spread thighs, he gave her a playful glare. "Were you this much of a pain in the ass for the guys in your past?"

"Yes," she replied without missing a beat.

"Really? Because you seem to enjoy riling me more than you do others."

"If you don't believe me, ask Shay."

Deke bit her right on the chin. His cat was unmoved by her little yelp, annoyed with her for taking Shay to her bed in the first place. The feline, still determined to withdraw from everyone around him, hadn't warmed to the idea of having Bailey around. But he didn't hiss and snarl so much anymore. He mostly just retreated to the corner and sulked.

Deke scraped her jawline with his teeth. "Speaking of Shay, I have a theory."

"Is it scientific? Because I don't like science."

Probably because it involved logic. "Not scientific."

"Then proceed."

He trailed kisses down the side of her neck, wondering if she had consciously realized that she'd ceased being uncomfortable when his teeth were near her vulnerable throat. "You get bored with guys very quickly. Shay was no exception—I could tell. But you kept dating him anyway." He circled her pulse with the tip of his tongue. "You did it to piss me off, didn't you?"

She sniffed, all haughty. "Partly. I don't like that you sit in judgement over me like you're oh so superior."

Frowning, he met her gaze. "I don't think I'm superior to you. I just think you've been sent here to do the devil's work, and it bothers me that you're not fighting your fate."

She let out an amused snicker. "Dude, you *so* think you're better than me."

"If you really believe that, why the hell are you in my bed right now?"

"Well, with your cock comes you—I have no way to change that."

He felt his frown deepen. "You're saying you tolerate me in order to have access to my dick?"

"Basically, yeah."

Dipping his face to hers, he shook his head. "You don't dislike me as much as you'd like me to believe you do." It was something he'd come to realize over the past few nights.

After sex, her guard tended to lower a little. She spoke of things she usually wouldn't. She forgot to plaster on her resting bitch face, and she didn't work so hard to conceal her surface feelings. He liked it.

Bailey pursed her lips. "We can go with that, if it matters so much to you. Won't make it true, though."

He took her mouth with a growl. Ate at it. Dominated every last crevice of it.

Rock hard once more, he entered her with one, smooth, purposeful thrust. "You drive me nuts. Make me honestly visualize cutting off your air supply with my own two hands. But I don't look down on you." Then he pounded into her until they both came.

The next morning, Bailey paused in humming along to the music playing over the convenience store's loudspeaker and glanced at Havana. "Sorry, what did you say?"

The devil's lips flattened. "I said—and you heard me just fine, you faker—I feel like you're keeping something from me."

Bailey *had* in fact heard her. But the Alpha didn't like to repeat herself, so naturally Bailey enjoyed making her do exactly that.

"Not a deep, dark, twisted secret," Havana went on, checking the price tag of the plastic skeleton she held. "But something's going on."

Returning a plush pumpkin to a shelf, Aspen nodded. "What aren't you telling us?" she asked, keeping her voice low so that their conversation wouldn't carry to other shifters—some were browsing the aisles; others were stocking the shelves. Like the rest of the premises on the street, the convenience store was owned by the pride.

Going for blasé, Bailey replied, "Nothing." Pushing her shopping cart forward a few steps, she took a long look at the bags of horror-themed confectionery. Bailey threw two bags into her cart—not for trick or treaters; for herself. They'd come to pick up some groceries, but they'd made a detour down the Halloween decorations aisle out of curiosity.

"Nothing my butt," said the bearcat as she and Havana caught up with Bailey. Aspen was the only one not pushing a cart, not needing help to carry a mere loaf of bread. "Why be so secretive?"

"Why be so insistent I share stuff? There are things you don't tell me,"

Bailey pointed out.

Aspen flipped a hand. "That's different."

"How?"

"It just is. Give up the goods."

"Fine." Bailey paused. "I'm thinking of taking up crocheting."

"*Bailey.*"

"What? It's true."

"Come on," Havana cut in, absently fiddling with the foot of the skeleton she still held. "We share things with you."

"Not everything," Bailey reminded her. "You both have stuff you only talk about with your mates. Do you ever hear me pushing for you to spill it all?"

Havana nodded. "Yes."

"All the time," replied Aspen.

"Your nosy questions are never-ending," Havana added.

Bailey frowned, perching a hand on her hip. "I haven't asked either of you a nosy question today."

Aspen shot her a look of disbelief. "Asking if I own a butt plug isn't nosy?"

"You think it is?" Bailey pursed her lips. "Huh. Weird."

"No, it isn't," the bearcat clipped. "God, would you just put us out of our misery?"

"What, like, shoot you behind a shed?"

Aspen fisted her hands. "*Tell us what you're hiding.*"

"A body."

Aspen threw up her arms. "I *can't* with you."

"I'm not hiding anything." Bailey just wasn't telling them everything. That was totally different.

Turning to the shelf beside her, Bailey grabbed a vanilla pumpkin-scented candle and gave it a sniff. Her sense of smell was acute enough that the candle's scent momentarily drowned out the store's smells of pine cleaner, fresh bread, and the warm foods being cooked at the small takeout counter.

"We'll find out what it is eventually," Havana warned. "And if it turns out you're doing work for Cesário on the side …"

Her brow creasing at the mention of their old boss from the Movement, Bailey glanced at her. "We retired, remember?"

Havana pointed the skeleton's arm at Bailey. "Don't think I don't know he calls and offers you the occasional job—ones that only *you'd* be crazy enough to take."

"He does *not* do that." Much. "I'd say no if he did. I adore Cessy and all, but retired means retired."

"You know he hates that nickname."

"Yes, I do know." It was exactly why Bailey used it. She returned the candle to the shelf. "Now … are you going to buy that skeleton or keep feeling it up like a weirdo?"

Havana frowned. "I'm not—We aren't changing the subject, Bailey."

"Don't tell me you're curious about bedding a corpse. There's a name for kinks like that, you know."

"Bailey, don't make me hurt you."

"Does Tate know you're into that? Ooh, do you have him pretend to be dead and stuff when you guys are getting it on?"

Havana's mouth tightened. "Do you have to be so inappropriate?"

"Inappropriate? *I'm* not the one violating a plastic skeleton."

"I'm not violating it!"

A male sigh drifted their way, edged with humor. "I see you're at it again," said Shay as he materialized beside Bailey.

She felt her brows meet. "At what?" Her inner snake roused slightly at the sight of him. The serpent liked him, but she'd never viewed him as a potential partner, only a temporary bedmate.

"Provoking the people around you," he elaborated, his eyes dancing. "It's like you can't help yourself. Or don't want to." He tilted his head slightly. "I'm thinking it's probably the latter."

"Is that why you dumped me and left me heartbroken?"

His lips twitching into a smile, he rolled his eyes. "I didn't dump you. We mutually agreed to move on. And you weren't heartbroken. You weren't *anything*. For all the emotion you showed, we might as well have been discussing whether to do the dishes then or later."

The same could be said for him. Which hadn't bothered her, because he was right—she hadn't cared. "Maybe I was hiding my heartbreak."

Shay snorted. "The only thing you were hiding was that you have the hots for Deke, but I see all." All smirky and shit, he nudged her. "Why haven't you jumped him yet?"

"I don't like to ambush and rob people."

Havana threw up a hand. "First of all, that's a lie. Second of all, it's not what he meant, and you know it."

Bailey bristled. "Excuse me, I'm no thief."

"You stole my wristwatch," said Shay, still smiling.

"No, you gave it to me," Bailey insisted. "You called it a parting gift."

His brow knitted, but his smile didn't fade. "Why would I give you my watch for any reason?"

"So I can always know the time *obviously*."

"You have an answer for everything, don't you?"

Aspen gave him a look of understanding. "Irritating, isn't it?"

He nodded, his eyes still twinkling with mirth. "Kind of, yes."

Bailey folded her arms. "Is that why you broke my heart?"

Another eye roll. "You were *not* heartbroken." Hearing his cell ring, he fished it out of his pocket as he said, "Do both you *and* Deke a favor, Bailey, and go jump his bones—by holding off on it, you're only delaying the inevitable." With that, he strode off as he answered his call.

"He's right, you know," Aspen told her.

"Yeah, he is," Bailey admitted. "I wasn't heartbroken."

The bearcat narrowed her eyes. "That wasn't what I was referring to."

Bailey blinked. "Oh. Well yeah, I did steal his watch," she confessed.

"I wasn't referring to that either."

"Maybe try being more specific."

"Maybe try being less of a dork," Aspen snippily shot back.

"Why?" Seemed unnecessary, really.

"I can do it myself," a new voice growled.

They all turned to see two of their pride mates turning the corner of the aisle.

Alex scowled at his pregnant mate. "It's heavy."

"It's a cart," snapped Bree. "I'm pushing it, not carrying it."

"Hey, you two," Havana greeted. "Everything okay?"

Bree looked at her, the image of exasperation. "It will be when he stops treating me like I'm made of porcelain."

"You shouldn't be overexerting yourself," Alex insisted.

The rubber sole of Bree's shoe squeaked as she swerved to face him. "How, pray tell, does shopping count as overexerting myself?"

"I don't know, but it does."

Eyeing the male wolverine, Bailey didn't bother fighting a smile. "I never thought I'd see you ruffled by anything." Like the rest of his kind, he was known for being both fearless and implacable.

He only grunted, not what anyone would call talkative or social. He didn't bother with many people and only seemed to enjoy the company of Bree, who was also the pride's primary omega. The pallas cat wasn't his true mate, but they were as tight as any predestined couple.

"His overprotectiveness was funny at first," said Bree, turning back to Bailey and her girls. "Now it's plain maddening. And I can't stop eating. I'm always hungry. *Always*."

"You don't look like you're overeating," Aspen told her.

Alex sighed. "The baby is basically devouring most of the goodness she takes in. That's how I know it's a wolverine. They're greedy even in the womb."

Bree swallowed, her expression pained. "I'm worried it might *eat* my womb, at this point."

Havana gave her a smile that was as compassionate as it was reassuring. "Soon you'll have your baby in your arms, and then it'll all be worth it."

"My arms?" Bree snorted. "If I'm lucky, sure. But something tells me that Valentina will take over," she mumbled, referring to Alex's mom—a badass woman who Bailey adored. "Or his Russian uncles. They're insisting on naming the baby, which will *not* be happening."

Bailey guessed that the three male wolverines were simply intent on ensuring that the kid had a Russian name as well. They weren't at all pleased with Alex's sister, Mila, for not giving her twins Russian names.

Alex put a hand on Bree's back. "Come on, let's finish shopping and then get you home."

The omega sniffed. "Fine. But *I'm* pushing the cart—I don't care what you say or do."

Bickering over the matter, the couple continued down the aisle.

Havana grinned at Aspen. "Camden will be like that when you eventually get pregnant."

"Tate won't be any less of a hoverer," the bearcat pointed out. "You'll try to kill him at least twice."

Havana sighed. "Probably."

As Bailey and her girls continued venturing down aisles, she and Havana tossed this or that into their cart as they went along. Bailey didn't grab much. Just some microwave meals, snack foods, and dairy products.

Eventually, they all reached the cash register, where they paid for and then bagged their shopping while the attendant—a pride member—bubbly jabbered on.

Bags in hand, Bailey led the way as the three of them headed outside. A little shiver skated over the back of her neck as the cool air hit her. Ugh.

They began a slow walk to Havana's cul-de-sac, chatting about everyday stuff, but the Alpha female watched Bailey closely. It didn't take a genius to sense that she wasn't gonna back down from pushing Bailey to confess all. She was merely giving her a break.

Once Havana was safely inside her home, Bailey and Aspen went their separate ways—the bearcat began making her way to the steakhouse to meet Camden while Bailey made a beeline for her apartment building.

Reaching the lot, Bailey walked toward the complex, her heels ticking on the black pavement as she passed vehicle after vehicle. She had to dodge the occasional puddle. The rain had thankfully stopped, but the scent of ozone and wet grass lingered.

Cold, she transferred her shopping bags to one hand so she could stuff the other in her pocket. The fairly large lot was bordered by bushes, streetlights, and narrow strips of grass. Right then empty of people, it was also quiet. Only the sounds of her footfalls and the nearby traffic noise could be heard.

Her plans for the evening were simple. Take a hot bath, dress in warm clothes, nuke and scoff down a microwave meal, and then meet Deke at his apartment. Where she'd hopefully got boinked until she couldn't think straight.

He was good at that. While he was deep inside her—touching her with desperation and urgency and so much need—it was easy to forget everything else. What *wasn't* easy was maintaining a "strictly sex" mental stance. Because curt and gruff though he might be, she was growing to like him.

He might be mean at times, but not to be *cruel*—just because he enjoyed sparring with her like that. That went both ways. And much as she might madden him, he never told her to get out of his sight or anything. Which was more than she could say for her parents.

Despite that they wouldn't be sexing each other up if it wasn't for the touch-hunger, he never treated her as if she was a faceless fuck. Never did or said anything that reminded her he wouldn't otherwise take her to his bed and that he was waiting for Dayna … which annoyed Bailey, because she'd prefer to have it straight in her head at all times. It wouldn't be good to get comfortable with him or—

A figure leaped out from between two cars—a blur of black that tossed something at her so fast she had no chance of avoiding it. Wet droplets landed on her face. Droplets that *burned.* Burned so bad it felt like her face was on fucking fire.

She cried out in both shock and pain as the boiling heat sank deep into her skin and ate at it. Corroded it. Made her fear that her flesh would melt off her face. The pain was out of this world—agonizing, unbearable, torturous.

A heavy weight slammed into her, taking her to the ground. The back of her skull smacked into the pavement, sending a wave of hurt through her head and causing her vision to briefly go dark. Standing over her, her attacker—it was a he, she distantly sensed despite the ski mask he wore—tried snatching her purse.

Her infuriated snake rose up with a vicious hiss and took control.

Ignoring the searing pain as Bailey's wounds became her own, the serpent bounded her head out of Bailey's collar and bit into the nearest ankle once, twice, three times.

He cried out. Backpedaled. Slammed into a car. A blaring, rhythmic alarm began to blare so loud it was deafening. He turned to flee.

The snake lunged and coiled her body around his leg, dragging him to the ground with her weight. Then she bit his calf, injecting yet more venom into his bloodstream, drinking in his pained cry.

He struggled. Kicked out. Spat words. Tried to crawl away.

But she was bigger and heavier than a full-blooded black mamba. He had no chance of escape.

He slammed his leg on the ground, trying to hurt and dislodge her. The snake contracted around his limb, feeling bones crack. His back bowed as a scream ripped from his throat.

More struggles. More kicks. More harsh words. But his attempts to fight quickly grew weak. He began to groan. Writhe. Scrape at the ground.

Ground that started to vibrate beneath her as footsteps thundered toward them.

People gathered around, crowding her. She let out a furious hiss that made them go motionless. Voices spoke, soothing. Familiar. Nonthreatening. *Valentina. James. Therese. Sam. Isaiah.*

She didn't care. Wouldn't have cared even if she understood their words. Her only interest was in her prey. He would *not* escape.

More footsteps sounded, and then: "Bailey! Bailey, fuck!"

The Beta female, the snake knew.

"I need you to make your mamba pull back," said Blair.

"Sam can't heal you while you're in your serpent form," Isaiah added. "She's too pissed; she'd bite him."

Inside the snake, her other half pushed for supremacy. Bailey, too, was enraged. But she wanted to surface. Heal. Be free of the pain that both she and the snake shouldered to each help spare the other.

But … their prey might escape if she shifted. That was not acceptable. He needed to pay.

Other voices began to plead with her. The snake ignored them all, until her Alpha female's voice joined the chorus and *demanded* that she shift.

With a low hiss of displeasure, the mamba withdrew.

Bailey was surrounded by people so fast it was almost dizzying. Hands gently rested on her, and then healing warmth fired through her system like sparks of electricity.

"You'll be all right, just breathe," Sam gently urged.

She gritted her teeth against the blistering agony that was her face, barely able to see due to her swelling eyelids, she lay still—not easing up her death grip on her attacker for even a second.

The whole time, people raged around her. Mostly her Alphas and Betas. A few kicked the guy whose leg she still gripped, including James and Luke.

Gradually, the blazing hurt faded and the swelling went down … until Bailey was fully healed and the agony was replaced by a storm of rage that burned in her gut as deeply as the acid had burned her flesh.

Fucking acid.

Bailey gave a spiteful squeeze of the broken leg she held, which only earned her a whimper. At this point, he was too riddled by the effects of her venom to react as she'd like.

"Thank you, Sam," she stiffly told the healer, speaking through gritted teeth.

He inclined his head, backing away to give her space to rise.

The moment Bailey stood, Havana hauled her into a hug. "God, you scared the shit out of me. Blair called to say you'd been attacked."

As the devil pulled back, Blair pushed clothes into Bailey's hands and said,

"I'm so fucking relieved you're okay. My inner bush dog is losing her mind about this bullshit."

The animal couldn't possibly be more furious than her snake. Even though her skin was chilled, Bailey's rage was so hot she barely felt the cold. Still, she dragged on her clothes. Aside from her sweater and bra—which had been protected from the rain-slicked ground by her coat—they were cold and a little damp, but they were better than nothing.

She turned to grab her shoes and coat from Blair, only to then realize that the bush dog had been frowning at the back of Bailey's shoulder. Her marked shoulder. *Shit*, she'd seen Deke's brand.

Blair flicked up her brow in question. Bailey gave her a narrow-eyed "say nothing" stare. The bush dog subtly lifted her hand in a gesture of peace.

Having put on her coat, Bailey slipped on her shoes as she skimmed her gaze over the people stood not far behind Blair. They were focused on Bailey's attacker, not on her body. *Good.* They might not have seen the bite mark.

Now dressed, she crossed to the asshole's side and studied him closely, itching to kick the holy hell out of him. By the looks of it, Valentina yearned to do the same—James seemed to be holding her back.

"He is weak to use such cruel weapon like acid," the female wolverine sneered, glaring at him. "He should have been put down like rabid dog long ago."

"At least he's in a shitload of pain and discomfort now," said Therese, standing beside Sam and watching dispassionately as the human vomited.

His face a study in ire, Tate looked at Bailey. "Do you recognize him?" he asked, holding the ski mask he'd clearly removed from her attacker.

She shook her head. She didn't recognize his scent either. A scent that told her he was human. "Does he have ID on him?" She had to force out the words. Her voice was thick and taut with an anger that had her in such a chokehold it was hard to speak.

"No, nothing," replied Tate. "Not even a phone or a set of car keys. Which means he either parked his car somewhere close, or he had a getaway driver who probably abandoned his ass when the whole thing went bad."

Holding Bailey's purse and shopping bags, Luke moved closer. "He's dying." His tone rang with the same malevolent satisfaction she and her serpent felt.

There was no antivenom for that of black mamba *shifters*, only mambas of the animal kingdom. Humans had no chance against her venom. Shifters could live through it, but not if they were injected with several large doses.

Cracking her knuckles, Havana flicked a look at Sam. "Heal him."

Betrayal an electric shock to her chest, Bailey hissed. "Fucking *heal* him?"

Havana gave her a placatory look. "We have questions that need answering. Once that's done, you can kill him—and I insist you make it as painful as you possibly can."

No such insistence was needed.

Sam crossed to the human, curling his upper lip in distaste. "I'm happy to say," he began, kneeling at the male's side, "that my healing him won't make the effects of the venom fade instantly. It'll take a little while."

That *was* a happy thought.

Members of the crowd shifted as someone pushed to the front. *Deke.* Her pulse leapt like a complete idiot.

He took in the entire scene, and his expression turned black as night. "What in the fuck happened here?"

Blair clenched her fists. "Bailey was the survivor of an acid attack. That's what."

He froze. His eyes hardened. A muscle in his jaw ticked. Then he moved. *Lunged.* Fisted the back of the human's sweater and snatched him off the ground.

"Don't kill him!" Tate ordered. "We need to know who put him up to this so we can deal with them as well!"

Deke went still again, the only movement that of his nostrils flaring. His gaze zipped to Bailey, flaring with a fury that spoke to her own. Then he tossed the unconscious human over his shoulder like he was a sack of spuds. "Fine," he said, his voice like gravel. "But I get to beat the shit out of him before Bailey delivers the killing blow."

That worked for her.

CHAPTER NINE

A manic rage burning in his gut, Deke strode into the cold, sterile room in which the human was being held. Located above the pride's antique shop, it was also the spare bedroom of the previous Alpha. Though Vinnie no longer had an official status, he liked to be very involved in pride business. Providing a space for people to be interrogated was one of the ways in which he contributed.

The only person in the room was the human. There had been no need to leave a guard with him. The particular cuffs holding him captive were made to withstand shifter strength, so he was going nowhere.

In a chair, the human writhed—his cheeks flushed, his eyes wide, his mouth covered by the strip of tape that Isaiah had slapped over his face earlier.

"Ah, you've almost shaken off the effects of the venom," Deke realized. "Good." That was all he'd needed to know, because the Alphas were ready to begin questioning the little shit.

Blue eyes dark with anger, dread, and defiance honed in on Deke. The asshole wasn't going to break easily. Not an issue. Because Deke was in absolutely no rush to get the whole beat-him-into-breaking part of the interrogation over with quickly.

The human deserved every bit of pain coming his way. Acid. He'd thrown fucking *acid* in Bailey's face. God, it was tempting, so very tempting, to just snap his neck there and then.

Deke clenched his fists. He tasted fury with every breath he took. It sat on his tongue like ash. Grated the back of his throat like razors.

His pacing cat, no less pissed, was practically foaming at the mouth. He might not have the time of day for people in general lately, but he was still protective of his pride. And Bailey wasn't simply any member. She was one who shared his bed and wore his mark—neither of those things were insignificant to the cat.

Deke glared down at the human, who eventually averted his gaze. "If you have any sense, you'll shove down that defiance. Refusing to answer our questions won't go well for you." He then stalked out of the room, down the hallway, and into the kitchen.

Several people stood around—the Alphas, Betas, Aspen, Camden, Isaiah, Vinnie, Farrell, and Alex. All were engaged in a debate, their words coming sharp and fast, unable to agree what the pride's next move should be.

At the mercy of her temper, Havana wanted to storm Westwood Pack territory.

Tate felt they should first question their captive to be sure that the pack had arranged the acid attack—it was clear that he didn't believe they had.

Some agreed with Havana. Some agreed with Tate … much like Deke himself.

Was it beneath the pack to have gone after Bailey that way? No. But they wouldn't have hired a human—*that* they'd have considered beneath them. They'd have done the deed themselves or sent a loner to do it on their behalf.

Only one person in the room wasn't throwing in their two-cents' worth. *Bailey*. She sat alone at the table. So quiet. So still. So very *not* Bailey.

Her facial features soft and her posture relaxed, she looked the absolute picture of serenity. But her rage was a feral thing that pulsed through the air.

She should have gone home, taken a shower, changed clothes, and rested. But Deke understood why she hadn't; understood her need to be part of the interrogation. In her shoes, he'd have insisted on it just the same.

Her gaze snapped to Deke as he began making his way toward her. She showed no reaction. Would probably react very little to anything. She'd pulled inward to keep a grip on her temper, and it was costing her.

His jaw tightened as he reached the mamba. The stench of acid clung to her. Mostly due to the stains on her coat. It made his cat's fur puff up.

Deke didn't ask if she was okay—it would have been a ridiculous question that didn't deserve an answer. He also didn't dare reach out and touch her for the same reason that the others were giving her a wide berth. She would not tolerate anyone getting too close until she'd calmed some. And it didn't seem as though that would happen any time soon.

He was about to inform her that the human had almost fully shaken off the effects of her venom, but then Havana whirled to face her and asked, "What do you think, Bailey?"

The mamba slowly looked up to meet the Alpha's hard gaze. "About?"

"Whether or not the jackals are behind what happened tonight," the devil replied.

Bailey stared at her, her gaze unreadable. Long moments of silence went by before she said, "It makes no sense that the pack would have lowered themselves—and that's how they'd have seen it—to hiring a human." Her voice was low and unnaturally calm. "But I'd still like to mention tonight's incident to them and see what they say." She plucked a small card out of one pocket and fished her cell from another.

Remembering that she'd been given a business card when approached, Deke asked, "Is that the number for the jackal?"

"Yes," she replied as she punched in the number. A ringing sound filled the air as she placed the call on speaker.

The phone rang several times before a voice answered, "Hello?"

Bailey licked her front teeth. "This is Amiri, I'm guessing?"

A long pause. "It is. And I recognize that voice. Bailey, yes?"

"Correct," she said, still eerily cool. "Not gonna lie, you're far from my favorite person right now."

Another pause. "And that would be because?"

"I'm not a big fan of people tossing acid in my face." The words were soft. Calm. Deadly.

Seconds of silence ticked by. "Excuse me?"

"Pretty sure you heard me just fine."

"You were attacked?" He sounded genuinely stunned.

"You should know. You orchestrated it."

"I assure you, my pack had no hand in it," he swore—not with any sense of panic in what the consequences might be, but casually … as one would when informing someone that, yes, it was in fact raining outside. Well, little worried jackals.

"You expect me to believe that?" Bailey asked him with a snort, but Deke sensed that she wasn't so doubtful.

"I can understand why you would be dubious. But truly, we have no actual wish to cause you harm. And what would we have to gain from it? We want your cooperation, not your anger. Angry mambas do nothing for no one."

Well, that was true enough.

As Tate approached her, Bailey said, "My Alpha wants to talk to you, Amiri."

"So," began Tate, folding his arms, "you're one of the jackals who thought to corner a member of my pride."

"Not to threaten or harm her," Amiri told him. "It is Roman we want. And I can assure you that we did not orchestrate what happened to her tonight. Such a thing would inevitably lead to war. If we wanted war with your pride, we would not declare it via a warning. We would simply come at you when you least expected."

"Then you would die," Tate stated, his voice a lethal blade. "Every last one of you."

"We are not your enemy, Devereaux."

"If that's truly the case, her attacker will verify it—we have him in our custody."

"He will verify it." Amiri sounded positive of that.

"If you have any more questions regarding Roman in the future, you bring them to me, not to Bailey," Tate stated, his tone non-negotiable. "If any of you go near her again, or anyone approaches her on behalf of your pack, I will take it as a declaration of war."

Amiri paused. "I will make my Alpha aware of it."

"Be sure that you do." Tate gave Bailey a nod, and she ended the call.

Leaning back against the counter, Vinnie blew out a breath. "Personally, I believe the jackal. I don't think his pack were behind this."

"Then he's right; the human *will* confirm it." Tate turned to Deke. "Is he still out of it?"

"No," replied Deke. "He was wide awake and squirming in his chair when I last checked on him."

Bailey slowly pushed out of her seat. "Then let's talk to him."

"Maybe you should hang back for now," Havana suggested.

Instead of snapping as Deke had expected, Bailey gave her a brittle smile and said, "Don't worry, I won't lose my temper. I'll wait until he crumbles before I kill him."

Havana hiked up a brow. "Can you say the same for your snake?"

Bailey nodded. "She went for the kill in the parking lot because she didn't want him to escape. But he's tied up now, so she doesn't have that concern."

Satisfied, Havana gently squeezed her shoulder. "All right, then we all go talk to him."

The Alphas led the way as they headed for the makeshift interrogation room. Deke walked behind Bailey, needing to be close to her while protectiveness was an ache in his bones. His cat needed it, too; needed to feel he was close enough to intervene should another threat abruptly come her way.

Inside the interrogation room, they all fanned out, facing the human. He swept his gaze over them, panic flaring in his blue eyes for a mere second. But then the defiance was back, and he jutted out his chin.

Alex stepped forward. The wolverine was often called on when interrogations were necessary. He had a knack for making people talk. "Name?" he asked their captive, his voice containing little emotion.

The human clamped his lips tightly shut.

Alex gave an indifferent shrug. "We'll have your ID soon enough."

They would. Deke had snapped a photo of the human and sent it to River so the male could search the police database.

"You're all shifters, aren't you?" It was a guess on the human's part.

"Clever boy." Bailey slowly walked toward her attacker, who leaned back slightly. She didn't stop in front of him, though. She moved to stand behind him, idly scraping a nail along his scalp.

He tensed. "I won't tell you anything, no matter what you do to me."

Alex scratched his temple. "I've heard that before. They all talk eventually."

"Well, look at this," Bailey drawled, her finger tugging the back of the human's collar away from his body. "We have an extremist in our midst."

Deke crossed to her, his lips thinning when he saw a tattoo of a familiar sigil. "You hate us so much you wear it on your skin, I see."

Havana rubbed her hands, a sadistic gleefulness shimmering in her eyes. "We just *love* having fun with your kind."

"I honestly can't wait to get started," Aspen told her, smiling.

"What faction do you belong to?" Tate demanded of him, crossing his arms over his broad chest.

Again, the human said nothing.

"It's fine. We'll have the info shortly." Bailey pressed her mouth to his ear. "What I most want to know is why you targeted me."

He swallowed. "Do whatever you want. I won't tell you a fucking thing."

Alex took another step forward. "Now that's where you're wrong. And I'm about to prove it."

The wolverine unsheathed his long, curved claws. Claws he then used on the human—slicing his arms, delivering shallow stabs to his thighs, disfiguring the sigil on his nape, carving 'I love shifters' along his forehead.

Camden joined in at one point. No surprise. He was a sadistic shit.

The whole time, the two shifters peppered the human with questions and gave him every attempt to end the torture by simply cooperating. But though their captive was clearly in a lot of pain and his defiance was being steadily drowned out by fear, he told them nothing.

Okay, that wasn't entirely true. He did answer some of their questions. But his responses were all lies—the deception was clear in his voice and body language.

Deke's phone began to ring. Digging it out of his pocket, he saw River's name on the screen. He exited the room and answered, "You got anything?"

"Yes," replied River. "He's not talking yet?"

"Not the way we'd like."

An annoyed grunt. "His name is Austen Perry. He's an extremist from one of the small, independent factions in these parts. They're not powerful, organized, or in any way connected to any of the main factions. They mostly stage protests and commit random attacks on shifters. But it isn't known to humans that Bailey is a shifter, so there has to be some other reason he targeted her."

Deke narrowed his eyes. "Such as he was hired directly, or his faction was hired and he drew the short straw?"

"That would be my guess. I'm going to send you a photo of his ex-wife and two children. Not sure if he'll care so much about his ex, but I doubt he'd be willing to risk his kids. He might speak up if he believes they'll otherwise be hurt."

"Appreciate it." Deke ended the call. None of the pride would ever hurt innocents, particularly not children, but Austen wouldn't know that.

Once he received the photo from River, Deke returned to the interrogation room. Austen was panting and sweating, his eyes glassy with pain and terror. Neither Deke nor his cat felt any sympathy for this person who had likely been involved in many attacks against shifters merely because they were "different."

"He still not cooperating?" Deke asked no one in particular.

It was Luke who replied, "Not in the slightest. He still thinks he can bullshit us." The Beta looked eager to pounce on the asshole.

Crossing to the human, Deke said, "You have a high pain tolerance threshold—I'll give you that much. I'm curious … Does your ex stand up so well against pain? What about your daughters?" He held up his phone so Austen could see the photo on the screen.

Bone-deep fear bloomed in his eyes. "If you dare hurt—"

"We don't actually *want* to hurt them, Austen," said Deke. "We're not like you. We don't target people without reason." He leaned forward. "So don't give us a reason."

Still standing behind Austen, Bailey dragged a sharp nail down the side of his face. "You're going to die here tonight. But if you answer our questions, they'll live; you'll die knowing they're safe. *Don't* answer our questions … and all four of you will be executed."

Austen squeezed his eyes tightly shut, his shoulders slumping in defeat. It was no shock that he didn't accuse them of bluffing. In the view of the extremists, shifters were monsters with no conscience or limits.

While Deke didn't feel good about threatening the man's family, he'd make such a threat if it meant finding out where the true danger to Bailey was coming from. He needed to eliminate that danger *yesterday*.

Opening his eyes, Austen swallowed. "There was a guy."

"What guy?" asked Deke.

"Just a guy. He came to one of our faction's hangouts. A bar called *Liberty*. Made small talk. Asked how I'd feel about giving a shifter a scare."

Bailey flicked his earlobe with her nail. "And what did you reply?"

Austen nervously licked his lips. "I said I'd do it for the right price."

Camden poked his tongue into the inside of his cheek. "I'm sensing that it isn't an unusual occurrence for you."

Austen raised his shoulders as much as the cuffs would allow. "Extremists get offers like that a lot. Not all the people who come to us hate shifters. They usually just have beef with one in particular; they want revenge, or for a point to be made."

And extremists didn't need to be convinced to do violence against shifters, Deke knew. "Why did he send you after Bailey?"

"He didn't say. Just said he had a 'friend' who felt that a certain shifter needed to be given a right good scare. He wasn't bothered *how* I did it, and he was fine with her receiving a little pain, but he didn't want her dead. He told me her name and where to find her. He never mentioned she was a snake," Austen grumbled.

"His name?" Aspen demanded through her teeth.

"He didn't give me one," Austen told her. "Or tell me anything about his friend, so I can't tell you who sent him."

The bearcat sidled up to her mate, keeping her gaze glued to the human. "What did he look like?"

"Average height. Bald. Stocky." Austen paused. "He paid me, insisted I don't delay in striking at the shifter, and then he left. That's it. There's nothing else to tell."

Tate cocked his head, his gaze probing as it bore into the human. "You're not even sorry, are you? You're about to die, but you don't regret what you did."

Austen sneered. "Why would I? You're abominations. You don't belong in this world. You should be caged like the animals you are."

Blair frowned. "I've never understood why humans think they're so much better than every species on this planet. I mean, really, what's so special about you? Because I don't see it. You call us monsters, but the truth is there's no race on this earth that's as destructive as humanity."

Austen's face reddened. "At least we're not the creations of Satan."

Vinnie flicked his eyes up to the ceiling. "Oh, Lord."

Bailey moved to stand in front of the human. "Out of interest, how much were you paid to come at me?"

"A hundred dollars," replied Austen. "But I'd have done it for free, really."

"For free, huh?" One of her slow, dangerous smiles took over her face. "Yeah, later it's going to be literally impossible for me to feel bad that my snake bit your dick."

"*What?*"

"If you have one, that is." Then Bailey shifted.

The last to leave the interrogation room an hour later, Bailey closed the door and inhaled deeply. She felt marginally better. Calmer. Could think clearer.

Oh, she still felt the hot burn of anger in her blood. But it had lost its steely grip on her emotional state. Well, getting a little revenge always did a wonderful job of improving her mood and clearing her mind.

It wasn't only her snake who'd had some fun with Austen. They'd all given him some special attention. Deke had done as promised and beaten the human bloody before her snake finished him off.

"You really think it wasn't the jackals who hired him?" asked Havana, clearly unconvinced.

"It's not their style," said Bailey.

Sighing, the Alpha female walked alongside her as they all returned to the kitchen. "You're right in that, but I'm not ready to dismiss them as suspects."

"It could have been Roman hoping to sic our pride on the jackals," Alex mused. "If the pack is wiped out, his problems are solved."

Blair's brows arched. "That's a possibility. From what I remember of him, he isn't bald or stocky like the guy who was at the bar. He is average height, though. He could have shaved his head and added some padding to his clothes to make himself look bigger."

Havana shook her head. "He's an asshole—no doubt about it. But he wouldn't arrange for someone to hurt Bailey like that. Stage a failed attack, yeah. But he wouldn't go any further than that. He wouldn't give someone permission to put her through pain."

"I agree." Aspen twisted her mouth. "It could be someone doing a little tit-for-tat. Jackson was attacked in the street. His brothers want to make the culprit pay."

Bailey felt her nose wrinkle. "None of them are bald, stocky, and average height. I guess they could have asked someone to go seek out an extremist-for-hire on their behalf, though."

"So could Ginny," Havana pointed out. "She isn't swimming in cash, but she could have scrounged up a hundred dollars."

As people began to speculate around her, Bailey sighed. She didn't want to discuss it anymore. She wanted to go home and shower—neither she nor her mamba had any chance of truly calming until they were no longer breathing in the astringent scent of acid.

She announced she was leaving, which quickly led to a bunch of people insisting on escorting her back to her building. It was … touching. They knew she didn't need *that* many guards, just as they knew she likely wouldn't be attacked twice in one night. Still, they wanted to escort her home safely all the same.

Once she'd slipped on her coat, she grabbed her purse and shopping bags. Her chest went all warm when she realized that Deke had earlier placed the dairy items in Vinnie's fridge so they wouldn't need to be trashed. She would have thanked the enforcer, but he shot her a *don't read anything into it* look even as he helped return those same items to her bags. Bags he then insisted on carrying, the pushy bastard.

She caught Blair watching them closely, her eyes narrowed. Ugh, she likely suspected that it was Deke who'd bitten Bailey. At least the bush dog could be trusted not to blab.

The walk back to her complex was completely uneventful. When Bailey and Deke stepped out of the elevator onto their floor, he didn't stop at his own apartment. No, he kept on trailing behind her.

Halting outside her front door, she cast him a quick look as she tugged her keys out of her purse. "What are you doing?"

He raised a brow. "What does it look like I'm doing?"

"Following me."

"Then I'm following you."

Snorting, Bailey unlocked the door and shoved it open. She dropped her keys into the entryway drop-zone basket, hung her purse on a hook there, and shrugged off her coat.

"Go shower," he told her, kicking the door shut. "I'll put your shit away in the kitchen."

She thought about objecting, but why bother? It wasn't like he wanted to put *his* shit in her cupboards. And she'd rather hop straight into the shower than first put all her shopping away.

Hanging her coat on the hook beside her purse, she shrugged. "All right, have at it."

He seemed surprised that she didn't fight him on it, but he said nothing. He simply marched straight into the kitchen.

After placing her shoes on the wrought-iron rack beneath her coat, Bailey began to head for her bedroom, loving how the heat from the oak wood beneath her feet seeped through her socks. One thing she adored about her apartment was the heated flooring. It had cost a whack, but it was worth every cent.

She doubted anyone would be taken off-guard by the eclectic feel to her apartment. There were lots of bold colors and shiny brass and carved wood. She had plenty of quirky pieces, too. Like the retro stereo planter, the vintage lava lamp, and the antique hanging rotary dial phone.

Inside her modern en suite bathroom that held hints of the French Renaissance period, she stripped naked and stepped into the shower stall. As the hot spray pounded down on her, she scrubbed her body and hair again and again, until the stench of acid was gone; until all she could smell was her coconut soap and her pine-scented hair products.

Done, she dried herself off, pulled on some sweats, dragged a comb through her wet hair, and then left the room. She found Deke still in the kitchen, a mug in hand. The scent of fresh coffee blanketed her.

His gaze swept over her, heating in a way that made her belly roll. "Have you eaten?"

Slipping onto a stool at the island, she shook her head. "I'm not hungry, though."

He tipped his chin at a particular cupboard. "There's a snake in there, by the way."

"Clive likes to play hide and seek." How he got into the cupboards she hadn't yet figured out.

Deke gave her a pointed look. "You told Havana you'd gotten rid of the snakes in the building."

"And I did." Sort of. "Clive's just a regular visitor. Like a stray cat, but not a cat."

He grunted and then took a sip of his drink. "Want coffee?"

"No. I want you to fuck me."

His muscles bunched, and his eyes darkened. "You got attacked earlier—"

"And I'm healed now. Also pissed. I like to work off my anger with sex. That's where you come in."

He lowered his cup to the island. "How do you wind down when sex isn't available?"

"Masturbate." She ignored his low curse. "Or go down to the bar and start a fight." Her eyes widened at the delightful thought. "Actually—"

"No, no barfights."

"But they're fun."

"No. We're gonna stay inside. I'm going to make you food. You're going to eat it. Then I'm going to make you come with my mouth before I fuck you."

That wasn't an offer she felt the need to refuse. Still, she had to ask, "What is it with you Hammonds and feeding people? Your mom is the ultimate feeder."

"Only when she likes someone." He arched a brow. "Now, do we have a plan or what?"

"I guess."

He snorted. "Don't sound too enthusiastic."

"Okay."

Sheer exasperation flashing across his face, he sighed. "Just so you know, I ain't a good cook."

"Who needs to cook when there are microwaves?"

He blinked. "Exactly. But few people would agree with us."

She shrugged. "I figure that's their problem."

Grunting again, he walked to the freezer and opened the door. "So, you like mac and cheese."

Considering the freezer was practically loaded with mac and cheese micro meals, it was no shock that he'd reached that conclusion. "You could say that."

He tugged one of said meals from the freezer.

Her snake watched him closely, not so sure she was comfortable having him in her private space. Well, she wasn't the trusting sort, nor was she accustomed to having men over.

But she didn't urge Bailey to make him leave. She liked this male who hadn't shied away when she'd delivered *a crap load of pain* to Austen. Liked that when Deke had first learned what happened to Bailey, he'd almost killed the human before anyone had the chance to question him. That his first instinct had been to eliminate a threat to Bailey was something the snake approved of.

Thinking of Austen made Bailey flex her fingers. That little shit stain was no loss to the world.

As part of her old job, she'd been in more dangerous situations than she could count. She'd been attacked with everything from knives to guns. But never acid. She hadn't seen it coming, hadn't—

"If you keep stewing on what happened tonight you'll never calm down," said Deke as the microwave whirred to life.

"It's not so easy." Bailey leaned her folded arms on the surface of the island. "I can still feel it. Smell it."

"The acid?"

She nodded. It was like the stench and burn of it was imprinted on her system.

Deke's jaw tightened. "Fucker deserved what he got." He angled his head. "You didn't agree with Havana."

"What?"

"She said she didn't believe that Roman could be behind the acid attack. Aspen agreed. You didn't. What's your opinion?"

"I don't think it was him. His nest overflows with assholes, but they do have some morals." Though not many.

He snorted. "I'm not so sure. They could have took you in when you were a kid. They didn't."

Bailey felt her brow knit. "Took me in?"

"You were a loner. They could have fixed that."

Ohhhhh, he hadn't yet figured out that she'd once been part of the Umber Nest; that, in fact, they were *at fault* for her being a loner. "Hmm."

His eyes narrowed. "What is it?"

"Nothing."

He kept staring at her, his eyes delving into hers. "Wait, that *was* your nest, wasn't it? The bastards banished you. Banished a child."

She only twisted her mouth.

Several harsh curses exploded out of him. "What possible justification could they have for that?"

"The Umber Nest … it isn't like most groupings of shifters."

"In what sense?"

"It's tight-knit for sure. But if you fuck up in a way that puts the others in danger, you're on your own."

"And you, then a child, fucked up?"

"No. My parents did." Too many times to count, actually. They'd had so many "last chances" it wasn't even funny.

His eyes blazed, two lasers of rage. "You're saying they made a child pay for her parents' sins?"

She licked her lips. "Yes. But that's another story." One she had no intention of telling. She rarely spoke of the people who were responsible for her birth but had done little for her. "A long, boring tale."

"I have time for you," he said.

Her throat went tight. "I'm already pissed off. Talking about what happened back then will only make me more pissed."

He held her gaze for endless seconds. "Then we'll table this discussion for another time."

She squinted. "Do you always pester your bed-buddies to share such personal stuff?"

"No."

"Why pester me, then?"

More moments of silence went by. "I want to know you."

"You know enough."

The microwave beeped.

Deke pulled out the meal, peeled back the cover, stirred the mac and cheese, and then returned it to the microwave. He pressed a few buttons, and it came to life once more. Planting his fists on the island, he said, "You'd better eat all this. You're going to need your energy for what comes next."

Her body perked up from head to toe. "Awesome. So long as it's sexual."

"It's sexual. But Bailey," he began, leaning across the island, "you can't keep that wall up between us forever."

"Ooh, I happily accept your challenge."

His lips quirked. "Yeah, you do that."

"On another note, I should warn you …"

"What?"

"Blair was stood behind me while I was dressing in the parking lot after shifting, so she saw the mark on the back of my shoulder."

He went rigid.

"I don't think anybody else did. I had my hair down, which will have helped cover it. And even if the others weren't focused on Austen, they aren't likely to have watched me dress." Shifters weren't bothered by nakedness—they stripped in front of each other all the time to release their inner animals—but they wouldn't openly stare at someone who was naked.

"I see," he drawled.

"I was careful when I was in the interrogation room—I kept my back to the wall while naked after shifting back to my human form. But I'd been too pissed to think about that earlier in the lot. Blair won't tell anyone, but I can't be sure that no one else saw the mark.

"If they did, well, you know how the pride likes to gossip, so whispers might start. Obviously, no one will know it's *your* brand. But they'll speculate, and they might wonder if it was you—if only because you almost killed Austen on the spot when you heard what he'd done."

He swiped his tongue over his bottom lip. "What do you plan to say if they ask who bit you?"

"I'll tell them to mind their own biz. Except for Havana and Aspen, because I trust that they'd keep it to themselves. In other words, you don't have to worry that all this will get back to Dayna. I just wanted to give you a heads-up so you won't be taken off-guard if anyone mentions it to you."

He crossed his arms over his broad chest, his expression pensive. "I doubt anyone else noticed the bite. They'd surely have asked about it. And as you said, their attention was locked on the human. It'll be fine," he decided with a nod. "There'll be no gossip. You're worrying for nothing."

CHAPTER TEN

Carving her hands into her hair, Havana glared at Bailey. "There are times I *really* want to hurt you."

Spooning some of her cereal, Bailey frowned. "Why?"

"Because you do things like share the bed of a guy you've been circling for *ages* and you don't say shit about it to me."

Hmm, see, it turned out that Deke was wrong. Someone else *had* noticed the bite on Bailey's shoulder. Vera, in fact. And that woman was the worst gossiper in the entire pride, so you could bet your ass the news had traveled through the pride's grapevine at top speed. Something Bailey had learned when she woke to countless missed calls and messages from people wanting to know if she cared to confirm or deny the rumor.

Bailey had ignored all of the aforementioned calls and texts, which resulted in Havana and Aspen turning up at her apartment before she'd even had the chance to finish her breakfast. Normally, all three of them would be at the center right now. But it was their day off work.

No sooner had Bailey opened the front door than they'd shoved their way inside and closed it behind them.

"*It was Deke, wasn't it?*" had been Havana's first words. "*He's the one who marked you.*"

Sighing, Bailey had gestured for them to follow her into the kitchen as she'd admitted that, yes, Deke had bitten her. She'd also let it slip that they'd been sleeping together for the past five nights, at which point both her friends had turned red in the face. And now they stood at the opposite side of the island from her while she finished what was left of her cereal.

Havana released her hair and lowered her arms to her sides. "Didn't we discuss that people don't hide newsworthy stuff from their BFFs?"

"I wasn't hiding it. I just didn't mention it. And I wouldn't call my sleeping with Deke 'newsworthy.'" Bailey gave an aloof shrug, adding, "It's no big deal."

"It's a *huge* deal," Aspen insisted.

Bailey arched a brow at the bearcat. "That so? You didn't seem to feel that way when you were oh so casually urging me to give him a helping hand with the touch-hunger."

Aspen spluttered. "I didn't think it would actually happen. You generally ignore my advice."

Of course she did. "Because your advice usually includes suggestions that will spoil my fun. You're always trying to sabotage my happiness."

"Now you're deflecting."

"I know."

Havana folded her arms, interjecting, "So is this thing between you and Deke a fling?"

"No." Bailey scooped up more cereal with her spoon. "We're just gonna be fuck-buddies until he's no longer a walking hard-on."

The devil shot her an incredulous look. "Fuck-buddies? Really?"

"Really." Bailey shoved her spoon into her mouth and chewed the soggy flakes.

"Since when do fuck-buddies mark each other?" Havana challenged, still dubious.

"We *haven't* been marking each other. He bit me, yes, but it was an accident." She saw no need to elaborate on how he'd had to keep renewing the bite in order for his cat to allow him to touch her. That the feline was having "issues" was for Deke to share or not to share. "Things got out of hand."

"Bullshit," Aspen blurted out. "He staked a temporary claim on you."

If her snake could have snorted in disbelief, she would have. "Deke is not possessive of me."

"The brand you wear says differently," said Havana.

Bailey felt her lips thin. "I told you, it was an accident."

Havana's face scrunched up. "Guys as ruthlessly controlled as Deke don't do stuff like that by accident, Bailey. He might tell both himself and you that he didn't *mean* to bite you, but that's a load of cock and bull."

Nu-uh. "Touch-hunger tends to send 'ruthlessly controlled' sailing out the window. Another guy I helped through it bit me as well. They get *seriously* primitive and animalistic."

"Granted." Havana lifted one finger. "But that doesn't necessarily translate to biting, does it? For Deke to brand you—"

"It didn't mean anything." Jeez.

"Yeah? Then why hide it? Why, if it's no big deal, did you keep it to yourself?"

"Because I knew you'd do exactly what you're doing: *make it into* a big deal, even though you know perfectly well that it's not always possessiveness that drives a person to mark someone."

"No," Havana scoffed, "you hid it from us because you knew we'd make you face that it is not whatsoever insignificant. You'd prefer to pretend that's not the case, because then you could keep on sleeping with him rather than get the urge to break things off due to your discomfort with territorialism."

Bailey inwardly groaned in exasperation. "He's not possessive of me. He'd have bitten me somewhere highly visible if that were truly the situation, and I wouldn't be sporting only one mark."

Aspen turned to their Alpha female. "Actually, she does make a good point. Dudes as dominant as Deke don't play around when they lay a claim."

"*And* let's not forget that he wants to keep our arrangement on the downlow," Bailey added, spooning more cereal. "He wouldn't want that if he really felt compelled to ensure the world knew I was off the market."

Aspen dipped her chin. "Deke's not a guy who advertises what's going on with his personal life, but he also doesn't take pains to hide it. *This* he hasn't been open about. Which doesn't gel with the idea that he essentially laid a claim on Bailey when he bit her."

Havana swatted at the air, apparently intending to disregard all that—likely on the basis that it didn't suit her argument. "Who specified that this would be a short-term arrangement?"

Bailey finished chewing her cereal before replying, "We both did."

The devil narrowed her eyes. "And that's all it is?"

"That's all it is."

With a sigh, Havana cut her gaze to Aspen. "Well, I suppose it's a start."

The bearcat nodded. "Yup."

Bailey frowned. "It's not a start to anything. It's temporary."

Havana gave a slight shrug. "If you say so. But I think more will come of this."

"Are you forgetting about Dayna? He's all entangled with her." And there went Bailey's stomach cramping again.

"He is." Havana grinned, adding, "But I don't think he will be for much longer. I believe there's a very high chance he's reconsidering keeping his promise to her."

Bailey felt her frown deepen. "Why?"

"Well, something you said last week got me thinking." The devil planted her palms on the island. "You pointed out that, despite the touch-hunger giving Deke an excuse to make a move on you, he actually kept his distance from you instead. So I asked myself … why would he do that? Why did he also do it the last time he was lumbered with touch-hunger? And then it hit me."

"What?"

"He didn't seek out an arrangement with you because he needs it to be something he can walk away from. He didn't want to find himself tempted to scrap his vow."

Aspen pointed at Havana. "That makes sense."

"But now here you two are sharing a bed," Havana went on. "That tells me that his vow isn't so important to him now. I'm not saying I think he has plans to break it *for you* specifically—I don't know what he feels for you—just that she doesn't have the same hold on him that she once did."

Given that, as far as Bailey was concerned, Deke was sticking to his word for the wrong reason, it wouldn't surprise her if he one day backed out. She wouldn't even be surprised if he was genuinely considering it now, though he'd given her no indication of it. But if he did shake Dayna off, Bailey doubted it would have anything to do with her. Or that it would change the fact that their arrangement had an expiry date.

"You know, it's kind of sad that it took for him to be riddled with touch-hunger before you two stopped circling each other and just got down to business," Havana continued. "But I'm glad he's stopped fighting the touch-hunger. Why *did* he finally stop?"

"He's helpless against my raw animal magnetism."

Havana rolled her eyes. "You know, I probably should have guessed that you two were shaking the sheets. I noticed he was doing better, so I suspected he was fucking someone. But I didn't assume it was you, because I figured you would have told us if you were bonking him. *Which you didn't.*"

"Are we still on that?" *Boring.*

"I should have suspected it was you, though, since he's not being subtle about eye-fucking you these days."

"I picked up on that as well," Aspen interjected. "So did several males in our pride." Her brows slowly slid together as her expression turned thoughtful. "And now I'm asking myself if it was his way of warning them off. After all, none would dare come on to Bailey if they thought Deke would freak about it."

"I'm having the same thought," said Havana. "He might not have openly claimed you, Bailey, but he made it clear in his own way that you weren't to be touched."

Aspen absently fiddled with her necklace. "You know, I'm not so certain he'll walk away once the touch-hunger subsides."

"Then you're moronic," said Bailey.

Aspen narrowed her eyes. "You're deflecting again."

"Can't help it."

Havana cut in, "I happen to agree with Aspen on this. What are you going to do if we're right and he does suggest that you two keep things going?"

"He won't." Bailey dumped her spoon in her empty bowl. "I was clear on where I stand, and so was he."

Aspen shot her a tired look. "Oh, please tell me you didn't give him the 'ground rules' talk."

Bailey's back straightened. "There's nothing wrong with having firm boundaries."

"No, there isn't," the bearcat allowed. "But it guts me that you're so set on keeping everyone at a distance."

"Just so you know, Bailey," began Havana, "I don't think you'll find it easy to do that with Deke."

Bailey felt her brow furrow. "What's that supposed to mean?"

"You've slept with dominant shifters in the past, but never one as dominant as he is," Havana explained. "Dudes like him respect boundaries. Until they don't. Until they decide that it doesn't suit them anymore and so they start being pushy and bossy. If he wants to plant himself in your life, he will—you won't be able to keep him out no matter what you do."

"He'd never want to do something like that." But even as Bailey said that, she recalled his warning …

You can't keep a wall up between us forever.

Bailey hadn't yet decided how she felt about him wanting to "know" her. Nor did her mamba. It made them slightly uneasy. They weren't used to people showing such interest in them.

In any case, she wasn't taking his words as an indication that he was looking for more than casual sex. Bed-buddies generally *did* like to "know" each other. And if Deke wanted more, he'd have just said so.

A cell began to ring, and Havana fished her phone out of her pocket. "Gotta take this. I'll be right back." She went into Bailey's bathroom to take the call in private.

Grinning like an idiot, Aspen said, "I think Vana's right. I think you won't manage to hold Deke at bay."

Bailey gave her a blasé shrug. "If you want to be wrong, that's fine. Not everyone can be brilliant like me."

The bearcat snorted. "I don't know if I'd use the word 'brilliant.'"

"Of course you're unsure. *You're* not brilliant."

"I'm freaking fabulous." Aspen splayed her hands on the island. "Whereas *you're* a pain in the ass."

"You say the latter as if I should be … you know … *sorry* or something."

Aspen let out a *pfft* sound. "Oh, don't worry, I'm well-aware that repentance is not your—"

"Don't start making up words again."

"Repentance is a word."

"Not in my mental dictionary."

"*Tell me you two aren't arguing*!" Havana bellowed from inside the bathroom.

"We're not arguing!" Aspen called out. "We're just talking about Deke!" She refocused on Bailey. "And *you're* doing your best to change the subject, because it's making you uncomfortable. You know I'm right, you know there's a chance Deke will cleave himself to you, and it's freaking you out. Ha."

Actually, Bailey had absolutely none of those worries. She knew where she stood with Deke and, what's more, where she'd *never* stand with him. "You're genuinely not bored of this conversation yet?"

"No. I find it fascinating."

"Well, that's just sad. No wonder Camden always looks like he's zoning out when you two talk. Your conversations are probably boring him to tears." Poor guy.

Aspen's mouth tightened. "I *far* from bore him."

"Oh yeah? Then where is he?" Bailey pushed her bowl aside. "Needs a break from your whiny-ass personality, does he? Ah, bless."

Aspen's nostrils flared. "You want me to knock you the fuck out, don't you? That's what this is."

"Oh, *please*. Like you could get the drop on me. You and your bearcat are—"

"Don't bring her into this. Unless you want her to kick your snake's butt."

"She couldn't kick her own ass, let alone my mamba's."

Aspen shifted.

So did Bailey.

Their animals clashed.

The bearcat stomped on the snake, who struck fast in retaliation—biting her face three times. They tussled. Hissed. Snapped their teeth.

"*I do not believe you two.*"

The animals paused—the snake wrapped tight around the bearcat's waist while said bearcat held the mamba's mouth closed.

Havana stormed over to them and perched her hands on her hips. "Do you not get tired of being a pair of idiots?"

They only stared at her.

"Back away from each other. God, if bearcats didn't have a peptide in their blood that made them immune to snake venom, Aspen would be dead a billion times over."

The bearcat slowly let go of the mamba's mouth.

Disappointed it was over, the snake reluctantly loosened her hold on her prey. Then sharp claws raked over her head. The snake hissed, displaying the inky black coloration inside her mouth, and then lunged—biting the bearcat's ear.

"Both of you stop *now*!"

Hearing his phone chime in a rhythm that told him it was a video call, Deke crossed to the nightstand and peered down at his cell. He wasn't all that surprised to see that the caller was Dayna. Lowering the basket of freshly laundered clothes on his bed, he rubbed his nape with a sigh.

He'd suspected he'd hear from her today. So far, he'd received several messages from gossipers, relaying that Bailey had been marked. Nobody had outright asked if he'd been the one to brand her, but some had hinted at it.

Deke hadn't replied to any of the texts, just as he never responded to gossip. Still, he'd known his failure to confirm people's suspicions wouldn't prevent either Therese or Gerard from rushing into contacting Dayna about it—they wouldn't want someone else to beat them to it.

Deke grabbed his cell and swiped his thumb over the screen to accept the call. Dayna's face appeared, her forehead slightly wrinkled, her eyes wary. Yeah, she'd received news of Bailey's mark all right. He'd put money on it.

"Morning," he said, sitting on the edge of his bed.

She gave him a quick flash of a smile—it was hesitant, strained, forced. "Good morning." The words were stiff and formal. "How are you?"

"Good. You?"

"I'm not sure yet." She sat on what appeared to be a chair and then carefully leaned her cell against something to prop it up. "It will depend on a few things." She pushed her curls out of her face. "When Therese told me a couple of days ago that your touch-hunger seemed less intense, it was more than obvious that you were sleeping with someone on the regular. I didn't ask you about it because I knew you'd say nothing. You never do."

Pausing, she leaned forward slightly. "But I need to know something, Deke. I need you to be straight with me on this."

"On what?"

Absently, she cracked her knuckles. "Is it the mamba shifter you've been sleeping with? Don't blow me off. Therese told me the snake's been marked. I have to know if it was you."

Deke inwardly sighed. He knew the truth would hurt her, but he wasn't going to feed her a line of bullshit. Nor would he claim to regret what he'd done, because he didn't—to lie would insult them both. The reality was that he'd brand Bailey again if needed. "It was me."

Hurt flashed in her eyes, and her throat bobbed. She cleared it with a cough. "Was it something you did on purpose, or did things just get a little wild?"

"The latter. The first time."

Her eyes went wide. "You branded her more than once?"

Although he could see she was misinterpreting the whys of his actions, he wasn't going to explain his situation. She'd *probably* be understanding. Maybe. But he didn't trust her enough to share his cat's issues with her. So, instead, Deke merely nodded.

Her eyes closed, and she dropped her head.

"Look, I'm sorry—" He stopped talking as her head snapped up, and she shot him a cold stare that made his cat bare a fang.

"You're *sorry*?" she scoffed. "I can't believe you did this to me! I feel like I don't know you right now."

Deke narrowed his eyes. He got that she was upset. He did. But there was no need for her to act as though he'd committed some huge betrayal.

They weren't in a relationship. Dayna had laid no claim to him. And none of what had happened had involved him breaking his promise.

She'd also once accidentally branded someone herself. He hadn't given her a hard time over it, despite the fact that back then it hadn't felt good. Nowadays, he wouldn't have cared at all.

She placed a hand on her breastbone. "Were you ever going to tell me?"

"Yes." Though he hadn't planned to do so until he came round to proposing they go their separate ways. He'd intended to do that once he'd given her another couple of weeks to mourn her recent losses.

A derisive snort popped out of her. "I'm not sure I believe that." She pressed her lips tight together, her expression stony and unforgiving.

His cat snarled, not liking that she'd expected *Deke*'s forgiveness when the situation was the other way around. And she really *had* expected it—there'd been no real apology, only a confession followed by, "*I got a little carried away, I'll try not to let it happen again*." Yeah. She'd *try*.

No fonder of double-standards than his cat, Deke found himself gritting his teeth.

"God, I feel so humiliated right now. How could you do this to me? Dammit, Deke, I *waited* for you."

"Like I waited for you," he clipped. "You said you'd be back in a year. You've been gone for over two and a half."

"Oh, so it's my fault you did this?"

"I never said that."

"Then what are you saying?"

"That I don't see that you have any right to act so fucking possessive and demand so much goddamn loyalty." His cat growled, backing him up on that. "If I meant that much to you, you'd have either come home or freed me from my promise at some point. You've done neither."

"I told you I'd come home!"

"You've been saying it for running up to three years. In all that time, you never made any concrete plans to back that up. You also fully expected *me* to let it go when *you* marked someone."

The corners of her eyes tightened. "So you decided to punish me? Is that what this is?"

He frowned, affronted. "You know me better than to ask that question." Deke didn't operate that way.

"I thought I did. But then I found out you *marked another woman*. You never branded me. Not once."

And that was why she was so pissed and upset, he realized. It was more a matter of jealousy and resentment.

Looking at him in disgust, she gave a disparaging shake of the head. "I don't see how I can trust you after this. Maybe we should just scrap the vow."

He shrugged, happy with that. "Seems like the best option to me." His cat couldn't agree more.

Her jaw went slack, and she blinked rapidly. Apparently she'd thought he'd beg her to reconsider and plea for forgiveness or some shit.

She licked her lips. "Deke, I—"

"There's no point in sticking to it anymore. We're just holding each other back."

Her mouth pinched as a sour expression slipped over her face. "In other words, you want the freedom to go fuck your slut whenever you want?"

His muscles stiffened, and his cat got to his feet with a growl. "Don't call her that again," Deke warned, his voice low and soft but lethal.

"So she matters to you?" Dayna asked, bitterness coating every word.

"All my pride mates matter to me one way or the other to some extent, including you. Whatever you might think, I want you to be happy. You wouldn't be happy with me, because it would mean leaving Evan. I get why you're finding it incredibly painful to do that. Well, now you don't have to."

"You could really walk away from this, *us*, so easily?"

"There hasn't been an 'us' in a long time."

She opened her mouth to argue, but then she took a long breath. "That much you're right about," she admitted, crossing her arms and gripping her elbows. "We stopped making an effort. But like you pointed out, it's been over two and a half years. We both kept our word all this time. We couldn't have done that unless what we were trying to build is worth exploring. To just give up on it seems wrong."

He felt his forehead wrinkle. "You just suggested we scrap the vow. You said you don't trust me anymore."

"You could earn my trust back. It might take a little time, and it would mean you'd have to get rid of this Bailey person. But you could do it."

"You talk like I owe this to you. Like by hurting you I now have no right to walk away." His mother was correct; Dayna used his sense of honor against him. "I'm done here."

She scooted forward on her seat. "Deke—"

"Take care, Dayna." With that, he ended the call.

He scrubbed a hand down his face. Much as that conversation pissed him off, he felt better. Lighter. Like he could breathe easier.

Pulling out of the vow had been best for them both. He did regret that he'd had to bring his plan forward, considering she was still in mourning, but he didn't lament that he was finally free of their promise.

So though she tried calling him again, he ignored it. And when she kept calling, he eventually switched off the ringer.

Well-aware that she'd soon call her friends to spill everything, he texted Bailey: *Just so you're aware, the entire pride will soon know that it was me who marked you.*

Her response came relatively fast: *Why?*

I admitted it to Dayna. She won't keep it to herself. And then Therese would eagerly share it with everyone else. If she didn't, Gerard would.

Three little dots danced on his screen. *You really told her?* asked Bailey.

It was the right thing to do.

Dude, you're so damn ethical. Don't you find it exhausting?

He frowned. *No.*

Huh. Weird.

Feeling his jaw tighten, he typed: *No, Bailey, it's not. Most people have ethics.*

I pity every one of you.

Snorting, he tossed his phone on the bed. He'd said it before and he'd say it again—the woman was a goddamn nut.

CHAPTER ELEVEN

Bailey was feeling blessed. Seriously. Because the mouth currently clamped around her pussy was an absolute champ at going down on a woman.

Another week had gone by during which she and Deke had shared a bed. His touch-hunger wasn't as severe now. That didn't mean he fucked her any less often or any less rough.

Bailey had zero complaints about that. Especially right then. Knelt on the base of his shower stall, he held her thighs wide open as he feasted. She could only cling to the edges of the bench on which her butt was perched, her hips angled toward him.

Around them, the hot spray pattered against tile, drummed down on his back, and steamed the air. Out of range of the spray, she might have felt cold—especially with droplets of water drizzling down her naked, goosebump-y flesh—if her nerve-endings didn't feel like they were blazing.

A wet flick to her clit made her gasp. No lie, Deke had a tongue that could enslave a person; could addict them like nothing else. Every velvet stroke of it pushed her closer to the orgasm that was almost on her.

Her head fell back as he rolled the tip of his tongue around her clit. A clit he then suckled on, his fingers digging into her skin. Oh God, oh God, she was gonna—

He pulled back.

Bailey's head snapped up. She glared at him, her gut clenching at the dark intent in his eyes. "Do *not* do that thing where you make me wait a lifetime to come."

His lips quirked. "But you like that game," he mocked.

"No one likes that game, you dick."

He gave her a wounded look that was pure bullshit. "That wasn't nice."

"You messing with me isn't nice. *I* didn't make *you* dance around an orgasm just now." She'd sucked him off when they first got into the shower.

"No, but you did almost spit out my come just to piss me off."

"*Almost,*" she stressed. "Almost, almost, almost."

"Not seeing what that has to do with anything." He latched onto a nipple and sucked hard, sending streaks of hot pleasure to her clit.

She sank her fingers into his hair, arching into the calloused hand that skated up her body and then palmed her breast. There was an *edge* in his grip. A greed that held a note of entitlement … like he was declaring with his touch alone that only he had the right to use her body for his pleasure.

He licked his way to the breast he cupped, using his hold on it to feed himself her nipple. He sucked, bit, and rubbed it against the roof of his mouth.

It felt good. So good. But she needed more. She ached inside, the sensation near unbearable. "Enough with the teasing, Boy Toy."

He released the taut bud and arched a reprimanding brow. "Now that's not my name, is it?"

"Whatever. Just do me."

He skirted his warm lips up her neck and to her ear. "You're not getting my dick until you say my name."

Grr, her snake wanted to bite him *so hard* right now. She gripped his solid shoulders tight, pricking his skin with her nails. "Don't push me, Hammond." His surname would have to do.

He hummed. "Close. Not close enough." Then he went back to playing with her breasts. Squeezing. Nipping. Shaping. Suckling.

Her defiance crumbling little by little, Bailey bit back a whimper. Her body felt tight and hot, caught in a state of such intolerably intense anticipation that she thought she might implode with it. "*Enough.*" Her voice came out raspy and thick.

He drew his teeth over her nipple. "You know what you've got to do."

She squeezed her eyes shut. "Deke."

"Again."

"What?"

"Say it again. And look at me this time." Deke had to fight a smile when her eyes flipped open and blazed into his, promising retribution. He'd expect nothing less. She was a mamba, after all.

Her upper lip curled. "Deke," she finally repeated.

He almost laughed. She'd said his name like it was a dirty word. He flicked her nose with his own. "Such a perfect little pout."

She frowned. "I don't pout."

Oh, she did.

"Now where's my orgasm?"

He stood, tugged her to her feet, and pulled her flush against him. "Coming right up," he said, cupping her delectable ass. Their breaths clashed as he slanted his mouth over hers. Ravenous, he kissed her deep and wet, greedy for everything she had to give.

His hard cock throbbed viciously. It was nothing to do with touch-hunger and everything to do with how badly he needed to sink into that exquisitely tight pussy he'd come to crave.

Her hand slipped between them and curled around his cock, startling a grunt out of him. He squeezed her ass tight, his mind's eye flashing with all the things he wanted to do to it.

She gave his dick a quick pump. "In me. Now."

He tugged her skilled fingers off his cock. "That's the plan." He spun her a little too roughly, his body screaming to possess her.

Letting out a muffled oath, she slapped her palms on the tiled wall to steady herself.

Deke pulled her hips back slightly and tilted them just right. He pushed the head of his dick inside her, groaning as her scalding hot muscles bitingly contracted around him. "Knowing my come's in your belly right now just makes me want to fuck you that much more." He drove his cock deep with a merciless forward-snap of his hips, seating himself to the balls.

She jerked, her breath catching in her throat. "Jesus."

He rode her hard, filling the air with the sound of flesh smacking slick flesh. The luscious scent of her need blanketed him, an electric zap to his senses. It sang in the stall's humid air, calling to him; drugging his mind; driving him to take her harder. So he did.

The tips of her fingers scrabbled against the wet tiles as she threw her hips back to meet every frantic thrust. She was never a passive participant. She took what she wanted. Demanded what she needed.

He grabbed her hand, lowered it to her pussy, and spread her fingers near her entrance. "Feel me taking you." Pounding faster, he gritted his teeth at the sensation of her fingers brushing over his shaft.

His eyes flew to the brand on the back of her shoulder, and his balls ached at the sight. That mark of his possession was straight-up porn for him. It shouldn't be. Didn't used to be. Initially, he'd viewed it as an inconvenient necessity; a way to prevent his cat from interfering.

That had changed.

He wasn't sure when. Perhaps it had been a gradual thing. Whatever the case, he now liked marking her. Even looked forward to it. More, it didn't bother his cat any longer.

Right then, Deke found himself disappointed that his brand didn't yet need renewing. The act of gripping her skin between his teeth, of biting down hard enough to leave a mark … fuck, his cock was pulsing just thinking about it.

Feeling his balls draw up tight, he caught a fistful of her wet hair and tugged her head back. "Play with your clit, baby. Make yourself come."

She didn't hesitate. She got right to it. And each time she rubbed or rolled her clit, her inner muscles spasmed around him.

He wasn't sure he could take it for long. He didn't want to come first. Didn't—

Fingers stroked over his aching balls.

Deke cursed as his release slammed into him with such shocking, violent force it stole his breath. His thoughts splintering, he kept on thrusting, pumping his come inside her … barely aware that she'd exploded right along with him.

It took some time for Bailey's brain to regroup after the dazzling orgasm that practically tore her apart. When she was finally able to think again, he was pulling his softening cock out of her. He brushed his lips over his bite in a barely-there kiss, making her pulse do a silly little spike.

Her pulse did it again when they got out of the shower. Why? Because the big lump didn't do his usual thing and toss her a towel—something he occasionally threw at her face, always snickering when she caught it wicked fast. Nope, this time he carefully wrapped a towel around her and began to pat her dry.

For long moments, she stood there, not knowing what to do. Clearing her throat, she finally said, "I can dry myself, you know."

"Clever girl." Pure sarcasm.

Dick.

He finished drying her off, dumped the luxury cotton fabric on the floor, and then none too gently lifted her.

She squeaked, fisting his own towel so tightly she almost tugged it off his waist. He carried her into the bedroom and dropped her on the mattress. She scraped her wet locks off her face. "You gotta stop tossing me around like I'm a damn doll."

"Why?" It sounded like a genuine query.

She rolled her eyes. And people thought *she* was difficult.

Deke gently threw a comb her way and then dried himself off while she dragged said comb through her hair. Done, he took it from her, returned it to the surface of the dresser, and then sank onto the mattress beside her.

Bailey frowned when he yanked the duvet over them, as if they were settling down for the night. She never slept over. Ever.

Still, she wasn't gonna shove off the covers. Nu-uh. She was cold, and his quilt was so much thicker than hers. She'd just lie here until she warmed up. Then she'd get dressed and leave.

The past week had been uneventful in every respect, really. There'd been no more attacks. She hadn't seen or heard from the jackals, Ginny, or Jackson's family again.

As for her and Deke … they each did their own thing during the day, and then she'd go to his apartment in the evening. They sometimes had dinner here together. Mostly, though, she ate before she showed up.

In that sense, nothing had changed. Yet it had. Because he'd started doing stuff he didn't do before. Like call her "baby" during sex. Like shampoo her hair. Like touch her outside of fucking and even *in public*—a little thing, maybe, but he used to act as if to touch her would have been to stick his hand in a damn fire, so it didn't *feel* little.

It also sort of flustered her. People generally weren't touchy-feely toward Bailey. Her past partners had given her plenty of personal space and hadn't been too tactile, sensing she preferred it that way. If Deke sensed it, he was choosing to ignore it.

He even sometimes dropped a kiss on her mouth before she left his apartment to return to her own. She called him on it each time. He never did anything but flash her a small smile that held a tinge of pity. Like it was both cute and a little sad that she thought she had a say in the matter.

Rather than annoyed, she found herself rolling her eyes.

One thing hadn't changed—her body still lit up like Vegas for him. And what kind of unfair bullshit was that?

She didn't have much time left to work off their chemistry, because their arrangement would end soon. Or *might* do. All things considered, she supposed there was a chance he'd be interested in scrapping their fling's intended expiry date. He wasn't tied to Dayna now, and he didn't seem anywhere near as annoyed by Bailey's presence as he used to be.

She kept waiting for him to tire of her. Not simply sexually, but in general. Bailey wasn't an easy person to be around—she owned that. Embraced it, even. But Deke just seemed to not care.

No matter how much she annoyed him, no matter how exasperated he became, no matter what she said or did … he never told her to go away. Never asked her to shut up. Never proclaimed that she was too much of this or too little of that.

Oh, he insulted her and stuff, but it was just playful shit talk. The dude might have little patience, but he never actually lost it with her. And she had to admit, it was nice to feel accepted. Her snake had grown to like and respect him for it.

Given that his sense of restlessness had eased and she rarely saw him scratching himself these days, she figured the touch-hunger would pass altogether in a week or so, maybe even less. She'd be relieved for him and his cat, but if he didn't wish to extend their arrangement she'd be secretly disappointed that they were parting ways.

It was kind of horrifying to realize that she'd actually grown to really *like* the guy. How in the hell had that happened? It wasn't as if he'd invested any effort into trying to make her warm up to him or anything. It just simply came to be.

He might be using her for sex, but he never made her *feel* used. On the contrary, he made her feel … good. It was in the small things he did, really.

He stocked mac and cheese micro meals for her in his freezer. He always gave her a mouthful of crap if he found out she'd skipped lunch and insisted she take better care of herself. And, knowing she hated the cold, he never put the thermostat low when she was here even though he burned hotter than the freaking sun.

A heavy arm draped over her as he scooted closer. She snapped her eyes open, only then realizing she'd closed them.

"Why are you slapping yourself?" he asked, his voice lazy, his breath fanning her hair.

"Trying to wake myself up a little. I don't want to accidentally fall asleep."

He only grunted. It had to make her terribly weird that she was becoming fond of those grunts. His sex grunts were her favorite, though.

Feeling her eyelids get real heavy, she forced them wide open. "I gotta go."

"'Kay," he mumbled.

But neither of them moved an inch.

"Really, I gotta go. Lift your arm."

"You lift it."

She frowned at him, but he missed it—his eyes were closed. "No, you do it."

"I'm tired."

"So am I."

"Then rest for a sec while you work up the energy. And don't wake me when you leave."

She sniffed. "Fine."

"Fine."

Bailey let herself relax as she waited for her body to catch a second wind. She'd get up in a few minutes. She truly would. Though it would be hard, because he was so warm and his duvet was a delight and she was sleepy from post-sex chemicals. She'd just rest her eyes for a sec. Just a sec …

Bailey wasn't sure what broke her dream, but it softly cracked as wakefulness pulled at her. As the cobwebs of sleep lifted, she let her eyes flutter open. Not *too* wide, though. It was kind of bright in here.

Licking her dry lips, she blinked several times to clear her fuzzy vision so she could check the time on her LED lamp. Only … her lamp wasn't there. Nor was her nightstand. A mahogany one stood in its place—taller than hers, and littered with receipts and chump change.

She tensed, awareness bleeding into her mind fast. An awareness that she was in Deke's bed, his chest to her back, his arm curled around her waist, his face buried in her hair. And it was *morning.*

"Fuck," she slurred.

He hummed, the sound all gravelly with sleep. "Figured you'd say that when you woke."

She let out a very Deke-like grunt, unamused by the hint of teasing in his tone. Her snake thought it was funny, though. She thought the whole damn situation was funny. When it was *not.* "Get off me."

"Later."

"Later?"

"Need to fuck you first."

Her stomach twisted. She debated his claim quite fiercely, but those hands of his—skilled and bold—changed her mind pretty quickly. Soon, he was taking her from behind, and she was loving it.

Then she went back to being annoyed. Which he seemed to find entertaining, the shithead.

Her movements quick and sharp, she washed and dressed. He did the same—though much more relaxed, as if this was the norm for them. Ignoring her protests, he then ushered her into the kitchen and onto a chair at his dining table before setting about making them coffee and cereal.

"Stop scowling," he told her, his eyes dancing.

"Don't wanna."

He pulled two mugs out of a cupboard. "It ain't a big deal, Bailey."

"I don't do overnight stays."

"Why not?"

"I just don't."

Deke didn't bother hiding his smirk. Bailey rarely got pissed at herself, accepting of her flaws and habits and quirks. But whenever she realized she'd subconsciously lowered her guard, she'd get all moody and snarly. That was exactly what she'd done last night or she wouldn't have been relaxed enough to fall asleep beside him.

He honestly hadn't realized until recently how much she made a point of keeping people at a distance. Maybe because she was so tightly bonded to Havana and Aspen. But he'd paid more attention lately. And he'd sensed that though she didn't mind befriending people, she was hesitant to make them *close* friends.

The more time he spent around Bailey, the more he came to realize that he'd harbored many misconceptions about her.

Because she treated life as if it were one big party, he'd fallen into the trap of believing that she didn't take it seriously. He'd been wrong. Bailey took the things that mattered most to her, the things that were within her control to influence or change or keep steady, *very* seriously—such as her responsibilities and her close friendships. Everything else? She shrugged it off rather than stress over it; laughed rather than dwelled; joked rather than whined.

He used to think she possessed no principles. But she'd guarded his secret that his cat was having issues. She hadn't liked that his marking her might hurt Dayna. And though she wasn't always sweet about it, she was honest. Also, though she cared little what people thought, she didn't consider their *emotions* unimportant. She was far more compassionate and understanding than she might appear.

Though she provoked people like she was born for it, it wasn't to be hurtful. Unless you'd pissed her off, of course. Mostly, she did it for two reasons.

One, yes, it just plain amused her. But also for the same reason that others might tell a lot of jokes or funny stories—it was really her way of connecting with others. She took it several steps further than most would, and he suspected it was to discourage people from getting too close. In that sense, it was her armor. Probably had been for a very long time.

That she was so dismissive of what most considered factual and rational made it easy to miss that she was highly intelligent and insightful. She just questioned things rather than accepted them as pure truths, likely due to her distrust of authority figures. And who wouldn't be so distrustful of authority when the adults in your life, including your Alphas, threw you away like you were nothing?

He still didn't know exactly what went down when her old Alphas banished her. He'd poked and prodded at her, wanting answers, but she'd resisted coughing up the info. Still, he felt he could safely conclude that her trust issues and hesitation to get close to people stemmed from her old nest's betrayal.

Once he'd set their coffees on the table, Deke carried the bowls of cereal over. Noticing she was still glowering, he leaned forward, planted a palm on the table, and then wrapped his hand around the back of her neck. "Ask yourself what difference it really made that you slept here and not in your own bed. Nothing has changed. The world isn't on fire. You didn't turn into a vase."

She mumbled something beneath her breath, still scowling. He couldn't say why he found it an adorable sight, he just did. So he gave her a quick kiss—or that was his intention. But the moment his lips touched hers, their sexual connection flared. He took her mouth, sweeping his tongue inside, gorging on her taste.

He'd known that fucking their attraction into dust wouldn't be an easy feat, but he'd thought he could at least take the edge off it by getting his fill of her. He'd thought that acting out his fantasies would give them a mundane feel and he'd eventually lose interest.

It hadn't quite worked out that way.

He knew her body well, but that didn't satisfy him. He wanted to know it even better. To become acquainted with every fine inch of it. To etch every curve and dip and weak spot into his memory. If he could only convince her to let him tie her to the bed so he could indulge himself that way, he would set about doing exactly that.

He'd pinned her wrists to the bed occasionally when he'd fucked her. She'd liked it, so he didn't doubt that she'd like being bound to the bed. The problem was that Bailey didn't trust easy. He believed she trusted him to an extent, but not enough to make herself that vulnerable to him.

Deke figured he'd have time to bypass those issues of hers, since he wasn't feeling a need to end their fling once the touch-hunger left him. He hadn't run that by her yet, though he would soon. He doubted she'd have an issue with it, considering she was more relaxed around him these days and wasn't showing any signs of wanting out.

She broke the kiss with a sharp nip to his lower lip. "Stop that," she said, the words a little breathy.

He arched a brow. "Stop what?"

"You're only supposed to kiss me when we're having sex or leading up to it."

He felt his mouth curve. "That so? Hmm. Does that mean I can't do this either?" He closed his hand around her breast.

She batted said hand away. "Yes, it does."

Even as his cat cast her an unhappy look, Deke smiled. He liked seeing her worked up. "Really? Anything else I shouldn't be doing?"

Her mouth firmed. "You think this is funny?"

"Yeah. It's not often I see you getting wound up about nothing." He frowned, pensive. "You know, I thought you just struggled with people being nice to you. But it's not simply that, is it? You struggle with any signs—physical or otherwise—of affection."

"So?" she snarked, defensive.

"So it makes me wonder why."

"Who needs affection? It's *blah*."

"Blah?"

"Yes."

His chest tightened. In other words, she hadn't gotten a lot of affection growing up, so at some point she'd told herself she didn't need it, and she'd eventually come to believe it.

Knowing she'd bristle if he showed her any sympathy or tried pushing her further, he went for playing the matter down. "Is it really affection, though, when what I'm mostly doing is groping you?"

She pursed her lips, thoughtful. "I guess not."

"Then it's not something you need to be bothered by, is it?"

"I guess not."

"Good. Then relax. Eat." He took the seat across from her, watching as she picked up her spoon. When she started to eat, his cat's tension eased and he settled down.

In spite of how withdrawn he'd become, the cat had grown to tolerate Bailey. Mostly, it was because the feline was a creature of habit. He got used to things. Didn't like change. Preferred routine. And the cat had become accustomed to Bailey's nightly presence, so now he didn't growl at her so much.

Catching movement out of the corner of his eye, Deke shot her a look. "You need to deal with *that* situation." He tipped his chin toward the garter snake slithering on his kitchen floor.

She shrugged. "I told you Clive likes to visit me."

"And I told you I don't want him here."

"Relax. He's just a snake."

Relax? Seriously? "He hissed at me yesterday."

"You were being rude."

"Rude?"

"You told him to get out. That's hurtful."

Deke frowned. "How can it have hurt him? He can't understand a word I say."

"How do you know? Because it's written in science books that animals can't understand humans? *Pfft.* Humans get stuff wrong all the time."

"I think, in this, they're correct."

"Then I can't help you."

"With what? I wasn't asking for help."

"But you need it." She wagged her finger. "You're too easily swayed."

"Because I believe scientific claims hold merit?"

"Yes."

Deke sighed. "Whatever." He dug into his cereal.

As they ate, she kept on scowling. Not at him. No, he suspected she was annoyed with herself for agreeing to stay for breakfast. He hadn't been so sure that she would.

Last night, he'd been awake when she drifted off. He'd sensed her body go heavy, heard her breathing change. He could have woken her, but he'd wanted her to stay. Wanted her to be there when he woke.

She didn't know, but he usually didn't sleep beside others either. Before now, he'd only ever made an exception with Dayna, because he'd known her so long and there had been a comfortable familiarity there.

One that was now gone.

His mother was delighted that he'd distanced himself from Dayna. Deke had thought she'd then cease trying to push him toward Bailey, but Livy was no less invested in her plan.

Once they were finished eating, he followed Bailey to her apartment so she could pull on fresh clothes. Since it was his new habit to walk her to her vehicle each morning, he usually came knocking on her door around this time to escort her outside. After the acid attack, he was taking no chances.

When they exited their complex a short time later, he caught sight of Gerard and Therese standing beside her car. The male noticed Deke, briefly tensed, and then all but shoved her into the vehicle.

Deke snorted to himself. He wasn't surprised that Gerard would attempt to hide her. Because though Dayna had ceased trying to contact Deke, she seemed to have talked plenty to her closest friends. Gerard had been quick to tell one and all that she was devastated Deke "replaced her." But the bartender had also claimed he thought it was for the best that Dayna and Deke were no longer bound by a vow.

Therese, however, hadn't been so fair or reasonable. She had—though not to his face—vilified Deke for doing this to Dayna while the woman was "knee-deep in grief," which was something of an exaggeration. Therese had also verbally flayed Deke behind his back for, by branding another, being unfaithful to Dayna—another exaggeration, since he and Dayna weren't in a committed relationship.

More, Therese had made out like Bailey was some kind of homewrecker, though the pride in general disagreed; they felt that the vow had been stretched out for long enough, and that if Deke and Dayna really had a future it would have been obvious by now.

He had every intention of confronting Therese at some point for the crap she'd spouted about Bailey, but he wouldn't do it here and now. His priority was making sure his mamba was safe.

"Why do you think the giant superhero turns green when mad?" asked Bailey.

Deke felt his brows draw together. "What?"

"I don't get it," she said. "People get red when angry. Why would he turn green?"

Deke didn't even want to know why her thought processes had led her there. So instead of answering her question, he asked his own, "What time does your shift finish at the rec center?"

Shuddering as the cool breeze brushed over them, Bailey looked at him askance. "Why?"

"Because I want to know."

"Why?"

"Because it'll affect what I have in mind for later."

"Which is what?"

He turned to fully face her. "We hit the diner together."

She blinked. "Huh?"

"Did I stutter?"

She simply stared up at him.

Yeah, okay, so they rarely ate together, let alone spend time together in public just the two of them. But it was no big deal, so she could stop looking at him like he'd suggested they take a trip to the moon.

"You eat out with your girls sometimes," he said. "What's the difference?"

"You're not one of them, for starters."

"Neither are Blair, Elle, or Bree. You've met up with them at the diner on occasions."

"But they enjoy my company. You don't."

He felt his brow pinch. "What makes you think that?"

"You used to threaten to choke and throw stuff at me. That sort of clued me in."

"Yeah, *used* to." Deke fisted her tee and hauled her close. "Though some would say it flies in the face of reason, I like having you around."

She leaned back slightly, eyeing him suspiciously. "You do?"

"Yeah. So. Diner. Six-thirty." He gave her a hard kiss. "Be there."

Still looking a little dubious, she said, "All right."

"You *bastard*!"

Deke's head whipped to the side. A short, dark-skinned woman was bearing down on them, her face flushed, anger in every step. He frowned. "Excuse me?"

She stopped in front of him, gave Bailey a thorough once-over, and then sliced her fury-filled gaze back to him. "I knew you were hiding something. And yeah, I entertained the idea that it could be a girlfriend. But I'd tell myself there was no way you'd ever do that to me." A bitter, self-depreciating smile pulled at her lips. "Huh. Turned out I was wrong."

Deke's gut stirred as suspicion pricked at his nape. Feeling his jaw tighten, he exchanged a look with Bailey, whose expression told him they were having the same thought.

The woman—*human,* he scented—threw up her arms. "Why did you even ask me to come here if you knew there was a chance I'd catch you with *her*? Or was that the point? You want to hurt me? Was this all a big game to you?"

Deke slanted his head. "And you are ...?" Not the most tactful way to handle the moment, no, but diplomacy really wasn't his strong point.

Her dark eyes went wide. "You *asshole*!" She shifted her attention back to Bailey and honed in on her hand. "No ring. Not a fiancée or wife, then, at least. He never told me about you, so I'm guessing he never told you about me."

Bailey scraped her teeth over her lower lip. "How about you tell me?"

The human perched a hand on her hip. "I'm Journee, the woman he's been exchanging 'I love yous' with for the past three months."

Shit. Deke blew out an annoyed breath.

"Online?" Bailey prodded.

"And over the phone," Journee clipped, batting at the corkscrew curls that slapped her face as the breeze picked up. "We met on Zing."

"Ah." Bailey sighed at him. "We should have thought to check other platforms."

"I don't have profiles on other platforms for anyone to clone," he pointed out.

"Doesn't mean he couldn't use all your info to create one in your name." Bailey turned back to Journee. "Zing's a dating website, right?"

"Ask *him*," the human sassed. "He knows all about it."

Bailey rubbed at the side of her neck. "Yeah, the thing he is … he actually doesn't."

Journee's face scrunched up. "What?"

"We should go somewhere and talk," Deke suggested.

The human's spine snapped straight. "If you've got something you want to say, say it here and now so I can go home and forget I ever came across your profile."

Fine. "I'm not the person you've been talking to. You were catfished, as they say."

Her smile was *all* mockery. "Yeah. Right." She looked at Bailey. "Don't buy this pack of bullshit. He just doesn't want you to know he's been talking to another woman while with you."

"He's telling the truth," said Bailey, her expression unusually somber. "Someone else came here recently claiming they were having an online relationship with Deke on NetherVille. We don't know who cloned his profile on there, but I'm betting it's the same person who's been talking to you."

Journee glanced from him to Bailey, her eyes narrowing.

"Seriously," Deke told her. "It wasn't me."

Journee's hand slid from her hip. "It has to be you, I—"

"You said I asked you to come here?" he double-checked.

She nodded. "Yes. You told me where you live. You asked me to come visit you this morning. Said to be here at eight, so here I am."

"And does it make sense to you that I would do that? That I would invite you here when I obviously already have a woman in my life?"

Her mouth bobbed open and shut. "I don't …"

"Surely I'd have asked you to meet me somewhere else. Somewhere there was no chance of you and Bailey running into each other." He paused, giving her a moment to fully consider it. "Why would I take that risk?"

Journee crossed her arms. "I have no idea. It turns out I don't know you as well as I thought I did." But there wasn't as much snark in her voice now. She didn't yet fully believe him, but the seed of doubt was firmly planted.

"The truth is, you don't know me at all, because we didn't once exchange a single message," he upheld.

She fished her cell out of her purse. "I'm going to call you. I want to see if your phone rings."

He waited in silence as she dialed. His shifter hearing easily picked up the rhythmic ringing. He pulled out his own cell and then held it up so she could clearly see that her phone was not whatsoever trying to connect with his own.

She swiped her thumb over the screen of her cell, eyeing him uncertainly. "You could have a second phone."

"But I don't. Have you spoken to who you believe is me on the phone?"

"Many times."

"And does my voice sound the same?"

She licked her lips, hesitating. "You could have faked it."

That was a "no." "But why would I? What would be the point, if I planned to meet you one day?"

Averting her gaze, she stuffed her hands in her coat pockets.

Bailey cut in, "You've been in contact with someone pretending to be Deke. Someone who sent you here knowing that what you'd discover would hurt you."

Journee swallowed. "This is for real?"

"Unfortunately, yes, it is," Bailey replied. "And it would really help if you could answer some questions for us. We want to find this guy and deal with him."

After long moments, the human finally nodded. "All right."

CHAPTER TWELVE

Tate cursed a blue streak. "We need to find out who this asshole is."

"Working on it," said Bailey, pissed beyond belief, her eyes on her computer as she worked to tackle the password for the dating website.

After their short conversation with Journee—who unfortunately had no info that could help them track their culprit—Bailey and Deke had headed straight to her apartment. She'd settled at her desk as he texted the Alphas and Betas, who promptly appeared. They'd all gathered behind her with Deke, who'd quickly filled them in.

Positively fuming on his behalf, Bailey wanted to rant her ass off. But that wasn't what he needed from her. Not right then. No, he needed her to be calm and use the skills she possessed that could help him. So she'd tucked in her anger and channeled it, using it to fuel her focus.

"There could be more profiles out there, couldn't there?" asked Luke, the same hard edge in his voice that could be heard in that of the others.

"Yes," said Deke, the word a whip. "Whoever's doing this could be having several online relationships while posing as me."

"He pretty much ended this relationship himself, didn't he?" said Havana, her heels clicking the hardwood floor as she paced back and forth. "He sent her here. He wanted you to know about her."

"Which means this isn't simply someone imitating you to land girls, Deke," Tate added. "He's fucking with you for certain. He could have instead deleted the Zing profile, and we'd have been none the wiser. But no, he kept it going, and then he made sure you found out about it."

"And he did it in a way that said he didn't give the world's first fuck about Journee's feelings." Blair sighed. "It must have been hard for her to realize she'd been played all these months."

Without looking away from the computer, Bailey said, "She tried to hide it by clinging to anger, but she was devastated. Whoever posed as Deke knew—" She cut off as the Zing profile opened. "Okay, I'm in."

Everyone shuffled closer, and Deke bent over to get the best view of the screen, his body so close his breath tickled her ear.

Bailey went on, "I half-expected him to have deleted the profile so that I couldn't hack into it. I mean, he knew in advance that I would try."

"Which probably means we can take what private info he provided to create the profile with a grain of salt," muttered Havana.

Pulling up his account information, Bailey gaped at what she read. "Oh come on, really?" The asshole had typed in *her* name and address.

"Ridiculous," scoffed Havana. "This whole thing is obviously some kind of damn joke to him. He knows there's no way Deke would suspect you'd created the profile." The devil paused. "You don't, do you?"

"Fuck, no," Deke firmly stated. "She can be a sly little thing and likes to play with people, but she wouldn't do something like this."

It was probably wrong that both Bailey and her snake took that as a compliment, but whatever. The mamba was as furious as her about the catfishing crap—in the serpent's view, only *they* got to fuck with Deke.

"Our boy hasn't changed his phone number," Deke noted. "New email address, though. You can hack into it, Bailey, right?"

"Yes, I just want to check his messages on here first." She skimmed through them quickly. "Journee's the only person he's been communicating with." And nothing in the flirty messages pointed to who he could be. "Once I've deactivated this, I'll do an online search for other profiles of you."

Straightening, Deke gave the mamba space as he watched her work. Her gaze was locked on the screen with lethal accuracy, her fingers zooming over the keyboard so fast they were a blur.

Six. It turned out there were six other profiles. Some were on dating apps, some were on social media platforms, and one existed in a private anti-shifter extremist group.

More, each had been created using the IDs of six pride members—namely Sam, Therese, Gerard, Cassandra, Shay, and Dayna.

Unfuckingbelievable.

His cat hissed and spat, raking Deke's insides with its claws, infuriated by not only the situation but by how they didn't have the name of the culprit.

"The son of a bitch sure does like pretending to be other people," mused Luke, his tone clipped. "You know, one of these six *could* actually be the culprit. Well, not Therese or Cassandra, considering the humans claimed they spoke to a male on the phone. But the others? It's possible. They might have used their own ID one time to paint themselves as a scapegoat so they wouldn't come under suspicion."

Scratching the back of his head, Deke grimaced. "I can't envision any of them doing it. This isn't a mere case of someone slashing my tire or keying my car. Whoever did this spent months creating profiles, charming women, and doing a whole lot of calling and texting and *lying*—it had to be exhausting. You don't do something like that unless you have a serious grudge."

Pausing, Deke shook his head. "None of the members of our pride he's effectively implicating have that kind of grudge against me. I've never had major beef with any of them, or anyone in the pride really. Okay, Dayna's likely feeling murderous toward me now, but she wasn't before."

"Just because you didn't have a huge fallout with anybody doesn't mean someone isn't super angry at you," said Bailey. "You might not even realize you did something to hurt or offend them. What one person will dwell over is something another person can laugh off."

Aspen folded her arms. "She makes a valid point."

Bailey shrugged. "Happens a lot."

Deke let out a doubtful snort that made her smile.

Bailey switched her focus back to the computer. On each profile, she checked every message, every post, every slice of info. There was nothing that pointed to who was playing these games. Nor was there anything informative to find in any of the emails in the various accounts.

Cursing in his head, Deke puffed out a breath.

Bailey turned to the Alphas. "So what now?"

Tate rubbed at his nape. "We have nothing that tells us who did this. Much as I personally don't believe these six people are anything but scapegoats, they should still be questioned." He cut his gaze to Deke. "I don't think you should be there for that."

Deke blinked, feeling his shoulders stiffen. "Say again?"

"Now that we've established that the person doing this wants to screw with you, we can be pretty sure they'll be paying close attention to you," said Tate. "They'll want to know they're getting to you."

Well, they were.

"If it is one of these six shifters," Tate continued, "they'll drink in every moment of you questioning them, Deke; drink in your anger and confusion and whatever else you're feeling. For them, it's a game—one they're winning. They'll be loving that they have this power over you. They'll be all smug at the idea that you're raging at not only what they've done but at having no clue who they are."

Deke sighed. "What you're saying is … you think that the best way to hit back at them is to act like I don't give enough of a shit to bother questioning any suspects."

"Exactly," confirmed Tate. "I think you should go on about your day as normal. Act like what happened with Journee ain't a blip on your radar. Make this asshole think they're gonna need to try harder to get to you, because we need them to slip up and make a mistake. And the sooner they do it the better. We don't know what their motive is, but we know that they want to get into your head and fuck with it. Don't know about you, but I personally don't feel inclined to do anything they might like."

Grinding his teeth, Deke reluctantly dipped his chin. "I'll sit out of the questioning." His cat growled, displeased at not being included.

Tate gave a nod of satisfaction. "I know this isn't easy for you, but it's the right move to make. He's several steps ahead of us. We need to fucking catch up. Fast."

Driving home from the center later that day, Bailey flicked a look at Havana via the car's rearview mirror. "Why are you scowling at your phone?"

The devil lifted her head. "I just heard from Tate. He and Luke questioned the six people implicated by our resident catfisher."

Twisting in the front passenger seat to look at the Alpha, Aspen spoke, "And?"

"And nothing." Havana pocketed her cell. "They all claimed they had no hand in the creation of the profiles, and none gave Tate any reason to believe they were lying."

Bailey felt her lips thin. "Shit."

She hadn't exactly been confident that Tate would identify the culprit during basic questioning—the asshole was too careful, he wouldn't easily give himself away—but she'd hoped that maybe he would have some luck. "I've gone backwards and forwards in my head trying to work out what's going on, but I'm stumped."

"Same here," declared Havana, returning her gaze to the scenery outside.

The long stretch of narrow road cut through a rural area. There wasn't much traffic at the moment. But there would be later when rush hour hit.

Looking somewhat sulky, Aspen said, "I'm not in the mood to cook tonight. Anyone else interested in grabbing takeout food on the way home? We could grab some for our guys, too, obviously."

"I'm in," Havana told her. "You up for it, Bailey?"

Flexing her grip on the steering wheel, Bailey awkwardly cleared her throat. "Uh, I can't. I've got plans."

"You have plans?" asked Aspen. "What plans?"

Scratching at her cheek, Bailey adopted a casual tone as she replied, "I agreed to meet Deke at the diner."

Havana leaned forward as far as her seatbelt would allow. "The diner?" she echoed, a spark of excitement in her voice.

"Yes." Bailey had thought he might cancel after what happened earlier—he'd looked eager to rip someone's face off. But she'd texted him before she left the center to see if he wanted to take a raincheck, and he'd told her he saw no need to cancel.

Aspen angled in her seat to face Bailey, all eagerness. "So, basically, you guys are going on a date?"

Bailey frowned. "What? No."

"Well, what else do you call it?" asked the bearcat.

"A simple meet-up."

Havana snorted. "Simple my ass."

Ugh, did these women need to complicate everything? "It's no different than when I go out for dinner with you guys," Bailey defended, paraphrasing Deke.

"Oh, it's very different, considering *we're* not fucking you," said Havana.

Bailey shot her a look in the rearview mirror. "What does that have to do with anything?"

The devil rolled her eyes. "It's a date, Bailey—admit it."

"It isn't, just as it isn't a date when he and I sometimes eat together at his place."

Havana raised a finger. "Those two things are not the same. One happens in public. The other doesn't. For him to take you out, he's making a statement to all and sundry—including you—that you're not a mere bedmate."

"But he's *not* taking me out," Bailey told her. "He asked me to meet him there."

"Don't split hairs. This is a date." Havana planted a hand on Bailey's headrest. "Let me ask you this: Did any of your other bed-buddies take you places?"

"They sometimes offered," replied Bailey. "I said no."

"Why?"

Bailey shrugged. "I saw no point in pretending that we had something we didn't."

"*And* you were managing their expectations. Right?"

"Well, yeah." It had seemed better to do so. And most of them had annoyed her snake anyway.

"You didn't say no to Deke. Why not?"

Bailey lifted her shoulders. "We have an arrangement complete with an approximate end date." One she did hope would be given an extension. "There's no chance of anyone getting muddled about where they stand."

"It's more than that."

It was, yes. He'd said something that made her chest go tight and warm and, more, caused her snake to melt a little. The words had taken Bailey so off-guard that she hadn't been able to think of an argument. She shifted in her seat. "He said he likes having me around."

"Aw," drawled Aspen.

"I *knew* he did," claimed Havana, smug. "I just knew it. A guy like Deke was never going to let a little goading hold him at arm's length."

"I'm sure your snake is delighted, considering he passed her test," said Aspen, a smile in her voice.

Bailey flicked her a sideways look. "What test?"

The bearcat sighed. "Bailey, you're a huge pain in the ass in just about every way possible. Your snake is no better—she's aggressive to just about everybody, even if she likes them. You push people to encourage them to give you space. *She* does it to see if they have the balls to get closer. If they don't, she decides they're useless."

"She did it to my devil and to Aspen's bearcat," Havana added. "Many times, actually. And when we didn't let her scare us off and she saw we'd accepted you as you are, she relaxed with us and let us in. So did you."

Bailey opened her mouth to deny it … and realized she couldn't. She hadn't given it any real thought before—self-reflection wasn't something she spent much time on, and she didn't much reflect on her snake's behavior either. "I didn't realize that's what she was doing," she mumbled.

"I know," said Aspen, her voice soft. "I take it she's not as determined to resist his charms anymore."

No, the mamba wasn't. She'd given him her silent approval … illustrating that, yes, he had in fact passed her little test.

"And neither are you." Havana gently poked Bailey's shoulder. "I think you pushed Deke so much harder than you do others to keep him away because you knew it would sting if he wrote you off and proclaimed he couldn't deal with you." She paused. "Has he hinted at keeping your little arrangement going?"

Bailey shook her head. "He hasn't mentioned the arrangement at all."

The Alpha let out a low hum. "So there have been no subtle 'remember this is only temporary' messages?"

"No. But Deke doesn't do subtle."

"True," Havana conceded. "And if he hasn't verbally reminded you that you two will soon part, that's pretty telling. I've seen how he is with you. Not lovey-dovey or gentle by any means, no, but Deke is not cuddly. What I'm getting at is … he gives you his full attention. He stays close, as if to leap between you and any threat if need be."

"And he spars with you in a way he doesn't with others," said Aspen. "He's *full*-on. He doesn't tone himself down. Like he lowers his guard with you; trusts that you'll take him as he is. You do the same with him." She reached over and tapped Bailey's thigh. "You'd like if he offered you more. Admit it."

Bailey cast her a brief, foul look. "Don't wanna. You can't make me."

Havana chuckled. "You don't need to be spooked by this, Bailey. It's a good thing, it—"

A *crack* split the air a mere millisecond before something slammed into the tire. The car juddered and then tilted downwards, the now-burst tire screeching as the vehicle swerved abruptly.

Her heart slamming against her ribs, Bailey yanked on the wheel with a shocked curse, struggling to regain control of the car. But its left side dipped off the edge of the narrow road, unbalancing it … and then the vehicle flipped.

For excruciatingly slow moments, it was as if they were suspended in the air. Like time itself had paused. And then the world went tumbling.

The breath slammed from Bailey's lungs as the safety belt snapped taut, hauling her against the seat with a vicious yank. Again and again the car flipped, whacking her body into the door, whipping her head from side to side. A billow of white bashed into her front, shoving her against the seat. But still, she was jerked and jostled.

There was an explosion of sounds—grinding, smashing, banging, crunching, startled female cries. All kinds of crap bounced around like pinballs and smacked into her.

Abruptly, the world stopped spinning. Her body stopped moving. The explosive sounds came to a halt.

Bailey blinked, her dazed mind struggling to assimilate what had just happened. Her primitive hindbrain was going nuts, but it was like her higher functions had shut down. She simply sat there, numb. Not even the shoves and bites from her frantic snake were penetrating her fog.

Beneath the ringing of her ears and the pounding of her heart was a hissing sound. Smoke? Air? She didn't know.

A warm wetness dampened her hair and dripped down her face. She knew it was blood. She could smell it—it mingled with the scents of gas, burned rubber, and the airbag's talcum powder.

A female groan.

The pained sound gripped Bailey's heart and made it skip a beat. Awareness steadily pierced her daze, and reality crashed into her hard.

A shot. A shot had rang out. And then the car had swerved like a nut and sailed over the edge of the road.

Bailey gritted her teeth. Anger and adrenaline surging through her, she shoved at the airbag until it deflated with a small gust of chalky powder. "Please tell me you guys aren't dead."

"Not dead," mumbled Aspen as Havana said, "Peachy over here."

Relief tumbled through both Bailey and her snake. "I say we get out of this car. Like *now*."

"I second that," said Aspen.

"Works for me," added Havana with yet another groan of pain.

Bailey wasn't feeling in any better shape. Burning twinges could be felt here and there, along with a massive ache in her head. And God, she felt like she'd taken a dozen punches to the chest, thanks to the belt and airbag. "I know I hit my head pretty hard, but I'm not imagining it that someone *actually* just shot out my tire to make us crash, am I?"

"No," Havana grunted, struggling with her safety belt. "No, you're not."

Motherfucking fucker. She dragged in a breath—which made pain flare through her already sore chest. "Okay. Just wanted to be sure."

CHAPTER THIRTEEN

The SUV had barely come to a halt when Deke ragged open its sliding side door. A sense of urgency clutching his chest, he leapt out, Tate and Camden hot on his heels. Deke distantly noted that Farrell and the Betas—who the Alphas had instructed to head to the scene of the accident—had already arrived, but he paid them no real attention. Ignoring everyone but the slender female sat at the roadside, he crossed straight to her.

She stood, and he framed her face with his hands, leery of hauling her close when he knew her body would be sore in places. He dropped his forehead to hers. "Baby." It was a gravelly whisper.

He'd been right beside Tate when Havana had called her mate to inform him of the incident. Panic had knifed through Deke's gut, and he'd snatched Tate's cell out of his hand and demanded that Havana put Bailey on the phone. His mamba had assured him that she was fine, but her words hadn't been enough to ease the wave of rage that had surged through him.

"I'm all right," Bailey muttered, laying a hand on his upper arm. "Just *mega* pissed."

She wasn't "all right" at all. She had a goddamn head wound that had bled bad enough to form a thick clump of sticky blood in her hair. There were also some cuts on her face and arms, and he would bet her chest hurt like hell.

His cat prowled beneath his skin, anger in every fluid step. She might not belong to the feline, but he still regarded her as under his direct protection. That someone would dare target her—*again*—made his blood boil.

Righting his head, Deke looked down the steep hill behind her and caught side of Luke and Blair studying the wreckage. Deke's lungs seized. The chunk of metal was positively fucked—windows gone, roof dented, doors hanging off.

And Bailey had been inside it.

He couldn't stop his hands from tightening their hold on her face.

She wrapped her fingers around his wrists. "Really, I'm fine."

He snapped his gaze back to hers. "No, you're not." But she would be once Helena, who was currently healing Havana, made her way over.

Tate had brought the healer even though his mate had assured him that none of their injuries were serious. Deke had been glad, not wanting Bailey or the other females to be in needless pain.

Skimming his gaze over both Havana and Aspen, he could see an array of cuts and bruises, though Havana's were healing before his eyes. Camden seemed to be insisting that Aspen had a broken rib, but the bearcat claimed it was merely bruised.

The crunch of gravel made Deke look to see Farrell approaching. Letting his hands slip away from Bailey, Deke half-turned toward the Head Enforcer. "Did you find anything?"

Farrell pointed to a spot on the opposite side of the wreckage and said, "A motorcycle was parked over there earlier, and there's evidence that someone was lying in wait."

"Someone who knew our schedule and is a crack shot," said Havana, her expression diamond hard. "We looked around after I called Tate, but the asshole was long gone by then."

"We were pretty sure they'd scampered, but we shifted and let our animals go check shit out." Bailey paused as Helena laid a healing hand on her shoulder. "There's no trail to follow, though."

"And we didn't pick up a scent," Aspen grumbled. "They used a scrambler." The pungent, scented sprays were designed to screw with a shifter's enhanced sense of smell, allowing people to hide their signature scent and protect their identity.

Right then, Luke and Blair clambered back up the hill.

"Tire was definitely shot out," the Beta male confirmed. "No other bullets appear to have hit the car."

Blair folded her arms. "I don't think this was an attempt to kill. If that were the case, the prick would have stuck around and either shot at the vehicle in the hope of making it go boom, or shot at Havana, Aspen, and Bailey to take them out. He didn't."

Luke dipped his chin. "This seemed more like another attempt at giving Bailey a scare."

"Doesn't matter what their motivation was," said Camden, his voice liquid menace. "They'll pay for this in blood."

"Too right they will," Deke agreed, clenching his fists.

His jaw tight, Tate looked from his brother to Blair. "You can get this mess cleaned up, right?"

"Consider it done," replied Luke, pulling out his phone. "I'll call on a few enforcers to give us a hand."

Tate gave a curt nod and then turned to his mate. "Let's get you home."

Deke, Bailey, Aspen, Camden, Farrell, and the Alphas piled into the nine-seater SUV. Like all the pride-owned vehicles, it had windows that were not only tinted but bulletproof.

Deke followed Bailey onto the rear row and sank onto the seat beside her. Her injuries were gone now, but streaks of dried blood remained on her skin and matted her hair. The scent taunted him and his cat, reminding them she'd been hurt.

Deke took her hand in his, ignoring the flicker of surprise in her eyes. So he wasn't the type to hold hands or link fingers or whatever. So what?

Farrell gave the horn a brief toot and nodded in goodbye at the Betas as he drove forward.

"I don't think the jackals did this," began Havana from the two-seat passenger row in front of Deke. "Don't get me wrong, I can easily see them running Bailey off the road to shake her up some. But they wouldn't have struck while I was with her. To target an Alpha is to start a war. The jackals claimed they don't want one."

"And if that's true, they would have had nothing to gain from what happened today," Aspen piped up, snuggling into Camden on the seat adjacent to the devil shifter. "Seems unlikely that they did it."

"Then I'd say either Ginny or Jackson's brothers were behind it," Farrell announced from the driver's seat. "I'm not saying that any of them were the shooter. They might have hired someone to do the job for them, just as the human extremist was hired."

Tate let out a hum. "I think it's time we question the three loners." Draping his arm over the back of the seat, the Alpha glanced over his shoulder at Deke. "Have River look up their addresses. Once we know where to find them, I'll send people to pick them up and bring them to us."

Deke fished his phone out of his pocket and quickly did as asked. "Done." With that, he pocketed his cell.

Tate slid his gaze to Bailey. "I'm assuming you still have the number for Amiri."

Suspecting where this was going, Bailey replied, "It's logged in my phone. You want to call him?"

Tate nodded. "After all, there's a chance it was their pack. A slim chance, yes, but it's there all the same. If it was them, this was essentially a declaration of war. As such, they'll have no reason to deny it."

It was a possibility, though Bailey personally doubted it. Jackals weren't known for playing guessing games. If this had been a declaration of war, they'd have stuck around to verbally make it clear, not fled the scene. Still, she handed her cell to the Alpha.

Flexing the fingers of her free hand, she cricked her neck. Her muscles were stiff and achy from the anger she couldn't quite shift. It was one thing that *she'd* been hurt. It was a whole other that her girls had also been wounded. She was seriously gonna skin some fucker alive when she had their name, and her equally enraged snake would put them through a world of hurt with her venom.

Tate placed the call on speaker. It rang a few times before a voice answered, "Bailey, good to hear from you. I hope you are calling with news about Roman."

"Not Bailey," the Alpha told him. "Tate."

A pause. "Ah. What can I do for you?"

"You can tell me if your pack are behind what happened today," said Tate, his voice silky with menace. "Bailey was ran off a road and crashed her car. My mate and one of my other enforcers were inside the vehicle. None are dead, but all are injured. I would like to know who's responsible for those wounds."

"I can tell you for certain that it was not my pack," Amiri firmly stated, a ring of truth in his voice that couldn't be ignored. "I have told you before, we have no interest in going to war with you."

"So you say. But you have to admit it doesn't look good for you that someone began targeting her right after you showed up."

"You must have your doubts, though, or you would have come for us by now," Amiri smoothly pointed out.

"Don't mistake that for me having a single fucking issue with shitting fury all over your pack. People die in wars. I will not take my pride into battle unless I am convinced it is necessary. If at any point I become convinced that you are behind the recent attacks, I will come for your pack. And I will fucking decimate it." With that, Tate rang off.

"Either someone from his pack acted without his knowledge, or they're unconnected to what happened," decided Camden, his voice flat, his eyes still hard. "Because that jackal was telling the truth."

Bailey dipped her chin. "Who are you sending to collect Jackson's brothers and Ginny?" she asked Tate as he passed her phone back to her.

"Farrell, Isaiah, Finley, and Joaquin," the Alpha male replied.

Camden's eyes narrowed. "Is there a particular reason why you're not sending me?"

"Yes," replied Tate. "It's for the same reason I'm not sending Havana, Deke, Bailey, or Aspen. You want blood. You're not particularly bothered at this point *who* you make bleed. And we have no proof that any of the three loners are guilty. They don't even seem likely suspects, since a few loners would be foolish to take on an entire pride."

Camden's nostrils flared. "If they are guilty—"

"It wouldn't surprise me if they tried provoking their captors into ending their life so they could escape the consequences," Tate finished. "You're too furious to hold back. It's better that others go grab them."

Bailey agreed with that decision. Camden was hyper-protective of Aspen, not to mention a sadistic fucker. He'd easily snap the neck of anyone he even suspected could be responsible for the injuries his mate had received. Really, so could Bailey. As such, it was definitely best all round that she wasn't being sent to collect the loners.

Havana sighed at Tate. "You're right that they'd be dumb to take us on. Seems both strange and improbable that they would, even to avenge Jackson. It's not like he's dead. He recovered, and he doesn't believe Bailey is responsible." She paused. "I take it you don't intend to hard-core-interrogate them, since they're not full-on suspects."

"No, I see no need for it," Tate told her. "I say we ask them some questions, all civil-like. If they lie, we can kick things up a notch. They'll be shaken up enough by being snatched out of their homes."

"Yeah, you don't need to tie someone up to intimidate them," said Farrell. "You just need to box them in."

Deke squinted, pensive. "The motorhome. We could drive it deep into the woods and question them there like we've done before with others. They'll be scared at the idea that they're in the middle of nowhere, where no one would hear them scream and their bodies could so easily be disposed of."

Tate's eyes sharpened with interest. "Yes, we can wait for them there. Farrell and the other enforcers can bring the trio to us. Bailey, I know your snake is a bloodthirsty creature who delights in biting people, but keep her from killing them unless it's necessary."

She gave him a look that said, *I make no promises.*

He only sighed.

Tapping his fingers on the steering wheel of the stationary motorhome a short time later, Deke spared Bailey a quick glance. Beside him, she was scratching at a splotch of dried blood on her cheek. The sight of the blood made his still-irate cat snarl.

Wanting to get right down to interrogating the loners, she'd vetoed taking a shower first. Deke had asked her to ride shotgun, wanting her close, and she'd agreed. It was a rare occasion when Bailey didn't toss "Why?" at him when he made a request of her. He wondered if he could consider it progress or she was simply distracted by her thoughts.

He'd parked the motorhome in a wooded area not too far from their apartment complex. It shouldn't be long before Farrell and the others arrived.

The Alphas, Aspen, and Camden were talking in the motorhome's small living area. The bearcat kept pacing, spitting out all sorts of plans she had for whoever had dared go after Bailey. Just as furious on the mamba's behalf,

Havana sat unnaturally still as she wished all manner of deaths on the guilty party. Bailey herself, however, had little to say. Which was an indication that she was *seething*.

Deke's anger had cooled during the drive, now overridden by the anticipation he felt at questioning the three loners. His Alphas were right in that it made little sense that said loners would take on so much more than they could chew. But edgy with the sheer helplessness he felt at being unable to protect Bailey from an attacker he couldn't ID, Deke needed to do *something*. Scratching suspects off his list would be enough for now.

It wasn't long before two cars pulled up outside. Deke slipped out of the motorhome, closing the door behind him. Isaiah and Joaquin urged Jackson's brothers out of one vehicle. Farrell and Finley hopped out of the other car … without Ginny.

Frowning at the Head Enforcer, Deke asked, "Where's Ginny?"

"No clue," replied Farrell, his voice too low to carry to their other captives. "But I did a walk-through of her apartment. Some of her things are missing—clothes, phone, ID, keys. I got the impression that she's been gone at least a week."

"A week?" Deke echoed. What the fuck?

"Either she's visiting someone," began Finley, "or she's in hiding."

Deke inwardly cursed and then turned to the male loners. Both were wide eyed, their dark hair tussled, clearly spooked. *Good*. They should be afraid. Because if one or both of them were behind what happened to Bailey, they'd die for it. And they wouldn't die easily or quickly.

He gave them a smile that wasn't in the least bit reassuring as he opened the door that led into the motorhome's living area. "In you go."

Somewhat reluctant, they slowly entered.

Farrell turned to the three enforcers who'd aided him in bringing the suspects to the motorhome. "Stay out here and keep a lookout for anyone who might stumble across us. Alert us if there's anything of note." With that, he then followed Deke into the motorhome.

As both took up a position either side of the closed door, Deke mouthed to Tate, "Ginny's in the wind."

Sprawled on the bench-sofa with his mate, Tate pressed his lips into a flat line. He then focused on the brothers and gestured at the identical bench-sofa opposite his. "Have a seat."

Neither loner looked as if they had any wish to accept the Alpha's invitation, but they nonetheless sat—their backs stiff, their gazes darting around. They clocked Bailey, who was kneeling on the front passenger seat, peering over her headrest. She gave them a little wave, her smile sweet, her eyes empty.

"I know your names, but I'm wondering which is which," Tate said to them.

"I'm Keaton," one said before tipping his head toward the male beside him. "This is Jarrett. What's all this about?"

Leaning against the wall, Camden cocked his head. "You have no idea why you've been brought here?" The casual question came out flat.

Jarrett shook his head. "No."

One hand braced on the kitchenette counter, Aspen let out a doubtful snicker. "Not sure I believe that, but I guess we'll soon see."

Tate leaned forward, bracing his lower arms on his thighs, and clasped his hands. "We're going to ask you some questions," he told the brothers. "Answer honestly, you get to go home. Simple."

Keaton swallowed. "Okay."

"Did you manage to uncover who attacked your brother and left him to die?" Tate asked.

"No." Keaton licked his lips. "We tried, but it was a dead-end. No pun intended."

"Hmm." Tate bit the inside of his cheek. "What does your gut tell you happened to him?"

"That it was likely a random attack."

"You suspected Bailey at one point, correct?"

Keaton hesitated. "Ginny thought there was a good chance that she was to blame."

"I'm not asking what Ginny suspected. I'm asking about you."

"I thought it was possible. At first. I mean, she made his life difficult for months. But everyone I spoke to who knew her, including Jackson, didn't believe it was something she'd do. They were all of the opinion that Ginny was capitalizing on what happened to have Bailey hurt."

Deke cut in, "Where is Ginny now?"

Keaton blinked at him. "I don't know. We haven't been in contact recently."

Deke narrowed his eyes. "Why not?"

It was Jarrett who answered, "She didn't like that we accused her of pointing fingers at Bailey just to get some revenge."

Aspen pushed away from the kitchenette's counter. "When did you last hear from her?"

Pursing his lips in thought, Jarrett shrugged. "About ten or so days ago. Did … did Ginny do something?" he asked, sweeping his gaze over every face.

"Possibly," said Bailey. "Or it could have been either—perhaps even both—of you."

Keaton reared back. "What?"

"Bailey has been targeted twice recently," Deke explained, his tone cutting as a blade. "There was an acid attack not long ago. And then today she ended up crashing her car after someone shot her tire."

Jarrett gave a wild shake of the head. "We had *nothing* to do with that."

Havana flicked up an unconvinced brow. "Really?"

"It wasn't us, I swear," Keaton asserted.

"You can speak for your brother?" Deke asked him. "You know for a fact that he didn't act independently?"

"He wouldn't do something like that," Keaton insisted.

Deke looked at the other loner. "Is he right to have such faith in you?"

"It wasn't me," Jarrett swore, a tremor in his voice. "Even if we had solid proof that it was Bailey who hurt Jackson, no way could I toss acid at her. That kind of shit is fucked up. And I wouldn't go shooting at her car either. I fight with tooth and claw, like any self-respecting shifter. My brother's the same. No way could he have done it."

"It wasn't us," Keaton vowed.

"And you didn't hire anyone to act on your behalf?" asked Camden.

Both brothers shook their heads hard.

Tate straightened in his seat. "We're going to check your cell phones. Particularly your texts and emails. Tell us in advance if there's anything we'll find that could … upset us."

Keaton rubbed at his nape, averting his gaze. "We might have typed some, uh, unflattering things about Bailey a couple of months back when we heard all she'd done to Jackson. But you'll see we changed our mind about her when you read the whole conversation."

He and Jarrett handed over their phones without argument, though neither looked pleased to do so. Bailey skimmed through one cell while Havana went through the other. Both made the same claims—there were no recent messages from Ginny, no *Bailey's at fault* conversations, and nothing whatsoever suspicious.

"Seems that you're as innocent as you claim to be." Tate returned their cell phones to them. "You're free to go."

Keaton and Jarrett exchanged a surprised look.

"If you'd like a ride, my pride mates will take you home."

The brothers politely declined the offer as they stood. They moved slowly at first, as if expecting someone to pounce any moment. When no one did, they rushed outside.

Closing the door behind them, Deke rolled back his shoulders. "Unless they months ago decided to fake an entire text-conversation to mislead us into believing they don't think Bailey's guilty, they're telling the truth."

"Ginny didn't feel the same way about Bailey, so I would have been very interested in talking to her," said Camden, sliding an arm around his mate's waist.

"Seems more than suspicious that she's out of reach," said Deke, as frustrated as his cat that they were unable to question her.

Tate nodded. "I think it's safe to say at this point that she's high on our suspect list."

They discussed the matter for a few more minutes and then decided to head home. Once they reached their complex, Deke herded an uncharacteristically quiet Bailey to her apartment and followed her inside. "Shower," he declared.

She blinked. "You're coming with me?"

"The scent of your blood is making me crazy. I want it gone."

"I can wash it off myself."

"I *want* to do it."

She shot him a quick look. "Careful. I'll start to think you like me or something."

His lips slightly kicked up. "That would be foolish."

Pleased that she'd cracked his black mood—which was ironic, really, considering she usually liked *putting him in* such a mood—Bailey snorted in amusement. Her own was no less foul. Similarly, her mamba was just as incensed. The anger that had earlier invaded and stiffened every muscle in their body was no longer so wild, but it hadn't left them either.

But when Bailey and Deke stood under the hot spray of her shower as he shampooed her hair so gently, careful not to tug on the bloody strands, she felt her tension begin to leach from her system. At the same time, though, she felt a little awkward. Which he must have noticed, because at one point he arched a questioning brow at her.

She shrugged. "I don't know what to do when you're so nice to me. It feels like there's something wrong with the world."

Again, his mouth quirked a little. "Maybe I just like to keep you on your toes." The humor drained from his face as he looked down at the bloody water on the base of the shower.

"I wasn't too badly hurt," she reminded him.

"You could have been," he clipped, not in the slightest bit placated. "And if Helena hadn't healed you, you'd be in a shit load of pain right now."

"Shame I'm not. You'd have made a hot nurse."

"Who says I'd have tended your wounds for you?"

She pouted and put a hand over her heart. "You'd have let others get too close to me while I was vulnerable?"

She thought he'd bark "absolutely" even if only to tease her, but he grumbled out a gruff and somewhat reluctant "no."

She blinked, and her snake almost jerked in surprise. "Really?"

He gave a defensive shrug. "So I'm protective of you. Sue me."

"Aw, you're such a sweetie pie."

He sent her a droll look. "Don't. Just don't."

She smiled. "But you're a joy to irritate."

"How about you kiss me instead?"

"Hmm, I guess I could do that."

The kiss was soft, slow, and lazy. Much to her surprise, so was the round of sex that followed when they stumbled into bed. And afterward, when he switched off the lamp and spooned her—very clearly settling down to sleep right there with her—she didn't insist that he leave and go to his own apartment. She lay a hand over his and closed her eyes.

God, she was turning into such a girl.

CHAPTER FOURTEEN

Four days later, Bailey stared down at the cereal she was struggling to eat, her stomach in tight knots. Deke sat across from her at the table, demolishing his own bowl of fruit loops, clearly unaffected by the elephant that had been circling them since they woke.

"*It's gone,*" he'd said when she'd woken to find him staring at her.

She'd known he meant the touch-hunger, because the last bit of restless energy he'd hummed with had dissipated. "*'Bout damn time,*" she'd replied. And when he hadn't followed it up with a suggestion that maybe they keep their little arrangement going, she'd considered punching him right in the junk.

Mean, sure, but she was feeling mean. Partly because she was annoyed with herself for not having the stones to make the suggestion herself. With anyone else, she might have, because she wouldn't have cared if they rejected her. But a rejection from Deke would burn like a bitch.

As they'd pottered around, they'd carried on as normal. Sort of, anyway. Bailey hadn't been her usual chatty self, disappointment a rock in her gut.

She'd known the touch-hunger was close to subsiding, of course. But she'd thought maybe she'd have a few extra days. She'd been prepared for it to happen sooner, but that didn't make this easier.

Not that she wasn't relieved for him and his cat. They'd suffered long enough. She was glad it was over. She was merely bummed that it wasn't the only thing that was over.

Super bummed, if she was honest.

And it did not help to know that, as he was now free from the vow he'd made to Dayna, he'd no doubt move onto someone else. Maybe not straightaway, but eventually. And, since he was not only her pride mate but a close neighbor, Bailey wouldn't be able to ignore it.

Oh sure, his cat—apparently still having major intimacy issues—wasn't up for letting other females into his life. But that wouldn't really be a factor for Deke. The feline had eventually let Bailey stick around, though somewhat begrudgingly, so Deke knew now that all he had to do was ask a woman to provoke his cat into wanting him to "teach her a lesson."

Giving up on the cereal she couldn't manage to chomp down, Bailey dropped her spool into the bowl and looked at him. He was focused on his breakfast, casual as you please, evidently unbothered that they'd be parting ways. *Lovely.*

Maybe it wasn't fair of her to be so bitter. It wasn't like he hadn't been clear where she stood with him. It wasn't his fault she'd come to hope that he'd change his mind about a few things. That didn't much help, however.

It didn't soothe her snake's resentment either. The mamba had grown to like and respect him, and it grated on her that he was so unaffected by the situation.

Bailey let herself have a moment to drink in the sight of the gorgeous bastard. She'd miss him—there was no pretending otherwise. Rough and rude, he was might not be anyone's typical idea of a "nice guy," but she didn't want or need nice. She liked him as he was, which galled her beyond belief.

Wanting to get the whole thing over with so she could go back to her apartment and throw some shit at a wall, she said, "So … you're better."

Chewing, he met her gaze. Those eyes roamed over her face, searching. Once he'd swallowed his food, he said, "The touch-hunger has finally passed, yeah."

Leaning back in her seat, she folded her arms. "Well, I'll miss your cock."

Humor lit his eyes. "No, you won't."

"I really will. I've grown kind of fond of it." Though she'd right now like to rip it off. Then he couldn't fuck anyone else. A gruesome and cruel thought, perhaps, but she wouldn't actually do it. Probably.

He took a swig of his coffee. "You won't miss it, because you won't be placed in a position where you'll find yourself missing it. It's not done with you. Neither am I."

She went still. "Not done?"

"That's what I said."

"And you're not joking?"

"I'm not joking."

"And you're sober?"

His lips thinning, he threw her an annoyed look. "Of course I'm goddamn sober."

"All right, there's no need to get testy." Doing a little happy dance in her head, she asked, "Are you one of those shifters who has a strict rule on how long he allows bed-buddy arrangements to go on?" She figured it was better to be straight on that.

He set down his mug, planted his lower arms on the table, and leaned forward. His gaze snared hers, focused and intent. "We're not just bed-buddies, Bailey. It started out that way, but things shifted at some point. We might not do couple stuff like go on dates or whatever, but what's between us ain't simple. Not anymore."

Struggling to think past the sheer surprise of his declaration, she quite simply stared at him. For a while, actually—she was at a loss for what to say. Her snake was equally stunned.

When Bailey could really *think* again, she asked, "So what is it that you do want?"

He ran his tongue along his bottom teeth. "I don't know what we have exactly. But I like it. I see no need to end it merely because the touch-hunger is gone. Do you?"

Feeling something in her chest expand, she swallowed. "No."

"Then we see where it goes."

Unable to shake off her befuddlement, Bailey rubbed at her brow. She was afraid to ask if this meant he harbored suspicions that she could be his true mate. Mostly because if he said yes, she wouldn't be able to agree.

Much as she liked Deke, she didn't believe he was her mate—nothing about him called out to her or her snake on that kind of elemental level. That didn't bother Bailey, though. She had no objections to imprinting on someone rather than bonding with her predestined mate. She knew plenty of imprinted couples who were solid and happy. But Deke … he wanted to find the woman who was destined for him.

Rather than mention any of that, Bailey said, "You know, not a lot of things surprise me. But hearing you say you want to see where this goes? Yeah, that's a shocker. At this point, I'd have thought you'd have hit your limit where I'm concerned."

"You drive me crazy—that will likely always be the case. But if you were any other way, I wouldn't like it." Straightening, he lifted his cup. "Maybe it makes me weird, but I wouldn't change you even if I could."

Warmth settled into her bones and wrapped tight around them. "I think that's probably the nicest thing any dude has ever said to me."

"I'm sure you'd have heard a whole bunch of sweet words over the years if you didn't have a habit of walking away from guys before there was a possibility they'd come to want more."

"I doubt it."

Deke didn't. Bailey might have a talent for irritating people, but she also tended to draw them in. Made them feel comfortable, even.

He'd heard countless people call her a "hoot." She could always be counted on to make others smile or laugh. At the very least, she could distract them from whatever was happening in their lives.

He took a sip of his coffee, lowered his mug again, and then once more caught her gaze. "Consider your ground rules null and void. The last thing I'll tolerate is space between me and my female."

Her brows inched up. "*Your* female?"

"Yeah. Mine. I won't share you, Bailey." He wasn't surprised that the proprietary note in his voice made her narrow her eyes. She generally didn't welcome possessiveness. But that was tough shit—she'd just have to deal with it.

"This might not be a heavy relationship, but it's something," he told her. "Something good. Like I said, we're gonna see where it goes. That means scrapping your rules, or we don't have a real chance of exploring this and making it work, do we?"

"I suppose not." She frowned as if something occurred to her. "What about your cat, though? Is he going to be okay with all this?"

Deke sighed. "He's still withdrawn and cranky as fuck, but he doesn't want you going anywhere. He's gotten used to having you around. He's protective of you—and not simply as a mere pride mate. To what will likely be your horror, he's even a little territorial."

"Huh." She puffed out a breath. "I wasn't expecting that."

"Neither was I, but it seems you've grown on him. So much so that, at the moment, you're the only person he doesn't protest to being around."

She cocked her head. "You still don't have even a tiny idea what could be causing him to pull back from everyone?"

"No. Tate has a theory. Thinks my cat could have withdrawn from everyone because the only touch he wants is that of his true mate. It's a possibility, but I feel as if it's more than that." He paused. "Is your snake on board with our decision?"

"Yeah. She likes how you treat me, so she likes *you*."

He felt his mouth kick up slightly. "I bet you never thought you'd say the latter."

"As it happens, no, I didn't. She's considered killing you more than once in the past."

"I picked up on that when she kept launching herself at me."

"Just so you know … I can't promise that will stop."

He full-on smiled. "I'd have been surprised if you could." And he'd have accused her of bullshitting him if she had.

After they'd finished eating, they loaded the dishwasher and switched it on. She then turned to him and said, "I better get going. I need to change before I head out."

As had become the norm since the morning after the "car incident," he and Isaiah would be following Bailey and her girls to the center in a separate car. Tate had ordered that the females have an escort to *and* from the center for the foreseeable future. As an added precaution, the trio had agreed to switch up their routines by changing their hours and using different routes.

Deke cupped her hip. "What time do you finish work?"

She rested her hands on his chest. "Noon. I'm only pulling a short shift today."

"Meet me for lunch at the deli, then."

"Why?"

He felt his eyelid twitch. "Because I'm asking you to."

"Why?"

"Because I just am."

"Oh. Okay."

Jesus, she'd never be anything close to easy, would she?

"What time?"

"Twelve-thirty."

She gave a curt nod. "Got it."

Pulling her flush against him, he dipped his head to hers and dragged her scent into his lungs. He skimmed his lips over a spot near her pulse. "Tonight, when I have you beneath me, I'm going to bite you right here." She was his to mark now.

"I might bite back."

He met her gaze. "You're welcome to."

"Your cat won't get mad?"

"Do you care if he would?"

"Nah, just curious."

He couldn't stop his mouth from twitching. "The last thing he'll be if you mark me is mad."

"Oh. Okay." She smacked a hard kiss on his lips. "Gotta go."

He gave her hip a little squeeze. "I'll be at your door in twenty. Be ready. And don't forget we're meeting for lunch."

Backing up, she pointed at him. "One-thirty, right?"

Quite aware she was screwing with him, he narrowed his eyes. "*Twelve*-thirty."

Her brows slid together. "I don't think that's what you—"

"Don't even."

Snickering, she walked off.

Bumping her shoulder into Bailey's, Aspen grinned like the smug little shit she was. "*Told* you this would happen."

"No, you didn't." With an airy sniff, Bailey moved her attention to the people skating around the rec center's gymnasium.

"Uh, *excuse me*, I said I believed that Deke wouldn't walk away after the touch-hunger was gone," crowed Aspen. "You called me moronic."

"Well, you are," Bailey told her.

Havana snorted, shaking her head.

"And," began Bailey still not looking the bearcat's way, "you didn't say you *believed* he wouldn't walk, Aspen. You said you weren't so sure he would."

The bearcat frowned. "Same thing."

"Nope, not really."

A huff from the bearcat. "You're picking at words. The point is, I predicted this. And I was right. You don't listen to me often enough. Why is that?"

"You bore me."

Aspen gave her a playful shove. "Bitch."

"Heifer," Bailey sassed, no heat in the word. She winced as a skater crashed into the wall near the retractable bleachers. *Ow.* They admirably managed to stay on their feet.

Skating sessions were surprisingly popular. Three rec center workers often supervised. This morning, it was her and her girls.

Shifters of all ages were skating around the gym—some confidently and expertly, others nervously holding onto each other or the cinder block wall.

Everything echoed in the gym—the voices talking and laughing, the music playing on the stereo system, and the sliding of the roller skates along the shiny wooden floors.

Havana squeezed Bailey's shoulder. "Personally, I am thrilled that you and Deke decided to give things a go. Livy will be on cloud nine when she finds out. I'm sure she'll also take credit for you two getting together."

"It wouldn't surprise me," Bailey mumbled.

The devil nudged her. "So, you happy?"

"About what?"

Havana sighed. "I mean, in general."

"Oh. Yeah."

"Good. I want that for you."

Bailey felt her brow furrow. "I'm always happy."

"You're always *lively.* Always smiling and nattering and laughing. That's not the same as being happy, when you feel all light and warm inside. I *knew* he'd be good for you."

Bailey raised a cautioning hand. "Don't get too excited. We didn't take each other as mates or anything. We're just gonna let nature take its course and see where we end up."

"Yes, but you *could* end up mated."

Aspen nodded, still grinning.

Bailey felt her nose wrinkle. "I don't know about that. I mean, everyone knows he hopes to find his predestined mate. I don't believe for one moment that it's me."

"Just because he hopes to find her doesn't mean he won't be open to imprinting on someone else instead," said Havana.

"Let's not get ahead of ourselves," Bailey told her, not quite as optimistic as her girls. Okay, it was more that she was *afraid* to be so optimistic. "Besides, did all three of us not once agree that it would be best if my mate isn't overbearing, controlling, and overprotective—all things that can be applied to Deke?"

"He does indeed have those traits," Havana allowed. "But it hasn't worked against you so far, has it?"

"We kept things light and easy, though," Bailey pointed out. "That's not going to apply as of today."

"Yeah, he likely didn't unleash the full force of his personality on you," Havana mused. "Now that you're taking things up a notch, he'll push and be bossy and try to fix all your problems because, hello, he's a dominant male shifter. You're capable of pushing back. You'll handle him just fine."

Aspen dipped her chin. "You've been handling him perfectly fine since the day you guys first met, haven't you?"

"I guess." Bailey watched as a skater landed hard on the floor a few feet away. She would have headed over to check on him, but the laughing juvenile scraped himself off the floor and hurried after his chuckling friends.

"You truly didn't think Deke would want more, did you?" It wasn't a question from Havana. It was a confident statement.

"No. As it happens, I didn't think *I'd* want more either. Truthfully, I don't want to want more. Things are simpler when I don't have other people's wants and needs to think about." Bailey then didn't have to worry she'd let them down or that they'd get sick of her. "But then he went and told me that he wouldn't change me even if he could, the asshole."

Havana smiled. "Oh, how dare he say something sweet."

"I know!" The dude was unbelievable.

Chuckling, Aspen slung an arm over Bailey's shoulders. "Did you throw something at him for saying something so nice to you?"

"No." But she should have.

"Ah, my girl is growing up." Aspen sighed, happy. "I was starting to think you'd be stuck in the Peter Pan stage forever."

Bailey frowned. "Is he the fox shifter we used to work with?"

"No, you donut. *Peter Pan*," the bearcat repeated, as if that would clear everything up. "The boy who could fly and lived in Neverland."

"Where's that? Don't think I've been there."

Aspen rolled her eyes. "Of course you haven't. It's a fictional place."

"How can someone live in a fictional place? And how the hell does he fly? Is he a bird shifter?"

"No, *he* is fictional too."

"Oh. That doesn't explain how he flies."

"He has—you know what, it doesn't matter." Aspen lowered her arm.

"Let's get back to the subject of Deke. You haven't told us how he is in bed yet."

Bailey pursed her lips. "Well … he doesn't snore or hog the covers. I count those as wins."

"Don't play stupid."

"But it's one of my favorite games."

"I've noticed."

"Then you're just mean for asking me not to play it." Bailey folded her arms. "My contentment should matter to you."

Aspen tipped her head to the side. "And yet …"

Havana shook her head, fighting a smile. "If it wasn't for me, you two would have murdered each other by now."

It was in fact highly probable.

Once their shift was over, they headed outside to the parking lot and made their way to the new car that had been assigned to Bailey. Like the last one, it belonged to the pride. Two enforcers, JP and Joaquin, waited in another vehicle parked nearby. The enforcers followed them until Bailey pulled up outside the Alpha pair's house, at which point the males went their own way.

Once Havana was safely inside her home, Bailey parked in the lot outside her apartment building. She and Aspen then parted. The bearcat made a beeline for their complex while Bailey headed to the deli to meet Deke.

Glad she'd slipped on a thick coat today, since it was pretty chilly, Bailey stuffed her hands in her pockets as she walked along the busy street. It was loud as usual. Horns beeped. Engines rumbled. Voices murmured. Footsteps slapped the pavement.

But it wasn't all the noise that made her snake coil herself to spring. It was the sight of Therese casually heading in her direction. The pallas cat had made an enemy of both Bailey and her snake after all the recent smack-talk she'd been doing.

Therese slowed to a stop in front of her, seeming awkward. "Hey."

"Yo." The word came out flat and unwelcoming, but Therese didn't let it faze her—she remained in place and flashed Bailey a nervous smile.

"How are you?" Therese asked.

"Good."

"I heard all about the crash." Therese absently prodded at the back of her golden braid. "Must have been scary."

"Why?"

Therese's bow mouth curved. "I probably should have known better than to think you were rattled by it."

"Hmm."

"Look, I'm sorry for talking crap about you." Regret glimmered in Therese's powder-blue eyes. "I don't truly believe you set out to seduce Deke so you could draw him away from Dayna for the heck of it."

Bailey flexed the fingers still tucked in her pockets. "Then why say it?"

"She's my best friend, just like Havana and Aspen are yours. You love them. It would hurt you to see them hurt, right? Dayna … she hardly ever cries, but she was sobbing her heart out and it killed me. I got pissed, and I handled it wrong." Therese sighed, distress lined into her oval face. "I'm sorry. Really."

Maybe, but Bailey couldn't say she was moved by the apology. Someone else might have nonetheless stiffly accepted it and got along with their day. She'd never pretended to be a forgiving creature, though. She wasn't going to start now.

And yes, part of the reason she wasn't feeling inclined to let Therese's behavior go was that Bailey wasn't the only person she'd talked crap about. "You need to throw a few sorries Deke's way. You made out like he cheated on her."

Therese raised a gloved finger. "I never said cheated, I said betrayed. He *did* betray her to an extent, Bailey. Wouldn't you have felt that way in her shoes if he marked another female?"

"In her shoes, I either wouldn't have been in Australia, or I wouldn't have been holding him to a vow I'd stopped sticking to by failing to come home when I said I would."

Therese grimaced. "I know her staying away makes it seem like she doesn't truly care about him. But she does, Bailey. He means so much to her. He really does." The blonde gave Bailey a serious look. "And she means a lot to him."

"As a friend, maybe." Though Bailey hadn't really gotten that impression from him, or from others in the pride. The case seemed to be that Dayna had been a lifelong friend of his, but not what you would call a treasured one.

"Friend?" Therese echoed, a pinch of astonishment in her tone. "Come on, you *have* to see that the reason he marked you was to get her attention and jumpstart her into coming back here."

Bailey blinked, mentally rocking back on her heels. What the fuck? "Nope, that's not how I see it." No one who truly knew him would. "Deke doesn't operate that way. He's—"

"A guy who does what it takes to get a job done," Therese finished, firm. Her eyes narrowed. "What I'm wondering is if you're in on it; if you agreed to him marking you so he could get a reaction from Dayna that would spur her into leaving Australia."

"His marking me had nothing to do with her," Bailey maintained, sure. Her snake was in full agreement—the mamba found the other female's claim ludicrous.

"I'm not buying that."

"I don't care if you do or you don't." It was no skin off her nose.

"I see that." Therese chewed on the inside of her cheek. "Let's say I believe that you played no part in his plan to make Dayna come home. I'd have to ask you why you'd share the bed of a guy who'll toss you aside if she ever shows."

Once more taken aback, Bailey rapidly blinked. Therese had to be joking. It wasn't like he hadn't been clear to one and all that he wasn't holding a candle for Dayna. "You can't honestly believe he'd do that."

"I'm shocked that you don't," Therese retorted. "He stuck to his vow for over two and a half years. You don't do that for someone unless you love them."

"He stuck to it for a long time, yes. But then he pulled away. You don't do *that* if you *do* love someone."

The blonde gave her head a small shake. "He wouldn't choose you over her."

"No?" Bailey took a step toward her, giving an aloof shrug. "Seems to me like he already has."

The corners of Therese's mouth tightened. "All I can say is … brace yourself, Bailey. I like you. I'll get no pleasure out of seeing you hurt. And by staying with him, you'll be taking a risk that won't pay off if she returns."

"I guess we'll see, won't we?" Bailey skirted around her and continued on to the deli, wondering if maybe the blonde's motive had been to make Bailey doubt Deke—perhaps at Dayna's prompting, or perhaps to strike out at Bailey to avenge an oblivious Dayna. Why else say positively idiotic stuff?

Over two and a half years *was* a long time to hold yourself to a promise, granted. And Bailey did believe that he cared for Dayna, just as Therese claimed. But love Dayna? Be open to taking the woman back? No, that didn't ring true.

He'd spoken of her many times to Bailey. There'd never been a sense of longing in his voice. His eyes had never dulled with the sadness of a lost opportunity or any such crap. On the contrary, he seemed at peace with the situation.

Maybe Bailey was only seeing what she wanted to see, only believing what she wanted to believe, but she didn't think so. Particularly since her serpent was of the same opinion as her.

Bailey would be genuinely surprised if Deke ever expressed any interest in reconciling with Dayna. She'd be equally surprised if the woman ever showed up, given she'd been gone so long and wasn't exactly his biggest fan these days.

Nearing the deli, Bailey noticed him sitting at the eating counter near the front window. He tipped his chin her way, and she flicked her hand up in a brief wave before then pushing open the door. She walked in and was immediately swarmed by the scents of cold meats, yeast, and spices.

It was right then that Cassandra stopped beside him, a tray in hand. Smiling, the woman boldly took a seat beside his and began chatting away to him.

Bailey felt her lips press into a thin line. She agreed with the general consensus—Cassandra had a little thing for Deke but didn't want anything permanent with him. That she wouldn't try to steal him out from under Bailey didn't make it any less irritating that Cassandra took any opportunity to talk with him. Or that the woman had settled at his side without waiting for an invitation, taking it for granted that he'd welcome her company.

Going by the look on his face, he *didn't* welcome her company right then. Not that that placated Bailey's mamba—the snake wanted to snap her teeth at both him and the female who coveted him.

Unable to hear what the female pallas cat was saying—it was loud with the music playing, the chatter of customers, and the orders being called out—Bailey began making her way to Deke, the soles of her faux fur-lined thermal boots scuffing the hardwood floor.

His gaze focused on her with each step she took, those perceptive eyes missing nothing as they swept over her face. His brow furrowed as she came to stand beside him. "What's wrong?"

She blew out a breath. "The world would be a nicer place if the only annoying person in it was me."

Cassandra smiled up at her. "Hey, Bailey."

It was hard to stop her upper lip from quivering, but Bailey managed it. "Yo." Flicking a look at the woman's tray, she asked, "Is that bubble tea?"

"It is," Cassandra replied. "They just started selling them here. I can't say whether or not they're good, because I haven't tried it yet."

Deke arched a brow at Bailey. "You ready to go order?"

Bailey shrugged off her coat. "More than. I'm starving."

Her eyes widening, Cassandra glanced from him to Bailey. "Oh, you … you two have a lunch date?" Her mouth curved into a lopsided grin. "Well, that sure is new." The leather-padded cushion creaked slightly as she slipped off the chrome stool. "I'm sorry, Bailey, I didn't realize you were meeting him here or I'd have sat somewhere else."

Deke drummed his fingers on the counter. "I'd say you're welcome to stay and eat with us."

"But I'm not," guessed Cassandra, still grinning.

"No, you're not," he confirmed.

The female pallas cat laughed.

"I mean that in the nicest possible way," he added.

"I know you do." Her shoulders shaking with silent laughter, Cassandra grabbed her tray. "You two enjoy your lunch." With that, she made her way to an empty table.

Deke stood and turned his full attention to Bailey. "So, who annoyed you? Tell me. I'll fix it."

Slinging her coat over the back of the stool, Bailey smiled. "Well, ain't you cute." Her snake thought he was plain adorable for thinking either she or Bailey would step aside to allow him to handle their problems. They *loved* handling problems.

He snorted. "Where's my kiss, anyway?"

"I don't know. Where did you last see it?"

He looked close to rolling his eyes. Instead, he took a step toward her and crooked his finger. She closed the tiny distance between them and let their mouths meet in a brief kiss that made him hum. Her belly predictably did a lot of idiotic flipping and twisting.

"Come on, let's go grab some grub," she said.

His hand splayed on her back, they walked to the deli's counter. As they joined the line of customers, Bailey strained to glance through the expansive glass case at the display of cured meats, condiments, and sandwich fixings. There was also a selection of bread and baguettes, and cellophane-wrapped desserts such as cookies. People could also order soup, sides, drinks, nachos, and potato chips.

He slid his hand up her back to rest between her shoulder blades. "Who annoyed you?" he asked again, the persistent bastard.

She swatted at the air. "Just Therese. I bumped into her on the way here. She apologized for all the petty smack talk. Then she claimed you marked me to provoke Dayna into hauling ass back to the US, and she wanted to know if I was in on it."

His brows snapped together. "What? That's pure bull. You know that, right?"

"I do. And I told her that."

Seeming satisfied that Bailey meant it, he nodded. "I'll have a little chat with her."

"You won't need to seek her out to say your piece," Bailey told him as they inched forward with the moving line. "I got the feeling she means to make her apologies to you soon as well."

He grunted. "On a more important note, did you talk to the others at the center and ask if anyone has seen Ginny like I asked?"

"I did. No one has a clue where she is." Most only came into contact with her at the center anyway, and Ginny was now barred.

"Enforcers will keep watching her place."

The problem was that Ginny likely knew that, which might explain why there had been no sign of activity so far. Surely the woman would have to come home eventually, though. She probably thought that Bailey's Alphas would call off the enforcers if she just gave them time. And what an incorrect assumption *that* was.

"As soon as she's back from wherever she's gone, we'll know," said Deke as the line once more moved forward. "The enforcers will nab her and take her to the Alphas."

And then Ginny would be none-too-gently questioned. Both Bailey and her mamba were looking forward to it.

Once Bailey and Deke had finally stacked their meals and drinks on a tray, they returned to the stools they'd claimed near the front window.

Deke unfolded the wax paper to reveal his baguette. "So," he began, pinning his gaze on Bailey, "tell me how you became a loner."

She blinked, stilling with her drink halfway to her mouth. "That came out of nowhere."

He shrugged. "Neither of us are into small talk, and there are a lot of things I want to know about you. Starting with this." He bit into his baguette and stared at her expectantly.

Bailey inwardly sighed. This wasn't a subject she much cared to touch. At all. Ever.

But … she'd have to tell him sooner or later, wouldn't she? Because they had no chance of building anything if she held back from him. "Okay." Her snake curled up, displeased. The serpent didn't like venturing down memory lane.

Bailey sucked a gulp of bubble tea through her straw and arched her brows at how good the Thai Milk concoction tasted. "So … the Umber Nest is basically made up of a bunch of people who don't care what's legal and what's not. My parents were pretty much a non-murderous, Bonnie-and-Clyde pair." She set her drink down on the counter. "Whereas most couples in our nest took their kids on jobs to teach them skills, mine felt that I cramped their style. I was often dumped with different people in the nest."

Deke's eyelids dropped, and his jaw tightened. "Dumped?"

"Yup." Exhaling heavily, she unwrapped her baguette. "The last time my parents left me to go on a job, they didn't come back." At first, she hadn't been worried. They'd often gone off to Vegas for the weekend to "celebrate" after completing a job—and they'd blown most of their "earnings" while doing so. "I later heard the job went wrong and they were killed by the people they'd targeted."

The aggravation in his expression gave way to sympathy. "Shit. I'm sorry, baby."

"Really, it had only been a matter of time—they were reckless as hell." She took a bite of her baguette, unable to truly appreciate the tastes of beef, mayo, onions, peppers, and crusty bread due to the topic of conversation. "Anyway … there's an iron-clad rule in my old nest. You can do as much illegal shit as you like. But if you fuck up and get caught, you and your children—who are sometimes targeted in place of their parents—will be banished to protect the nest from dealing with retaliation for the crime committed. So I was taken to Corbin, and the rest is history."

Deke's face reddened. "Fuckers," he spit out. "They should have been helping you work through the grief of losing your parents, not tossing you away to protect their own asses."

"Corbin and my girls helped me work through my grief. To be honest, my parents' death didn't hit me as hard as what it might have if we'd been a normal family. I wasn't close to them. Never had been."

"Why?"

"They loved me, but I was an after-thought to them. They were, like, *super* tight. Too wrapped up in each other to make emotional room for anyone else. So I got passed around from person to person. Like I was a pet that they needed others to watch over while they went off to do this or that."

Anger flared through Deke's gut and rushed through his cat. "Basically, they had no issues treating you like you were an inconvenience, even though they knew it had to hurt you."

Chewing on her food, she inclined her head in confirmation.

He couldn't imagine such a scenario. He'd grown up with loving parents who'd never once made him doubt how important he was to them. He and his siblings had been their priority. Bailey? She hadn't been anyone's priority but her own. That made his throat ache.

She licked along her lower lip to swipe away the dab of mayo there. "At one point, I stopped caring that they didn't want me around. *I* didn't want *them* around. And I did my best to piss them off when they were there." She took another bite of her baguette. "I was pushing them away, I guess. But they pushed first."

Jesus, no wonder she made no attempt to bond with people. She'd never really had bonds growing up. She'd been passed around like a fucking parcel, no one asking to keep her with them; no one insisting her parents step up. Emotional isolation was what she knew. Anything beyond that and she was out of her comfort zone.

"I truly do think I was better off with Corbin," she said, her brow briefly pinching in annoyance as an onion slipped out of her baguette. "I don't wish the nest hadn't banished me."

He heard the ring of truth there, knew she meant it. "But what they did had to have hurt all the same." They'd effectively abandoned her.

"It stung, sure, but I was used to being dumped on other people, so it probably didn't affect me as deeply as it would have other kids. Really, I don't wish they'd kept me with them. And while I obviously regret that my parents are dead, I'd be lying if I said their loss shaped me. You can't lose what you never had. They were there, but they weren't parents."

Their deaths might not have shaped her, but their failure to parent her had played a huge part in making her the person she was today. A person who didn't form attachments. A person who didn't expect people to care for her. A person who'd look shocked as all shit when a guy told her that he wouldn't change her.

As far as he was concerned, her parents were assholes, but that wasn't something she needed to hear. "I'm glad you had Corbin, your girls, and Camden."

"So am I." She set down her baguette and grabbed her drink again. "Now let's talk about something else. Something fun and not boring."

Knowing it had been difficult for her to open up and appreciating that she had, he didn't push her to keep going. If she needed a change of subject, he'd give it to her. "Like what?"

"Your cock."

He sighed, figuring he should have expected she'd say something along those lines. He leaned toward her and lowered his voice as he said, "We can talk about what I intend to do to you with it later."

She grinned. "I'm *always* up for these conversations. Do tell."

CHAPTER FIFTEEN

Breathing in the scents of greenery, tree bark, and stagnant pond water the next day, Bailey glanced around. Any human who stepped out onto the complex's communal yard would no doubt be horrified by the state of it. The grass was overgrown and weedy. The bushes were thick and untamed. Leaves and wood fragments floated on the surface of the pond.

More, the clusters of tall trees were covered in moss and territorial claw marks. And the rockeries were nothing like the decorative ones often seen in backyards; they were messy and chaotic. But this place was a pallas cat's playground.

They might not claim territory like most breeds of shifter, but they needed space for their animals to run. Bailey herself often let her snake loose here to explore and relax. She wouldn't be doing that today, though. Because she didn't quite trust that her serpent wouldn't end up fighting with Deke's cat.

Yes, he intended to give the animal a little freedom. Since the feline had recently developed the habit of picking fights with his pride mates, the other shifters who'd been playing in the garden had already left. His cat still had no interest in interacting with others … which was why Bailey disagreed with Deke's current theory.

Turning to him, she said, "I don't see how this could possibly be a good idea."

"My cat won't hurt you." Deke jiggled his head, adding, "Unless you come too close."

"That right there is the problem. I'm apt to push the broody little shit."

"He resents being called that."

"Doesn't make it untrue." She sighed. "Are you sure you don't want me to head inside?"

"I'm positive." He whipped off his tee, baring all that likable taut skin stretched over hard muscle. "As much as he might not want physical contact with you, he does like having you close; he considers you his. Which you are." Deke's gaze dipped to the wickedly visible brand on the column of her throat.

He'd marked her a few times the previous night. Her inner thigh and the crook of her neck both also now sported bites, but the one on her throat was the deepest. He'd wanted no one to miss that she was taken, he'd explained.

Possessive ass.

Not that she could talk. The brand she'd left on his jaw was far from subtle. Well, she believed in tit for tat.

Deke quickly shed the rest of his clothes and dumped them on the ground. "Try not to piss him off." He shifted in a smooth, fast movement.

As if to properly settle into his form, the cat shook his thick, gray, white-tipped fur. A small, stout ball of fluff. That was what he looked like. And super cute with his grumpy expression and little tufty ears that had small patches of creamy white fur.

She loved the snow-leopard-type spots that dotted his forehead. They were as dark as the stripes on his cheeks and the rings on his bushy, black-tipped tail.

His amber eyes landed on her; their pupils round, not vertical. There was nothing welcoming in that gaze. It said, *Stay the hell back, I'm not in the mood.*

She smiled. "Hey, cranky pants."

He flashed a fang.

"You realize you only prove my point when you snarl, right?"

He let out a rumbly, somewhat haughty sound and then padded away.

She watched him explore the yard. He ran through the tall, wild grass. Took time to mark trees and rocks. Pawed the edges of the pond.

At no point did he play. Intent on changing that, she picked up a couple of little stones that sat near a rockery. Aiming for a spot on the ground near the cat, she threw a stone. It hit home, startling the feline, who predictably hissed at her.

She gave an innocent shrug. "What?" She threw another stone—again, not *at* him, just close to him.

He let out a *super* loud growl that would have chilled a lesser female.

"I ain't afraid of an itty, bitty thing like you."

Rumbling yet another growl, he stalked toward her.

"Yeah, come on, show me what you got."

Nearing her, he swiped out a paw, but his claws were sheathed. It was a clear warning to leave him be.

Instead, she fished the ball of string she'd brought from her pocket and then sat on the ground, spreading her legs wide. Unwinding the ball, she tossed the string at his feet.

He glared down at it, sniffing.

She began wiggling the string and then dragged it toward her just a few inches.

He lunged, slamming his paw on the string.

She tugged on it again, swiping it out from beneath his paw, and slowly pulled it toward her once more.

Like before, he pounced on it.

Smiling, she did it again. And again. On and on it went, until he was between her legs, rolling on the ground as he bit at the string he'd managed to grip with his claws.

She kept on lightly tugging at it just to keep him focused on it. Which was likely why he didn't react when he soon after rolled so close to her that his back crashed into her leg. Rather than freaking out over the physical contact, he stayed like that for long minutes, chewing on the string. The whole time, her snake sulked that she couldn't join in the fun.

Eventually, he got bored and jumped to his feet. Though he fired a moody look her way, he didn't snarl. And then bones were snapping and popping as he shifted.

Mirroring her position, Deke pulled her onto his lap so she straddled him. Swiping her hair away from her face, he lightly touched his nose to hers. "You got him to play."

"I wanted to channel his aggression into something positive."

His gaze lowered to the abandoned string. "You planned it out."

"Yep. I didn't tell you, because then *he* would have known about it. Did you notice he didn't get all snarly about the physical contact? Him resting back against my leg was only minor, sure, but I'd still call it progress."

"It was progress." Deke slid his arms around her. "He's currently lazing in my head, more relaxed than he's been in a while. Thank you for that."

"No thanks needed. My motives aren't entirely selfish." She paused. "Ever."

His mouth curled. "So this wasn't simply about helping my cat?"

"No. See, my snake wants to tussle with him. But I don't see that going well. She has it in her head that he won't harm her, but I don't want to take that chance. She'd bite him without hesitation if he so much as scratched her. Then he'd be in pain for hours. We can't risk it. So I'm also helping him for her sake, too."

"I appreciate it, whatever your motives." He gave her a quick kiss. "Gotta get dressed. It's fucking freezing out here."

She stood, allowing him to rise to his feet. He dragged on his clothes fast, and she couldn't blame him. It was seriously nippy. Her ass felt chilled after sitting on the cold ground.

He closed his hand around hers and led her toward the door.

Her brow creased in surprise. "I never took you for a hand-holder."

He gave a careless shrug. "You're so easily distracted I can't be sure you won't wander off. This way, I know you're with me."

"Oh, this is a form of supervision?"

"Pretty much, yeah." Stifling a smile at her unimpressed huff, Deke opened the door wide and then pulled her inside. He wouldn't admit it, but he liked taking possession of her hand; liked that he had the right to.

As they reached the elevator, he went to press the "up" button. It wasn't necessary. The doors slid open with a *ping*.

His mother stepped out and full-on grinned at the sight of him and Bailey. "Well hello, you two." Her eyes dropped to their joined hands, and her grin widened. "Don't you look cute together."

Deke grunted, seriously fed up of the smug looks Livy kept gifting him. In her view, *she* was the reason he and Bailey were now together. Yeah. Because baked goods totally seduced women.

Livy pointed at them. "Don't forget you're coming for dinner tonight. I'm making pot roast."

"I'll bring your dish with me," Bailey told her. "That Devil's Food cake was *to die for*, by the way."

Deke frowned at his mother. "You're still taking her food?"

Livy shot him an arch look. "Is that a problem?"

He felt his mouth tighten. "You don't need to anymore."

"Why, does she no longer eat?"

Bailey snorted.

Sighing, Deke shook his head. The two women were impossible.

Livy waved. "See you later on."

As he tugged Bailey into the elevator, she said, "I really like your mom."

He'd noticed. "She likes you, in case you didn't guess."

"It was hard not to pick up on that." Bailey hit the button for their floor. "We're still going to the Tavern tonight, right?"

They'd made plans to meet the Alphas, Betas, Aspen, and Camden there. Hauling her close, he buried his face in her neck and nipped at her pulse. "I'd much rather we spent the evening alone at my place."

"What, for a change? Because we *never* do that."

He gave her earlobe a punishing bite. "Snarky little shit, aren't you?"

"Among many other things. Don't you just feel endowed with good luck now that you have me in your life?"

Deke smiled. "Something like that."

Leaning against the wall a few feet from one of the Tavern's pool tables, Deke had to fight a grin. Alex wasn't someone who tended to amuse people. He spent most of his time scowling and growling and generally being antisocial. But as he fisted the pool cue tight while glaring at a smiling

Bailey, Deke couldn't help but want to laugh. "I think that's the first time I've ever seen you lose."

The wolverine cast him a dark look.

Sitting on a stool near a high-top table, Bree smirked. "He's gonna sulk about it all night. Watch."

Alex frowned at his mate. "I'm a dominant male shifter. We don't sulk."

"Oh, what a lie." Bree winced and put a hand to her swollen belly. "Ow. This kid is strong. They kick like a champ."

Alex placed his hand over hers, his expression softening in a way Deke had never before seen with the tough-as-fuck male.

"Do you have the nursery ready yet?" Blair asked the soon-to-be parents, leaning back into her mate, who had his arms curled around her.

"Oh, yeah," replied Bree. "Everything's ready. Except me. I'm still adjusting to the fact that I'm pregnant."

A mask of concern slipped over Alex's face. "Want to go home?"

The female omega's brow furrowed. "No."

Alex let his hand slip from her belly. "You shouldn't exhaust yourself."

"There's really nothing tiring about sitting here watching other people play pool." Bree dug into her purse and pulled out a pack of beef jerky. "Here. Stop bothering me."

Bailey tapped the end of the pool cue on the floor. "So, who's next?"

"Me," declared Luke, disentangling himself from his mate. "But I'm not playing against you."

"Why?" asked Bailey. "Because you know you'll lose."

"Yes," he readily admitted, taking the cue from her.

On a chair beside Camden, Tate chuckled at his brother. "At least you're honest."

Just then, Havana and Aspen—who'd taken a quick trip to the restroom—reappeared.

"I don't know," Aspen said to the Alpha female. "Probably my favorite book, a luxury tent, and a bottle of pink gin."

"What?" Bailey asked them.

"We're talking about what three things we'd want to have with us if we got stuck on an island," explained Havana. "I said a kettle, a fishing net, and a lighter. What would you want?"

Bailey looked at her as if the answer were obvious. "A helicopter, an aerial map, and some snacks for the journey home." Her forehead creased. "Why would you want to stay on the island?"

Aspen's lips thinned. "We wouldn't *want* to stay, it's—Ugh, you're spoiling the game."

"You call this a game?" Bailey shot them a disappointed look. "You guys are sad."

Something that suspiciously sounded like a chuckle came out of Camden.

Aspen rounded on her mate, narrowing her eyes. "Did you just laugh?"

The tiger shifter cleared his throat. "No."

Deke idly stroked a hand down Bailey's hair. "Wouldn't you also need a pilot to get off the island?"

She shook her head. "Nope, I wouldn't need help."

He felt his brows knit. "You can fly a helicopter?"

She shrugged. "It isn't that hard."

Uh, yeah, it was. But so were most of the things she could do. They really did need to talk about where she'd learned those skills.

Crossing to the mamba, Blair gently nudged her. "How's your snake handling being branded?"

"She doesn't mind, since he wears *my* mark with pride," Bailey replied.

"He really does." Blair lifted her shoulders. "And why wouldn't he? You're awesome."

Bailey smiled, delighted. "I know, right?"

The Beta female laughed.

Hungry, Deke cupped his mamba's hip and said, "I'm gonna go order some food. You want anything?"

Bailey joined her hands. "Hmm, barbeque chicken wings would go down nicely."

"Ooh, they sound good," said Blair, her eyes lighting up. "Same for me, please."

Deke gave the bush dog a nod and then refocused on Bailey. "Did you hear that?"

His mamba frowned and looked around. "What?"

"Blair said 'please.'"

"Uh … yes, she did."

"And it didn't hurt her to be polite, did it?"

Bailey studied her. "No, she seems fine." The mamba then stared at him, her expression one of blank incomprehension. "Is there a point to this conversation?"

He sighed. "Forget it."

"Already forgotten. I got bored fast."

Feeling his mouth twitch, Deke shook his head. "I'll be back in a few minutes. Behave while I'm gone."

"You say that like I stir shit for a living."

"You do."

She gave a small shrug. "It keeps me entertained. Isn't that what's important?"

"No." Deke gave her ass a quick tap and then began to make his way to the bar. He exchanged hellos or tips of the chin as he shrugged through the crowds and skirted tables. The Tavern was as busy as usual, and most patrons were members of his pride.

As he arrived at the bar, Gerard headed over and stiffly inclined his head. "What can I get you?" he asked, formal but without any of his usual suppressed hostility. Possibly because Deke no longer had any designs on the woman that Gerard never quite got over.

Deke placed his order and then paid with his debit card.

"I'll have one of the waitresses send the food over when it's done," Gerard told him.

"Appreciated." Deke turned to leave and almost crashed into Shay, who stood with Cassandra and Sam.

Shay's lips curved into a smug smirk. "Now that's a whopper of a brand on your jaw, Deke." Thrusting out his chest, he crossed his arms. "I knew you'd end up in Bailey's bed eventually. I just knew it."

Deke threw him a tired look. "Don't gloat, it doesn't suit you."

"Of course it does." Shay raised his shoulders. "And why would I not gloat?"

"Because it's a dick move."

"A dick move is lying to a close friend," Shay corrected. "You tried convincing me that you weren't into Bailey."

"It's not like you believed me."

"That's not the point. You hurt my feelings."

Deke almost crossed his eyes at the false wounded look on his friend's face. "No, I didn't. Stop being an ass." He shifted his attention to the other two pallas cats. Taking in how close Cassandra stood to Sam, Deke had to wonder … "Are you two on a date?"

She gave him a sheepish smile.

"I wore her down," Sam proudly declared.

Deke felt his mouth hitch up. "Man, I didn't doubt for a second that you wouldn't."

Cassandra slid the healer a mock look of exasperation. "You are somewhat persistent, I'll give you that. The thing is, Deke, I—" She cut off as her gaze flew to something behind him, and her lips parted in shock.

"What?" Deke spun. He almost did a double-take at the totally unexpected sight he found. He felt his jaw go hard as anger blazed through him. That same anger made his cat jump to his feet with a snarl. "You are shitting me."

A tremulous smile tugged at Dayna's lips. "Hey." She took tentative steps toward him, her eyes shining, and put a hand to her chest. "God, it's been too freaking long."

Conscious of the nearby conversations stuttering to a halt as people became aware of her presence, he asked, "What are you doing here?" The words came out toneless.

"It took me several days to get my ducks in a row, but I'm back." Her smile ramped up a little. "Back for good."

Unfuckingreal. He felt his nostrils flare. No, she didn't get to do this. She didn't get to reappear in his life now that he'd moved on.

Over two and a half years she'd been gone, and not once during that time had she appeared even for a mere visit, let alone to declare that she was home. No, it had taken for him to meet someone else before she felt motivated to return. *That* was why she was here. Not simply because he'd walked away and she wanted him back—no, if she'd cared for him that deeply she'd have done a lot of things differently—but because she felt replaced and didn't like it.

It stung. It did. They'd been good friends once. Friends didn't pull this shit.

If she had told him she'd met someone while in Australia, he would have accepted it. He would have wished her well and let her go. The last thing he would have done is turn up to mess with her head.

She licked her lips. "I'm sorry I took so long, I just … it wasn't easy to leave Evan."

"Dayna—"

"I know this has to be a bit of a shock. I thought about calling you, but I wanted to surprise you instead."

It was a surprise all right. Just not a good one.

"It's so great to see you again in person." She went to hug him.

"Don't," he bit out, his cat bristling at the idea that she'd *dare* touch him.

"You're still upset with me," she noted, her face falling. She squared her shoulders. "We have to talk, Deke."

Actually, no, they didn't. "We said all we needed to say during our last video call."

"That wasn't a real conversation. It went downhill fast. And that was my fault, I know. Things got a little heated. We said things we didn't mean—"

"*I* didn't. I meant everything I said to you."

"I'd imagine you did. Again, it was my fault. I was out of line. Being hurt was no excuse," she added, oh so reasonable and regretful.

It was fake, and he knew it. Knew her too well to buy the little act. She was saying what she thought would make him properly hear her out, nothing more.

"I know I have a lot to make up for—"

"Dayna, stop."

"—but I will, Deke. I will."

"Maybe you would. But it doesn't matter anymore." His cat let out a rumbly noise of agreement, done with the female in every sense.

She hitched in a breath. "Don't say that."

"I didn't back out of the vow because I was upset with you for suggesting it first. I didn't do it on impulse. The truth is I'd made the official decision to back out long before that. I simply hadn't want to tell you that at a time you were grieving."

Hurt flickered across her face. "You don't mean that."

"Why else would I say it?"

"To … I don't know." She flapped her arms, her lips pinched. "I can't understand why you would have wanted to back out before we argued."

"You can't? Seriously?" Was she being funny?

"I took longer than I said I would to come home, I know, but not because I don't care for you. You knew that. I told you over and over."

"You did. And it mattered once. Little by little, it mattered less and less. Until it didn't anymore."

Her expression soured. "You're saying your feelings for me just … faded over time?"

"Yeah. That's what I'm saying."

Giving her head a disbelieving shake, she took a fast step toward him. "I don't believe that. We can get back on track, Deke."

His cat sliced out his claws, annoyed that she wasn't listening. "That's not going to happen. I'm not interested in revisiting the past. It's over. Done."

Her eyes blazed. "*No, it isn't.*"

"I've moved on. You should do the same."

"Moved on?"

"Yeah." He angled his face so she could see the brand he wore.

Her jaw set into a hard line. "You and the snake shifter are all cozy now, is that it?" she sniped. "What happened to only fucking her while you worked off the touch-hunger?"

"That was how it started. It's not like that anymore. But even if it was, I still wouldn't want to start anything with you."

She gaped, her eyes pained. "How can you say that to me?" She balled up her hands. "You kept your promise for *years*—"

"And more fool me, Dayna."

She snapped her mouth shut, twin flags of red bleeding into her cheeks, her breathing picking up. "Where is she?" she demanded. "The bitch you're fucking?"

"Oh, that would be me," said a new voice.

Deke tensed. *Shit.*

CHAPTER SIXTEEN

So *this* was Dayna.

Bailey hadn't heard much of the conversation. She'd only come over to see what was causing people to gather near the bar. When she'd approached the crowd, she'd heard the unfamiliar female point out to Deke that he'd kept his promise for years, to which he'd replied: "*And more fool me, Dayna.*"

Surprise had slammed into Bailey, and her snake had done a double-take. The last thing they'd expected to find was his ex … whatever she was. Not quite a girlfriend, but more than a bed-buddy.

A hot ball of anger had swiftly formed in Bailey's gut. That the skank had turned up now, after staying away for so long, was full-on shitty. She hadn't come to him when he'd wanted her to; no, she'd come when he wanted someone else. She hadn't cared that this might hurt him, or that it was downright unfair to him.

Despite that Bailey had itched to step in and dish out some bitch slaps, she might have instead kept her mouth zipped and simply observed. But if Dayna felt like taking her on—and her demand to know Bailey's whereabouts said that was exactly what she had planned—Bailey was *all* for it. Her snake was eager to bury her fangs in the little skank.

The redhead's eyes flared as they dipped to the bite on Bailey's throat. Fresh and deep, it made a statement that the feline couldn't miss. Ha.

Well, it was hard to like this person for obvious reasons. More, knowing that the woman had kissed Deke, touched him, had him inside her, made icy blades of jealousy stab Bailey in the chest. The same emotion rubbed her snake's nerves raw.

Feeling like messing with the redhead, Bailey chose to play dumb. "Who are you?" she asked, keeping her tone bored.

Rigid, the feline pinned her with a fevered glare. "Who am I? I'm Dayna."

"Dayna ...?" Bailey prodded, letting her brows squish together.

A low, cat-like hiss slithered up the bitch's throat. "The woman whose man you marked," she spat.

"*Your* man?" Ensuring she appeared appropriately confused, Bailey looked at him. "Does this female have a claim to you?"

"No," he stated, his tone firm and unyielding.

Bailey slid her gaze back to the redhead. "Huh. I'm confused. Wait, are you the one who's been in New Zealand for years?"

Her face flushing, Dayna's fingers retracted like claws. "Australia. And yes, that's me. He and I made a commitment to each other."

"No, actually, you both committed to a promise," Bailey corrected. "A promise *you* broke when you didn't come back exactly when you swore you would."

"I'm here now. And I'm staying."

Bailey tipped her head to the side. "Funny how you only decided to do that *after* he branded someone else and told you he was done with you. Felt the need to come piss all over what you feel is your territory, did you? How cliché."

"Deke isn't *territory* to me. He's someone I care about."

"Maybe. But you're not really here for his sake. You're here because you can't stand that he's moved on—it's written all over you in bold letters. I sure hope you're not expecting me to step aside and let you have him. 'Cause yeah, I won't do that. He's mine now."

"Yours?" Dayna snorted and notched up her chin. "I think not. He might have marked you, but he hasn't been sharing your bed for long. I know him far better than you do—and not just in a biblical sense. We grew up together. We were friends for years before we were lovers. We have the kind of bond you can't begin to understand."

"If that's true, why is this happening right now?"

Dayna's head jerked slightly. "What?"

"If you care so much for him, this whole scene wouldn't be playing out, because you'd have let him go years ago so he could live his life. Instead, you held him to you all this time. That's pretty damn selfish whatever way you look at it."

The redhead's mouth flattened. "You know nothing."

"I know that there's no way you're back for good. It would have taken you a lot longer to get your affairs in order if you honestly meant to relocate here after a long stay in a whole other country among a whole other pride. You're here to win him back and convince him to move to Australia with you."

Dayna blanked her expression. "You're wrong."

"You'll swear that on your nephew's life?"

The feline hesitated, her eyes blazing. "You don't get to talk about my family."

"Just did. Might do it again."

"You're a mouthy little bitch, aren't you? I'm not understanding what he sees in you."

"I suck cock really well."

Dayna scowled as Aspen and Havana moved to stand a few feet away, both all smiley and casual.

Aspen waggled her fingers at Dayna in hello. "I'm just making sure I have a good view of Bailey wiping the floor with you." She gestured at them to ignore her, adding, "As you were."

Dayna returned her gaze to Bailey, a glint of dark amusement now dancing there. "They really think you have a shot against me? Oh, how precious."

Gerard rounded the bar fast. "Dayna, how about we go sit down," he proposed, crossing to her. "It's been a while since we've talked in person." He didn't look very surprised to see her, so maybe he'd known she was coming.

The redhead didn't even look his way. "Maybe later, Gerard. I need to deal with this slut first."

Bailey's snake whipped her tail as she hissed long and loud.

"Uh," began Therese, materializing beside Gerard, her eyes wide, "he's right, Dayna, you two should go catch up. I'll come along, we can all have a drink and—"

"Maybe later," Dayna repeated. "I'm busy here."

Deke cursed. "Dayna, take the out your friends are giving you and walk away. Whether you see it or not, they're trying to do you a favor. You'd be a fucking fool to take Bailey on, and they know it."

Bristling, the female pallas cat fired him a glare. "You should worry about her, not me."

Sighing, Deke gave a half-shrug. "Don't say I didn't warn you."

Dayna blinked. "You're not going to forbid me from touching her?"

"The last thing Bailey needs is for me to protect her," he replied. "And she'd ream my ass if I tried anyway."

Bailey cast him a smile, glad he wasn't pulling the dominant male overprotective routine. "You understand me so well."

Rolling her shoulders, Dayna settled her gaze on Bailey again and took two confident steps toward her, leaving mere inches between them. "You have no claws, so I'll be fair and keep my own sheathed."

"That's pretty thoughtful of you," said Bailey, her voice dry. Her inner snake reared up, more than ready to take this bitch down.

"Not thoughtful. I simply don't need that extra edge. I've fought snake shifters before."

"But not me." Bailey snapped out her fist and connected hard with Dayna's face, shattering her cheekbone, making her head whip to the side.

Shocked into stillness, the feline stayed like that for long moments. Then, slowly bringing her hand to the injured side of her face, she righted her head to once more glower at Bailey.

With a snarl, Dayna made a grab for her hair.

Bailey threw up her arms, blocking Dayna's own, and then headbutted her. Hard.

Bone *cracked*. Dayna cried out. And the fight was officially on.

For Deke, there was nothing easy about hanging back while his woman went head-to-head with another shifter. The fight was *not* pretty. Both females had abandoned technique in favor of fighting dirty and catty.

Fists flew. Palms slapped. Feet kicked. Teeth bit. Nails dragged across skin. Hair was fisted and yanked.

Even as he stood tense as a goddamn bow, Deke couldn't help but join his cat in admiring how Bailey moved. She was fast. Fluid. Sinuous. As if her bones were malleable and bendy.

It made it hard for Dayna to both land and avoid blows, so his mamba quickly dominated the fight. And he had to admit, it gave him a surge of pride that clashed with the primal need to *take* that flowed through him. Yeah, he got off on watching her brawl.

Around them, the pride kept their distance, all looking on the verge of their proverbial seat. Many tried staying neutral, but others egged on whoever they were backing. Neither Havana, Aspen, Blair, Bree, or Elle made any bones about yelling at Bailey to "fuck that bitch up."

Even Camden shouted an occasional—and somewhat sadistic—piece of encouragement, such as "Punch her in the tit, Bailey! Right in the tit!"

The mamba didn't need to be told twice. She did as advised and then delivered a harsh punch to her opponent's jaw.

Staggering backwards, Dayna spat out a glob of bloody spit that nearly landed on Therese's shoes. Panting, she then scowled at Bailey, her split upper lip curling, revealing a couple of blood-stained teeth. "Are cheap moves all you—"

"No smack talk, please, it bores me." Bailey went at her again.

He knew Dayna. Could read her well. So he spotted the slight gleam of uncertainty in her eyes that told him she was inwardly scrambling. A strong fighter, she wasn't used to being outclassed by her opponent. But Bailey was showing her up big time, and she wasn't even going full-throttle.

He'd seen his mamba fight before—not only in mere barfights, but in life-

or-death battles. She was a master at various combat techniques. She could very quickly disable a challenger without breaking much of a sweat.

But here and now, Bailey wasn't bringing out any fancy moves or aiming to end the fight. Nope. She was dragging it out, quite clearly enjoying herself.

Especially right at this moment, as she ragged an *actual* chunk of hair out of Dayna's head. Hair she then shoved into the mouth Dayna opened in a cry of pain.

His cat bared his teeth in approval of his female's viciousness, but he didn't like that she was wounded. A bruise was forming beneath one eye, and she had a wicked cut above one brow. There was also a crimson stain on a patch of her hairline, and a matching stain on her top from when Dayna had very briefly unsheathed her claws in a rage after Bailey tore out her earring.

Her wounds had *nothing* on Dayna's. The feline honestly looked like she'd gone a couple of rounds with a feral alley-cat. Vicious scratches crisscrossed over her face, including over the eyelid that was swelling courtesy of her broken cheekbone.

Her nose was also broken, as was a rib or two—he'd heard the distinctive *cracks*; watched members of the crowd flinch while others grinned. Her mouth was almost grotesquely swollen, and her hair looked like a bird's nest.

She was also tiring and breathing hard. It had to be sheer pride that kept her from backing down. Both Gerard and Therese were yelling at her to concede the fight, but she was ignoring them.

Sweat beading her forehead, Dayna sliced out her claws again.

Bailey snorted. "Thought you didn't need the 'extra edge.'" She bent backward, avoiding the clawed hand that swung at her. But she wasn't able to avoid the kick to her knee. If she'd been standing straight, she might have done no more than wobble. But due to her position, the kick knocked her flat on her ass.

Bailey didn't jump to her feet as he'd expected. She crouched, planted her palms on the floor, twisted her hips, and swiped out a leg … taking Dayna's own legs out from under her in a smooth, superfast move that the pallas cat stood no chance of evading.

Bailey snatched Dayna's stiletto off her foot and rammed the heel right into the feline's thigh. Dayna all-out wailed in pain.

Deke winced. "Fucking Jesus. Wasn't expecting that."

Beside him, Tate grunted. "Your mamba always does something in a fight that I don't see coming."

Her jaw clenched, Dayna kicked out at Bailey with her other leg, making her rear backwards to avoid the spiked heel. Dayna then leaped to her feet. So did his mamba.

"Finish the little hoe bag, Bailey!" Aspen shouted. "Stop playing with her!"

His woman sighed at the bearcat. "You always want to spoil my fun."

Refocusing on Dayna, she twisted her mouth. "Another person would advise you not to fuck with them again. But me? I personally will welcome any future challenge from you. So keep 'em coming. They'll all end the same way, of course. You'll lose in a spectacular fashion. But it's the participation that counts, I think." She lunged, shifting in mere milliseconds.

Her snake dove between Dayna's legs, sprung up behind her, and coiled around the feline's body *super*fast—pinning her arms to her sides. The hissing mamba then bit into the unswollen side of Dayna's face.

Many of the crowd sucked in a breath while others chuckled. Deke exhaled a sigh of relief, glad it was over; tired of watching his woman take blow after blow.

A cursing Dayna stumbled around, striving to free herself from the serpent's hold—to absolutely no avail. Soon enough, her struggles weakened and her steps slowed.

Apparently satisfied that her foe was no longer a threat, the snake unwound her slim, gunmetal-colored body from Dayna as she slid down to the floor. Dayna dropped to her knees, swaying and mumbling as Gerard and Therese rushed to her side. The mamba paid them no attention; she slithered over to Deke and began to climb his body.

At one point, such a thing would have made him tense. Not now. She was his, just like Bailey.

Once she'd twined the lower half of her slender body around his arm, she settled the rest of her weight over his shoulder. Deke reached up and gave her coffin-shaped head a brief stroke.

"Aw, how cute," said Bree, her lips curled.

"You could have stopped it!" Gerard shouted at Tate, crouched beside Dayna. "You saw that Bailey was playing with her. You saw the extent of her wounds. You did nothing."

Tate frowned at him. "Interfering in a fight between shifters is simply not done—you know that. You wouldn't have wanted me to do it if Bailey was losing."

Gerard gestured at Dayna, who was now unconscious. "Look at her, she's a mess!"

Havana sighed. "She's also being healed by Helena as we speak. Don't be so dramatic."

Standing, he slammed his gaze on Deke. "This is *your* fault. All you had to do was give Dayna ten minutes of your time. Then there would have been no fight."

Bailey's snake hissed at the other male in warning—a move as protective as it was territorial.

Gerard froze, his mouth snapping shut. Well, no one wanted veins full of venom, did they?

Deke met the mamba's gaze. "You gonna shift back?" She flicked out her tongue and settled her head on his shoulder. "That's a no, I take it. Stay still while Sam heals you, then."

He thought she might ignore him, but though she watched the healer with her unblinking stare, she didn't make any aggressive moves when he rested his hand on the lower half of her body.

"She'll need to shift," said Luke. "You can't walk down the street with her like that."

True. But no amount of urging from anyone—or even orders from Tate—made the snake budge an inch, let alone subside.

Havana snickered, amused. "You might as well give up. She's in protective mode. She won't shift until she's sure Deke is in a place of safety."

"It's kind of sweet," said Aspen.

Luke rubbed at his nape. "Meet me in the back alley, D. I'll bring a car around and then drive you back to your complex."

Tate nodded. "We'll take care of this situation. Go. Get her out of here before she goes for Gerard's throat."

Happy to leave, Deke gave a curt nod and accepted Bailey's purse and balled-up clothes from Blair.

When he slid into a car a short time later, the mamba didn't alter her position, so he had to be careful not to hurt her with the seatbelt. It wasn't until he was in his apartment that she moved. Having slithered down to the floor, she shifted in a flash.

Standing a mere foot away, Bailey stared at him, her gaze inscrutable. "You mad at me for hurting her?" Her tone was carefully neutral.

"Not in the slightest." Tossing her purse and clothes on the sideboard near the front door, he drank in every naked inch of his female, feeling his dick stir. The patches of dried-blood that covered her now-healed wounds pissed him off even as they brought to the surface his earlier and very primitive need to *take* her. Because they reminded him of how magnificently she'd fought.

What fueled that oppressive need to be inside her was the memory of how she'd staunchly refused to stand aside for Dayna. Bailey had instead firmly stated her own claim to him—a claim she'd defended; *fought* for. That meant more to him than she could know.

And now he had to have her.

His hands aching to grab her, touch her, stamp his fingerprints on her, he lowered his zipper. "Come here."

Surprise bloomed in her eyes—a surprise that was quickly drowned out by the sexual heat that bled into them. A flush swept up her face. Her nipples peaked. Her breathing picked up.

The atmosphere between them quickly became thick. Hot. Electrically charged.

"Now, Bailey." He whipped off his tee. "I want in you." The words were guttural. Barely human.

She didn't make him wait. She launched herself at him. Literally.

He caught her, slamming his mouth on hers, licking his tongue inside. She curled her limbs tight around him as they feasted on each other. In no mood to go slow or gentle, he roughly spun and backed her against the front door. He swallowed the breath that gusted out of her as he closed his hand around her breast.

In the biting grip of a lust so carnal it burned, he ground his cock against her clit over and over. She dug her nails into his back, feeding him soft, greedy moans that fisted his shaft.

Feeling like he might explode with how desperately he needed to be deep in her body, he tore his mouth free. "This is going to be fast." He slid her upwards and sucked a nipple into his mouth, liking her sharp intake of breath. He released the taut bud with a flick of his tongue.

And dropped her on his dick.

A zap of dark pleasure shooting up her spine as his long, thick cock abruptly stuffed her full, Bailey felt her head fly back and hit the door. *Mother of all that was holy.*

His eyes liquid pools of raw lust, he held her thighs up and open as he drilled into her. Every heavy, upward roll of his hips tunneled his cock impossibly deep.

Tucking her face into the crook of his neck, she gripped his broad shoulders and pretty much hung on for the ride. And it was a *rough* ride. Unrestrained. Explosive. Heart-pounding.

Already she could feel her orgasm building—a gathering heat in the pit of her stomach that threatened to sweep outward and consume her at any moment.

Her senses were filled with him. With his warmth. His weight. His scent. His pounding thrusts. His grip so blatantly possessive she wondered how she could have worried that Dayna might sway him to choose her.

Even though he hadn't rushed to his unconscious ex's side, a part of Bailey had thought he might be mad at her for what she'd done. Because she hadn't merely defeated Dayna, she'd toyed with her. And the redhead had been part of his life since he was a kid—it would be normal for him to feel so protective of her that he'd be unhappy with Bailey for wounding her.

But he hadn't been angry. Hadn't admonished her. Hadn't even scowled at her. And now he was fucking her like need was a fever in his blood. His shaft chafed her clit again and again just as his sleek, hard chest rubbed at her taut nipples.

"Look at me, Bailey."

Drunk on feel-good chemicals, she lazily lifted her head.

"That's it," he said, staring at her intently. Hungrily. Possessively.

Feeling his cock throb and thicken, she knew his release was close. So was her own. It was a wonder she hadn't yet fractured.

He groaned. "Yeah, mark me."

It was only then, as a faint scent of blood drifted to her, that she realized she'd dug her nails deep enough into his skin to break it.

He stole her mouth with a hotly sexual kiss that went right to her core. A core that heated, spasmed, tightened. And then it contracted as wave after wave of almost unbearable pleasure engulfed her so intensely it trapped a scream in her lungs.

Deke's growl poured down her throat as he slammed harder, faster, deeper. He broke the kiss with a curse as he planted his cock deep and exploded, filling her with hot bursts.

As their orgasms subsided, he dropped his forehead to hers while they strived to catch their breath. Trembling, she said nothing, her mind blissfully empty.

Finally, Deke pulled away from the door and carried her to the bathroom. Only then did he withdraw his cock from her body. He cleaned her up, ignoring her offer to do it herself, and then perched her on the counter. Having grabbed and dampened another cloth, he began to clean the little streaks of dried-blood from her skin, gentle and thorough.

"It offends me that she blooded you," he said, his jaw hard. "If I hadn't known you'd be pissed at me for interfering, I'd have stopped the fight before it could start."

Bailey shrugged. "If it hadn't happened tonight, it would have happened some other time. You heard the way she talked. She considers me someone who stole you from her. She no doubt had every intention of confronting me at some point." Idiot.

He dumped the wet cloth in the hamper. "You're probably right about that."

"What exactly did she say to you before I made my way over? I didn't hear a lot." She felt her blood pressure go up as he relayed it all to her. Her snake slapped the floor with her tail, wishing she'd bit the woman twice. "Ballsy little skank, isn't she?"

He rubbed at the corner of his brow. "Maybe I should have expected her to do this. But considering she'd managed to go two and a half years without seeing me in person, I didn't think she'd turn up and declare she was here to stay and wanted us to be together."

"She shouldn't have bothered. You're mine."

His eyes gleamed with something soft and warm.

When he just stared at her for long seconds, she frowned. "What?"

"I like hearing you say it. That's what." Snatching her off the counter, he took her to the bedroom, where he then roughly dumped her on the bed with a teasing smile that made her chuckle.

"Do you think anyone knew that Dayna was coming?"

"She talks a lot to Gerard and Therese. Neither seemed shocked to see her, so I think they knew." He dug his cell out of his pocket and placed it on the nightstand. "Or, at least, they knew she might turn up sometime soon."

Bailey twirled her hair around her finger. "If Therese *did* know—or at least suspect that it might happen—it would explain the stuff she said to me yesterday about how you'd sling me aside if Dayna ever showed up."

He snorted and began shedding the rest of his clothes. "I suppose it's my own fault that they'd believe that. I stuck to my promise for too long." A long exhale left him as he lay beside her on the mattress. "She'll go back to Australia when it hits her that this was a waste of time."

"Don't be so sure," Bailey warned, leaning into him as exhaustion crept up on her. "I really don't see her letting go easily." The feline had declared before the entire pride that, in so many words, Deke would be hers. That she'd had no qualms about doing it so publicly meant she was quite confident that she could win him to her side—why else would she have risked being rebuffed in front of everyone?

"I made it clear that I've moved on."

"I don't think she believes that you truly have. I think she believes as Therese does—hell, it might have even been Dayna who first tossed out the theory. I think she believes you marked me to spur her into coming home."

His brows snapping together, he gently hauled her closer, his hold protective … as if to shield her from any hurt that that viewpoint might cause. "That's bullshit, baby—I made that clear to you yesterday."

"*I* know it's bullshit. But I think Dayna believes it's true."

He shook his head. "If she thought I'd only done it to get her attention, she wouldn't have been jealous when I confirmed via a video call that I'd marked you."

"Just because she was jealous doesn't mean she thought I meant anything to you. No female would ever be blasé about their sort-of-man branding another woman."

His gaze turning inward, he absently smoothed his warm hand up her thigh, over her hip, and up her side … only to then backtrack in yet another smooth glide. "You might be right that she didn't take it seriously. She seemed genuinely shocked just now when I told her I was truly done."

"Of course she was. You were slowly pulling away over time, but she didn't sense it. She had no idea you weren't in the same mental place as her. For Dayna, you backing out of the vow has come out of nowhere. She probably thought that her turning up here would be enough to change your mind; that you'd feel she'd proved you're important to her."

He sighed, put out. "She couldn't have just texted me and said she'd made arrangements to come home?"

"It wouldn't have had the same impact. Nor would turning up at your apartment to speak with you alone. She wanted to make a statement—not just to you, but to anyone who thought they could take her position in your life."

"She always was a little dramatic," he griped.

Snuggling into him, Bailey lazily skimmed her fingers through the small tufts of his hair. Her eyelids were going heavy, but she kept them open, wanting to finish their talk. "I don't believe she's here to stay."

"Neither do I. When you challenged her to swear on her nephew's life that her plan wasn't to lure me to her side and then talk me into going to the land down under with her, she evaded it."

"For her to come all this way, she must have been confident that her plan would pay off; that she's so important to you that you'd choose her over anyone else." Bailey's mouth thinned at the thought.

"She's wrong." He gave Bailey's hip a little squeeze and snared her gaze with his, silently insisting she heed him. "Even if there was no you, I wouldn't have been interested in starting something with her. But there is a you, and you're who I want."

"Understandable. I'd want me, too."

A slow smile curved his lips. "You were fucking magnificent earlier, all vicious and merciless. The way you move when you fight …" He nuzzled her, grazing her pulse with his teeth.

Bailey couldn't control her grin. "I knew you liked watching me fight."

"My cat likes it, too." Deke met her gaze again, tucking her hair behind her ear. "He approves of how fierce you are."

"Typical pallas cat." When he nipped at her jaw just because, she nipped him right back. "You really do like to bite, don't you?"

"Not usually. But you have very markable skin." He breezed his finger over the bite on her throat. "I like this one most of all."

As it happened, so did she.

Hearing his cell chime, he retrieved it from the nightstand and swiped his thumb over the screen. "It's a message from Tate. Havana wants to check that you're good—she apparently texted you a few times. Oh, and it turns out that Gerard scooped Dayna up off the floor and whisked her away after we left."

"Really?" asked Bailey with a yawn, watching as he rattled off a quick text, likely confirming that she was fine.

"He'll do his best to convince her that she's better off without me. I hope he succeeds."

"If he does, it won't be something that happens overnight."

"Maybe not." Deke placed his cell back on the nightstand and then moved back to Bailey, curving an arm around her. "But she won't approach me to declare her feelings again. Dayna is a proud creature. She won't come begging for scraps from my table. Particularly after I embarrassed her tonight by rejecting her so firmly in front of God and everyone—she wouldn't give me the satisfaction of thinking she's broken up over it."

"If she's really so proud, she won't scuttle away with her tail tucked between her legs either. She'll do something."

"Probably. She's not a bad person. Not even close. But if anyone lashes out at her ego, she has to lash back. She's always been that way."

"I'm just as big on revenge, so I get it." Bailey couldn't fight the yawn that cracked her jaw. "Damn, I'm wiped."

The set of his mouth softening, he dragged her closer and dropped a kiss on her nose. "Then sleep. We'll talk more tomorrow."

"'Kay." She let her eyes close. "Night."

"Night, baby. Sweet dreams."

CHAPTER SEVENTEEN

Even with the incessant drone of the roof's HVAC unit and the muted street sounds coming from below, Deke heard feet clambering up the exterior ladder. He knew it would be Isaiah, since the shifter was scheduled to take the next shift.

Most enforcers did surveillance duty. Usually from a low seat on the rooftops of the various pride-owned stores. None of the pedestrians below ever noticed them. Why would they bother looking up?

As Deke rose to his feet, the wind swept toward him, pulling at his clothes, rattling the deli's sonar panels, and showering him with the smell of car exhaust and the stomach-rumbling scents coming from the street's eateries. He hadn't eaten lunch yet, so he was damn hungry.

Finally, Isaiah reached the rooftop. He tipped his chin at Deke as he crossed to him, his shoes scuffing the concrete floor. "Anything worth noting?"

Deke shook his head. In particular, he'd kept a lookout for Ginny, who—according to the enforcer watching her apartment—still hadn't returned home. "All seems normal. The only bit of action was the Phoenix Alpha female, Taryn, arguing with her mate's grandmother outside the florist." He was pretty sure the old woman's name was Greta.

Isaiah's mouth curved. "Is it just me, or does the grandmother not seem to age?"

"Kye swears she'll outlive them all," he said, referring to the Phoenix Alpha pair's son.

"He's gonna have to leave his pack soon. He's too strong a born-alpha for his wolf to tolerate being ruled by another shifter for much longer, even if that shifter is his father."

Deke nodded. "I don't know if he'll definitely join our pride, though."

The problem with many breeds of shifter was that two alphas couldn't exist in the same group without fighting. Pallas cats didn't have that issue, so Tate and Havana had offered for Kye to join their pride so that he wouldn't be far from his family.

"There's a chance he could instead begin his own pack," Deke added.

Isaiah's brow pinched. "He's only, what, twenty-one?"

"Shifters younger than that have done it."

"True." Isaiah paused. "How's Bailey?"

"Good." Her fight with Dayna had been the talk of the pride for the past four days. His mamba had expected to receive the cold-shoulder from some, but none were iffy with her. All she'd done was answer a challenge—she'd had every right to do so. Yes, she'd been unnecessarily vicious, but no one was judging. Pallas cats didn't really *have* room to judge anyone for being so brutal.

Isaiah planted his feet. "Have you seen or heard anything from Dayna?"

"No. She hasn't reached out to me in any way. I didn't really expect her to. Her pride is hurt, and my mother threatened her with certain death if she didn't leave 'her boy' alone."

Isaiah chuckled. "Sounds like Livy."

"According to Tate, Dayna said that though she's upset that I rejected her, she'll accept and respect my decision." The Alphas had paid her an official visit a few days ago to welcome her home—a welcome which wasn't genuine from Havana, but she'd been civil. "Apparently, Gerard sat with her the whole time and held her hand."

"Gerard?"

"That's what Tate said."

Isaiah twisted his mouth. "It wouldn't surprise me if he's jumping on this opportunity to try and win her back."

"Maybe. Whatever the case, he's keeping her occupied. That suits me fine."

"I take it she hasn't given Bailey any more trouble."

"Wisely, no, she hasn't. Dayna claimed to our Alphas that she has no intention of challenging Bailey again because it would hurt me and also get in the way of me and Dayna ever being friends again one day."

Isaiah snorted. "She's just worried she'll get her ass kicked again."

Deke dipped his chin. "I think she's taking the high road to save face and hide that she's hurt." It was Bailey who'd put forward that theory, and he agreed with her. "All I care about is that she stays out of Bailey's way. So far, she has." It was made easier by how Dayna lived in the other pride-owned complex. Though the two females had caught sight of each other once or twice from afar, neither had made a move to cross the distance.

"She'd be a fool not to, because Bailey will just humiliate her all over again if Dayna pushes her buttons or starts another fight."

His mamba would—not merely because it wasn't in her nature to back down, but because she wouldn't hesitate to assert her claim to Deke. It soothed the jagged wound to his pride that Dayna had caused when she kept him dangling for two and a half fucking years, never making his importance to her clear.

"I'm sorry I missed the brawl," Isaiah added with a smile. "I've been repeatedly told it was highly entertaining."

That it had been. "Where were you anyway? Tate said he invited you to meet us at the Tavern that night but you made excuses not to come."

His smile fading, Isaiah licked his lips. "I was busy. Genuinely."

"Doing what?" His scalp prickling, Deke narrowed his eyes. "What's going on, Isaiah? Is it about Lucinda?"

Isaiah looked away at the mention of his true mate. Deke knew of shifters who'd recognized their mate at first sight. The enforcer in front of him was one of them. He'd spotted her from afar two years ago, but he hadn't approached her, because she'd been snuggled up against another male. Instead, Isaiah had learned everything he could about her.

Lucinda wasn't a shifter, she was human. She was also engaged to a man she'd been involved with for several years. As such, Isaiah had kept his distance and watched over her, no doubt hoping she'd separate from her human fiancé at some point.

"She's pregnant," Isaiah blurted out.

Deke went still. "What?"

"She was getting IVF treatment," said Isaiah, his voice like crushed rock. "It worked."

Deke felt his eyes close. Just as shifters couldn't produce offspring with someone who they hadn't claimed as their mate, humans who were the predestined mates of shifters could only reproduce with other humans through IVF. "Fuck, man, I'm sorry," he said, opening his eyes.

Isaiah scrubbed a hand down his face. "I'm done keeping tabs on her. I have to stop for my own sanity. At this point, I've accepted that I'll never have her." He pushed his shoulders back. "That's why I'm entering into an arranged mating."

Deke felt his lips part. "The fuck?"

"I signed up to FindYourMatch.com the night I declined Tate's invite to the Tavern."

Mentally rocked, Deke stared at him in silence. The website in question was run by shifters to help pair up any who sought to enter an arranged mating. Apparently, it was very popular and had led to many successful arrangements. "Wait, are you sure this is a good idea?"

"I've been considering it since Lucinda first started IVF treatment. I knew then, deep down, that I was never going to have her. But my cat held out hope. He's always felt she'd choose us over her human partner if only we'd tell her we exist. But I'd never barge into her life, break it to her that we're mates, and upturn her world like that. And I don't see her leaving her fiancé of five years to pursue something with me—a total stranger."

"And now that she's pregnant, your cat's hope is gone," Deke guessed.

Isaiah nodded, his throat bobbing. "He couldn't accept her now that she's carrying another man's child—he feels betrayed. But he's struggling to emotionally let her go."

"You think taking a mate would be the answer?" asked Deke without judgement.

"It was my dad who put the idea in my head. My parents entered into an arranged mating, as you know. He said the moment he branded my mother, his cat considered her under his protection and intellectually understood she belonged to him, though the animal didn't immediately immerse himself in the mating. The rest came with time."

"Your theory is that if you claim a woman, it'll make your cat officially let Lucinda go," Deke realized.

"Dating someone won't be enough—I've tried it, he doesn't acknowledge them. But if I claimed someone, it would force him to take notice of them, to engage with them, to cease dwelling on what he can't have. And it would fill the void in him that Lucinda can never fill."

And also fill that same void in Isaiah. "You don't worry he'd lose his shit and reject whoever you claim?"

"No. He might not emotionally accept the female as his mate in the beginning but, as my dad's cat did with my mother, he'd place her under his direct protection and feel territorial on an elemental level—there'll be no way for him to fight it if she's branded." He held Deke's gaze as he added, "I've put a whole lot of thought into this. It isn't a decision I made lightly or simply because I was hurting. I wouldn't consider it if I wasn't sure it would work out."

Fair enough. "If it's what you want, we'll all be behind you. What comes next?"

"I have to finish the process I began a few nights ago. There's a long-ass questionnaire to fill in. It's very detailed and covers everything—not merely basic stuff such as your likes and dislikes, but your bedroom habits, how many kids you want, your preferred parenting style—the list goes on and on." Isaiah rubbed the side of his neck. "It's not easy to be that open and honest, so it's not a questionnaire anyone can work through quickly. I'm almost done."

"And you can guarantee that all your information won't be shared?" Because if it was leaked to the shifter world, it could be used against him.

"Yes. Not even any potential matches will receive a copy of the completed questionnaire."

Knowing Isaiah wouldn't sound so positive unless he'd made certain of it, Deke moved onto his next question. "What will happen once you've completed it?"

"I'll submit it. The site will suggest possible matches for me based on my answers. I'm only allowed to choose one to contact. If after an exchange of messages we'd both like to meet, we'll do that. If we choose not to, I can reach out to any other possible matches." Isaiah inhaled deeply. "Hopefully there'll be at least one. You know as well as I do that not all shifters are fond of pallas cats. That might go against me."

It might indeed. "If you do find a possible match and the meet goes well, do you have the opportunity to date them for a while?"

"No, the founders of FindYourMatch are very clear that it's not a dating site, it exists only to help advocate arranged matings. As such, I wouldn't even meet with a potential match alone—both of us will have one of our Alphas present. I suppose it's to ensure that shifters aren't using the site to merely hook up. The female and I would have to decide there and then if we wanted to go forward with the mating."

In that case, the process was similar to when Alphas got together to make such arrangements for the purpose of securing alliances or other such things. "I must admit, I didn't expect this. But I can see why you'd choose this option. I hope it works out for you."

"So do I." Isaiah paused. "I don't visualize myself having any problems imprinting on someone. I've never been set on finding my true mate. Maybe because my parents are happy without theirs." He gave Deke a probing look. "What about you? Could you imprint on someone?"

"It isn't something I hoped to do. I wanted to find my true mate. But …"

"But Bailey is making you reconsider whether that's so important," Isaiah finished, the far too insightful asshole.

Yes. Deke couldn't imagine letting her go. Wasn't sure if he could. And, in truth, he didn't want to.

Not that he'd said as much to her. His mamba was skittish and guarded. He wasn't certain how she'd react.

Plus, there was the little problem that, in order for imprinting to happen, his cat would need to be on the same page as Deke. At the moment, the animal still had issues upon issues.

"She wasn't supposed to make me reconsider it," Deke grumbled.

Isaiah's lips twitched. "Bailey often does things she isn't supposed to."

"Very true."

They chatted for a few more minutes before Deke headed to the ladder that would take him to a narrow alley. He climbed down and then strode out of the alley and onto the street. Intent on grabbing lunch, he went to push open the deli door … but then Therese stepped out.

Instead of skirting around him, she remained in his path, cleared her throat, and gifted him a nervous smile. "Hi, Deke."

He only grunted.

She winced. "I know I'm probably not your favorite person right now, but could we talk?"

"If your intention is to pass on a message from Dayna—"

"It's not, I just wanted to give you a heads-up about something." She huddled a takeout bag close to her chest. "I thought you should know that she and Gerard are back together now."

The pair had moved fast. "Why did you think I needed to know?" It had zilch to do with Deke.

Her mouth bobbed open and closed. "I didn't want you to get sucker-punched with it."

"Nice of you." But the news wouldn't have had any impact on him no matter how he'd learned of it.

"Listen, I shouldn't have said the bitchy stuff I said when you and Dayna split. She was just so sad. A mess. I was mad on her behalf and … well, I'm sorry."

"Are you also sorry for trying to convince Bailey that I would set her aside for Dayna?"

She raised her shoulders. "I thought you would. I thought you loved Dayna."

"You thought wrong."

"Why would you have marked Bailey if it wasn't to get back at Dayna?"

His cat bared a fang at the note of demand in her question. "Well, that's none of your business now, is it?"

She sighed, her shoulders slumping. "I take it you don't accept my apology."

"It wasn't a real apology. You're not sorry for what you said. You're not warning me about Dayna and Gerard for my sake. She told you to pass on the news to me and report back how I reacted. Well, you can tell her that I genuinely wish her and Gerard the best."

Therese studied his face. "You really mean that? You're truly done with her?"

"Yes. Do us all a favor and get that across to her." He tipped his chin to the side, gesturing for her to move out of his way. Once she did, he stalked into the deli and joined the line.

In front of him, Luke and Blair turned their heads.

"Oh, hey," she said.

Luke's brow creased as he took in Deke's expression. "Who put that look on your face?"

"I'm just goddamn sick of people playing games," replied Deke, thrusting a hand through his hair. "Therese was sure to let me know that Dayna and

Gerard are once more an item—something Dayna undoubtedly put her up to."

"Ah," said Blair. "Sounds like she's hoping to make you jealous. I hope not, because it isn't fair to Gerard if she's using him and toying with his feelings."

Luke pursed his lips. "You never know, they could be serious about making another go of things. But I doubt it."

Blair's nose wrinkled. "I might have bought it if they weren't making such a claim literally *days* after Deke publicly proclaimed he was done with her. It doesn't seem genuine to me."

The doorbell pinged behind him and then … "Deke?"

He tensed, recognizing the voice. *Shit.* Very hesitantly, he turned to face Maisy.

She lifted a placatory hand. "I know, I know, you don't want to get to know me. That's fine, it's not why I'm here." She moved closer. "He called me again using another number. Deke Two, I mean."

The sense of urgency in her voice made Deke frown. "What happened?"

"He said he missed me and wanted us to meet," Maisy elaborated. "I don't want anything to do with him. But I was curious about who he really is, what he looked like, if he was young or old or whatever. So I agreed to meet him at a place of his choosing. But I didn't go inside. I looked through the café window and took a picture of the guy sitting at the table where he'd said he'd wait for me." She held up her phone. "Do you know him?"

Studying the photograph on the screen, Deke felt his face harden to stone. "Yeah," he bit out. "Yeah, I know him."

A short time later, Deke felt his muscles bunch as a knock came on his Alphas' front door. Luke briefly met his gaze before rising from the plush armchair and breezing out of the living room. Deke glanced at Tate, who stood in front of the fireplace; his stance dominant, tension rolling off him in waves.

After his conversation with Maisy, Deke and his Betas had headed straight to the Alpha pair's home to relay what they'd learned. Home alone, Tate had then summoned the pride member who Maisy had snapped a picture of … so it was no surprise to Deke when Luke reentered the room with Sam at his back.

The healer wore his default half-smile, his face and posture as open as usual. It was only when he took in the others' expressions that a line dented his brow. "Is everything okay?"

"Yes, fine," Tate told him, his voice carefully neutral. "We just need to speak to you about something. Have a seat."

"Okay." Sam gingerly perched himself on the opposite end of the sofa from Deke. "What's going on?"

Tate folded his arms, his body language relaxed rather than confrontational, but his sober gaze telling the healer he meant business. "Where were you yesterday at noon?"

Sam blinked. "Um, having lunch at a café about half an hour's drive from here," he easily replied. "Why?"

Tate's eyes narrowed slightly. "Were you alone?"

"Yes. I would have had Cassandra with me, but she was busy."

The Alpha cast Deke a *the floor is yours* look.

Deke turned to Sam. "I had a visitor today. Someone who says you were supposed to meet them at the café yesterday."

Sam frowned. "What?"

"According to them, you called them and requested that they be there," Deke added, watching him closely.

Sam's back snapped straight. "That's a load of crap. I wasn't there to see anyone. I always go to that particular café on Wednesdays, and I always eat alone."

Luke stirred in his armchair. "This is a routine thing for you?"

Sam nodded hard. "I go to visit my human aunt and then stop off at the café on my way home—she used to own it, so I like to go there." He swept his gaze over everyone in the room. "Who the hell is claiming I wanted to meet them?"

Deke dug his tongue into the tip of his canine tooth. "Remember how your name was used to create one of the fake profiles of me?"

"Yes," the healer replied. "Tate asked me about it. I told him that it wasn't me."

"This person contacted one of the women he'd been 'dating' while posing as me," Deke went on. "He asked her to meet him at noon the previous day at that café; told her he'd be sat at the corner table near the restrooms. She took a picture of him and brought it to me to see if I recognized him." Deke paused. "It was a photo of you."

Sam shook his head hard. "I was at the café, yes, but I did *not* arrange to meet her or anyone else."

"Do you always eat at that particular table?" Blair asked from where she was perched on the armrest of Luke's chair.

Sam gave a sheepish shrug, his cheeks going pink. "Yes. I used to sit there as a kid with my mom when we'd go there together, so I like to eat at that table." He cut his gaze back to Tate. "I *swear* to you, it was not me who contacted the human; I had nothing to do with the fake profiles." His eyes lit as he clicked his fingers. "Talk to Cassandra. I invited her to come with me yesterday morning, but she couldn't make it. If I'd planned to meet anyone else, I wouldn't have done that, would I?"

Tate bit the inside of his cheek, saying nothing for long moments, his eyes raking over the healer's face. "Thank you for answering our questions," he finally said. "You can go."

Sam blinked, seeming surprised that he'd been so easily dismissed. He slowly stood, swallowing hard, and then mumbled goodbyes before leaving.

Deke exhaled heavily, tossing an arm over the back of the sofa. "That went pretty much how I thought it would."

When he'd first spoken to Maisy, he'd been open to the idea that Sam could be their culprit. But the more he'd thought about it, the more his point of view had shifted. Because if there was one thing their boy had been very careful to do, it was mask his identity. It made no sense that he would suddenly be prepared to remove that mask.

Deke went on, "I wasn't sure how Sam could have been lured to the café, but I was pretty certain he was set up."

Blair gave a slow nod, her fingers absently doodling patterns on her mate's nape. "I can't see Sam being our guy. It seems to me that someone knew his routine and used it against him."

Tate unfolded his arms, a muscle in his jaw flexing. "The fucker is playing games again."

Luke idly drummed his fingers on Blair's thigh, saying, "He probably expected Maisy to barge in there and make a scene. Sam would have then reported it to us. The situation didn't unfold as our boy expected, but the end result was the same." He looked at Deke. "He got your attention."

Deke cricked his neck. "And I'm now supremely pissed off." Later that evening, that same anger flamed in Bailey's eyes when he brought her up to speed.

Straddling him on his sofa, she clamped her lips shut and shook her head. "I can't *believe* this motherfucker. Does he not have anything better to do with his life?"

Deke slid his hands up her thighs. "You would think he would, but apparently not."

"I cannot tell you how much I want to pound my fist into his balls. If he even has any. Goddamn coward hides behind his designated scapegoats." She clasped her hands together. "Can we peel off his nipples when we find him? Like, seriously?"

Sensing it was a genuine request, Deke couldn't stop his lips from curving despite his mood. She always managed to do that. Always managed to crack through the stubborn wall of his anger, no matter how black his mood. "I doubt anyone would try to stop you, even though our boy has got to be someone from the pride."

For his cat, that was the worst part. The betrayal slashed at him. If you couldn't trust pride, who could you trust?

Bailey let out a sigh. "Poor Maisy. He would have used her all over again. If she'd marched into that café and confronted Sam, only to realize she'd approached the wrong person yet again, she'd have been wrecked that our boy played her a second time."

Which he evidently didn't care about. "I don't get why he won't just stop. He could have left the matter alone. Could have quit while he was ahead. He didn't. I know he wants my attention, but why? What is he getting out of all this on a personal level?" Deke just couldn't see it.

"Questions for the ages. If he's so intent on being up here in your head"—she tapped his temple gently—"all I can think is that you must be up in *his*. If it was someone who had a thing for you, I really don't think they'd go about it this way, so it can only be someone who has beef with you." She sighed. "I don't know why people cling to grudges."

Deke did a slow blink. "*You* cling to grudges." Tighter than anyone he knew.

She waved that off, as if it wasn't relevant. "Well, I say we don't give him what he wants; that instead of thinking and talking about him, we focus on something else."

"I'm up for that."

"Groovy." She tipped her head to the side. "Whatever shall we talk about?"

He cupped her hips and tugged her closer. "You."

Her brows lifted. "Me?"

"There are lots of things I'd like to know about you."

"Hmm, like what?"

"Tell me where you learned how to hack and fight and build bombs and fly helicopters," he urged, but she went still, her expression closing over. "I don't know what it is you're hiding, but you can trust me, Bailey. I swear to Christ, you're safe with me; anything you share is safe with me." He gave her hips a gentle squeeze. "Let me in a little more, baby. I won't make you regret it."

CHAPTER EIGHTEEN

Uncertain, Bailey dug her teeth into her lower lip. Did she trust Deke? Yes. He'd never given her a reason why she couldn't. And it was well-known that he never broke his word. But this wasn't a simple secret, and it was instinct to clam up and say nothing.

Names of ex-members of the Movement were leaked from time to time. Every one of those people were then either hunted by extremists or tracked down by the human law authorities. Humans generally didn't interfere with shifter business, but extremists weren't shifters. They fell under a different law system, and so any shifters who wronged them were expected to pay for it.

As such, ex-members rarely shared their past occupation. Havana had told Tate, but they were mates—his loyalty was therefore primarily toward her. She didn't have to worry that he would ever betray her.

Luke was made aware of their past because she and her girls trusted that he'd hold his silence, even if only out of loyalty to his brother. Like Deke, he was a man of integrity. And just as she couldn't foresee the Beta ever breaking her confidence, she couldn't envision Deke doing it either—particularly not when it would endanger her.

Her gut told her she could trust Deke, and her snake agreed. Nonetheless, Bailey hesitated. Why? Because she doubted he'd believe her.

Not that she thought he underestimated her in the same way he once had. But she still wasn't certain he'd buy that she'd given eight years of her life to *any* cause, let alone one so noble. She wasn't certain he'd believe she had it in her. If anyone else displayed such incredulity, it wouldn't bother her. But with Deke, it would sting.

There was only one way to find out how he'd react, though, wasn't there?

Deciding to take the risk, she cautioned, "You can't tell a soul."

Clasping her hands, Deke gave her an earnest look. "I won't say a word to anyone. Whatever you tell me will remain between us."

Puffing out a breath, she sat up straighter. "We were members of the Movement once. Me, Havana, Aspen, and Camden." She held her breath, awaiting his response.

His brows arched slightly. "That sure answers a lot of questions. How did you become part of it?"

Bailey scrutinized his expression, surprised. There wasn't even a hint of skepticism there. "We were recruited," she replied, still not yet trusting that he was taking her seriously.

"Huh." He swiped his tongue along the inside of his lower lip. "I can see why you'd have caught the Movement's attention."

She felt her brows slide together. "You can?"

"You're strong. Fearless. Loyal. Sharp. You have your own mind but respect the chain of command. That you're also a loner without a mate would have ticked their boxes." His forehead creased when she stared at him. "What?"

Bailey shrugged. "I thought you might struggle to trust that I was telling the truth."

"Once upon a time, I'd have doubted you," he admitted. "I'd made too many incorrect assumptions about you. But now, yeah, now I can easily believe it. You're a person who'd commit to something you wholeheartedly believed in, especially if you thought it would make a difference to others." He squeezed her hands. "Thank you for your service."

Relief slipped through her bloodstream, and her snake's tension eased away. That had *not* gone as either of them had expected. Not that they had any complaints. "You really can't tell anyone. The only people in the pride who know are Tate and Luke."

"I told you, you can trust me."

"I know I can, or I wouldn't have shared it with you. But I also know that you're close to your family, who are all about being open with each other. I can imagine it would bother you to keep major secrets from them."

"Not if those secrets simply aren't their business or need to be kept private. I love my mother, but I'm not blind to the fact that she struggles to keep things to herself."

Bailey felt her mouth quirk. "She's awesome. You're lucky to have her."

His expression softened. "Yeah."

"What was it like to grow up in a family where you're the only dominant?"

"Fine, mostly." Releasing her hands, Deke skimmed his palms up her arms and settled them on her shoulders. "But you feel like you have to tone yourself down; keep the more intense parts of you dormant until you're around other dominants. Only then do you really let the full force of your personality stretch out."

"Did it make you feel like the odd one out?"

"Sometimes. But my parents knew that, so they did their best to counter it. Still, it didn't always work. I couldn't even have a real spat with my brothers over trivial things because at some point my level of dominance overwhelmed them; then they'd cringe and cower, which made me feel like a sack of shit. So I had to bite my tongue a lot and put a chokehold on my temper."

Bailey felt her lips part as realization dawned on her. "No wonder you don't bother with tact and have so little tolerance. You spent too long holding back words and crushing your emotions."

"I guess you reach a point where you're just done with toning down your responses."

"You sure never did it with me," she muttered, fisting the bottom of his tee.

"You didn't need me to. It was one of the reasons I was comfortable around you—though you probably wouldn't have guessed that. No matter what I said or did, you didn't get upset or cower or yell or anything. It was freeing. I could just be who I was around you. I think you get how that can mean something to a person."

She swallowed. "I get it."

Slipping his hands from her shoulders to the sides of her neck, he said, "Come here." He tugged her forward, and their mouths met in a slow, languorous kiss that made her toes curl. Pretty soon after, he used his fingers to shove her into an orgasm that had her toes curling all over again. She then rode him right there on the sofa, impaling herself on his cock over and over until they were both engulfed by a release that made their thoughts splinter.

Oblivion was a marvelous place.

Picking up yet another bat from the rec center's outdoor tennis court at closing time the following day, Bailey flicked Camden a look. "Anyway, I just wanted to let you know that I told him. If *you'd* shared our past history with someone, *I'd* want to be made aware of it." A cool breeze swept over her, ruffling her hair and gently shaking the wire fence separating the court from the parking lot adjacent to it.

Noticing that Camden was eyeing her closely, she frowned. "What?"

He shrugged. "I'm just surprised you told me. It's not often you put yourself in other people's shoes and imagine how they'd feel." He grabbed a tennis ball from the ground. "Your sense of empathy isn't exactly fully developed."

She shot him a sharp smile. "Hello, Mr. Pot. I'm Black Kettle. Nice to meet you."

"Hey, I ain't judging—I'm aware that I'm no better at empathizing. If it wasn't for Aspen, I'd probably do all kinds of cruel shit on a daily basis. She's pretty much my conscience; brings out what little good I have in me." He threw the ball in the container near the wall that held several others.

Bailey felt her nose wrinkle. "I don't think me and Deke bring out the good in each other."

"No, you bring out the good *and* the bad."

"You say that like it's a positive thing."

"Because it is."

"How?" It didn't *sound* positive.

"It means you bring out who he really is—no masks, no frills. He does the same for you."

Huh. "I never really thought of it like that."

Camden turned to fully face her. "Look, you once did me a favor. You pestered me to stop hesitating in telling Aspen what I felt. You opened my eyes, made me confront a few things, and gave me the push I needed. So now I'm going to do the same for you. I repay my debts—Aspen harps on that it's important." He rolled his eyes.

Bailey shoved the bat into the box with the others and then set her hands on her hips. "Okay."

"I know what it's like to be abandoned by the people who are supposed to protect you. It makes you pull inward. Makes you see bonds as a threat. You and me lucked out, though. We found people early on in our lives who taught us that not everyone will leave us."

She gave a slow nod. "Havana and Aspen saved us both." They'd essentially made her and Camden see that they didn't have to be perfect to make people stick around.

"For me, it was really just Aspen—I didn't listen to anyone else; didn't care what they thought. She stopped me from fully closing myself off to the world. But I still don't bother with outsiders unless she asks it of me. I've got the only person I really need. Her." He paused. "You're more willing to take chances on people than I am, but you don't really open up to them."

"I've opened up to Deke."

"Not all the way. You're still keeping a part of yourself locked away because you're not really expecting what's between you two to pan out in the long-run. You think you'll part ways at some point. Don't deny it—I know you too well not to sense where your head's at."

Bailey shifted from foot to foot. "It's not that I think we'll *definitely* part ways. I just don't fully trust that we won't. He wants to find his true mate. I don't believe that's me. Neither does my mamba."

"Honestly, I don't think you're his predestined mate either. But does that have to matter?"

Not to Bailey, however … "It will if he's intent on seeking her out. And I don't know if Deke, being as honorable as he is, would find it disloyal to imprint on someone instead of wait for his mate."

Pursing his lips, Camden briefly inclined his head. "I can see why that would play on your mind. He is far too noble—it must be tiring."

"I know, right?"

"But there's a chance he'll choose you instead. You want that. Want it badly enough that you'll easily get spooked if you get it, because—with the exception of Havana, Aspen, and yeah me to an extent—no one ever *chose* to keep you around."

She folded her arms, feeling vulnerable.

"What I'm trying to say is … If he does offer you what you want, *don't panic.* Think. Don't backtrack. Don't pull away. Don't immediately assume it won't work. Or ignore my advice and fuck it up—your life, your choice. But then you'll do what you said *I'd* do if I didn't push past my own issues: you'll spend the rest of your life wondering if you made the right decision." He jabbed her forehead with his finger. "Be smart."

"Does this mean you care if I'm happy?"

His brows pulled together. "Let's not get crazy."

She laughed. "You were just returning a favor."

"Right." He looked around the court, checking that no other equipment was lying around. "We're done."

Bailey nodded. "Let's go back inside and check—" There was a *whoosh* a mere millisecond before scalding heat blazed across her cheek, making her flinch. *Bullet.*

She and Camden dived to the side and then took cover behind the corner of the building, barely escaping the other bullets that near-silently whizzed by.

It took her military-trained mind a split second to work out where the shooter must be hiding. So when the fucker stopped firing and her enhanced hearing picked up the thudding of feet fading away, she darted out from behind the building and ran for the fence with Camden at her side. They scaled it fast, and then he shifted.

Ignoring the burning pain in her cheek, she followed the white tiger across the parking lot and into the small wooded area beyond it. Adrenaline pounded through her and kickstarted her heartbeat.

The big cat was far faster than her as they rocketed through the maze of trees, following the noise and scent—*human*, she sensed—of the shooter, so the tiger was soon out of her sight.

Her pulse leaped as she heard a guttural roar followed by a cry of *such pain* up ahead of her. Bailey tracked the sounds, skidding to a halt moments later. A male dressed in black lay flat on his front, claw marks spanning his back and tearing through cloth and skin, screaming as the tiger ragged him backwards with the jaws he'd clamped around the shooter's leg. Well, ow.

The male was desperately reaching toward the rifle on the ground mere inches away from him, but the tiger kept on hauling him back. The human twisted onto his side, pulling a handgun out of seemingly nowhere, and aimed it at the tiger.

Bailey was on him fast, snatching the firearm. As he stared up at her, his face a mask of sheer agony, she whacked his head hard with the butt of the gun. He slumped to the ground, his eyes closed.

Panting, she looked at the tiger. "You can let him go now." She wasn't entirely surprised when the big cat did no such thing. "We need to get him back to the center. It'll be faster if one of us carries him than if you're dragging him."

The tiger dropped the leg with a put-out snarl. Bones snapped and popped as his body shifted shape, and then a naked Camden stood there glaring down at the human. He fisted the fucker's torn sweater and, without a word, began none-too-gently hauling him toward the center. Bailey grabbed the rifle and then followed Camden.

When they stalked into Corbin's office soon after and dumped the human on the floor, Havana, Aspen, and Corbin sharply turned their way. They stiffened. Gaped. Spluttered. And then they jumped into action. Havana crossed to Bailey, Aspen went straight to her mate, and Corbin crouched down beside the human.

"What in the hell happened?" asked the Alpha female.

Rage a hum in her blood, Bailey replied, "To sum up … that asshole shot at me while I was in the tennis court, me and Camden sprinted after him, Camden's cat took him down, and then we brought him here after I knocked him unconscious with this." She held up the handgun, wanting to hit him with it all over again. Her snake was leaning more toward fucking his system up with her venom.

"Bastard," Corbin growled, searching the human's pockets. "No ID or phone. There's a set of car keys, though."

Camden flexed his fingers, his expression blank in a way that told Bailey he was *seething* inside. "I didn't see a vehicle," he clipped. "He must have parked it somewhere in or near the woods."

"I'll go see if I can find it," said Aspen, all business.

"I'll go with you." Camden shifted again and then preceded her as the pair prowled out of the office.

Pacing, her face flushed with anger, Havana looked at Bailey. "I'll call Tate." A deadly calmed laced her voice. "You should call Deke. He'll want to hear about this from you."

After setting down both the rifle and the handgun on Corbin's desk, Bailey took a long breath, doing her best to suck in her fury. She could lose her shit later, when they had the answers they needed. For now, she needed to adopt some of Havana's icy composure.

She also needed to do as Havana said and call Deke.

He answered the call after only a few rings. "Hey. I'm almost at the center. You ready to leave?"

She hadn't known he would be one of the enforcers who would follow her car home today. "Uh, I need you to not go AWOL."

A pause. "What happened?"

She scratched her uninjured cheek. "Well … someone might have shot at me while I was at the tennis court outside the rec center."

"*What?*"

"I said shot *at*, not shot," she quickly added. "Their aim was a load of my ass. Apart from a graze on my cheek, I have zero wounds."

"Not the fucking point, Bailey." There was a loud rumble in the background, like he'd slammed his foot on the pedal. "I'll be there within minutes. Did you see the shooter?"

"He was hiding in the woods, but me and Camden caught up to him and brought him to the center."

"You *pursued* someone who was armed?" he asked, the words jagged with a pissed-off snarl.

"Of course I did. *You* would have pursued him."

Another pause, and then Deke cursed. "Do you recognize him?"

"No. He has no ID on him. He's human—that's all I know for sure at this point." She frowned on hearing the screech of tires coming down the phone. "Don't drive too fast, we don't need you crashing."

"What I don't need is my woman having bullets fired at her."

That, too.

It wasn't long before he appeared in the office with Isaiah hot on his heels. His posture stiff, his muscles bunched with tension, Deke made a beeline for her. His jaw clenched tight, he cupped her neck so gently, his touch barely there, as he examined the graze on her cheek.

"It's healing fast," she told him. "It'll be gone within a few hours."

Hauling her close, he palmed the back of her head and wrapped his free hand around her nape. "Fuck, baby." He dragged in a breath, taking in her scent as if to reassure himself that she was alive.

Bailey swallowed, unused to anyone other than her girls giving that much of a crap about her safety. She smoothed her hands up his back. "I'm okay." It was an awkward attempt at comforting—she'd never been all that good at it.

"What do we know so far?" he asked no one in particular.

"His name is Richard Fleming," Aspen replied. "Me and Camden found his wallet in his car. I texted his details to River. He's digging for more info on our friend as we speak."

"I searched his phone," Camden added. "His text-conversations make it apparent that he's an extremist. He told a fellow extremist that he got a 'job' to give a lone shifter a scare. He wasn't given strict instructions on *how* to go about it; he was told to be creative. But instead, he planned to kill Bailey to impress the higher-ups in their faction."

Deke let out a low growl that rang with fury.

Aspen took up where her mate left off. "If he has the ID of who hired him, he didn't mention it to his buddy, only added that he'd met the guy at a bar. It's probably the same dude who hired the last extremist."

Scraping his hand over his nape, a visibly upset Corbin shook his head. "I know you might want to consider the jackals, but I don't see them associating with extremists. Gut them open like a fish, yes, but not giving them work."

Havana nodded, her temper barely controlled. "Ginny could have asked a friend or paid someone to hire an extremist for her. Unfortunately, we can't question her, because she's still nowhere to be found."

"No one here I've spoken to has seen or heard from her," said Corbin.

Isaiah piped up, "I don't even slightly suspect Jackson's brothers. They were terrified of us." He paused and looked around. "Is Tate not here yet?"

Havana rolled her shoulders. "He's on his way. He's bringing Luke, Blair, and Farrell with him."

Camden's phone chimed. He whipped out his cell and frowned down at the screen. "That was River. Our guy here is definitely an extremist and has quite a criminal record. Much like the last extremist we detained, he's seriously small fish. His faction doesn't officially exist—it's just a bunch of hateful humans who've banded together and commit petty acts."

Just then, Fleming stirred, squirming slightly.

Deke narrowed his eyes. "Someone's awake." He crossed to the human and rolled him onto his back.

Wicked fast, the male put a small vial to his mouth and knocked back the contents.

Deke frowned. "What the fuck?"

Everyone crowded around the human as he began coughing and groaning.

Bailey lifted the empty vial and sniffed it. She reared back. "Poison. He poisoned himself." She sneered, as furious as her snake with the little shit for taking such an "out." "Typical extremist behavior when they're captured. He must have kept it in a hidden pocket or something."

Deke fired questions at him, but the bastard ignored them and then started seizing. Within moments, Fleming was dead. "*Fuck*." Deke whirled around and thrust a hand through his hair.

Grinding her teeth, Bailey clasped the vial so tight it hurt. She would have thrown it at Fleming's goddamn face if it wasn't for the fact that he'd feel no pain.

Around her, the others went on a rant. Camden even kicked the body, his fists clenched. Bailey remained silent, the sour tang of rage in her mouth.

Tate, the Betas, and Farrell soon arrived. Needless to say they were all pissed that the human not only couldn't tell them anything but had escaped punishment.

His hands on his hips, Luke scowled down at Fleming. "Someone needs to get rid of both his body and his car."

Soothingly rubbing his mate's back, Tate gave a curt nod. "I need you, Blair, Farrell, and Isaiah to take care of it."

"Will do," Luke told him.

Blair looked at Tate. "Are you going to call the jackals again?"

Tate scraped a hand down his face. "I don't see any point. The conversation will go the same as the previous two did. And, honestly, I don't believe that they were behind this."

"Neither do I," said Corbin. "*One* scare to send a message, maybe. I could even accept that they might choose to do it twice just to make it clear that they mean business. But three is overkill, and I don't envision them having anything to do with extremists anyway."

"Plus, they'd know we'd take it as declaration of war if we were positive it was them," Tate continued. "So they'd surely hire a lone-shifter mercenary to get the job done and vanish in a flash, not hire small-time extremists who—given that their strength and speed is no match for ours—are more likely to get caught and overpowered."

"My money's on Ginny," said Blair. "If for no other reason than it's mighty suspicious that she's in the wind."

They all discussed it some more. Aside from Deke. He found it hard to think past the rage vibrating in his bones.

Finally, his jaw hurting from how tightly he'd clenched it, he exhaled heavily and turned to Bailey. "Let's get out of here." He and his cat wanted her away from this place; wanted her in their den where she'd be safe.

Her brow furrowed. "My car—"

"I'll have someone pick it up for you tomorrow. I need you with me, where I can see you."

She looked like she might argue, but then she sighed. "Okay."

The Alphas, Aspen, and Camden followed them in Tate's vehicle as they made their way home.

Her gaze on the window, Bailey said, "This isn't going to stop until we make it stop, is it? At first, I thought they might call it quits at some point, since their only intent is to scare me. Yet, they haven't stopped, even though they've surely got better stuff to spend their money on."

His grip tightening on the steering wheel, Deke said, "The reason they might not have stopped is that you *aren't* afraid. You're not on edge or hiding or even keeping a low profile. You carried on with your life as usual while also taking sensible precautions."

Bailey frowned, looking thoughtful. "Good point." She puffed out a long breath. "I'm not going to give them what they want and withdraw from the world, but I am going to stay away from the center until this is over. It's a special place for a lot of people. A place they need to feel safe. I won't put it or them at risk. I don't want the members to be afraid to go there."

Deke had already anticipated that she'd make such a decision. "From now on, consider me your personal bodyguard."

"How did I know you'd say that?" she muttered rhetorically, her voice dry.

"Because you know me. You know I protect those who matter to me. And you matter."

"It's still a little weird when you say nice things to me. Everything feels out of sync."

He might have smiled if he wasn't so pissed.

"You matter to me, too." She cleared her throat. "Just thought you should know."

His chest tightening, he gave her thigh a soft squeeze.

When they finally reached their complex, he guided her up to their floor and into his apartment. They hadn't been there more than ten minutes before his parents turned up.

The image of worry, Livy barged inside and went straight to Bailey. "I just heard what happened. You poor thing."

Noticing the casseroles she held, Deke frowned. "You brought her food again?"

Livy offered him a haughty look. "I'll bring her whatever I like." She then went back to fussing over his mamba.

His father chuckled. "Just let it be, son. She likes mothering your Bailey. I think she senses that the girl hasn't had a lot of that in her life." He eyed Deke. "How are you doing?"

"I'm ready to burn shit down," Deke told him.

Clarence laid a supportive hand on his shoulder. "You'll find out who did this soon enough. Until then, all you can do is try your best to keep her safe. But don't take on any blame for the danger dogging her heels. I know you dominant males have a tendency to shoulder unnecessary blame. It isn't your fault that you can't put a stop to what's happening—a man can't kill an enemy he can't see."

Deke grunted and then followed his mother and Bailey into the kitchen. Livy was still fussing, even though his mamba seemed completely unsure what to do about it. He glanced at Clarence as he noted, "Mom really does like Bailey."

"Initially, I think your mom infiltrated her life so she could push her toward you. But she's grown fond of Bailey. So have you."

Deke felt his lips thin. "I'm sure Mom crows about that every chance she gets."

Clarence smiled. "Oh, she does. You know how much she likes to be right."

Havana, Aspen, and their mates turned up shortly afterward. Both females seemed spooked and were clearly intent on checking on Bailey, who increasingly calmed as the hours went on.

Deke, however, couldn't find any such calm. He might be outwardly controlled, but he was a raging storm on the inside.

His feline was no more collected—not on the outside *or* the inside. The animal restlessly paced and hissed and occasionally swiped at the ground with his paw.

Since no one took Deke's hints to leave him and Bailey in peace, he eventually split the casseroles between everyone. His parents left shortly after they'd eaten, but Havana and Aspen would have lingered for a while longer if their mates hadn't pressured them to leave. Finally, after hugging Bailey tight, the females agreed to head home.

Not tired, his mamba declared that she was going to throw on a movie. As he didn't want her to be alone, he lay on the sofa with her as she watched it. He couldn't follow the plot, couldn't concentrate on the scenes playing out on the screen. Much like his cat, his mind was still hectic after what happened earlier. The occasional growl slipped out of Deke when he thought back to how the human had cowardly—

"Stop thinking about it," she admonished with a huff as she rolled over to face him.

He frowned. "How can I *not* think about the fact that someone is gunning for you?"

"Easy. You focus on something else. Want me to flash you my boobs?"

He delved his fingers into her hair as he remarked, "You're good at compartmentalizing things. If there's shit going down, you're able to mentally set it aside. Where does that come from?"

"Years of living a double life when I was part of the Movement, I guess. I've been shot at before, you know. I'm used to it."

"I don't see how there could be a way of getting used to having bullets fired at you like it's no biggie."

"You'd be surprised."

He curved the arm she lay on, so the back of her head was tucked into the crook of his elbow. "Do you miss it?"

"Being shot at?"

"No. Being a member of the Movement."

She hummed. "Sometimes. But I wouldn't work for the group again. I've been offered jobs on the sly, but I always turn them down. Don't tell Havana and Aspen about it—they don't know." A scowl took over her features. "You know, I share things with you that I don't even tell them. I can't tell you how much that vexes me."

He felt his lips hitch up. "You're cute when you get mad at yourself. You should be able to handle that you instinctively trust me with your secrets, though. I thought you were tough," he teased.

"I *am* tough. Now that anyone would believe it if they saw me right now. Look at us, cuddling on a sofa while confiding in each other. It's sickening."

He bit back a chuckle. Even his cat was amused, though he didn't cease pacing.

She poked Deke's chest. "I blame you. You dazzled me with your cock, and what should have been a short fling became *this.*"

He flicked her nose with his. "Would you go back and change anything if you could?"

"No," she all but grunted.

His mouth curved a little more. "Vexed about that, too, huh?"

"Must you get such joy out of my frustration? That doesn't seem normal to me."

"You get joy out of mine."

"And?"

He rolled his eyes. "Can we turn this movie off?"

"Why?"

"Because I want to take you to bed."

Her face scrunched up. "I'm not tired yet."

"You will be after I'm done fucking you raw."

Her pupils dilated. "You basically plan to fuck me to sleep?"

"Pretty much, yeah."

"I don't see that working."

"Challenge accepted." In a matter of moments, he was hefting her over his shoulder and carrying her to his bedroom. There, he did exactly as promised.

CHAPTER NINETEEN

The next morning, Bailey woke tucked up against Deke's back, her arm tossed over him, his fingers loosely curled around her hand. It was a rather abrupt awakening. Like a beeping alarm had pierced her dream.

She wanted to groan. It felt too early to be awake. Her thoughts were all sleep-cottony, and her body felt heavy and lethargic. Still, much as she felt tired, she didn't feel *sleepy*.

She sluggishly rolled over, scooted closer to the nightstand, and weakly lifted her cell phone. *7:11am.* Definitely too early, considering she wouldn't be going to work.

She chucked her phone back on the nightstand and then let herself flop onto her back. Deke stirred with a tired grunt and rolled onto his own back.

Why her snake was in a wonderful mood, she had no clue. Didn't even care. She needed more sleep, needed …

Her thoughts trailed off as she became aware of something. Something that made her pulse skitter and her mind clear *fast.*

Tensing, she slowly turned her head to look at Deke, only to see he was doing the same to her. They both stared at each other, shock parting their lips.

"Holy shit," she breathed, because she was wearing his scent … and he was wearing hers.

Imprinting. They were imprinting on each other.

She mentally scrambled, her brain short-circuiting for a moment. Her heart began working overtime in her chest as her fight or flight instinct kicked in. She wanted to jump from the bed. Dress. Leave. Take time and space to process.

Camden's words drifted to the forefront of her mind …

If he does offer you what you want, don't panic. *Think.*

Bailey took in a fortifying breath, telling herself to calm her tits, striving to think through the riot of emotions in her system. Deke might not have done as Camden spoke of and verbally offered her what she wanted, but … Deke being in a mental space that had sparked imprinting to begin was a definite indication that he was prepared to do it.

Right?

Right.

Or maybe not.

She wasn't sure. The imprinting process was too poorly understood. Just because they had the emotional potential to take things to a whole other level didn't necessarily mean it was what he wanted.

Don't backtrack. Don't pull away. Don't immediately assume it won't work.

She should probably be annoyed that Camden had pretty much predicted how she'd react in such a scenario.

Her snake was having no such crisis. The serpent was completely relaxed, utterly content with the situation and finding Bailey weird for doubting that Deke would commit to them.

Really, the only way Bailey would know where his head was if she outright asked him. She cleared her throat and positioned herself on her side. "Okay. So. What do we do?"

Rolling to face her, he studied her expression. "Scared?" The question was whisper-soft.

"A little," she admitted. "You want to find your true mate. You used to talk about it to people often."

"I didn't have *you* back then. Now I do."

Hope whipped to life in her stomach. "You're not upset about this?"

"Not even close." He palmed her face, breezing his thumb over her lower lip. "Baby, I'm not the flight risk here. That's you." He searched her eyes, his focus so intent. "Do you love me?"

She sucked in a long breath. "Uh … well … I mean, it's … I … Why are you smiling?"

"You love me," he asserted, confident.

"What?"

"If you didn't, you'd have just said no. That you're all flustered means you do but you're struggling to admit it." He lightly flicked her bottom lip with his thumb. "Will it help if I tell you I love you first?"

She swallowed so hard it was audible. "Maybe."

He nipped her chin. "I love the shit out of you, crazy though you make me. Now it's your turn."

Bailey nervously chewed on the inside of her cheek. "Iloveyou," she blurted.

His smile widened. "Now that we've gotten that out of the way, let's get back to the imprinting situation. What do you want to do?" he asked, throwing her own question back at her.

"Bite you really hard."

He chuckled even as his eyes heated. "In other words, I don't have to convince you not to fight this?"

"No, but your cat is another matter. Is he flipping his lid right now?"

Deke shook his head. "Tate was wrong in what he thought. My cat didn't withdraw because he was angry at not having his true mate."

"Then why?"

"He was pissed at himself, because he'd started to resent the people close to him. So many were mated and moving onto the next stage of their lives while he was alone. He was even mad at his true mate for eluding him, irrational as that may be. And … he was mad at you."

"Me?"

"He wanted you from the beginning, but you disregarded his strength and authority," Deke explained. "That changed recently, though. And you let me in. Started to trust me. You even played with him. Little by little, you made him feel less lonely, less bitter. More settled. Until he felt part of something; felt important to someone."

She swallowed. "My snake would get lonely sometimes. Then she'd haughtily decide she didn't need anybody. But the loneliness would trickle back in eventually, because all she'd really done was push it aside. You made it go away, and you earned her trust."

"So, to sum up, our animals are good with us imprinting. Also, *we're* good with it. Yes?"

"Yup."

Pure male satisfaction flooded Deke's body. That, and a healthy dose of relief. He'd worried his skittish little mamba would flap on realizing they were wearing each other's scent. He'd been braced for it, but she'd surprised him. His cat loved that he now wore her scent; was rolling around in it. "Then all that's left to do now is celebrate it."

Deke fisted her hair and brought his mouth crashing down on hers. He sank his tongue inside, seeking the taste of his mate. *His mate.* Their bond might not be alive and kicking yet, but she still belonged to him.

And she loved him.

It had been a hell of a shock upon waking to realize they were imprinting on each other, considering his cat's issues and Bailey's guardedness. But he hadn't been shaken in a negative way. A bone-deep satisfaction had poured through him like warm syrup, filling every crevice, settling in good and proper, and making him face that he loved the goddamn bones of the woman now moaning into his mouth.

He shuffled closer to her, his cock so hard it hurt. Everything primitive in him urged him to take her, dominate her, own her so completely she'd see no way out.

Still feasting on her mouth, he pushed her onto her back and then lowered his body over hers, giving her his weight. The level of skin-to-skin contact tantalized his nerve-endings. He brushed his dick over her clit, making her gasp into his mouth.

She shook her head, tearing her lips free. "Don't tease. Not now. Can't take it."

Neither could he. Nor did he have the patience for it. He needed to be in her. Right fucking there and then.

Deke hooked his hand behind her knee, hiked her leg up, and lined up the head of his cock with her entrance. He snared her gaze and held it tight. "Mine." He snapped his hips forward, ramming his dick as deep as it could go, groaning through his teeth as her fluttering inner muscles clasped him tight. "You're mine now, Bailey."

She curled her free leg around his waist and gripped a tuft of his hair, her eyes blazing into his. "And you're mine."

The possessiveness in her tone made his lungs burn. "Yeah, I fucking am." He rutted on her, unleashing the primal need to *take*; giving free reign to the carnal hunger that twisted his insides. "I won't let you go." Not for anyone, not even for his cat.

"Right back at you," she said, scratching at his shoulders.

He groaned at the sting. "Harder." He wanted her to break the skin. Mark him. And that was exactly what she did, causing the smell of his blood to blend with the drugging scent of her need.

Spitting out a curse, he quickened his thrusts, still slamming hard. Her pleasure-drunk gaze locked with his, completely unguarded, hiding nothing.

He licked at her pulse. "Once our bond snaps into place, I'm going to leave my claiming mark here." It was tempting to do it right then, but it wouldn't have been fair to her. Not when the bond wasn't yet complete.

That didn't mean he wasn't going to mark her at all.

Bailey jolted as sharp teeth sank into the spot beneath the hollow of her ear. That he'd bitten her again was enough to feed the unbearable ache in her pussy, but then he sucked hard, his clear intent to leave a bruise … and the territorial act made pleasure burst over her in giant waves that dragged a scream from her throat.

He groaned into her ear, ramming harder, his cock throbbing against her rippling inner muscles that clamped down on him. Moments later, he exploded.

For a short while, they lay there, panting and trembling. When she finally emerged from her post-orgasm daze, she stroked his back. "I'd have been sad to part with your cock, so I'm glad it won't come to that."

His lips curved against her neck. "I think I'm jealous that you're more emotionally attached to my dick than you are me."

"Well, it's a very nice appendage."

Bracing his weight on his elbows, he released the leg he'd hiked up and then met her gaze, his own all warm and lazy and dark.

"What?" she asked when he kept staring.

"Nothing. Just taking a good, long look at my mate."

She gave him a teasing smile. "I'm betting you would never have guessed the day we first met that you'd ever refer to me as your mate."

No, he wouldn't have. "You'd be lying if you said *you* saw it coming. I think maybe my mother might have believed it could happen, but that's it." He skimmed his nose along her jaw. "We'll stop by my parents' place later and tell them. They'll give us a lump of shit if they find out through the grapevine."

"We can visit them on our way to Havana and Tate's house. We're having a movie night there, remember?" Bailey always gathered with her girls on Halloween, which was one of her favorite days of the year. Now she had another reason to love it: It would be the anniversary of when she and Deke started imprinting.

Her lips thinned as she thought on how she just might come to loathe the day if they fucked this whole thing up somehow. "Disclaimer: if the bond doesn't progress or it regresses and breaks, I'm going to haunt you like a living poltergeist."

He did a slow blink. "I guess it's a good thing that it won't come to that."

"You sound very sure it won't."

"You and me … It wasn't an easy road for us to get here. Several things had the potential to knock us off this path, but we kept moving forward. That's not going to stop now. I'm all in. You're all in. Our animals are all in. Nothing's going to change that. So I'm not worried that the bond won't fully form. Neither should you be."

Funnily enough, she wasn't worried. Wasn't braced for it all to mess up. She simply wasn't prepared to take for granted that it wouldn't. She didn't like taking *anything* for granted, particularly not the people who mattered to her.

Bailey danced her fingers along his nape, both she and her snake content in the knowledge that he had no intention of fighting that he was theirs. Okay, so he wasn't theirs completely just yet—they needed the bond to solidify the whole thing. But they were mates all the same even now.

Bailey loosely hooked her thighs over his hips. "People are going to call you nuts, you know."

He tilted his head. "Why?"

"Because time and time again people have told me that if anyone claims me as their mate it'll mean they're out of their mind. I don't disagree."

"Oh, I don't doubt that I'm signing up for a lifetime of being psychologically toyed with. You wouldn't be you if you weren't testing my sanity. But I've told you before, I wouldn't have you any other way."

"Aw, that's sweet. No one would ever believe you say such nice stuff to me. They'd accuse me of bullshitting." She frowned. "They do that a lot."

"Because you lie a lot."

"Only when I'm bored. That doesn't count."

"It really does."

She huffed. "At least I don't build bombs anymore to keep me mentally occupied."

"You used to build bombs when you were bored?"

"I don't like having nothing to do. You know that."

"I'm curious, did members of the Movement ever regret teaching you that skill?"

"No. But some did lament that they'd passed on their secret to making a homemade lethal poison. Not that I used it on any of the members. They were simply scared I would, what with mambas being vehicles of vengeance."

Deke studied her for a long moment. "You're far more deadly than most people will ever assume, aren't you?"

"You say that with approval."

He dipped his face to hers. "I like deadly." He took her mouth, soft and slow … but the kiss quickly kicked up a notch, and soon enough he was fucking her like a savage all over again.

Life was a blessed, blessed thing.

Smiling at the cute little giggles coming from the nearby trick or treaters, Bailey rapped her knuckles on the Alphas' front door. All the children walking from house to house appeared to be members of the pride—it wasn't always easy to tell, since some wore masks.

Spotting Isaiah sitting on his own porch, Bailey gave him a quick wave. Chewing on what was most likely candy, he saluted her.

Havana swung open her front door and beamed at them. "Hey, guys. Come in, come in." She stepped aside, excitement pouring off her, and then closed the door behind them. "Movie is ready. Snacks are laid out. Candy bowls are full for the trick or treaters and …" She trailed off, her nostrils flaring—no doubt sensing that Bailey and Deke now wore each other's scent. Her eyes went wide. "Oh my freaking God! *Aspen!*"

Chewing on something, the bearcat walked out of the living room to join them in the hallway. "What, jeez?"

"Sniff up," urged Havana, her smile bright.

Aspen looked from her to Bailey to Deke. "If one of you has farted—"

"No farts," said the devil with an impatient flap of her hand. "Now sniff."

"You'd better not be lying to me." Aspen stepped closer and took a delicate sniff. Her eyes bulged. "*Oh.*" Then she was jumping up and down, her hands clasped in delight.

Bailey looked at Deke. "I'm not sure if they're happy for me or just pleased they'll have someone to help ensure I don't destroy the world."

He chuckled. "It might be a bit of both."

"What's going on?" asked Tate, coming down the stairs.

"Bailey and Deke are imprinting!" Havana replied.

The Alpha male's brows winged up. "Yeah? Congrats." He shook Deke's hand and gave Bailey a smile. "I'd like to say I saw it coming, but I wasn't sure how things would go. There's nothing predictable about any situation that involves Bailey."

She inclined her head, proudly conceding, "Too true."

Right then, the doorbell rang.

Since Bailey was closest to the door, she pulled it open. Two couples and four children stood on the porch. Only the kids were dressed up.

The "vampire" Dillon and the 'witch' Emilia were the twin children of Alex's sister, Mila, and her wolf-mate Dominic. The couple were part of the Phoenix Pack, as were the Betas with them, Jaime and Dante. Bailey hadn't before seen the "angel" or "grim reaper" standing behind the twins, but she was guessing that they were the Betas' offspring, given the resemblance.

"Trick or treat!" the little ones sang in chorus.

"Happy Halloween, kiddos," said Bailey.

Havana sidled up to her, a bowl of candy in her hand. "Don't you all look adorable!" She bent a little and held out the bowl, and the children pretty much descended on it.

Bailey and Havana exchanged brief greetings with the adults.

"How are you not a walking icicle?" Bailey asked Dante, who wore only a tee and jeans.

The huge hunk of a guy shrugged, replying, "It isn't that cold."

"Oh, it absolutely is," said Jaime, huddling in her coat. "But Popeye here never seems to feel it. I worry there's black magic at work."

Havana snorted. "How come you guys decided to come trick or treating around these parts?" she asked the wolves. "Not that you aren't welcome or anything."

It was Mila who explained, "Dillon's best friends with Bastien, and Emilia adores little Juliette, so they wanted to stay together. Since my monsters weren't prepared to skip trick or treating, we all came as a group."

Dominic plucked a piece of candy from his son's pumpkin bag, earning himself a very adult growl. "You gotta learn to share, boy."

"No, I don't." Dillon snatched it back and returned it to his bag.

Bastien, who'd pushed his way to the front, gazed up at Bailey. "You smell a bit like one of my pack mates, Savannah. She's a viper shifter. What are you?"

"A demon straight from the bowels of hell," she deadpanned.

Havana shot her a glare. "*Bailey*."

She lifted her shoulders. "What? People have said that to me."

Jaime laughed. "Bastien, get over here."

Juliette did a little curtsy. "Thank you!" Then she scrambled off the porch with the other kids.

All the adults said their goodbyes, and then Havana closed the door.

Turning, Bailey realized that the others were no longer in the hallway. She tracked their voices into the living room, finding Tate and Deke standing near the patio doors while Camden sat on an armchair with Aspen on his lap.

The tiger shifter looked up at Bailey. "I hear a congrats is in order."

After a few moments of silence, she asked, "Are you going to *say* congratulations?"

"Maybe later." He grunted when Aspen playfully socked his arm.

"Okay," began Havana, "someone needs to be on trick or treat duty."

"I'll do it," Bailey volunteered.

The devil sighed. "Someone other than Bailey."

Affronted, she frowned. "Why not me?"

"When unsupervised, you scare the kids and then eat the candy they would have taken."

"It'll otherwise go to waste."

Aspen lifted a hand. "I'll do candy duty."

Havana smiled at her. "Thank you."

"What are we watching?" asked Deke, striding across the room.

"First, *Hocus Pocus*," Havana told him. "We have to watch it every Halloween. It's the law. Before we get started, who wants drinks?" She took everyone's order and then headed to the kitchen with Tate.

Deke dropped a kiss on Bailey's mouth. "Need to answer a call of nature. I'll be back in a sec."

As he strolled out of the room, she sank onto the sofa and grabbed a chip from a bowl on the coffee table.

"I'm so happy," Aspen told her, beaming.

Bailey blinked. "About what?"

The bearcat seemed to be fighting the urge to roll her eyes. "That you and Deke are imprinting on each other, dufus."

"Oh." Bailey tossed the chip in her mouth.

"Did you freak out when you first realized?" Camden asked her.

"No. I might have, but I followed your advice not to panic." Bailey smiled. "You'd have been proud of me."

He snorted. "Let's not go that far."

She only laughed.

Aspen looked at her mate. "Wait, you gave her advice?"

"You told me I'm supposed to repay any favors," he reminded her. "She once did me a favor by giving me sound advice, so …"

Aspen's face went all soft, and she gave him a quick kiss. "You know, not only can you be super sweet at times, you're not as mean and rude as you used to be."

Tate hollered Camden's name. "Need help carrying these drinks!"

The tiger didn't respond in any way, nor did he move.

The bearcat raised a brow. "You're going to ignore him?"

"I don't want to get up."

Aspen sighed. "I take back the whole you-not-being-so-rude these days." She slid off his lap. "Go help him."

Rolling his eyes, Camden pushed to his feet and then left the room.

Aspen flopped into the chair and refocused on Bailey. "I thought there was a chance you and Deke would imprint, but I figured it wouldn't happen for a *long* time—you're just so cagey and stuff. He apparently smashed down your defenses, huh?"

"Something like that," said Bailey.

Aspen bit her lip. "Do you worry that, since imprint bonds can be broken, he'll always have that 'out'?"

"No. Because Deke doesn't commit to anything half-heartedly, and neither do I."

"That's true. And he obviously means a lot to you if you were able to push past your panic and follow Camden's advice." Aspen paused. "I was clearly right in what I said not so long ago—you're growing up."

Bailey flicked her head to the side. "Huh?"

"You never used to follow anyone's advice. I feel like you're maturing."

"I'm already mature."

Aspen barked a laugh, looking like she expected Bailey to join in. But her smile faded when it didn't happen. "Oh, you're serious. Wow."

Bailey paused with another chip halfway to her mouth. "You think I'm not mature?"

"I can see that you don't so, honestly, I'm not certain the word means what you think it does."

"So you disagree with my opinion, in other words."

"Yep. Totally."

Bailey shook her head hard. "You can be so mean."

"You're deflecting yet again."

"I'd stop if I could."

Aspen let out a snort. "No, no, you wouldn't."

"Correct. But who cares?"

"*I* care."

"So?"

Aspen bared her teeth. "Do you want me to slap you again? Is that where this is going? Because I'm up for it."

Bailey smirked. "Bring it, bitch."

Deke exited the half-bath in the hallway to see Tate and Camden walking out of the kitchen, bottles of beer in hand. "Need help?"

"We're good," the Alpha told him. "But *you* may need it," he added, his lips twitching.

"With what?"

"Bailey. That you're now her mate won't stop her from driving you crazy."

Deke felt his lips curve. "At least she takes an interesting route."

Tate snickered. "Do your parents know about the imprinting yet?"

"Yes. Me and Bailey stopped by to see them before coming here. My mother *never* would have forgiven me if she'd found out second hand." The woman was beyond excited, and he was quite certain that she'd have made several calls by now, spreading the news.

"Are they good with this? With Bailey?" A careful question from Camden.

Deke felt his brow pinch. "Why wouldn't they be?"

The tiger shrugged. "Some people make snap judgements about her and then don't look beneath the surface. They brand her 'trouble' and write her off."

Like Deke had once done, he thought with an inner frown. It would likely always make him feel like a complete asshole. "My parents like Bailey a lot. More, they like her for me."

"So do I," Tate cut in. "You need someone who'll challenge you and not care that you're an intolerable ass at times."

Deke blinked. "Uh, thank you?"

A low, angry hiss came from the living room quickly followed by an animal yelp of pain.

Deke sighed, knowing what that meant. "Here we go again." He entered the room, not whatsoever surprised to see Bailey's mamba and Aspen's bearcat having an ugly brawl. The lower half of the snake's body was curled tight around the bearcat's neck, and said bearcat was chewing on the mamba's head.

Havana shrugged past Deke, growling. "You can't go without fighting for this one night?"

The animals paused and looked up at their Alpha female.

"Let go of each other *now*!"

The bearcat released the mamba's head just as the snake began to uncurl her body from the other animal's neck. But then the snake bitch-slapped Aspen's animal with the end of her tail, and the bearcat pounced on her like a feral lion.

"*I said stop*!"

Finally, the animals broke apart and shifted back to their human forms. They began tugging on their clothes fast while Havana lectured them. A lecture that cut off when the doorbell rang again. Warning them not to resume fighting, the Alpha headed for the door.

Fastening her fly, Aspen looked at Deke. "I don't know if you're brave or stupid to take *that* on," she began, jabbing a finger in his mate's direction, "but you have both my admiration and sympathy all the same."

Shoving an arm into the sleeve of her sweater, Bailey grinned at her. "You love me really."

"In a manner of speaking," said Aspen. "But when Z-Day arrives—"

"Oh, Lord," muttered his mamba.

"—you'll be the first person I eat when the food runs out."

"And then you'll carry a piece of me always, wherever you go. How sweet."

"How fucked up," Deke corrected. "Now come sit down."

Bailey held up a finger. "One sec." She hurried into the hallway.

Moments later, there was an almighty roar followed by terrified squeals.

"*Bailey!*" Havana yelled.

"Fear builds character," said his mate.

Aspen exhaled heavily and slid her gaze back to Deke. "You sure you want to be bound to her for life?"

"I'm sure," he said, smiling, knowing he'd never been more certain of anything.

CHAPTER TWENTY

"Uh … I have no words."

Hearing the voice of his Beta male, Deke's cat lifted his eyelids to see Luke hanging out of a window that overlooked the communal yard. Not liking that he'd been disturbed, the cat bared his teeth.

Curled around the spot on which the feline was sprawled on the ground, his mate lifted her head and flicked out her tongue.

The Beta lifted his hands. "It's just not often you see a black mamba snuggling a pallas cat." He retreated inside and closed his window.

Now wide awake, the feline rose and did a long stretch. He nudged his mate's head, wanted her to shift back, and then he retreated to allow his other half freedom.

Crouching on the ground, Deke ran his hand along the snake's smooth scales. He thought he'd need to coax her to shift, but the animal subsided. Probably because she didn't like the cold any more than Bailey did.

His mate stood upright. "They didn't fight." She fist pumped. "Success."

Deke rose to his feet. "I told you my cat wouldn't hurt her." The animal happened to adore the serpent and wanted only to cosset and protect her.

"I wasn't worried that your cat would harm her. I was worried that my snake would bite him. She's kind of a bitch."

Looping an arm around Bailey's waist, he tugged her close and gently tapped the tip of her nose. "You can't call her that."

"Why not?"

"She's mine now, so no one gets to talk shit about her."

Bailey snorted. "Whatever. Now move. My lady bits are getting cold."

He released her with a chuckle, and they crossed to the bench on which they'd piled their clothes. Once they were dressed, Deke hauled her against him once more. She melted into him with a small shiver that made him smile.

Two days they'd been mates. He was impatient for imprinting to progress to the next stage, where they'd be able to feel each other's emotions. He wanted to be *that* in tune with her. Wanted to feel her inside him. And, like his cat, he couldn't fucking wait for the bond to form.

Deke wasn't sure what currently stood in the way of it taking shape. Bailey swore she had no other secrets, and he didn't feel that she was holding back anymore. He had no secrets of his own, and his every guard was down where she was concerned.

The pride's overall response to the imprinting had been positive. In most people's opinion, Deke deserved to finally have someone who put him first and made him happy. And they liked the idea that Bailey—who would probably be surprised to know that many of the pride were fond of her—finally had a special someone of her own.

But there were some people who, though not *against* the pairing, didn't believe it would last. As they saw it, Bailey couldn't be "tamed," and they believed that Deke would eventually tire of how high-maintenance she could be. Those people didn't realize that he felt no need or wish to tame her, or change her in any other way.

If they knew her as well as he did, they'd get it. They'd understand why her quirky ways amused rather than annoyed him. Since Deke wasn't a person who explained himself, he hadn't bothered enlightening the skeptics. They'd see for themselves that they were wrong in time.

Breathing in her scent, he licked along the life-giving vein in her throat. "Before we began sharing a bed, there were times I imagined using this vein as a chew toy."

"You wanted me dead?" she asked, her hands clamped around his upper arms.

"On the *verge* of death—never beyond. I'm not a monster."

"Mean." She frowned when he swept a hand down her back to cup her ass. "Hey, watch the butt."

He felt his lips twitch. "Still sore?"

"Don't act like you care."

"Of course I care. I don't want you in pain."

She palmed his cock through his jeans. "Then why did you happily shove that thing up my non-entry zone last night?" She lowered her hand with a sniff.

"That thing?" he echoed. "I thought you were fond of my dick. Anyway, you liked it when I fucked you there."

"I did—I won't deny it. I don't see a reason to. But that does not alter that I'm sore, or that you're pretty smug about it."

"I like that we both have the reminder that I've now claimed every part of you." He nuzzled her neck. "As soon as you're not sore anymore, I'll be doing it again. You're so tight and hot up there. It makes—"

"I'm going to fart next time. Then we'll see if you like it so much."

He laughed, throwing back his head.

"I don't know why you think I'm joking."

He honestly wouldn't put such a thing passed her.

"Now can we go inside? I don't have a coat."

He dabbed a kiss on her mouth. "Yeah, we can go inside."

They retreated into the building and made their way to the elevator. As they entered the lobby, he noticed Isaiah, Farrell, and Finley outside having what appeared to be a terse conversation.

Isaiah idly swept his gaze over the complex and incidentally caught Deke's eye through the window. The look on the enforcer's face made Deke's instincts stir.

He put a hand on Bailey's back. "I want to head outside and find out what that's about. You coming?"

She juddered. "No. Too cold. And it's probably a boring enforcer thing. I'll meet you upstairs. You can bring me up to speed then."

He waited until she was in the elevator before he exited the building and crossed to the small group who stood in the lot. All three shifters turned to him, their expressions sober. "What's going on?" asked Deke.

"Maybe nothing," replied Farrell. "Maybe something."

"I'm on perimeter duty today," said Finley.

Ever since the acid attack, an enforcer would prowl the land on which the apartment buildings and the parking lot were situated. "You spotted someone hanging around?" Deke guessed.

"From a distance, he looked a little like Bailey's cousin—the guy who crashed your dad's party," Finley explained. "But I'm not positive that it was him. He stood too far away for me to get a decent look at him. Whoever it was, he didn't do anything suspicious. He just seemed to be nosing around."

"We all know it's not unusual for people to do that," Isaiah chipped in. "It's most often lone shifters who've heard that our pride provides lodging and protection for loners."

Deke nodded. "They find it too good to be true, so they like to get a feel for the place and question our loner tenants." Bailey, Havana, Aspen, and Camden had done that very thing when they first showed up.

"Yes," said Farrell. "But whenever there are occasions when enforcers are on patrol, any loners nosing around don't come too close."

"He scampered once he realized I'd noticed him," said Finley. "But that might be because he thought I'd otherwise chase him away. Bailey's cousin would be a fool to breeze around like he doesn't have jackals on his ass, so I truly doubt it was him. But it's my job to report anything that could possibly be of note, so that's what I did."

Deke gave her a nod. "It was the right thing to do." Like her, he found it improbable that Roman was lurking around, but he wouldn't dismiss the idea.

As Finley's gaze snagged on something to his left, Deke looked to see Sam walking toward his building huddled in a coat, staunchly avoiding making eye-contact with anyone.

"It's sad about Cassandra and Sam, huh?" Finley sighed. "I really thought they made a cute couple."

Deke had heard through the pride's overactive grapevine that the healer had gotten positively wasted at the Tavern last night, drowning his sorrows after Cassandra allegedly chose to end their relationship. Apparently, her cat simply wouldn't except the submissive male as a partner.

"I know a lot of people are angry with her, feeling she was careless with his feelings by giving a relationship a try when she knew her cat's stance on the matter," began Isaiah, "but I don't know if that's entirely fair. I mean, some dominant animals in such situations do change their mindset if they grow fond of someone."

"They do," agreed Farrell. "So I think people are being a little harsh on her." He cut his eyes to Deke. "What do you think?"

"I think it's not my business," replied Deke, to which the Head Enforcer gave him a *You're so boring* look.

After they'd rounded up the conversation, they headed in different directions. Deke began walking toward his building, his step almost faltering when Dayna slid out of a car up ahead of him. She swallowed as their gazes clashed, gripping the strap of her purse hard.

Another female might have kept her pace slow so that their paths didn't cross, but Dayna was made of sterner stuff. Instead of walking passed him, she stopped a few feet away. He did the same.

His cat's upper lip peeled back. He had many good memories of Dayna due to how long they'd known each other. But the most impactful memories for the animal were those of this female goading and hurting his mate.

Licking her lips, she looked up at Deke, her expression unreadable. He had no idea how she'd reacted to the news of he and Bailey imprinting on each other. He hadn't asked anyone about it, and no one had volunteered the information.

She and Gerard were apparently still cozy—and getting cozier as the days went on—so maybe she wouldn't be all that bothered. Deke hoped so, because at this point the only thing he held against Dayna was that she'd hurt his mate. The rest just didn't matter. As he'd told her, he'd moved on.

She gave him a tremulous smile. "Hi, Deke." The words were low. Soft. Laced with awkwardness.

He briefly tipped his chin in greeting. "Dayna."

"I heard about ..." Trailing off, she scraped a hand through her hair. "Congratulations. I'm pleased for you." Hesitating, she jiggled her head.

"Okay, maybe not *pleased* pleased. It's hard when I spent so long thinking of you as mine. That doesn't just switch off overnight, even if you want it to. But I'm glad that you're happy."

The latter sounded true enough, but there was a note of resentment there that told him she'd prefer if his happiness didn't stem from his relationship with Bailey. "I hear that you and Gerard are making another go of things."

"It could work this time round. We're both older now. Wiser." She scraped her teeth over her lower lip. "He offered to come to Australia with me."

"I'm not surprised."

Her brows hiked up. "You're not?"

"He never stopped caring for you, Dayna. He'd follow you anywhere."

"Unlike ..."

Unlike him, yes.

Looking skyward, she let out a short, low, self-depreciating laugh. "We weren't meant to be at all, were we?"

"No."

Meeting his gaze, she pressed a fisted hand to her thigh. "I didn't want to see it. Maybe I clung to you because, for me, you were safety. I could rely on you. You might be a rude ass, but you're a dependable one. You kept me anchored at a time I needed it. For that, I thank you."

He inclined his head.

"Maybe we can one day be friends. I don't foresee it happening any time soon. But ... yeah, maybe one day."

His cat snarled, unprepared to be anything close to friendly with a person who'd once attacked his mate. Honestly, Deke didn't know if he could get past that either. "Maybe."

"Your mamba wouldn't like it, huh?" There was a slight bite to her voice.

"Bailey wouldn't feel threatened by it, if that's what you mean. She knows who she is to me."

"She did seem very sure of her place in your affections when she gave me a dressing down." Her lips drew into a tight line, her eyes hardening.

"She only did what you'd have done if the situation was reversed."

Dayna seemed as though she'd argue, but then she exhaled a resigned sigh. "Yeah." She paused. "It must be weird for you. Imprinting on someone who, if the stories are true, was once your sort-of-nemesis."

"Life takes us by surprise that way. It doesn't feel weird, though." It felt right.

"I wouldn't have pictured you with someone like her. I don't mean it in a cruel way. Truly. I just mean I wouldn't have envisioned you settling down with someone who's allegedly the ultimate extrovert. Loud, bubbly people generally annoy you."

"It's different with Bailey. Everything is." Because he loved her.

Hurt briefly tightened her face. She forced a cough. "Well, I won't keep you any longer. See you around."

"I hope things work out for you and Gerard."

"I hope … I hope you manage to keep the happiness you've found." The words were strained but seemed partly genuine.

"I will." He had no intention of ever letting Bailey go. "Take care." With that, he skirted around her and returned to the building.

From her seat on the sofa, Bailey heard her apartment door open just as she ended her phone call. She knew it would be Deke before he came loping into the living area, since he was the only other person who had a key to her apartment.

Letting out an annoyed sigh, she held up her cell. "There are so many gossips in this pride it's almost painful. I got to hear all about how you and Dayna were talking out front. Like they expected me to rush downstairs and order you away from her out of fear that she'd win you back to her side." She crossed her eyes.

His expression hardened. "That would never happen."

"I know." Bailey didn't feel in any way insecure in her relationship with Deke—he would never allow it. "I was told that the conversation appeared to be stiff but civil. I'm quite sure people were disappointed by the lack of drama."

"They were probably hoping that you and Dayna would have a Round Two, considering most found your first fight so entertaining."

She placed her cell on the coffee table. "Hmm, maybe."

"I half-expected her to march right past me with a huff, but she didn't." Deke sank onto the sofa beside Bailey. "She swallowed her pride—not easy for her—and had a real conversation with me."

"About what?"

"You and me, mostly." Angling his body to face her, he draped his arm over the back of the sofa. "She claimed to be sort of pleased for me and said she hoped I'd keep what happiness I'd found."

"Do you believe she meant it?" Bailey asked, mirroring his position.

"Yeah. I think there's still a little bitterness there, but I do think she doesn't wish me ill. And she seems to genuinely intend on trying again with Gerard."

Bailey felt her nose wrinkle. "I'm not so sure it's for the right reason. He's familiar to her. Safe and comfortable. And his feelings for her will soothe her battered pride. She needs that to get through what's currently happening."

"Hmm," was all Deke said, busy tracing the bite on her throat with his fingertip.

"But that's not to say it's destined to end. Only that I don't think she has as easily moved on as she'd like everyone to think. Are you even listening to me?"

"No. I'm wondering if I should leave two claiming brands on you. See, I want anyone who lays eyes on you to see that you're very much taken. But I also want you to have such a mark on your inner thigh."

She shook her head in wonder. "I never would have thought you'd be so possessive. You never struck me as particularly territorial." Her snake hadn't expected it of him either.

"I wasn't until you."

"Not even a little?"

"No."

She felt her lips press into a thin line. "I find that hard to believe, considering."

"Considering what?"

"The promise you made to Dayna. A promise you kept for over two and a half years."

He pinned her gaze with an unblinking stare. "If it had been you who'd asked me to wait a year while you went to Australia, I'd have said no."

Well, that was a direct shot to the heart. "Why?"

"Because I wouldn't have been able to handle that you were out of my sight. I wouldn't have been okay with the idea of you sleeping with other men, even if it was to alleviate touch-hunger." He palmed the side of her neck. "I would have gone with you."

Oh. "Well … we're mates, so—"

"Even before imprinting started, when we weren't positive this would go somewhere, I would have gone with you."

Warmth filled her expanding chest, and a grin pulled at her mouth. "*I'd* find it hard to be away from me, so I totally get where you're coming from."

He rolled his eyes.

"Now," she began, folding her arms, "want to tell me what Farrell and the enforcers were talking about earlier?"

He twisted his mouth. "Finley *may* have seen your cousin hanging around the lot. She's not positive. As you know, loners show up to check things out and speak to tenants, so it's not a weighty incident that a stranger was spotted."

Bailey twirled her ankle. "I know his criminal history would suggest he has little self-preservation, but I don't think Roman's dumb enough to not lie low at a time like this. He's good at hiding. It's what he does when things go to shit. And why come back when Tate made it clear that our pride wouldn't help or shield him?"

"We mentioned once before that it's possible he'd want revenge against you for refusing to help him."

"I know, but I don't agree with that theory. People refuse to help him all the time. To my knowledge, he doesn't pay extremists to give them crap. Plus, he's a compulsive gambler. He spends—or, more accurately, wastes—whatever cash he has in casinos. He isn't going to put some aside to place in the pockets of anyone, let alone extremists, for something unnecessary. Sending people to give me a scare isn't necessary. And he'd know it'd take more than all the recent attacks to rattle me anyway."

"True," Deke allowed. "It would be a waste of his time and cash. I agree that it likely wasn't him who Finley saw. She herself doubts it; she reported it all the same because it's what she's supposed to do."

Her phone began to ring. Bailey snatched it off the table and answered, "Yo?"

"Oh my God, Bailey," began one of her neighbors, "did you hear that Deke and Dayna had some kind of confrontation in the parking lot?"

For the love of all that was both holy and unholy. She started moaning. Whimpering. Panting. Groaning. Rasping "Oh, yes" over and over.

When the line went dead, she snickered and placed her phone back on the table.

Deke sighed, exasperation plain on his face. "Was that the first time you did that, or have you done it to every person who called to give you gossip just now?"

She bit her lip. "Do you want, like, an honest answer?"

"Of course I do, or I wouldn't have asked."

"You'd be surprised how often people don't actually want honesty. A lot of the time, they just want you to say what they'd feel most comfortable hearing."

"Well, I don't. I want the truth."

"Why?"

"Because I prefer honesty."

"Why?"

His eyelid twitched. "Because I just do."

"Then, yes, that was the first time today I faked an approaching orgasm down the phone to one of the gossipers."

"Really?"

"No."

He threw his head back and muttered something unflattering.

"Oh come on, I bring light to your life. Admit it."

He once more fixed his gaze on hers, and his face went all soft. "Yeah. Yeah, as it happens, you do."

CHAPTER TWENTY-ONE

A puff of hot air blasted Bailey's face as she pulled open the dryer door. *Nice.* She wafted it away and then began pulling out her warm clothes and dumping them in the washing basket beside her.

Her building's laundromat facilitates were located in the basement. Rows of industrial washing machines and dryers lined one of the off-white walls. The air would have been uncomfortably hot if it wasn't for the overhead fans and the air conditioning. Particularly since the small, high windows always remained closed.

Humming to herself, she crossed to one of the folding tables, pushed aside the stray glove sitting there, and then set down her basket. Still humming, she tossed the dryer sheet in the garbage can beside the vending machine that contained detergent, softener, dryer sheets, and even snacks for those intending to hang around while their clothes finished their cycles.

Personally, Bailey didn't like hanging around here. It wasn't exactly a relaxing place to sit. The plastic chairs weren't comfortable, and it was damn noisy. The whirring of the dryers and ceiling rotary fans blended with the gurgling of the washing machines and the *tings* of buttons and zips clacking against the metal drums.

As Bailey returned to her clean laundry, the creaking of hinges made her peer over her shoulder.

Carrying a basket overflowing with clothes, Cassandra strolled inside. Her step faltered when she noticed Bailey. "Oh, hey."

"Yo."

The feline made a beeline for a spare washing machine, the heels of her shoes clicking along the tiled floor that needed a good brush. The bright florescent lighting bore down on the pieces of lint and particles of detergent powder.

Bailey lifted a tee out of the basket, wrinkling her nose as a little static zapped her fingers. "I'd ask if you're okay, but I'm not good at comforting people."

"Comforting?" Emptying her basket of clothes into a washing machine, Cassandra looked at her askance. "Most people want to snipe at me, not offer comfort." Sighing, she closed the machine's door a little too roughly. "To be fair, they're right to be mad at me."

Bailey snapped out her tee and then neatly folded it. "I don't know about that. I mean, it isn't your fault that Sam likes you more than you do him. That sort of thing happens." She placed her tee on the table and then plucked another out of the basket. "And there's nothing you can do to change that your cat wasn't along for the ride." Still, most of the pride considered her public enemy number one.

"But I shouldn't have agreed to date him," muttered Cassandra, adding detergent. "I knew she was unlikely to accept him."

"Did you warn him of that in advance?"

"Yes."

"Then he knew where he stood with you from the beginning." Bailey placed her newly folded tee on top of the other. "You were clear that things might not work out."

"The way some see it, I gave him false hope by giving in to his pushy attempts to convince me to go on a date. That wasn't my intention. I just thought we could maybe give it a shot."

"I personally don't see any wrong in it. It's how most couples end up together." She and Deke had done it. "No one knows from the outset how it's all gonna play out, do they? There's always a risk it'll go bad. Sam knew that even without you warning him."

Having added softener, Cassandra whipped a coin out of her pocket. "The way he's acting, you'd think I'd pledged to be at his side forever."

Bailey added a sock to her fast-growing pile. "He's hurt, and his ego probably isn't all too happy either." It likely didn't help that everyone was all *Poor Sam.* No one wanted to be pitied when they were dumped.

"I hate that he's hurting. I never wanted that. Everyone's acting like I set out to do it."

"They're just super protective of him. Shifters usually are toward healers."

Clearing her throat, Cassandra jerked her head to the side to move her bangs away from her face. "On a whole other note … how are things going with you and Deke?"

"Couldn't be better."

"The imprinting is progressing, then?"

"Not in leaps and bounds, but a little." Every now and then, she'd feel a spark of emotion that wasn't her own. So she didn't doubt that she'd soon be able to tap into his emotions at all times.

"That's good." Cassandra briefly grimaced at the speckles of powder on her fingertips as the washing machine came to life. "I wouldn't worry about it being so gradual. I know a couple whose imprinting process was sluggish, then all of a sudden *pow* the bond clicked into place."

"I'm not worried. The bond will form when it forms."

Silence fell as Cassandra washed her hands in the stainless steel sink. As she tugged some paper towels from a dispenser, she turned back to Bailey. "I could tell that you guys were attracted to each other back when you first met, but I didn't foresee you mating."

"I'm pretty sure no one did other than Livy—she swears she knew I'd be perfect for him."

Cassandra's lips pressed into a thin line. "There was a time she swore I was 'the one' for Deke," she said a little too casually. "It was back when I helped him through a touch-hunger phase. She only started all that because she wanted to pull him away from Dayna, though. Livy didn't care who she pushed him toward so long as they convinced him to pull out of the vow."

Carefully folding a camisole, Bailey felt her eyes narrow. "Did *you* think you were 'the one' for him?"

"God, no." Cassandra flapped her hand and tossed the balled-up, wet paper towels in the trash can. "Don't misunderstand me, he's a great guy. He's not someone I can see myself in a relationship with, though." She said it as though it would otherwise be a possibility. Like he wasn't very much permanently unavailable.

Feeling her lips twitch, Bailey planted her hands on the table. "You're one of the people who think me and Deke are destined to crash and burn, huh?"

Cassandra blinked. "That amuses you?"

"Sorta."

"Can I ask why?"

"Sure."

"Then why?" Cassandra prodded.

"Oh, well, dominant females don't like to be wrong *ever.* They get all sulky when it happens. And, you see, you're wrong."

"You really are very confident that you and Deke will make it work, aren't you?"

"Well, I have no intention of letting him go, so …"

Cassandra's mouth curled. "I like that he has someone who won't let him doubt his worth to them. You clearly won't do that, unlike a certain female I could mention."

Bailey grabbed a hoodie from the basket. "Let's *not* mention her."

"Okay, I'm good with that." Cassandra paused as a machine buzzed loud, the tumbling laundry abruptly cutting off. "Well, I need to get going. See you later."

"Later." Bailey winced as she touched the hoodie's boiling hot zipper. *Rookie mistake.* She dumped the piece of clothing on her pile and then blew on her smarting finger. Once the sting faded, she fished a tank out of her basket and folded it.

Hinges creaked again. She placed her tank on the pile and went to look—

A threatening *whizz* of sound. A sharp piercing sensation in her back.

Bailey whirled fast with a hiss of fury, her snake unfurling in an instant.

A familiar person stood at the door, tranquilizer gun in hand. *Motherfucker.* Disbelief beating at her, she lunged toward them—or would have. A dart buried itself in her chest before she had the chance. She ragged it out and again went to lunge … but then a heavy lethargy began to descend on her while a tingling feeling skipped over her skin.

Colors smudged as her vision blurred and darkened. Feeling like she was wading through concrete, she took one shaky step. And another. And another. But then her knees buckled, her legs gave out, and she landed hard on her ass.

The world tumbled and shook and spun as her head swam, her belly churned, and her body became dead weight. Then darkness pulled her under.

Luke's brows flew up. "Really? Wow."

Standing in the lobby of his building, Deke frowned. "Why 'wow'?" He didn't think it would be considered surprising that his own mate would have agreed to move in with him.

"I thought she might fight you on it. Mostly just to screw with you."

"It may seem like life is a joke to Bailey, but she takes the things that matter seriously," Deke told him, feeling defensive on her behalf.

"Yeah, I sensed that about her," the Beta assured him. "You can see it in the way she's so dedicated to her position as Havana's bodyguard. Well, maybe *you* didn't see it at first. You initially seemed to have a blind spot where she was concerned."

Deke felt his mouth tighten, annoyed he couldn't deny it. "I resented her for making me want what I couldn't have."

"Ah. I suppose I should have seen that." Luke tilted his head. "How did she manage to work around your cat's earlier aversion to physical contact?"

"In a way that only Bailey could have made work."

Luke snickered. "How's your cat doing these days?"

"Better now that he no longer feels alone. That was at the crux of his problem. He was lonely, and so he began feeling bitter when others around him mated. Then he became angry at himself for that bitterness. So he pulled back from everyone, which only made the loneliness worse. It was a vicious cycle."

"I think it's easy for us to take for granted how difficult it can be for our animals when they have no mate to anchor them. Just because they don't experience the full range of human emotions doesn't mean they don't feel things very deeply and acutely."

Deke nodded. "Loneliness creeps up on them way sooner than it does on us."

"An animal like your cat, who grew up in a home where he was the only non-dominant, will have felt very alone in many ways. That would have made him crave finding an equal and being part of something."

That was exactly how his cat had felt. "Now that he has what he wants, I don't foresee him having another 'nobody come near me episode.' The only thing bugging him of late is that the imprinting bond hasn't yet formed. He's simply impatient to be fully mated to Bailey."

Luke's mouth hitched up. "I'll bet you're just as impatient."

Deke smiled, unrepentant. "Of course I am." His smile faded as he looked out the window and caught sight of Gerard and Isaiah carrying a limp Dayna toward the front door. "What the fuck?"

Swearing beneath his breath, Luke yanked open the door to let them in.

"We need either Helena or Sam," said Gerard, urgency coating every syllable. "*Please* get one of them down here fast."

Luke pulled out his phone. "On it."

Isaiah and Gerard placed a seemingly out-cold Dayna on the lobby's sofa. It was only then that Deke got a good look at her. He felt his lips part in shock. Her face was swollen and badly bruised. More, she had one hell of a gut wound … like she'd been sliced deep by a knife or claw. "Jesus Christ. What in the shit happened?"

"We don't know," said Isaiah. "She was in her car outside. I saw Gerard making a mad sprint to the vehicle and followed him. We found her like this. I think she's been drugged. I found this near the pedals." He held up a tranquilizer dart.

Luke took it from him and sniffed the tip. "Pretty sure it's the drug that not only knocks you out but temporarily suppresses your ability to shift."

"A scrambler was used," Isaiah chipped in. "Whoever shot her in her car covered their tracks."

Luke swore again. "I'll call our Alphas."

Deke turned to Gerard. "Why were you running for her car?"

"She called me," the other male replied, kneeling beside her, his gaze locked on her face. "She said she was in her car in the lot. But her voice was all slurry and weak and … *Goddammit, look at her.*" He scraped a hand through his hair.

Deke took a step toward him. "What exactly did Dayna say on the phone?"

Gerard swiped a hand down his face. "She said my name. Twice. Told me where to find her. Then I guess she passed out."

Just then, the elevator *pinged.*

Helena came rushing out of it and went straight to Dayna.

Vera followed at a more sedate pace, her eyes widening when she clocked the state of the female on the sofa. "What in the world …" She touched her neck. "Will she be all right?"

"She will now," said Helena, using her healing skills as they spoke. "Who did this?"

Luke shrugged, pocketing his phone. "We don't know yet."

Vera let out a *humph.* "I think we all know who'd happily do this to Dayna."

Deke felt himself stiffen. "Don't even think about pinning the blame on my mate for this."

"She's perfectly capable of hurting someone this way," Vera insisted, though she lowered her gaze.

"It wasn't her," Deke stated, his cat rising to his feet with a snarl.

Vera stroked her wrist. "How can you be sure?"

"Because she's in the basement doing laundry." *Alone*, he thought. She was alone. While someone was wandering around with a tranquilizer gun.

Unease making his heartbeat pick up, he whipped out his phone and called her. No answer. He tried again. Still no answer.

"What is it?" asked Isaiah, sidling up to him.

Deke felt his nostrils flare. "Bailey's not answering." Egged on by his cat, he ran down the hall, passing the elevators, and skirted the corner. Instantly, an overpoweringly floral scent shot to his head like brain-freeze. *Scrambler.*

His gut knotting, he realized the whole area here—all the way to the nearby side exit—had been sprayed with it.

He vaulted down the basement stairs and then threw open the door. His stomach sank. *No Bailey.* Her basket sat on one of the folding tables beside a pile of clothes. Her cell phone lay on the floor. More, the usual scents of warm fabric, chemicals, bleach, and hot metal were absent, buried beneath the scrambler's floral smell.

His cat lost it, letting out rumbly growls that were so loud Deke's ears rang.

Fuck, fuck, fuck. With panic flapping inside him like a crazed bird and his heart pounding a mile a minute, Deke flicked the security camera a quick glance and then darted back up the stairs. He shoved open the side exit door, finding the alley empty. The scrambler's scent trail ended here, but there was no sign that a vehicle was parked there recently.

Hurrying toward the security office, he called Finley, knowing she was on perimeter duty.

"Hello?" she answered.

"Have you seen anything of Bailey?"

A surprised pause. "No, nothing."

He clenched his free hand into a fist. "Who has exited the building in the last half hour?"

"Um, I don't know. I don't keep track. I noticed a few. Valentina. Evander. My sister. That's all."

"Did you see any vehicles parked in the side alley of my building?"

"No, not while I was passing."

Cursing again, Deke hung up as he burst into the security office. Ignoring the sickly strong floral scents—*fucking scramblers*—he focused on the wall-mounted monitors. Nothing but black screens.

Deke spat several harsh expletives and slammed his hand on the desk. He switched the CCTV back on and then dialed Tate's number as he rushed back to the lobby. "Where are you?"

"On my way," replied the Alpha, sounding like he was running.

Deke swallowed, trying and failing to beat back the dread and panic that battled for supremacy inside him and his cat. "I'm pretty sure whoever attacked Dayna has Bailey."

Tate swore. "We're almost there."

Deke ended the call just as he reached the lobby. "They have Bailey," he announced to no one in particular. "Whoever did this has her."

Luke gaped. "Are you sure?"

"Positive," Deke bit out, shoving his cell back in his pocket. "She's gone. Her phone is still there. And a scrambler was used—its trail ended in the side alley."

"Son of a bitch." Luke reached back to clasp his nape. "The cameras—"

"Were all turned off," Deke finished, putting his hands to his head. "I switched them back on."

"So, what, this was supposed to be a distraction?" Luke asked, waving a hand toward Dayna—who was now healed but still unconscious. "A way to keep us focused on something else so they could take Bailey?"

"That was more than a distraction. It was personal." Dayna had taken some brutal hits … and whoever did it to her might well do the same to Bailey.

Deke swallowed around the hard lump of dread in his throat. He wanted to race outside, hop in his car, and find her … But driving aimlessly would achieve nothing. It wouldn't help *her*.

"Bailey being gone only adds weight to the idea that *she* did this to Dayna," claimed Vera. "She could have set this up to look like she'd been taken."

Grinding his teeth as a wave of anger washed over him, Deke glared at the woman. "If Bailey wanted to hurt Dayna, she'd do it. But she wouldn't do it on the sly. That's not who she is. She'd *own* what she'd done."

"Like it or not, this stinks of Bailey," Vera persisted. "Mambas are merciless creatures. They always get even. No one else would want to hurt

Dayna this way."

Growling, Deke made a move toward the woman. He halted when Luke slid between them and said, "Vera, you're letting your personal issues with Bailey color your opinions here. If you've got nothing helpful to say, get the hell out of here."

Her back snapping straight, the woman marched out of the building.

Dragging in a breath that should have been calming but failed, Deke rubbed at his face. "She's probably not the only one who'll think that way."

"Probably not," agreed Isaiah. "But the majority won't. It's a well-known fact that Bailey owns her shit. Someone else has beef with Dayna. Someone who also has an issue with Bailey. Who?"

Deke crossed to the male still kneeling at Dayna's feet. "Gerard? *Gerard*?" Finally, the male looked up at him. "Do you have any idea who did this?"

He shook his head, but his eyes flickered.

Deke tensed. "You know something. You do."

Gerard licked his lips. "I-I'm not sure—"

"Who would have done it?"

He dropped his head. "It can't have been her," he said more to himself.

"Who?"

"She was pissed when I told her, but she wouldn't have done something like this."

"Who?" Deke growled.

"The plan was simple. So simple. The *results* were supposed to be simple. But no one reacted how they should have. Nothing went as it should have."

Deke fisted the back of the guy's long-sleeved tee and yanked him to his feet, pinning his gaze. "*What fucking plan*?"

The front door swung open and slammed into the wall.

The Alphas rushed inside with Aspen and Camden on their heels.

Tate took in the scene. "What happened here?"

"I don't know," replied Deke through his teeth. "But Gerard here knows *something*."

Havana folded her arms, her face a mask of rage. "Spill."

And then Gerard began to talk.

CHAPTER TWENTY-TWO

The curdling of Bailey's stomach nudged her out of sleep. She felt her forehead crease. Jesus, she felt awful. Dizzy. *Off.* Her throat was dry as a bone, and her head pounded like a drum.

More, she ached in too many places to count, more particularly her wrists and the back of her neck. But that wasn't what set off her inner alarms and brought awareness racing back to her, it was the fact that her snake was going nuts—hissing, striking, whipping her tail.

Her pulse doing a little hop, Bailey resisted the urge to freeze. She knew she wasn't alone. She could hear soft breathing coming from across the room.

Tranqs, she remembered. She'd apparently been not only drugged but taken. And now she was bound by her wrists and ankles to what felt like a chair.

Oh, someone's ass was getting caned.

Her mind jumped to Deke. Had he realized she was missing yet? Would he know who'd taken her?

If their imprinting had been a little more advanced, he'd have felt her lose consciousness.

Her snake sprang, pushing at Bailey's skin, wanting out; wanting to kill.

Zero point in that.

Bailey recognized the smell oozing from her as that of a shift-suppressant drug. Its stench almost overrode the scents of dust, mildew, stale air, and the woodsy scent of a familiar female. A *traitorous* female.

Bailey probably would have panicked if this was the first time she'd found herself bound to a chair. It wasn't even the second. And if there was one thing she was good at, it was getting out of shit. Which was fantastic, considering she had a habit of getting herself *into* shit.

And it was definitely time she got herself out of this particular pickle.

She blinked several times to clear her fuzzy vision and then lifted her head, inwardly wincing as her stiff neck cracked. *Ow.*

The sound made the female sat near the opposite wall look up from her cell phone. "You woke sooner than I thought you would." She didn't sound too concerned about that.

She *should* be. Because she was in for a world of hurt.

"Oh, I wouldn't bother trying to free yourself—that rope is shifter-resistant."

But hopefully not Bailey-resistant. She rolled her throbbing neck and then glanced around, taking in the stacks of chairs, tables, and other various things. It was a storage room, she realized. One she recognized. "We're still in our apartment building." It was the other half of the basement.

"Yup. No one really comes in here unless they need to get something out of storage. It isn't worth screaming, by the way. As you know, every room in the complex is soundproof." Therese pointed at her phone. "That's why I need to watch the damn CCTV footage to know what's going on outside. Someone noticed the cameras were off and switched them back on. I hacked into the security system; I'm good with technology."

Well, how lovely for her.

"Don't count on anyone coming here to look for you. They won't assume you're hiding here," Therese added, idly stroking a hand over the tranquilizer gun on her lap.

Bailey frowned as she repeated, "Hiding?"

"When they find Dayna dead, they're going to conclude it was you and that you then faked your own kidnapping and ran off."

Whoa, back up. "You killed Dayna?"

"Of course not. But she was as good as dead when I left her after our little argument, so she'll have croaked by now."

And apparently Therese felt that that wouldn't make her responsible for the woman's death. Huh.

"You're not wondering why you're bound to a chair?"

"I suppose I am a little curious."

Therese crossed one leg over the other. "You know, back when I was a kid, I was teased a lot for being latent. Like it was my fault. Like it was a weakness on my part rather than a simple error of nature."

Shifters did tend to be assholes toward those who were latent.

"The only friend I had was Dayna. She never really saw me as an equal, though. I was more of her sidekick; always in her shadow. Dominant and beautiful, she cast a *big* shadow. I didn't really mind. I'm not a person who feels the need to stand out." Therese's jaw hardened. "But I *did* mind that she made a move on the only guy I had any interest in."

"Deke," Bailey easily guessed. It had to be him. Why else would Therese have come for her?

"He was one of the people who *didn't* tease me. If he caught anyone giving me crap, he intervened and chased them off." Therese lightly drummed her fingers on her thigh.

Ah, the glows of hero worship.

"Dayna knew how much I liked him," said Therese, "but she came onto him anyway. I was upset and angry and felt betrayed. And she just … waved it off. Said I'd never land him anyway so what did it matter?"

Bailey remained silent, subtly working to untie the rope securing her wrists together. It was not gonna be a quick process. Not when the knot was tight and she had Therese's eyes on her.

"I was *delighted* when she left for Australia. I thought he'd be free of her. But they made that damn vow," Therese said through her teeth. "She wanted me to 'look out' for him while she was gone. What she really meant was that she wanted me to spy on him. I was, of course, happy to help."

Bailey could guess why. "You could tell her whatever you wanted her to believe; poison her mind against him."

"I tried. It didn't work well." Therese pressed her lips together. "She had too much faith in Deke to believe that the 'rumors' I claimed I'd heard of him bedding other women could possibly be true. But I thought it would only be a matter of time before she and Deke parted. Except … weeks became months, and months became years. It was maddening for both of us."

Bailey felt her brow pinch. "Us?"

"Me and Gerard. He loves her. Really loves her. He wanted another chance with her. But he couldn't talk her into detaching herself from Deke. We needed to do something."

"What *did* you do?" Not that Bailey really cared, but keeping Therese focused on telling her story—which she seemed relieved to be able to do, as if she'd held it in for what felt like too long—meant she wasn't paying too much attention to Bailey's movements.

"Little things at first. We would each tell her that we saw him having drinks with human women or leaving bars with them. She was skeptical, though. She called up a few other pride mates to ask if they'd noticed Deke hanging with other females. They, of course, said no." Therese curled her fingers into a fist. "We needed to have what looked like concrete proof that he had other women in his life."

"Enter the fake profiles," Bailey drawled as realization hit her. "That was you. You set them up. You pretended to be Deke."

"It was Gerard's idea." Therese lifted her shoulders. "Who better to pose as Deke than someone who knew him inside out? A simple voice-changing app enabled me to sound like a guy over the phone."

So this hadn't been about striking at Deke. It had been about hurting

Dayna.

"Gerard was *so sure* Dayna would be so furious about the profiles that she'd fly over here, confront Deke, break it off … and then of course Gerard would make his play."

"And as Deke would be free, you could make your own," Bailey mused.

"You say that like I was delusional to think it would work. Well, here's something you should know, then," she added with a smirk. "Gerard overheard Deke talk to Shay about how he would have dated *me* if it wasn't for his promise to Dayna."

Bailey inwardly snorted. That didn't seem likely. He looked at the woman with utter disinterest—he had done for as long as Bailey had been part of the pride. So she was getting the distinct feeling that Gerard had lied to secure Therese's assistance.

A small movement caught the attention of Bailey's peripheral vision. A movement that came from beneath one of the chairs. A similar movement came under Therese's chair.

Bailey didn't need to look to see what it was. Didn't need to. She'd mastered the art of looking without *looking.* She knew exactly what little creatures were hiding here. And it was hard not to smile.

"Don't get me wrong," began Therese, "I didn't believe it would be easy to convince him to act on what he wanted—he's not a guy who'd be good with sleeping with his ex's BFF. But Gerard's theory was that once Dayna railed Deke for 'cheating,' he'd be so furious with her for not believing his protests that he wouldn't care if sleeping with me might ruin my friendship with her. Still, I was skeptical. So when touch-hunger struck him, it seemed the perfect time to expose the profiles and get things moving."

Anger spiked through Bailey. "You meant to take advantage of his situation?" *Cruel little bitch.*

"A few subtle prompts were enough to encourage Maisy to surprise him with a visit." Therese's expression turned sullen. "She was the only person who acted as they *should* have. Dayna believed the profiles were fake, not real. Worse, Deke turned to *you* for sex."

"And you didn't like it; wanted to punish me. Hence the acid attack." Bailey gritted her teeth as her snake lunged *hard* to battle the drug. It didn't work. "Was Gerard in on it?"

"No. He wasn't mad that Deke marked you. He was thrilled. He thought that would be enough to send Dayna spiraling; to spur her into freeing herself from the vow. But she still didn't want to pull away from Deke. Not even when he basically dumped her via video call. Not even when he made it clear to her that he wanted you."

"You didn't like hearing that, so you sicced extremists on me again."

Therese sneered. "He barely even knew you, yet he made you the freaking focal point of everything."

"Is that why you sent Journee his way and then later made the call to Maisy? You wanted Deke's attention to switch from me to you, even if he didn't know it *was* you?"

"Well, it worked." She glanced down at her phone. "No one has left yet, unfortunately. But they will eventually. Which is excellent, because your ride will be here at some point tonight. And then you'll be gone for good. From my life, *and* from Deke's."

Bailey's insides seized. "Ride? What ride?"

CHAPTER TWENTY-THREE

"T-that's all," Gerard stammered. "That's everything."

His hands set on his hips, Deke glared down at him. "You are fucking *kidding* me with this shit," he growled, his cat raring to maul the bastard.

Gerard flinched, his shoulders tensing, sweat dotting his forehead. "I just wanted to come between you and Dayna; I never planned for anyone to get hurt. That was *never* supposed to happen."

"But it did, and you did *nothing*."

"That's not true. When I realized it was Therese who was hiring extremists—which I didn't find out until after the car crash—I made her promise not to do it again."

"That makes it better, in your opinion?" fumed Havana, a vein pulsing in her temple. "Maybe you didn't notice, asshole, but she broke that promise."

"And still, you did *jack*," Aspen spat, holding herself stiffly as if she'd otherwise pounce. Not even the hand Camden was sweeping up and down her back soothed her.

Grinding his teeth, Deke once more blasted Gerard with a glower that made the coward recoil. "Was anyone else in on this?"

The other male shook his head. "N-no, no one."

"What about the person she used to hire extremists for her?" asked Deke.

"She just paid random guys off the street to go do it," replied Gerard.

"Are you sure? Because the scrambler's trail ended in the side alley, but Therese's car is in the lot—I can see it from here. So either she had assistance or another mode of transport. Who would help her?"

"I-I don't know. If she dragged anyone else into this, she didn't tell me."

"Maybe she rented a vehicle," suggested Blair in an unnaturally flat tone, cracking her knuckles.

"At least we know she's alive, Deke," said Tate, his eyes flinty. "You might not have an imprinting bond, but you'd *feel* her death. It would reverberate through you."

"I swear, I never meant for things to go this far," Gerard vowed.

"And yet," bit out Camden, "you didn't do a damn thing to stop the runaway train."

Gerard pulled his shoulders up to his ears, lifting shaking hands. "What could I do?"

Deke leaned toward him. "Warn us where the danger was coming from so I could protect my mate!"

"She wasn't your mate back then," Gerard pointed out in a defensive mumble. "Look, I fucked up, I know, but—"

"*And* you set up others to take the fall for the profiles," Luke reminded him.

Gerard shrugged. "I knew they'd be able to prove they were innocent."

As if that made it okay? Unreal. "What about Ginny?"

"Therese wanted you to suspect the loner, so to scare the woman into relocating fast she made up some bullshit story about how Bailey planned to have her killed."

A low moan escaped the female sprawled on the sofa.

Gerard crept closer to her. "Dayna?"

Her eyelids flickered several times and then lifted. Her brows squished together. "Gerard, what are—" She stopped speaking, awareness flooding her eyes. "Where is she? Where's Therese? Fucking bitch tranq'd me after I parked in the lot, started hitting my face with the butt of her gun and then tried to gut me."

Gerard's eyes fell closed. "God, I'm so sorry."

Havana loomed over him. "Where is she? Where would she have taken Bailey, Gerard?"

Dayna stiffened. "Therese has Bailey?" She shot to an upright position. "What the hell is happening here?"

"Where, Gerard?" demanded Havana, ignoring the redhead's question. "*Think*."

He spluttered. "I'm not sure, okay? I mean, there's one place she might have taken her, but it's a long shot, really."

Deke took a lurching step toward him. "Where?"

"A bar that extremists frequent called *Liberty*," the male replied. "She once talked of selling Bailey to them, but she said it laughing. Like it was a joke. I don't think she'd go that far."

Deke shot him an incredulous look. "She almost killed her best friend, Gerard. I don't think she has many limits at this point." He made for the door, aware that several people were hot on his heels. Pulling out his phone, he looked up the bar and found its address. "I'm going to—" He stumbled as a hot flash of fury surged through him.

"What's wrong?" asked Havana.

He put a hand to his chest. "I just felt her. A quick flare of anger." He dashed outside and hurried toward his car, hearing Tate shouting out orders for some pride members to follow in other vehicles.

"Bailey's no easy prey, Deke," said Camden, keeping pace with him. "Therese made a mistake in taking her. She doesn't know what Bailey is capable of. Your mamba will be alive when we find her. And we *will* find her."

Deke nodded. Yes, they would. He'd accept nothing else.

Therese smiled down at the screen of her phone. "Ah, people are running to their vehicles now. They're off to look for Dayna's killer. *You.*"

Unfortunate, but Bailey wasn't holding out hope of a rescue anyway. She didn't need one. The knot binding her wrists was almost loose enough that she'd soon be able to free herself. She simply needed to be careful how she went about it, since she didn't want to get tranq'd again.

Therese still held her gun securely in her lap. Any abrupt movement from Bailey would earn her nothing but a damn dart to her chest. Lucky for her, there was a great way to distract the little bitch to give Bailey time to get out of this freaking chair. But there was no sense in launching that part of her plan until her wrists were free, since she'd need a few moments to also untie her ankles before she could rise.

Intent on keeping Therese occupied, Bailey spoke again. "So, you're not going to tell me who my 'ride' is?" She'd asked once already, but Therese had only responded with a smug grin. She did that same thing yet again. *Bitch.*

Choosing another subject that would hopefully keep Therese occupied, Bailey said, "All right. I don't suppose you're interested in telling me why you killed Dayna, are you? Sorry, *almost* killed her? I'm curious."

"Her plan was to leave for Australia next week. She'd invited Gerard to go with her. He was so excited. He literally couldn't wait to start a life with her." Therese swiped her tongue between her teeth and lower lip. "But then, earlier, she had a change of heart. She broke it off with him."

That wasn't much of a shocker. It hadn't seemed logical to Bailey that Dayna could have truly moved on in a matter of days.

"She told him she should never have hopped back in his bed; that it was a mistake; that she still had feelings for Deke. Gerard was devastated. I didn't know until he texted me while I was in the car with her." Therese stood, gun still in hand, and pocketed her phone. "I asked her why the hell she'd leave him behind. You know what she said?"

Well, obviously not.

"She'd changed her mind about going back to Australia so soon." Sucking in her cheeks, Therese shook her head. "See, she thought she still had a shot of being with Deke. Yup, she believed that there was no chance you and him would imprint *all* the way; that it was only a matter of time before the process regressed and he was free of you."

"She hoped to then slide in and 'comfort' him, I'm guessing."

Therese's hand clenched the butt of her gun. "I've been furious with her several times in my life. But hearing her say she wasn't prepared to let him go, that he loved her but didn't see it, that she wouldn't leave until she'd *made* him see it …" Cheeks reddening with anger, Therese ground her teeth. "She intended to make him hers for good this time. Everything I'd done would have been for *nothing* if she'd succeeded. Well, now she can't have him. And I'm not going to let *you* do it either."

"Just how do you think you can ensure that?"

"Sell you to extremists. They'll do with you what they will." Therese smiled. "They're scheduled to collect you later. I arranged it all this morning when I bought this delightful gun from them along with some nifty darts. They're always happy to sell shift-suppressant drugs."

This woman *so* needed to have her asshole stapled shut. "Do they know *you're* a shifter?"

"Of course not. They think this building houses humans and that I discovered you're a lone shifter in hiding."

"And however will you manage to get me out of here without anyone seeing?"

"In *that*, of course." She gestured to a plastic, wheeled waste container that was most certainly big enough for a person to fit in. "As soon as your buyer turns up, I'll wheel you out, and then you'll be on your way."

Her fingers smarting from fiddling with the knot, Bailey took a moment to flex them. Just a little longer and it would be undone. "People will look for me."

"Oh definitely, since they'll want to make you pay for Dayna's murder." She smirked. "They won't find you, though."

"Deke won't for one moment believe I did it. Neither will anyone else who knows me well."

"Maybe not." She shrugged one shoulder. "It won't really matter, though. You'll still be gone."

"And you'll be dead for what you did."

Therese snorted. "No one will know I had anything to do with it."

"Gerard will. It won't be hard for him to figure it out."

"He won't care what happens to you. He hates you for hurting Dayna at the Tavern."

"But he'll care that *you* hurt her, so what makes you think he won't give you up?"

Therese flicked her hand. "He can't blab all without exposing his own part in our plan. He'll never do that. Besides, I don't think he'll be that bothered to find her dead, considering she'd broken his heart all over again."

Bailey cocked her head. "And you really think that Deke will just fall into your arms if I'm not in the picture?"

"Maybe not straight away, but eventually."

God, the woman was literally delusional where Deke has concerned. Her insistence that she could have him might sound idiotic to others, but Therese truly believed every word she spoke. She so needed to believe he could one day be hers that she'd swallow anything anyone told her that would give her hope. It was almost sad.

"I'll be there for him while he's hurting from the reversal of the imprinting process, I'll—"

"Achieve nothing," Bailey finished. "He's known you pretty much all his life. If he wanted you, he'd have done something about it by now."

Therese's cheeks went crimson. "Gerard heard him say—"

"Oh, I wouldn't be too sure you can trust Gerard's word. He told lies to Dayna to get his way," Bailey reminded her. "You think he wouldn't have done the same to you?"

"He didn't lie to me. No way."

Bailey's pulse skipped as the rope around her wrists loosened enough that she'd be able to shake it off. *Boom.* "Whatever. Believe what you want. But I'm telling you, this whole thing was a waste of time. Nothing will come of it. Deke won't be yours. Ever."

"Maybe not," said Therese. "But at least you'll be dead. I'm assuming the extremists will kill you—they might have other plans, to be fair."

"I won't end up in their hands. I can assure you of that."

Therese snickered. "Oh, you can? And how's that?"

"Because I know something you don't." Bailey let out a distinctive hiss—a call that went answered. Dozens of snakes who were secretly nesting there zipped out of the shadows and lunged at Therese. She cursed and squealed and kicked out, but they were undeterred as they pounced and bit and lurched at her. Their venom wouldn't kill a shifter, but it would sure hurt them.

Taking advantage of the distraction, Bailey shook off the rope loosely curled around her wrists and then worked on the knots binding her ankles to the chair. In the meantime, Therese shot at the snakes once, twice, three times. Only one dart hit home. She kept pulling the trigger even though she was clearly out of ammo.

Lovely.

Her ankles free, Bailey pushed to her feet and knocked down the chair. She snapped off one wooden leg as she let out another hiss—this one lower, calmer. The snakes melted away, and a panting Therese glared at her.

Bailey just smiled. "Don't worry, I'm not going to kill you. Not straight away, anyway. After the little attacks you arranged, I owe you some *serious* pain. And I have to be honest, Therese, I'm going to genuinely enjoy subjecting your ass to it."

Deke clenched the steering wheel as battle-adrenaline fizzed through him—another emotion that wasn't his own. But it didn't surge through him like her anger had done. This was more like a gentle flutter of sensation.

"You all right?" asked Tate, riding shotgun. "You just went stiff as a board."

Deke swallowed. "I felt her again. For the slightest moment, I felt pure battle adrenaline."

"She's likely fighting," Havana piped up from the backseat. "Bailey will *never* roll over and take anyone's shit. You know that."

Cursing, Deke pressed his foot harder on the pedal. An electric sense of urgency seemed to run through each and every vein in his body and heat his blood to unbearable levels.

His cat was in a blind panic. Like Deke, he knew their mate was strong and fierce. Both man and animal were confident in her ability to take care of herself. But none of that dimmed their fear for her.

"You know," began Aspen from beside her Alpha female, "I'm surprised Therese managed to get Bailey out of the building so easily all while covering her tracks so well. I mean, Gerard was the mastermind behind everything other than the extremist attacks—she didn't even pass on suggestions for how they should scare Bailey; only advised them via who she sent to hire them to 'be creative.' Yet, she made her final move fluidly and quickly, outsmarting us all, and even squeezed in a lethal attack on Dayna."

"I don't think the attack on Dayna was planned," said Camden, holding his mate's hand. "But given that Therese had a tranq gun *and* a scrambler on her person, not to mention another mode of transport ready to roll, her abduction of Bailey was definitely top of her schedule."

"Yup," said Aspen. "And despite having such a small window of time to make everything happen, Therese achieved it. I wouldn't have thought she …"

Deke didn't hear the rest of what Aspen said, becoming lost in his own thoughts as his instincts stirred in unease. He and his cat froze as understanding slapped them. "*Fuck.*" He eased his foot of the pedal and, seeing his opportunity, did an about turn with a screech of tires.

Tate planted a palm on his window to brace himself. "What the hell are you doing?"

"She isn't at the bar," Deke told him, speeding back down the road. "Tell

Luke and the others to stay en route there to be sure, but I'll bet my ass she's not."

Havana leaned forward, frowning. "What? Why?"

"She's still at our goddamn building somewhere." It would explain every damn thing.

"How can that be possible?" asked Tate, texting someone—probably the others who were heading for *Liberty*.

"Because Aspen's right," said Deke. "It all went too smoothly, too quickly. It took precious moments out of what time Therese had to switch off the cameras and spritz a scrambler trail as well as disable Bailey, yet she pulled it all off *and* managed to get Bailey out of the building and drive off with her—all without being seen. How? Her car hasn't moved, and Finley didn't see an unfamiliar vehicle enter or exit the lot, let alone any car park in the alley where the scrambler's scent-trail end."

"Extremists could have snuck past our enforcers and collected them," Tate suggested.

"Collected Bailey, sure. But Therese would have no reason to go with them, would she? She could have stayed behind. It would have made the most sense." Knowing that Isaiah was still at the building, Deke contacted him using the car's built-in Bluetooth system. "I want door-to-door searches to be done of the complex. I think Bailey's still in there somewhere with Therese. Find her."

The enforcer swore. "Got it."

"And guard every exit," Deke added. "Therese may try to smuggle her out while less people are around."

"She'll never succeed—I won't allow it." Isaiah then hung up.

"I told the others to keep driving to the bar," said Tate, setting his phone down on his thigh. "They'll check it out, just in case you're wrong."

"I'm not wrong," Deke asserted.

The Alpha squinted. "How can you be sure?"

"I felt her earlier for a split second. It was a strong sensation. So strong it *almost* felt like my own emotion." Seeing the green traffic lights turn amber, Deke accelerated fast and sped through them before they could turn red. "I sensed her again a few minutes ago. It was weaker, but I don't think it means *she's* weak."

"You think distance dimmed the emotion's vibrancy," Tate correctly guessed.

"Yes. I think we were driving away from her rather than towards her, and I'm rectifying it right fucking now."

Aspen scooted to the edge of her seat. "Where exactly in the building could Bailey be?"

"We know she's not in the lobby, laundry room, or security office," said Deke. "At the moment, that's pretty much all we can be certain of."

"It seems dumb to hide in the building rather than make a run for it," began Havana, "but in actuality, it's not that stupid at all. None of us considered it until now."

"But we *did* consider it eventually," muttered Tate. "So Therese's plan isn't what I'd call smart, just cunning. Cunning doesn't always pay off." He looked at Deke. "Did you know she's pretty much obsessed with you?"

Deke gave a quick shake of the head. "Don't get me wrong, she made it non-verbally clear that she'd be willing to share my bed. But she was subtle enough about it that it didn't make things awkward and it failed to set off my alarms. I didn't suspect her of being behind the profiles."

"Really, it was Gerard who was behind them," Havana pointed out. "He told her what to do, and she did it. If he hadn't pulled her into his little plot, I don't think she'd have done anything like that off her own back."

"She acted alone when hiring extremists, though," said Camden.

"Because nothing was happening the way he said it would. She lost faith in him. Took the matter into her own hands." Havana blew out an impatient breath. "How long before we're back at our building?"

"About twenty minutes," replied Deke.

"Hopefully, one of our pride will have found her before then," said Tate.

"Yeah, hopefully," said Havana. "It'd be a bummer if Bailey leveled the building or something."

Tate twisted his neck to look at his mate. "What?"

Camden explained, "It was what Bailey did last time someone abducted her. Got free, snapped their neck, and destroyed the building. The time before that, she set the location on fire after kicking her captor's ass. No ropes or cuffs or other binds can keep her where she doesn't want to be."

Deke studied him in the rearview mirror. "You're not worried for her safety at all, are you?"

"No," replied Camden. "Because I know exactly how lethal your mate is. She could deck someone in one move. *One*. She brawls for the fucking pleasure of it—nothing more. She can kill just as fast and efficiently. She simply prefers not to, because it isn't as fun for her. And with Therese, she won't make it quick and clean. Bailey will punish her in a brutal fashion. And by the time she's done, Therese will rue the day your mate was born."

CHAPTER TWENTY-THREE

With an almighty curse, Therese threw the gun at Bailey, sending it hurtling through the air.

Chair leg still in hand, Bailey sharply leaned to her left, easily evading the firearm that would have otherwise smacked her in the face. Adrenaline dancing through her bloodstream, she rolled her shoulders and let out a speculative hum. "You're slower than I thought you'd be."

Therese bared her teeth and kicked off her shoes. "You're dead."

"No, dear, that's you."

The feline charged with a yell.

Bailey swung the chair leg like it was a bat, slamming it into Therese's head, sending it whipping to the side. *Ha.* Her inner snake writhed restlessly, eager but unable to join in the fun.

Bailey struck out with the wooden leg again. Therese caught it and dragged it toward her, bringing Bailey closer … and then cried out as Bailey's forehead butted her nose hard. There was a distinct *crack*, and then blood laced the air.

Smiling grimly, Bailey didn't give the cursing woman a moment to recover. No, she threw aside the chair leg and went in hard, fast, and brutal; intent on making this bitch *hurt.* Bailey slapped and punched and scratched and kicked and bit.

It wasn't pretty. Wasn't "fair." Wasn't anything close to merciful.

She wasn't aiming to kill. Wasn't even aiming to disable. This was not a mere fight. This was a punishment. A prolonged, tit-for-tat beating. Only when she felt ready would she end the feline.

Pallas cats were fierce and didn't go down easy. They'd fight to the bitter end and very rarely surrendered. But Bailey had way more fighting experience than Therese would ever know. She'd battled far tougher opponents. Had *beaten* said opponents.

With a chuckle of delight, Bailey grabbed the feline by her hair and ragged out a chunk. Therese roared a scream of rage and pain. Bailey's mamba drank in the sound, wanting more.

Her hair sticking up all over the place, Therese took out the hair tie, wincing as it pulled on what would now surely be a very sensitive scalp. "You duel like a girl," she sneered. Her eyes beginning to swell and bruise courtesy of her broken nose, she gently dabbed at one of the catty scratches spanning her face.

"Duel?" Bailey let her lips curve. "Sweetie, I'm just playing with you right now." She sharply elbowed Therese's throat, making her breath catch, and then slammed several heavy blows into her ribs.

Pain rippling across her face, Therese retaliated fast. But, as sinuous as any snake shifter, Bailey was a master at dodging hits and delivering surprise-blows.

The bitch only managed to land a few punches—one to Bailey's temple, one to her neck, another to her jaw. The adrenaline pumping through her system dimmed the pain, but Bailey knew she'd feel it later.

Blood, anger, and pain laced the air. The sounds of grunts, curses, snarls, flesh ramming into flesh, and fast and heavy breathing echoed in the space.

A scowl twisting Therese's face, she seized Bailey's arm and yanked hard.

Sucking in a pained breath as her shoulder was wrenched out of its joint, Bailey delivered yet another ringing slap to Therese's face—the side that sported a gaping cut on its cheekbone—and then stepped back. She'd barely righted her dislocated shoulder before a screeching Therese came at her, swinging her balled-up hand.

Bailey blocked the arm and shot out her fist, crashing it into Therese's split lip. She followed it up fast with another punch to the ribs which made the feline jerk backwards, her breath gusting out of her.

Her bloodshot eyes blazing, Therese sliced out the claws of one hand and slashed at Bailey's face. *Fuck*, it was like being scratched with razor-sharp knives.

"Now we're even," taunted Therese, gesturing at her cheek. She swiped out her claws again, raking Bailey's chest, cutting through cloth and grazing skin.

Her inner snake hissed in fury and gave her an encouraging nudge, urging her to kick things up a notch and take this bitch *down*. But Bailey just wasn't ready yet. Snarling, she whipped up her leg and caught Therese's groin.

Coughing out a choked moan, Therese reflexively bent forward even as she staggered backwards. With an enraged cry, she grabbed one of her high-heeled shoes from the floor and hurled it at Bailey's head.

Narrowly escaping a heel to the eye, Bailey let out a dark chuckle. "You look like a spoilt little kid throwing her toys across the room because things aren't going her way."

They went head to head again, vicious and determined, until their knuckles were bloody and swollen. They swore, grunted, gasped, and snarled.

Bailey knew she sported some wicked slashes and puncture wounds, but she gave zero fucks—especially when it was *nothing* compared to her opponent's injuries. Ignoring the stings, aches, and throbs, she kept punching and slapping the piss out of her abductor. Again and again, her snake pounced within her, wanting out.

Pausing for a moment, Therese wiped at the blood dripping from her nose and down to her lips. "I don't think I've loathed anyone quite as much as I loathe you right now." The words came out all weird due to her broken nose.

Bailey felt a cruel smile curve her mouth. "Aw, thanks. I can't tell you how much that means to me." She snapped out her fist again.

Therese threw up her arm to block the blow. Missed. Grunted as the balled-up hand connected with her jaw.

With a maddened war-cry, the feline tried slicing her claws diagonally across Bailey's upper body from breast to hip, but Bailey jerked back to avoid the swing.

A gleam of uncertainty in her eyes, Therese licked her lips. It was easy to see that her anger had started to give way to fear. So it was no surprise when she began to ease back, blocking and dodging rather than attacking. Bailey didn't let up, kept her strikes harsh and swift, relishing each and every cry of pain.

Panting and clearly tired, Therese was soon struggling to land a blow. Struggling to *avoid* blows that came her way. She kept blinking hard and swaying, seeming lightheaded—likely due to the blood loss and brutal head-punches.

"Dayna's right, you know," Therese fairly rasped. "You and Deke won't fully imprint." She went to deliver a palm-strike to Bailey's face.

Easily dodging the clumsy strike, Bailey caught the feline's wrist and yanked it backwards in a sharp, merciless movement and … *crack*.

Therese coughed out a pained curse and stared at the break in what appeared to be shock.

"I'd say that you'll soon see I'm wrong, but you won't be around long enough for that." Not releasing the now-broken wrist, Bailey sank her teeth into Therese's fingers. The warm, coppery taste of blood slipped over her tongue. A dark satisfaction filled her snake.

Tears welling up, Therese went to strike out with her free hand, but Bailey dealt her a solid punch to the spot behind her ear. A glaze fell over Therese's eyes as they lost focus. She weaved and then landed hard on her butt. Heaving in breaths, the feline didn't try to stand, looking all hollowed out.

But she did viciously kick at Bailey's ankle.

Avoiding the foot, Bailey stomped hard on Therese's thigh, grabbed a dart from the floor and then rammed said dart into the bitch's boob.

Flinching with a cry, Therese swung up her arm, but Bailey gripped the limb and punched the side of her elbow to dislocate it. Therese gaped at the injury, seeming stunned.

Looming above her, Bailey took in the sight of her opponent. Therese's savagely-clawed face was contorted with pain, her swollen and bruised eyes two swirling orbs of hatred. Blood was everywhere—it dripped from scratches, poured from her nose, trickled out of her mouth, seeped from head wounds, and stained several patches of her clothes. More, she'd plastered a hand to her ribs as she hauled in mounds of air, every breath seeming to hurt like hell.

All in all, she was clearly in a crap load of pain. As such … "My work here is done."

Maybe someone else would have felt sorry for Therese right then. Maybe they would have given her mercy. But this woman had too many things to pay for, in Bailey's opinion.

An acid attack.

A car crash.

An attempted shooting.

The near-death of her supposed BFF.

Catfishing human women.

Messing with Deke and telling lies about him.

Setting up several pride mates to take the fall for her crimes.

And an intention to sell Bailey to anti-shifter extremists, not giving a single damn that they would beat, torture, and eventually kill Bailey once they were done with her.

So, no, Bailey wasn't feeling merciful.

Bending, she hummed. "The question is … should I actually kill you now, or should I leave you for dead as you did Dayna so as to stretch out the pain a little longer?"

Letting out a grating growl, Therese reached up and stabbed her claws into Bailey's side.

Mother of fuck. "Death it is." Bailey rammed her fist into Therese's already broken nose. The feline's head snapped back with the force of the blow and hit the concrete floor hard.

Bailey snatched the broken chair leg and rammed it into Therese's chest, staking her. The woman arched, choking on a silent scream, her eyes going as wide as the swelling would allow. Her body writhed, her legs kicked, her hands slapped at the makeshift stake. Soon, her movements became slow and weak and pitiful, until the life finally bled from her eyes.

Inhaling deeply, Bailey straightened and stepped back. Taking a few moments to regulate her breathing, she rubbed at her shoulder. It was tender from where it had been earlier dislocated.

Eager to find Deke, knowing he'd be worried, she trudged up the set of stairs and shoved open the basement door. Stepping out, she realized there was a lot of activity going on. She could hear muffled shouting, feet thundering, and the chiming of multiple cell phones.

Padding around the corner, she noticed Helena standing just outside the door of the communal yard, talking to someone out of sight. Catching sight of Bailey, the healer did a double-take.

Bailey gave her a weak salute and mouthed, "Yo."

Her eyes bulging, Helena turned to whoever else was out there and yelled something. She then dashed inside and hurried over to Bailey. "My *God*, where were you?"

Before the back door could swing shut, Deke was pushing through it. Relief flickering in his eyes, he made a fast beeline for Bailey. His lips tightened as he took in the injuries that Helena was in the process of healing. "I'll fucking kill her."

"You're too late for that party," Bailey told him. "The deed has been done."

The moment Helena stepped back, Deke hauled Bailey close and buried his face in her neck. "Jesus, baby."

She held tight to him, breathing him in. He said nothing more, but she didn't need words; *felt* his fear for her, felt his anger that she'd been taken, felt his relief that she was well and in his arms.

She was distantly aware of Helena making a call to Havana. Though part of Bailey wanted to speak to her honorary sister and assure her that she was fine, Bailey didn't move. Neither did Deke. They just continued to hold each other.

"What happened?" he asked, his mouth against her neck.

Without drawing back, she gave him a quick account of all that transpired.

"You staked her?"

"At least I didn't shove it through her eye and into her brain. Thought about it. What did I miss?"

Still holding tight to her, he gave her a bullet-point summary. Meanwhile, people began to gather around them as it became clear that she'd been found. The crowd enlarged little by little as the news circulated. Soon, Havana and Aspen were shrugging through it.

Deke was not whatsoever impressed when his Alpha female snatched Bailey from his arms. Like *literally* snatched her from him. The devil was hellishly strong.

Babbling about how much she was gonna kick Bailey's ass for going missing, Havana hugged her hard. She reluctantly passed her off to Aspen, who gave his mamba just as fierce a hug.

"Where's Therese?" asked Tate, his voice dangerous, as he came up behind his mate.

In answer, Bailey slid the storage room door a glance.

Tate descended the steps fast, a bunch of people following behind him, including Havana, Aspen, and Camden. In passing, the tiger gave Bailey a casual tip of the chin … like she'd come back from a damn daytrip. He also shot Deke an "I told you so" look.

Deke cast him a narrow-eyed "Fuck you" look in response. Needing his mate close, he drew her to him once more and breathed deep, filling his lungs with her scent. The fear that had seemed to weave itself into his cells hadn't yet began to dissipate.

Tate jogged back up at the stairs and gave Bailey an odd glance. "And people call Camden a sadist. Not that they're wrong. Or that I have an issue with it."

Havana huffed at Bailey. "I should be mad that snakes are still nesting here—yeah, I noticed them—but I can't find it in me to care right now. That might change tomorrow."

Feeling Bailey stiffen against him, Deke tracked her gaze and noticed Gerard and Dayna hovering nearby.

"You have been a very busy boy," said Bailey, her voice cold.

Gerard flinched and opened his mouth to speak, but then he clamped his lips shut.

Bailey looked from him to Dayna. "You know, you make a perfect couple. You don't care who you hurt so long as you get what you want. Oh, and just to be clear, Dayna … me and Deke *will* imprint all the way, so don't stick around waiting for something you'll never have."

Tate caught Farrell's eye and gestured toward Gerard. The Head Enforcer nodded at the silent signal and swiftly detained Gerard, who didn't bother fighting him.

Bailey turned to Tate. "Extremists may turn up here soon, depending on whether or not they first try to contact Therese—they might hang back if they receive no answer. She intended to sell me to them."

Havana spat out a rough curse. "What exactly went on down there? I want every measly detail."

Wanting to get his mate upstairs so he could tend to her, Deke cast his Alpha female an annoyed glance. She totally missed it, focused on Bailey.

After his mamba finished recounting everything, he cut in, "If you have more questions, call her later, she's done here."

Ignoring Havana's snort, he guided Bailey up to his apartment—a place that would soon be theirs, since she was scheduled to move in at some point in the following few days. Inside, they showered together, saying nothing. It wasn't until afterwards, when he wrapped a towel around her, that Deke touched his forehead to hers and said, "I'm so pissed at myself right now."

She curled her arms around his waist, careful not to dislodge his own towel. "You think you should have sensed that Therese was so majorly and creepily into you," Bailey guessed. "Why? No one else did. She made sure to hide it. Not even Gerard realized the extent of it, or he would have anticipated that she'd turn violent toward Dayna."

"I didn't even realize that all the fuckery going on around us was related. I wondered about it a time or two, but I couldn't think of anyone who'd target us both and in such different ways. Especially when the profile bullshit started way before any extremists came at you. I couldn't make it fit." He righted his head. "If I'd sensed how Therese felt, or I'd considered that Gerard might resort to—"

"If, if, if. Come on, Deke, you're not omniscient. No one is. *I* didn't cotton on to what was happening either. Like you, I recently thought that maybe the same person was behind it all, but we were struck at in varying ways at different points in time. It didn't line up for me, so I didn't think on it too hard. Do you blame me for that?"

"You know I don't. And I get what you're saying." He slid his fingers into her wet hair. "But I'm still angry at myself."

"The blame belongs to Gerard and Therese—be angry at them."

"Oh, I am," he fairly growled. "I could have happily tore him to pieces if my priority wasn't finding you. And as for Therese … part of me regrets she's dead, because now I can't make her pay."

"I did that well enough for both of us."

"I can believe that." He pressed a kiss to the tip of her nose. "Camden assured me that you'd be fine. But how could I not be a fucking wreck? You were gone, and I couldn't find you, I—"

"Lived your own nightmare," she finished. "I know. I wish I could kill her all over again for that."

He exhaled heavily, trying to relax into his mate as she nuzzled his throat. But it was fucking hard when she—the only woman he'd ever loved, ever would love—had almost been *killed.*

"How about I get dressed, and you let out your cat so I can give him some snuggles?"

His pacing cat stilled, more than interested. "He'd like that."

"Then let's do it." She led the way into the bedroom, where she quickly pulled on a long tee. "Now you can …" She trailed off, her brow furrowing as her head cocked to the side.

Deke, too, was frowning. "Is that the TV?"

"Uh-huh."

His lips thinned. "I already know what I'm going to find before I open the door. Or should I say *who* I'll find."

They both padded out of the room, down the hallway, and into the living area. As he'd expected, Havana and Aspen were sat on the sofa watching a movie. They gave both Bailey and Deke a tip of the chin before sliding their gazes back to the TV.

He sighed. He should have anticipated this. Whenever something happened to one of the girls, the other two turned temporarily clingy. "Do your mates know you're here?"

"Probably not," hedged Havana, still looking at the TV.

"But they'll guess when they can't find us," added Aspen.

With a heavy exhale, Deke turned to his mate and dropped a kiss on her forehead. "I'll be right back, I need to put on some clothes."

"Don't bother on our account," Aspen told him.

Ignoring that, Deke returned to the bedroom and slipped on some sweatpants and a tee. He then picked up his cell and rattled off a text to both Tate and Camden, asking that they come take their mates home. He wanted time alone with Bailey to—

A yowl came from the living room quickly followed by a grating hiss.

"I cannot *believe* you two!" yelled Havana.

Letting his eyes close, Deke dropped his head with a groan.

CHAPTER TWENTY-THREE

A month later

Half-propped up against the headboard, Deke watched as his mate swallowed his cock again and again. It was a beautiful sight—her lips stretched around him, her face flushed, her sleek back arched, her delectable ass up in the air.

He'd woken to the feel of her tongue licking at his shaft from base to tip, which had to be the best alarm in existence. She'd gone easy at first, lapping and playing. But the moment she'd taken his dick into her mouth, she'd gotten right down to business.

She sucked hard and fast, taking him deep with each pass, doing wicked things with her tongue. And now he had his fingers buried in her hair, *so close* to snatching the control and fucking her throat raw.

She was good at making his composure erode. It was how she'd ended up with a claiming mark on her neck before the imprinting process was complete.

It was exactly two weeks ago when he'd been riding her hard that his control had vanished, his possessiveness had taken over, and his teeth were then buried deep in her flesh before he knew it. Bailey hadn't freaked on him for leaving a claiming mark so soon, no, she'd returned the favor.

It had been right then that the imprinting bond appeared. Up to that point, the process had dragged its heels. It was as if both he and Bailey had needed the other to back up their words with actions before they could truly trust the claiming would really happen.

That was Deke's theory, anyway.

After all, Bailey didn't find it easy to believe that people would want to keep her around, and she'd worried a part of him would prefer to find his true mate.

As for Deke … After Dayna had kept him dangling on a carrot with fake promises for so long, he'd needed more than verbal assurances to feel sure of Bailey's intentions. More, he'd needed to be certain his cat wouldn't have a relapse and suddenly withdraw from everyone—including her.

All of that could have interfered with the progression of the imprinting process, so their claiming each other would have been exactly what was needed to complete it.

Whatever the case, they were now officially mated. Something that neither he nor his cat could be more pleased about. They'd had the mating ceremony mere days later, and the after-party had been a blast. It was—

He groaned as she suddenly began bobbing her head faster, her lips tightening around him. "Jesus, baby." He ground his teeth as the head of his cock bumped the back of her throat. "Take me deeper. *Fuck*, yeah."

Unable to help himself, he began jutting up his hips to meet her mouth. She didn't pull back. She took it. Sucked even harder, as if determined to suck the come right out of his balls. Knowing he'd blow his load if he didn't put an end to it now, he used his hold on her hair to snatch up her head. "Get over here and ride me."

She pouted, her lips red and swollen. "Always so bossy in the mornings."

Yeah, well, he didn't really have the patience to do anything but rut on her when he woke hard as a rock. "You gonna make me wait?"

Straddling him, she positioned the broad tip of his dick at her entrance. "No. I want to come." She dropped down on him.

He hissed as her pussy swallowed every inch of his dick, so gorgeously hot and slick he could live there. *Heaven.*

She planted her hands on his chest and began impaling herself on him over and over.

"That's it, use my dick to get yourself off." He reached out and palmed her breasts, wanting to feel them bounce in his hands as she rode him. His release would hit him soon. So would hers—he could sense through their bond how close she was to exploding.

Being so connected to her had taken some getting used to, but he liked it. Especially at moments such as these, where he could feel her rising pleasure; it amplified his own by a thousand, and vice versa.

A growl crawled up his throat as she briefly and deliberately tightened her inner muscles around his shaft. "Do that again."

She did, smiling wickedly.

Feeling his balls tighten, he released one of her breasts and dove right for her clit. He rubbed it, rolled it, flicked it, plucked it.

Her glazed eyes turned glassier. Her face flushed deeper. Her downwards thrusts became frantic.

Then it happened. She threw her head back, choking on a scream as her pussy clenched and rippled around him.

As an echo of her orgasm danced down their bond, he grabbed her hips and started slamming her down on his cock, thrusting upward each time. His mind blanked as his release hit, making jets of come burst out of his cock and fill her.

Breathing hard, she let herself fall forward and sprawl over him. "I don't know who I love more," she slurred. "You, or your cock. You're both so wonderful."

He felt his lips kick up. "*Me*. You love *me* more."

"You sure?"

"Yes."

"Okay." She began idly stroking his chest, petting and relaxing him in that way she sometimes did after sex—his cat looked forward to it. Her lips curved against his skin. "You're purring. Such a pretty kitty."

He bit her shoulder.

Her head shot up, and she glared at him. "Ow, that hurt."

Using his fingertip to trace the claiming mark on her neck, he said, "It's not nice to tease your mate."

"It's not nice to abruptly shove a finger up their butt during sex," she shot back, "but you've done that to me more times than I can count."

His mouth curving again, he skated a hand down her back to palm the aforementioned butt. "How can I resist when you have such a beautiful ass?" He doodled circles on the smooth globe, disappointed to find that the indentation of his teeth were gone. He'd bitten her last night, though not hard, so it was unsurprising that the mark had already healed. "And don't act like you don't like having my finger up there."

"A little warning would go a long way, though."

"But there'd be no fun in warning you."

"So it's revenge for how often I torment you?"

He pursed his lips. "Pretty much, yeah."

"I can respect that. Revenge is good."

Snickering, he loosely gathered her hair in his hands, loving how luxuriously soft it was. "You would say that."

Humming, she pressed a kiss to his mouth. "I gotta go clean up. In fact, we both do." She rose from the bed and stretched. "We need to eat, dress, and shower … though not in that order. We have a party to attend."

Rising, he followed her into the bathroom. "I'm surprised Bree got Alex to agree to throw one. I mean, I know it's to celebrate the birth of their daughter, but he's not a guy who likes parties." The wolverine was far too antisocial to enjoy them.

Nodding, she edged into the shower stall. "There isn't much he wouldn't do for Bree, though. He's gone for her. Like you are me."

Deke flicked up a brow as he joined her in the stall. "Gone, huh?"

"Yup." She squealed as he switched on the shower, making cold water pour down on her. "You're such an asshole!"

He chuckled. "A *gone* asshole, apparently."

She juddered even as he heated the water. "That was cruel."

He rolled his eyes. "Stop whining. You're alive, aren't you?"

"I get closer to death every day—we all do—so it's more like a slow journey toward death than 'life.'"

Deke could only shrug. "If you say so."

When they exited their apartment a couple of hours later, Bailey smiled as they walked straight into a party. Rather than have the entire pride celebrate at the Tavern as usual, Bree and Alex had chosen to break tradition and throw an apartment-block party—possibly so he could close himself inside his bedroom when he'd hit his socializing limit. As such, people were everywhere.

Clusters of them stood in the hallway. Others gathered inside apartments or stood in the open doorways. Those who weren't dancing to the music blasting were talking with others while drinking and nibbling on finger foods.

The whole pride was thrilled by the birth of Aurora Velentia Devereaux. Only a few weeks old, the baby wolverine—yes, Alex had been right in his prediction of what breed of shifter she'd be—was spoiled rotten already. Her arrival had sure brightened what had been an otherwise dull time for the pride, thanks to the Gerard and Therese extravaganza.

No extremists had turned up to collect Bailey, so she could only think they'd first attempted to contact Therese and then gotten suspicious when she hadn't answered or returned their call. Lucky for them, or they'd have been eradicated by the pride.

Before being kicked out of the pride, Gerard had been appropriately punished. Bailey hadn't had any part in that, since she hadn't trusted that her snake wouldn't rise and kill him, but she was pretty sure Deke had had some "quality time" with him.

Without a goodbye to anyone, Dayna had returned to Australia literally days after Therese attempted to kill her. Bailey couldn't lie, she'd totally fist pumped. It was best for the woman's health that she'd accepted the simple fact that she'd never have Deke. If she'd pushed the matter, Bailey would have dealt with her in a manner that made Therese's attack on Dayna seem like a tickle-fest.

Right then, Bailey looked up at him. "Where's the buffet?"

"Mom said it would be in Valentina and James' apartment," he replied.

"Then that's where we're going, I'm peckish." She said her hellos as they began shrugging through the crowds. Deke took the lead, ensuring people edged out of the way so she wouldn't get jostled, which her snake found sweet.

They didn't get far before they came across Shay, who beamed at them. Bailey grinned right back. But Deke? No.

"What's that frown for?" Shay asked him, his brows sliding together.

Deke's nostrils flared. "My cat is growling. The sight of you still irritates him."

A mischievous glint in his eyes, Shay smiled. "You mean because I know what your mate—"

"*Shay*." She poked his shoulder hard. "Don't play with him. Only *I* get to drive him and his cat insane. No one else has that right."

Shay's brows lifted. "That's fair."

"I think so."

Deke sighed. "Get out of our way, asshole."

Shay moved aside with a chuckle. "Cranky bastard."

She and Deke once more advanced through the throngs of people. When they finally stepped into the elevator, it was to find a makeshift bar there. Manning it, Finley arched a brow. "Hey, guys. What are you having?"

After he pressed the correct button on the panel, he and Bailey both grabbed a beer as the elevator began its descent. No sooner had they opened their bottles than the shiny metal doors glided open. They filed out and, again, found themselves surrounded by people.

Deke once more shouldered his way through pride members, ensuring Bailey could squeeze by without problem. As she caught sight of Cassandra across the hall, she gave her a quick wave. The blonde returned it, looking somewhat stiff and uncomfortable.

Bailey didn't fail to notice that not many people stood close to her. Cassandra had been getting the cold shoulder ever since Sam went to stay with his relatives in another pride for a short time. Most people blamed her, which Bailey didn't think was fair.

Apparently, neither did one of the enforcers, JP—he'd started dating her recently, and things seemed to be going well with them. He stood beside her right then, his body language daring anyone to give her attitude.

Hearing Deke bid someone a hey, Bailey looked to see James and his mother, Ingrid. Both were fussing over the baby girl he held.

Smiling, Bailey gently skimmed a finger over her super-soft cheek. "She is far too adorable." Her snake flicked out her tongue, liking the new-baby scent.

"She is," agreed James, his mouth curved.

"You look proud as punch," Deke said to him.

"I am." James gazed down at her, rocking her gently. "I don't often get to hold her. If my mate isn't hogging her, it's Alex or Elle or Damian or my mother. Even Bree struggles to get some time with our Aurora."

"Don't whine," Ingrid told him. "It's unattractive on a grown man."

Three males materialized, none of whom were pride members. Or cats. Or sane.

Alex's uncles.

"Deke," boomed Isaak in greeting. "You look well," he said in his thick Russian accent, patting Deke's back.

"You claimed mamba, I hear," said Dimitri, briefly cutting his gaze to Bailey before refocusing on Deke. "You have my admiration and respect."

Deke frowned. "Uh … thanks, I guess."

Sergei melted at the sight of the baby James was still cradling. "Ah, if it isn't our beautiful Galina."

James sighed, his eyelid twitching. "That's not her name."

Sergei adjusted his collar. "It is fitting one for Ivanov wolverine."

"First of all, she's a Devereaux," James reminded him. "Second of all, the name Aurora is—"

"Not suitable," Sergei finished.

"Not Russian, you mean."

Isaak cut in, "Same thing."

James frowned. "No. No, it isn't."

Dimitri leaned into Isaak and said, "Poor babe deserves pity, having psychopathic cat for step-grandfather."

James looked honestly close to punching one of the brothers—maybe all three. "I'm not a 'step' anything. Like it or not, I'm the father of your niece and nephew. Accept it."

Ignoring that, Isaak patted Dimitri's shoulder in reassurance. "Little Galina will have us. We will be there for her. She will learn ways of wolverines from us."

"Mama will help," Sergei threw in.

James gave them a pointed look. "That dysfunctional mother of yours won't be around Aurora without supervision—I can tell you that now."

And just like that, the chests of all three male wolverines puffed up in affront.

"Dysfunctional?" Isaak echoed in a tone that *dared* James to repeat himself.

The pallas cat lifted a brow. "Would you prefer I called her the embodiment of all evil?"

Isaak ground his teeth. "If it is really death you seek, dumb cat, I will—"

"Please do not tell me you are arguing *again*," interrupted Valentina, appearing out of nowhere.

Dimitri frowned at her. "He called Mama dysfunctional. Can you believe that?"

Well, Deke could. From what he'd seen of Olga, the woman had a dozen screws loose. And she had no issue drugging her mate to make him stop talking. She made Bailey seem sound of mind.

Sergei sneered at James. "You disgust me, feline. How can you show no respect for person who birthed woman you tricked into thinking she is your mate?"

"There were no tricks," James upheld, looking bored. "Valentina *is* my true mate. Let it go already."

"Lies," Isaak declared. "Nothing but lies."

James slid him an exasperated look. "I'd ask you to be normal, but I don't think you know what that is."

"*Enough* of this foolishness," Valentina interjected, slashing a hand through the air. "I am—" She cut off as Havana and Aspen barged out of the stairwell door squealing like little girls. The answer of why quickly became apparent when Blair chased after them like a crab, several of her limbs all disjointed—including her neck.

Bailey scrambled up Deke's back so fast it was impressive—particularly since she didn't even spill her beer. Looping one arm and both legs around him, she shuddered. "*Creepy*."

Deke snorted, his lips quirking. Spotting Isaiah leaving a nearby apartment, Deke cupped his mate's calf as he crossed to the enforcer.

A chicken wing in hand, Isaiah frowned at Bailey, though his eyes were lit with amusement. "There a reason you're all the way up there?"

Clinging to Deke like a monkey, she replied, "Of course." But she didn't expand.

Deke took a swig of his beer. "Any progress with FindYourMatch.com?"

"Ooh, yeah, what's going on with that?" Bailey asked the enforcer, who'd recently made the entire pride aware of his plans to enter an arranged mating.

"I was sent the names of three possible matches," said Isaiah. "Each has what you'd call a basic profile and a photograph on the website, so I checked them out."

"And?" prodded Bailey.

"One stood out for me." Isaiah bit some meat off his chicken wing. "I had River do a little digging, but he couldn't find more info on her than I already know."

"What kind of shifter is she?" Deke asked.

Isaiah's mouth hitched up. "A breed that will never fear pallas cats, so I knew I wouldn't have to worry that she'd care what I am. I contacted her. We exchanged a few messages. She's agreed to meet with me."

So far so good, in that case. "When?"

"Soon. Tate will come along, as will her Alpha male. We'll probably—"

"*Dear God, will you never stop*?" bellowed Damian, his face red as he glared at his sister further down the hall.

"*Until the world accepts that I'm right about you and brands you the monster you are, no*," Elle yelled right back. "*No, Beelzebub, I will never stop*."

Damian threw up his arms. "I *can't* with you."

Feeling his lips curl, Deke peered up at his mate, expecting to see her laughing. She wasn't. Her eyes were glazed over as she stared into space. He squeezed her calf to get her attention. "Are you in a mental world of your own again?"

She hummed. "I'm just wondering if colors look the same to everyone else as they do to me."

Deke felt his brows draw together. "What?"

"Well … we can't know for sure that we all see the exact same thing when we look at a color, can we?" she asked. "*My* version of yellow could be different from yours, and we'd have no clue. And before you go thinking that our eyes can be trusted to see things exactly as they are, just note that leaves are not really green."

Honestly, he had no clue why her brain latched onto crap like this, and he'd given up trying to figure it out. "I'd tell you to look it up, but you don't like reading about anything that involves science."

"Because scientists lie." She slid off his back and moved to stand before him. "They shape our view of the world with bullshit from when we're young so we'll miss the truth even when older."

"I really don't think that's the case."

"Because they've successfully brainwashed you." She gently patted his cheek. "It's so sad."

Ignoring Isaiah's chuckle, Deke fisted her sweater. "No one has brainwashed me, least of all scientists. They deal in logic—something I'm aware you fail to grasp."

"Preaching logic is another way to shape and control you. *Do what's rational, follow the rules, blend with the flock.*" She cupped his chin. "Don't let them trap and rule you."

Jesus Christ. "There is no trap."

"You have so much to learn, young grasshopper. Stick with me, kid. You'll be fine. I'll open your eyes to reality in time."

"My eyes are wide open."

"And seeing only what scientists tell you to see. *Hello, brainwashed.*"

He released her sweater and threw up a hand. "Okay, this conversation is just plain over."

"It's a good sign that my questions make you uncomfortable. It means you're starting to believe I might be right but you're not ready to face it yet. I can work with that."

"There's nothing to—" Deke stopped speaking and dragged in a breath. "You know, I don't know why I bother appealing to you with rationality. It's not like I'm unaware it won't work, or that you've ever pretended to care for logic. I signed up for crazy, and it's exactly what I'm getting."

She smiled. "But you love me anyway."

He felt his expression soften. Gripping her hip, he pulled her closer.

"More than I thought I could love anyone, even if you are fucking certifiable."

"Hmm, prove it and kiss me."

"That I can do."

ACKNOWLEDGEMENTS

There are always so many people to thank …

My husband, my children, my cats (it doesn't feel right to leave them out), my amazing PA Melissa Rice, my badass edit Donna Hillyer, my fabulous cover designer who also happens to be my very talented son, and all those who read and support the Olympus Pride series - thank you all so much!!! You make shit happen. My shit happen. Which I mean in the best possible way.

Stay safe and take care

S :)

ABOUT THE AUTHOR

Suzanne Wright lives in England with her husband, two children, and two Bengal cats. When she's not spending time with her family, she's writing, reading, or doing her version of housework—sweeping the house with a look.

TITLES BY SUZANNE WRIGHT

The Deep in Your Veins Series
Here Be Sexist Vampires
The Bite That Binds
Taste of Torment
Consumed
Fractured
Captivated
Touch of Rapture

The Phoenix Pack Series
Feral Sins
Wicked Cravings
Carnal Secrets
Dark Instincts
Savage Urges
Fierce Obsessions
Wild Hunger
Untamed Delights

The Dark in You Series
Burn
Blaze
Ashes
Embers
Shadows
Omens
Fallen
Reaper
Hunted

The Mercury Pack Series
Spiral of Need
Force of Temptation
Lure of Oblivion
Echoes of Fire
Shards of Frost

The Olympus Pride Series
When He's Dark
When He's an Alpha
When He's Sinful
When He's Ruthless
When He's Torn

The Devil's Cradle Series
The Wicked in Me

Standalones
From Rags
Shiver
The Favor
Wear Something Red – An Anthology
The Pact (coming October 2023)

Printed in Great Britain
by Amazon

20013662R00159